S0-AXO-536

In The Time
Of Famine

Michael Grant

Copyright © 2011 Michael Grant
All rights reserved.
ISBN: 1463645082
ISBN-13: 978-1463645083

LCCN:

DEDICATION

The book is dedicated to the millions of nameless men, women, and children who suffered and died in the *an Gorta Mór,* the Great Hunger of 1845-1850.

ACKNOWLEDGMENTS

In researching this novel I read many excellent books on the Irish Potato Famine. But I especially relied on historian Cecil Woodham Smith's seminal book on the Irish Famine entitled *The Great Hunger*. I highly recommend this book to anyone who has a serious interest in the history of the Famine.

Special thanks to Sandi Nadolny and Elizabeth Nardone for their careful and meticulous reading of the manuscript. Nevertheless, if there are any errors in this book, the fault is entirely mine.

CHAPTER ONE

September 1845
Ballyross, Ireland

The rains were steady and relentless the summer of 1845. At the time, most thought little of it. What else could one expect from the vagaries of the harsh, unpredictable climate of western Ireland? But tenant farmers, superstitious and fearful by nature, were always on the lookout for portents of misfortune. A crow flying too high, an owl abroad in daylight, or a deformed newborn calf was enough to send men scurrying to the parish priest for explanations. These men of the soil, who barely eked out a living in the best of times, viewed the unusual rains of '45 with vague dread and foreboding.

Now it was mid-September and, in spite of all their prayers and entreaties, the rains continued unabated. Since dawn, black clouds had been scudding across a heavy gray sky promising yet more rain. A damp wind, funneled by the mountains to the west, swept across the valley, causing the wheat to roil like waves in a golden sea. In a field, two men, bracing against the stiff wind, swung their scythes, slowly wading through the golden waves one-step at a time. They worked in silence—the only sound was the moaning of the wind in the wheat, the soft swish of scythes, and the occasional *caw, caw* of a distant crow.

To look at these two men one would never suspect they were brothers. Michael, almost six feet tall, towered over his younger brother by more than a foot. He had thick curly black hair and dark blue eyes that never failed to send shivers through the bodies of the young girls in the village. He possessed a natural grace and bearing not often found in peasant stock. He swung his scythe in a graceful, rhythmic arc as though the tool were an extension of his body.

Dermot, short and compact like their father, had close-set eyes that gave him the vague look of an imbecile. His unruly hair, the color and texture of straw, didn't help matters. The same girls who nudged each other and giggled when they saw Michael, snickered in derision at Dermot. With a scowl that seldom left his face, Dermot hacked at the wheat with choppy, uncoordinated strokes as thought he'd never gotten accustomed to the shortness of his arms and legs.

Reaping was hard on the body, but Michael didn't mind. He was young—he'd just turned twenty-four—and his body was hard from toiling in the fields since he was nine. Besides, the rote nature of the work freed his mind to think of other things. And what he was thinking about now, and had been thinking about for the better part of three years, was an idea so fantastic, so daft, so daunting in its implications that even now he could barely grasp it.

Just the night before he'd dug up the box again to reassure himself that he did indeed have the money. The sight of all those shiny coins never failed to take his breath away. He could scarcely believe he'd amassed such a fortune. One by one he counted the coins. Then he carefully put them back in the box and reburied them. He sat there for a long time in the darkness with his back against a tree, reflecting on what he'd gone through to earn them.

After the harvest, when the wheat and the potatoes and the corn were in, there were long winter months when there was little to be done but wait for the spring and a new season of planting. Most farmers welcomed this annual respite from grueling fourteen-hour days in the fields and holed up in their cottages, content to snuggle close to their warm turf fires, smoke their pipes, and sip their jars of "poteen"—a potent homemade whiskey. Michael, forgoing these meager comforts, took this opportunity to go out into the countryside to find work.

In a rural land where the preferred currency was barter, earning coin was a formidable task at best. Still, day after day he trudged from village to village in the cold and the rain. He begged, cajoled, and employed his considerable charm to convince merchants that he was a trustworthy lad whom they could count on to pick up and deliver their goods on time and in prime condition.

It was lonely work traveling the roads for such paltry wages. He cut expenses by eating whatever a passing field had to offer and sleeping in a ditch or barn instead of an inn.

He'd gone as far as Dublin, but most trips were no more than twenty miles from Ballyross. Sometimes he was taken advantage of by merchants who paid him less than the agreed price. Others cheated him out of his money entirely. But he refused to give up. He soon discovered who the honest merchants were and hauled their goods day and night in the cold and the wet. For three long years he did that and now, finally, after collecting a shilling here, a half-crown there, he'd saved enough.

By all rights he should have been happy, but to his dismay, now that the time to make a decision was at hand, he found himself wavering. Making decisions—big or small—was not something the son of a tenant farmer was accustomed to doing. Michael's life—indeed the life of every tenant farmer—was simple and preordained. A man was born. He worked his father's rented fields, ate his father's food, and slept in his father's cottage until he married. And then the cycle started all over again when his sons were born.

But Michael wanted none of that. He was convinced that there had to be more to life than tending rented fields and living in constant dread of being turned off the land at the whim of a landlord. There had to be a better place and Michael knew where that place was: *America.*

Da must be expectin' it, he told himself as he swung the scythe. *He knows I've been workin' and savin' money. Sure he'll be all right. He'll have Dermot.* Michael glanced at his younger brother listlessly hacking at the wheat and knew that was a lie. The God's truth was Dermot would be no help at all.

"Is it time yet do you think, Michael?" Dermot's scowl had given way to a wide, lopsided grin.

The question brought Michael out of his musings and he was grateful for the momentary reprieve from making a decision about America.

"You've been askin' me that all day. When it's time Da will come get us."

Michael pretended not to care, but the truth was, he was as excited as Dermot. There were only three times when the fiddles and the poteen were brought out—weddings, wakes, and the end of harvest. And the reason for Dermot's uncharacteristic excitement was because tonight Michael's best friend, Bobby Ryan, was getting married.

"Will Old Genie be there do you think?" Dermot asked.

"Isn't he always?"

"I like it when there's a fiddler." Dermot leaned on his scythe and stared dreamily off into the distance. "I get to put me arms around the girls when we dance."

"You mind how you hold the girls or you'll be gettin' married yourself."

Dermot reddened. "Don't be daft."

"Is there anyone you have an eye on then?" Michael asked, amused at his brother's sudden discomfort.

"No. You?"

Michael shook his head.

Dermot leered. "What about Moira Boyle?"

"Shut your gub," Michael said sharply. "She's marryin' Bobby."

"Aye, but she was sweet on you. Why didn't you marry her?"

"Get back to work or Da will have us here all night and we'll miss the weddin'."

As he went back to his mowing, Michael asked himself that same question. *Why didn't he marry her?* Moira was certainly pretty—with gray eyes and hair the color of a raven. And she was willin'. God knows she was willin'—in the barn, in the field, down by the river. And God knows he was willin' as well. And why not? He didn't know if it was love, but when he lay with Moira he was transported from his dreary world to a world of pleasure and joy that was almost painful.

But it wasn't enough. She was seventeen and pretty now, but in ten years, if she didn't die in childbirth, she'd be a tired old woman and him a tired old man. He could accept even that, if only she had something more to offer than her beauty. One night after an exhausting bout of lovemaking, as they lay on a haystack staring up at a sky filled with stars, he'd said to her, "Moira, do you think there's a better life somewhere away from here?"

He might as well have asked her if she'd fancy flying to the moon on the back of a pig. She sat up and, leaning on one elbow, snapped, "What kind of talk is that, Michael Ranahan? Tis here we live and we'll do like our das and mams have always done. I don't like it when you talk queer like that."

That was almost six months ago. And it was the last time he made love to her.

"Thank Jasus, here he comes," Dermot said, wiping his brow with his sweat-soaked cap.

Michael glanced over his shoulder. In the distance, a wagon approached trailing a plume of brown dust.

"By Christ, we're goin' to a weddin'!" Dermot danced an awkward jig on the newly mown wheat.

"You'd best keep workin' by Christ or it's no place you'll be goin'."

From atop the wagon Da set his short, thick legs wide apart to maintain his balance as the slow-moving wagon lurched across ruts in the uneven field. He was a small, compact man with a weather-beaten face that made him look a decade older than his forty-eight years. Wild, unruly gray hair stuck out from under a shapeless, wide-brimmed hat that covered his eyes.

He squinted at the two figures at the far end of the field. Even from this distance, and with his poor eyesight, he could easily tell his two sons apart by the way they handled the scythes. Watching Dermot you'd think he'd never swung a scythe in his life. But Da knew better. It wasn't incompetence at work here. It was the devil's own laziness.

Da reined in the horse beside his two sons and inspected the field. "Is this all you've got done then?"

"The blade needs sharpenin'," Dermot said, trying to keep a straight face.

"And what's your excuse?" Da asked his eldest son.

Michael made no attempt to hide his grin. "There's gonna be a weddin', Da."

Da's ruddy face darkened. "In my time no one got married before the harvest was in. And we didn't stop the mowin' till dark. And—"

He stopped talking when he saw his two sons grinning at each other like a couple of eejits. "Get in the wagon the pair of you. Sure you'll be useless the rest of the day."

Chapter Two

Birthdays and anniversaries were never a cause for celebration for the Irish peasant. They were just another day in the week and the work had to be done all the same. But a wedding was something special—a welcome, if short, reprieve from the flint-hard life of tenant farming. For a few hours there could be joy and hope, the promise of children. The promise of renewed life.

Tenant farmers were the poorest of the poor. They lived in hovels not their own. They worked land not their own and barely survived from harvest to harvest. Still, when there was a wedding, everyone found a way to make a contribution to this most happy day.

Now, as the sun, making its only appearance of the day, sank behind the western mountains, friends and neighbors converged on the cottage of Brian Boyle, the father of the bride. They deposited their meager gifts of buttermilk, pans of boxty, and jars of poteen on the wedding table by the door.

Tapping his foot to keep time, old Genie Connor sawed his way through a jig while a handful of young men and women whirled around a blazing bonfire. He was not the most talented fiddler in the county but what he lacked in ability, he made up with enthusiasm.

Within an hour the red sky had given way to blackness and the night air, damp and chilly, brought everyone close to the warmth of the raging fire. Michael, warming his hands, stood with his friends, watching the dancers.

Pat Doyle, a giant of a man with flaming red hair, eyed the dancers wistfully. "Sure it seems like only yesterday I was married meself. Now I have six wee ones at home."

Barry Scanlon, a man with large protruding eyes that gave him a look of perpetual surprise, handed him a jar of poteen. "For the love of God, Pat. It's a weddin'. Don't be thinkin' such cheerless things."

"What are ya talkin' about, man? Getting' married was the best thing I ever done," newly married Martin Duane offered.

"You've got a wife *and* her old mam in the bargain," Jerry Fowler said, taking his turn at the jar. "If that's the best thing you've ever done, I'd not like to see the worst."

Duane shrugged, not sure if he should take offense at Fowler's remark. That was the impact Jerry Fowler had on a lot of people. He delighted in saying things, cutting, insulting things, that coming from anyone else would surely provoke a fight. But if challenged, Fowler, a man of uncommon good looks and a persuasive charm that never failed to fool the unwary, would always feign surprise that his remarks had been taken wrong.

Scanlon, breaking the uncomfortable silence, said, "Pay no mind to Martin. He's not been right since he was kicked in the head by Lord Attwood's mule."

Over the ensuing laughter, Michael, who was not fooled by Fowler's oily charm, said, "Taking his wife's mam in was the decent thing to do. Of course it's not somethin' the likes of you would understand."

Fowler turned his winning smile on Michael. "Ah, for the love of God, man. Can you not recognize a jest when you hear it?"

Doyle, knowing how Michael felt about Fowler, snatched the jar from Fowler and shoved it at Flanagan. "Shut your gub the two of yez."

Matty Flanagan took a sip, grimaced and nodded at Genie. "You know with every nip, Genie's soundin' better and better."

Just then, Dermot danced by with a red-headed girl, hopping up and down, hopelessly out of sync with the rest of the dancers. His short legs could barely keep up with the taller girl, but he wouldn't let go of her waist.

Someone passed the jar to Michael. He took a swig and winced. Homemade poteen was never smooth, but this batch was particularly harsh. He passed it to Martin. The young farmer took his swig and shuddered. "Jasus, tis pig piss!"

A sweating Dermot elbowed his way into the group. The air was chilly, even by the fire, but the exertion of dancing had brought a sweaty sheen to his flushed face. "Give it here."

Martin handed him the jar. "Maureen send you off?"

"There's plenty of girls. Who needs Maureen Brady?"

Doyle winked at the others. "She sent him off."

Michael noticed his brother's eyes were getting glassy. "Go easy on that," he said. "We've the field to finish tomorrow."

"Don't you worry about me." Dermot took a swig and passed the jug to Fowler and disappeared into the crowd of dancers as Bobby and Moira danced by.

"I wouldn't mind bein' in Bobby Ryan's bed this night," Fowler said, leering at the couple.

"Mind your tongue," Michael said sharply.

Fowler's eyes glistened from the poteen. "And what's it to you? Are you still gettin' it from her then?"

Michael lunged at Fowler, but Pat Doyle grabbed both of them by the collars and yanked them apart. "Now, now. Tis a weddin'. We'll have no fightin' here." He shook Fowler. "And you mind your tongue. It's the woman's weddin' day and you'll not be disrespectin' her or you'll answer to me."

Fowler pulled loose and held up the jar. "May they both live to be a hundred." He winked at Michael and moved away.

"You'd do well to stay away from him," Scanlon whispered to Michael. "He's a dangerous one, he is. They say he once stabbed a man to death in a fight in Cork."

"If he did, it was in the back," Michael answered.

Doyle shoved the jar into Michael's hand. "Have a sip and calm yerself."

An angry Michael pushed the jar away and watched Fowler move among the dancers, mumbling remarks that made the girls blush and the men scowl uncertainly. There had been bad blood between them ever since Michael had taken Moira away from him a year ago. To hear Fowler tell it,

Michael had stolen his one true love. The truth was Moira was terrified of Fowler and she'd told Michael that Fowler had hit her on more than one occasion.

As the night wore on and everyone got louder and the dancing wilder, the older people and young ones drifted home to their beds. The young men and women, not wanting to see this festive night end, tossed more logs on the fire and kept dancing. And old Genie and his fiddle was happy to oblige—as long as someone kept his jar filled.

Michael moved off to be by himself. He'd always enjoyed weddings and looked forward to a dance with the girls and a drink with the men, but tonight he felt as though he didn't belong here. Weddings, he knew, led to other weddings and now, as he watched the young people paring off—including Dermot and Maureen—it occurred to him that he wouldn't be here this time next year for their weddings and already he felt like an outsider. He'd grown up with these people, shared their good times and misfortunes. But that was all about to end. *If he went out to America.*

For the second time tonight a knot of uncertainty clenched his stomach. The first time had been earlier in the evening when he'd watched Moira and Bobby dancing together and wondered if he'd made a mistake letting her go. Who was he to think she wasn't good enough for him? Who was he to think he could cross that great ocean and live in a strange land? And who was he to think he could be anything but a tenant farmer? America was far away. He knew no one there. Where would he live? How would he earn his keep?

"Michael, you look so sad."

13

Moira, suddenly standing in front of him, took his hands and pulled him to his feet. Michael cursed himself. All night he'd been carefully avoiding her, but distracted by his thoughts, he hadn't seen her approach. By the way she was swaying he knew she'd had too much to drink.

"Michael..." Her eyes glistened and she threw her arms around him.

He pushed her away gently. "Moira, tis a lovely weddin'. I hope you and Bobby will be very happy."

"We will." She wiped her eyes with a sleeve. "We could of had a good life together, you and me, if—"

"You're Bobby's wife now. Don't be talkin' like that."

She sniffled. "You're right, Michael, and I'm gonna make him a good wife. At least he appreciates me."

"As well he should." Michael lowered his voice. "Moira, what happened between you and me is no one else's business. Isn't that right?"

"Aye."

To make sure he was getting through to her, he added, "It would go bad for both of us if anyone found out."

"Aye, it would." Even through a poteen fog she recognized the truth in that statement.

"There's a good girl." He gently pulled his hands from hers. "Now go and find your new husband."

"I will." She leaned close to him and for a moment he thought she was going to kiss him, but instead she whispered, "You're a no good bastard, Michael Ranahan."

"I am. Indeed, I am."

She nodded solemnly and moved off unsteadily.

To shake his melancholy, Michael took a couple of turns around the bonfire with several girls, but his heart wasn't in it. Just as he made up his mind to go home, he saw Bobby Ryan heading toward him and the big man didn't look at all happy. *Ah, Jasus,* Michael thought. *She's gone and blabbed her mouth and now I'm in for it.*

Bobby Ryan was two inches taller than Michael and at least fifty pounds heavier. Michael had always appreciated the man's physical size when they'd been on the same side in a fight. But he didn't feel that way now as he watched the big man lumbering toward him, unsteady on his feet. Bobby had tears in his eyes. Was it something his wife told him or was it the poteen? Michael couldn't tell. He sighed in resignation and braced himself for the fight that was sure to come.

Bobby stepped up to Michael, his barrel chest heaving with emotion. He looked down at Michael for a moment and then threw his arms around him. "Me old friend," he squeezed Michael in a crushing bear hug. "Thanks for everythin'."

"I didn't do anythin'," Michael said, his voice muffled in Bobby's chest.

Bobby let Michael go and slapped two beefy hands on Michael's shoulders so hard it made him wince. "I know you and Moira... well, no matter"—he wiped a tear from his eye with his sleeve—"I'm a very happy man this day."

"So am I, Bobby." Michael exhaled in relief. "You have no idea."

After the drunken groom lumbered off, Michael tried to slip away, but each time he kept getting pulled back to dance by one of the girls.

He was taking a breather on the sidelines, talking to Doyle and Scanlon, when Fowler danced by holding Moira very tightly. Michael glanced around looking for Bobby, wondering why he would let his brand new wife dance with the likes of Jerry Fowler. Then he saw Bobby curled up under a tree sound asleep.

It's none of my business, he told himself. Then Fowler and Moira danced by again and Moira looked at him with pleading eyes and he realized that Fowler wouldn't let her go.

Michael grabbed Fowler's arm and pulled him away. "All right, Jerry. I think Moira's had enough dancin' for tonight."

Fowler's eyes gleamed brightly in the firelight. "Ah, is it your turn then?"

"Go home and sleep it off, Fowler. You never could hold your jar."

As Michael turned away, Fowler took a swing at him and caught him on the side of the head. Michael ducked and drove his fist into Fowler's exposed belly. As Fowler doubled over, Michael came down on the back of his neck with both hands. Fowler dropped to the ground.

Suddenly Pat Doyle's huge arms were around Michael's chest and he was thrown to the side like a sack of flour. "That's enough the two of yez."

He dragged Fowler to his feet. "Jerry, it's time for you to go home now. There's a good lad."

Even in his drunken state, Fowler knew better than to challenge the big man. He shot a cold grin at Michael and stumbled off into the darkness.

"Thanks," Moira said to Michael.

"Why don't you wake your husband and go on home," Michael said.

"Aye, I think that's a good idea."

Chapter Three

When the sun came up—it was the first time Michael had seen a rising sun in weeks—only he, of all the revelers, was awake to witness it. Enjoying the solitude of the moment, he watched the sun paint the peaks of the eastern mountains a golden hue as the birds took to the air in search of a meal. The fire had long since burned to embers and the dancers slept where they'd fallen. Old Genie, his back propped up against a tree, hugged his fiddle and snored softly. The morning air was chilly and wisps of morning fog swirled among the trees. Michael moved among the tangle of sleeping dancers until he found his brother with his head resting in Maureen's lap. He nudged him with the tip of his brogue. "Come on little brother, time to go to work."

Dermot opened one blood-shot eye and ran his tongue over his parched lips. "It was a good weddin', Michael. Countin' yours, there was only three fights the whole entire night."

It had been a good wedding, but now it was time to pay the piper and it was a brutally long day mowing wheat with a poteen hangover. Dermot, even more irritable than usual, cursed the wheat, the scythe, the land, and his life in general. In contrast, Michael was in high spirits. He didn't know he'd been whistling until Dermot croaked, "For the love of God will you stop that infernal noise?" The reason for Michael's euphoria was that while he'd sat watching the sun come up, he'd finally made up his mind.

He was going to America, by God, and that was that.

Dermot straightened up. "Jasus, me head's killin' me. Let's take a blow."

Dermot flung the scythe to the ground and flopped down on a pile of mown wheat. He rolled over on his back and held his head with his hands. "God, I'm fecken dyin'."

Michael leaned on his scythe and surveyed the field. "We'll be done by sunset."

"And we'll be back tomorrow to bundle it up. It's destroyin' me I tell ya."

Michael had long ago learned to ignore his younger brother's chronic complaining. As Dermot droned on, Michael's attention focused on a flock of sheep in the distance—small white dots, slowly moving across a mottled green hill. Then his gaze shifted to the light and dark patterns the wheat bundles made in the next field. In the field beyond, two cows slowly clomped down the hill toward a flowing stream. It suddenly occurred to him what he was doing. He was looking at—*things*. It was as though he were trying to commit to memory the land that he would soon leave forever.

Forever.

Such a forbidding word. It was a word he'd never used about himself before. Death was *forever*. Burning in hell was *forever*. But the simple truth was, when he left this land, he would be going away—*forever*.

His eyes swept the landscape with its infinite shades of green. It truly was a beautiful land. The land that he was born on. The land that his Da was born on, and *his* Da before him. Michael felt a tightening in his throat. He would miss it. *Forever*.

He looked over his shoulder and saw a wagon coming across the field.

"Da's comin'."

Dermot sprung to his feet too quickly and clutched his head. "Oh, Jasus…"

As Da reined in the wagon, Dermot swung the scythe too low and the blade struck a rock with a loud metallic *twang*.

Jasus, Mary and Joseph!" Da jumped down from the cart, snatched the scythe from Dermot, and examined the blade. "If you break it, how am I to pay for another?"

Dermot shrugged.

Da felt the anger rising in him. What was it about Dermot that just a mere shrug could make his blood boil? He was about to say something to him, but changed his mind. Instead, he turned to his eldest son. "Come on, we've supplies to pick up."

"Why can't I go?" Dermot protested. "You always take him."

Michael wiped his forehead with his sleeve. "Take him, Da. I'll finish up here."

"I'll do no such thing. He'll disappear and I'll have to do all the work meself." He shoved the scythe into Dermot's hands. "When I get back I want to see three more courses done. And mind you leave something for the Pooka."

Michael turned away so his father wouldn't see him grin. Unlike his superstitious father, Michael did not believe in fairies and hobgoblins. Da, on the other hand, was firmly convinced that the Pooka, which was said to be a small, deformed goblin, demanded a share of every crop at the end of the harvest. And a terrible fate awaited those who defied him. Da made sure that several strands of wheat, known as the "Pooka's share," were always left in every field. Michael thought it extravagant to leave so much food for the crows to eat, but he could never convince his father of that.

As Da guided the horse out of the field and onto the road, he glanced back and saw Dermot hacking at the wheat. "Will you look at the fury in him?" he said, shaking his head in dismay. "Sure you'd think he was attackin' the devil himself."

Michael would never say so, but he agreed with his father. For as long as he could remember, Dermot had always been angry. He didn't know why, but he was, and Michael had just learned to live with it.

"Ah, go easy on him."

"Don't you be tellin' me how to deal with me own son."

Michael fell silent. He didn't want to upset his father any more than he already was. Especially today. Until this moment he'd told no one about his plans to go to America, not even Dermot. But tonight he would announce his plans to the family.

21

Michael looked up at the low clouds rolling in from the west. "Looks like more rain," he said, changing the subject.

Da squinted at the sky and his brow furrowed with unease. "In all me years I can't remember a wetter summer." He flicked the reins and the horse picked up the pace. "It's a black sign and that's a fact."

The village of Ballyross was essentially an afterthought. Lying almost in the center of a wide sweeping valley dominated by mountains checker-boarded with stone-walled fields, it had once been nothing more than a crossroads dissecting the valley. Then, an enterprising miller set up a grinding mill next to a swift flowing river. Soon a general store appeared across the road to sell to the people who sold their wheat to the miller. Then a grog shop appeared to quench the thirst of all those buyers and sellers. Then a Catholic church sprang up to save the souls of farmers bent on swimming to hell on a river of drink. Not to be outdone, a Protestant church with an even higher steeple appeared at the other end of the road to tend the souls of the Protestant gentry and protect them from the drunken papist bastards. One by one more tradesmen appeared to satisfy the needs of the growing community and, before anyone knew what was happening, Ballyross was a full-blown village.

Michael was carrying a sack of flour out of the general store when he saw Lord Somerville's gleaming black landau coming up the road from the train station. He stopped to admire the graceful carriage with the Somerville coat of arms emblazoned on the door in gold leaf lettering. As the landau passed, he caught a glimpse of a young woman inside and sucked in his breath. She brushed an errant lock of auburn hair away from her forehead and glanced at him—or rather through him. Michael had never seen anyone more beautiful in his entire life.

"Who's that, Da?"

"Young Emily. She's been called home."

Michael vaguely remembered a little girl with freckles who used to play in the Manor House garden. She'd gone away a long time ago and Michael had forgotten all about her. "Little Emmy?"

"*Mistress* Emily to you, me boyo."

Michael watched the carriage disappear into a cloud of dust and felt an odd stirring within him.

Da saw the expression on his son's face and felt a sudden press of dread. "Get any thought of her out of yer head, Michael. She's not for the likes of you."

Michael slammed the sack into the back of the wagon. "And why not? Because she's the landlord's daughter and I'm just a tenant farmer?"

"Never you mind," Da said, frightened by that kind of talk. A man who didn't know his place was bound for trouble. "Go fetch that other sack."

Michael stomped back into the store, leaving Da to wonder, once again, what was the matter with the young people today.

The sprawling Somerville estates, less than two miles outside the village of Ballyross, had been home to six generations of Somervilles since the first Somerville, Lord Thomas, arrived in Ireland at the turn of the eighteenth century. Over the years, succeeding generations of Somervilles had occupied the house, adding extensions to the original Georgian mansion until it had become a majestic example of architectural eclecticism that was admired throughout the west of Ireland.

The carriage turned onto a long, well manicured road leading up to the manor house. Emily, her face a mask of resignation, stared at the imposing home perched on the crest of a long, sloping hill. It had been ten years since she'd last seen it and nothing, it appeared, had changed in that time. The tall, majestic oak tree she'd swung from as a little girl was still there. So, too, was the hill where she'd rolled snowballs until they were giant rounds of snow taller than she. The gate she'd swung on—and broken more than once—was still there, freshly painted and in good repair. This had been her home once, a place she loved. Now it was to be her prison.

As the carriage wheels crunched to a stop on the freshly raked gravel driveway, the front doors opened and a short, stout woman came rushing out. Nora, the family's retainer for over fifty years, rubbed her hands on her apron expectantly as Emily stepped out of the carriage.

"For the love of God will you look at you," Nora said, beaming. "You're all grown up, Emmy— I mean, Miss Emily."

Emily hugged Nora, genuinely glad to see the old housekeeper. "Well, I should hope so, Nora. It's been ten years."

"Did you have a good trip then?"

"As well as can be expected."

Nora heard the strain in the young woman's voice and nervously rubbed her hands in her apron. "Well, I'm glad you're home safe just the same."

Emily glanced toward the front door and stiffened.

A tall, ramrod straight figure with thick white hair and bushy eyebrows, partially concealing intelligent gray eyes, stood in the door. He flashed a hesitant smile and came down the steps toward her.

"Welcome, Emily."

Emily made no move toward him. "Hello, Father."

Somerville stopped as though he'd been slapped in the face. Self-consciously, he cleared his throat and clasped his hands behind his back.

Nora pulled her shawl around her, as though feeling a sudden chill. "Well, don't be standin' there gawkin'," she snapped at two young servant girls, who were indeed gawking at the beautiful young woman standing before them. "Get the bags into the house." She averted her eyes from her embarrassed master and took Emily's arm. "Come inside, child. You'll catch your death out here."

The manor's great room was indeed great—in size and in the splendor of its furnishings. Heavy tapestries of finely weaved patterns hung from walls covered with burgundy and sage green wallpaper imported from the Far East. Massive Oriental rugs added a touch of much needed warmth to the cold flagstone floors. Plush couches and armchairs, built by the finest furniture makers in Dublin and London, filled the room. Perched on delicately wrought tables were collections of screens, fans, and porcelain and lacquer figures from China.

Two huge Waterford chandeliers, hanging from chains attached to the wood beamed ceilings above, cast a soft warm glow to the otherwise cold room.

The fireplace, with ornate basket grates as tall as a man covering the opening, was the focal point of the room. Lord Somerville was standing at the fireplace warming his hands when Emily came in.

"You wanted to see me, Father?"

Somerville turned to look at his daughter and caught his breath. She'd taken off her bonnet and traveling coat and he was getting his first good look at her in ten years. She looked so much like her mother that it was unnerving. She had the same flowing auburn hair, the same intelligent green eyes. And she was the same age—twenty—when he'd married her mother. Somerville tried to push the thought of his dead wife out of his mind, but it was no use. She was always with him. Even after all this time, he still couldn't think of her without heart-numbing grief.

"I trust your trip was uneventful?"

"What does it matter?" Her tone was icy. "I'm here, aren't I?"

Ignoring the sarcasm in her tone, he said, "Perhaps you should take a nap. You must be tired from your long journey."

"I'm not a child. I don't take naps anymore." Emily started toward the door. "Is Shannon still here?"

"Yes, but he's getting old and cantankerous. I don't think you should—" He didn't finish the sentence because she'd already gone. Alone, once again, Somerville turned back to the fire and glumly poked at a log.

Since she'd been a child, Emily's remedy for unhappiness had been to take to the fields with her horse. Racing across a meadow with the wind in her hair and feeling the strength of the horse beneath her, and the delicious, terrifying fear that she might fall off, never failed to make her forget what it was that had made her unhappy.

She walked into the barn and the familiar, pungent smell—a not unpleasant blend of horse manure and hay— brought back a flood of agreeable memories that she'd long since forgotten.

A young man was stacking bags in the corner of the barn. She recognized him as the same one she'd seen staring at her in town. In spite of his ill-fitting, threadbare clothing, he was handsome in a rustic sort of way. But she had no interest in men, especially after what happened in London. And she certainly had no interest in a common bog trotter.

"You," she said imperiously. "Saddle my horse."

Michael looked up and smiled. "Yes, mum. Which one?"

"Shannon."

"Oh, I don't think that's a good idea."

"I didn't ask your opinion. Just do as you're told."

As he saddled the horse he kept glancing at her as she paced back and forth, pretending she didn't know he was staring at her.

He led the horse out of the stall. "All ready, mum."

Michael helped her mount the horse. "You're makin' a terrible mistake," he said. "He's very cranky these days."

Emily stared down at him in astonishment. "*You* are impertinent."

"And *you* are spoiled."

"What's your name?" she sputtered. "I'll have you discharged immediately."

"Michael. But you can't get me sacked. I don't work for the Manor."

"Then why—? How—?"

Michael slapped the horse's rump and it bolted out of the barn. "Have a good ride."

He watched her gallop away and, again, felt an odd stirring within.

Chapter Four

At sunset, as if to mock the farmers already anxious about the queer weather, the sun appeared just moments before it disappeared behind the western mountains. Da, Michael, and Dermot watched it go down in silence as they trudged up the road toward their cottage. They moved slowly, their bodies weary from a backbreaking fourteen-hour day in Lord Somerville's fields. Da and Michael veered off toward a small potato patch in front of the cottage, while Dermot continued toward the house.

"And where do you think yer goin'?" Da called after him.

"To me dinner. I've done me work."

"You've done the landlord's work," Michael said. "Now it's time to do ours."

The arrangement between landlord and tenant was quite simple and quite harsh. In exchange for the right to build a tiny cottage and plant potatoes for his own consumption on a patch of land supplied by the landlord, a tenant farmer agreed to grow money crops for the landlord. And it was understood that the landlord's crop came first. It was a barter system in its simplest form, and it was a system that weighed heavily in favor of the landlord. Everything on the land belonged to him, including the cottage and any improvements made by the tenant. Tenants, who had virtually no rights, could be thrown off the land with little cause. With no place to go, and no land to grow the all-important potato, "ejectment"—as that dreaded fate was called—was a certain death warrant.

Dermot glared at the field of tall green stalks. "I'm sick to death of spuds."

Da's face flushed in anger. "You won't be sayin' that when they fill yer belly this winter."

Father and son glared at each other. To break the tension, Michael grabbed Dermot in a headlock and playfully pulled him toward the field.

"Look at these fine, healthy plants, Dermot. Sure they're almost ready for harvestin'. Then you can sit on yer arse and do nothin' until—" He looked up at the drumbeat of horse hoofs and saw Emily, astride Shannon, galloping across a field toward them.

To Michael's practiced eye it was clear that the horse was out of control. Then he saw why. Shannon had the bit in his mouth and Emily couldn't control him. The horse was headed straight for the stone wall surrounding the potato field and for one terrifying moment Michael thought Shannon would break both his and Emily's necks by crashing into the wall. But at the last instant, he leapt over it.

Stalks and chunks of potatoes flew as the horse's hooves churned the soil. Michael positioned himself in the path of the horse. As it passed, he snatched the reins. Shannon reared and, eyes wide with fright, struck at him with lethal hooves.

"All right now..." Michael said soothingly. "It's all right, Shannon..." The prancing horse snorted, his eyes white circles as he strained against the reins. But Michael's soothing manner soon calmed him. He rubbed his hand across the horse's trembling muzzle. When he was sure that the animal was under control, he turned to survey the destroyed plants.

"It's potatoes growin' here," he snapped at Emily. "Not weeds to be trampled underfoot."

Emily yanked at the reins, not sure of what surprised her most—his impertinence or his angry tone. "Let go of my horse, you clod."

When Michael didn't let go, Emily swiped at him with her riding crop, but he snatched it from her hand. He was about to fling it into the field when Da stopped him with an angry shout.

"*Michael!*"

Standing rigid with shock and anger, Da glared at his son in outraged disbelief. To think that a son of his would speak to the master's daughter in that manner was inconceivable.

Michael glared back defiantly. For a moment he considered flinging the riding crop into the field anyway, but instead, he turned to Emily and with a forced smile offered her the crop. She snatched it, nodded to Da, and rode off.

"You mind yer place, Michael Ranahan," Da rasped in a voice constricted with rage.

"Is it my place to stand by while my betters destroy my property?"

"Yer property? Dermot said scornfully. "You own nothin'. Sure it's all hers—and her Da's."

Michael was about to lash out at Dermot, but he suddenly realized his brother was right. "It's not ours," he said more to himself than to his brother. "None of this will ever be ours."

He glanced over Da's shoulder at the pitiable cottage they lived in—more a pile of mud and thatch than a real house—and the miserable patch of ground where they grew their potatoes. Now, more than ever, he was certain that he'd made the right decision to go to America.

"Ah, what does it matter who owns what?" Da said. Such talk of ownership, he knew, was pointless. And dangerous. Hadn't he seen what happened to tenants who forgot their place? Hadn't he seen cottages "tumbled" and families evicted for challenging the authority of the landlord?

"As long as we have a roof to put over our heads and a field to plant our spuds," he said in a voice trembling with emotion, "what does it matter who owns what?" He pointed to the crushed stalks. "Get this cleaned up, the pair of yez," he mumbled. "I'm off to see Lord Somerville."

Da dreaded going into the Manor House because every room was filled with costly vases that might shatter from a good sneeze, dainty tables that could break if you looked at them crooked, and all manner of dishes and little porcelain statues that vibrated ominously when he stomped by in his big brogues. He lived in fear that he would break something and spend the rest of his life paying for it. He'd tried walking on tiptoe once, but he'd lost his balance and had almost fallen against a china cabinet full of fancy blue dishes. Still, in spite of his trepidation, he was here because he had something very important to ask Lord Somerville.

Nora, the housekeeper, led him down a dark oak-paneled corridor and stopped in front of an imposing set of double doors. "Wait here." She knocked softly and opened the door. "Sir, it's John Ranahan to see you." She stood aside and motioned for Da to go in.

Da swept his cap off and came in with his arms tightly by his side. The room was many times the size of his own cottage. And every wall, he noted with awe, was covered with books stacked on shelves all the way up to the ceiling. He, himself, couldn't read, but still, he wondered how it was possible for any man to read so many books in just one lifetime. He glanced down and to his horror saw that he'd tracked mud onto the carpet. He quickly stepped back onto the stone floor and promptly bumped against an umbrella rack. The umbrellas and walking sticks, clunking against each other, made a god-awful racket, but mercifully the rack didn't fall over.

Da glanced fearfully at Lord Somerville, who was sitting at a large desk writing. Thank God he hadn't noticed. Da exhaled softly and concentrated on remaining perfectly still. As landlords went, Lord Somerville was better than most. He'd always been fair with him and treated him with respect. Still—he glanced around fearfully—he didn't want to think what would happen if he broke something.

"Yes, Ranahan, what is it?" Somerville asked without looking up.

"Yer Lordship..." Da began hesitantly. "If I could take a minute of yer valuable time... it's about the land...."

"There's no problem, Ranahan. You and your boys are doing a fine job."

"Yes, sir. Thank you, sir. It's just that—"

"Speak up, man."

"I wish to rent more land, yer lordship," he blurted out.

That got Somerville's attention. He put his pen down and sat back in his high-backed chair. "How many acres?"

"Two."

Somerville studied Da in silence. Then he said, "Why do you want more land?"

"It's for the sons, ya see. They're grown men now. Soon they'll marry and they'll need a bit of land to put up a cottage and plant the potatoes."

Somerville got up and stood by the fireplace with his hands clasped behind his back. He stared into the flames for a long time before he spoke. "You're one of my best tenants, Ranahan, so I'm going to give you some advice. If I let you rent the acres, keep them for yourself. This cursed country is going to ruin, dividing and dividing the land until there's not enough to support a crow. God knows I'm as guilty of that as any man."

And Somerville knew the reason for this ill-advised practice. Money. Dividing the land into smaller and smaller parcels meant more rental money, but when the parcels got too small they couldn't yield enough to support the tenant, and soon landlord *and* tenant were ruined.

Da couldn't have understood any of that. But even if he did, he still would have wanted the land. What choice did he have?

"Will you rent me the land, sir?"

Somerville was still staring into the fire. In the glow of the firelight Da saw a deep sadness in Somerville's eyes. He'd seen that look often, ever since the wife died, but now the sadness seemed even deeper. He wondered if it had anything to do with the daughter. There had been rumors, but Da was not one to listen to them. All he knew was that she was young and, if she was anything like Dermot, she had to be a handful.

Somerville sat back down at his desk and picked up his pen. "See me after the harvest, Ranahan."

"Yes, sir. I will. God bless you, sir."

Da backed toward the door, careful not to knock anything over. He didn't relax until he was well clear of the house. Then he spit into his calloused hands and rubbed them together. Lord Somerville didn't say no and Da took that as a good sign. His heart pounded with joy, certain he'd just secured his sons' futures.

A tenant farmer's home was called a "cottage"—a word that conjures up images of quaint thatched roofs and roses spiraling up whitewashed walls. But a 19th century Irish tenant's cottage was anything but charming. Most cottages were windowless, one-room dwellings of mud walls covered by a roof of sod or thatch, which the family shared with pigs and chickens.

The Ranahan cottage was slightly better than that. For
one thing it was cleaner. The day they were married, Mary
Ranahan announced to her new husband, "John Ranahan,
there will be no animals in this house." She made him build a
shelter alongside to house the animals. He grumbled about
the great waste of money and space but he built it all the
same.

The cottage was brighter because she'd also made him
knock a hole in the wall to create a window—even though
anyone with any sense knew that a window was useless.
Wasn't it just one more opening for the wind to blow
through?

And the Ranahan cottage was larger. After the birth of
Michael, she made her husband break out one wall and
expand the cottage. Even with all that, it was still a very small
home for so many Ranahans.

There were, all together, six of them living under the one
roof: Da, Mam, Michael, Dermot, and Da's mother and father.
There would have been more, but one son, born a year after
Michael, died in childbirth. Another boy of the fever when he
was five. And a sickly little girl who died before her third
birthday. They never knew what killed her.

The whitewashed walls helped brighten the interior of
the cottage, but it was still gloomy. At night, the only light
came from a meager turf fire and a flickering candle. The
ceiling, barely six feet high, gave the cottage a cave-like
quality. From years of turf fires, smoke had been absorbed
into the thatch, and now the smell permanently permeated
the stuffy air. The dirt floor was covered with straw which
Mam replenished daily. There was little in the way of

furniture—three pallets for beds, a long table flanked by two wooden benches, a chest, and a couple of stools by the fire. And there was little in the way of decorations—a crucifix over the fireplace, and on the walls a few faded pictures cut from a discarded book. In the fireplace, an all-purpose iron cooking pot, used for everything from boiling the potatoes to heating water for the impending birth of a baby, rested on the glowing turf.

One-half of the one-room cottage served as sleeping quarters and was separated from the other half by a tattered cloth hung on a piece of rope strung across the room. Even so, there was no hope of privacy. Three straw-covered pallets, just inches apart from each other, filled the small space. Da and Mam shared one, Granda and Grandmam another, and Michael and Dermot the third.

As lacking as these accommodations were, other families had it worse. Sometimes twelve to sixteen adults and children shared a space the same size or smaller with pigs, chickens, dogs, and any other farm animal that made it into the house before the front door was shut for the night.

As Mam tended to the pot of boiling potatoes, Michael sat at his place at the table, nervously tapping the rough-hewn top with his fingers. He shot furtive glances at his family, trying to assess their mood. Dermot was sitting opposite him, still sulking about not going to town this afternoon. Nothing new there.

Granda sat opposite him, staring off into the middle distance, lost in his own thoughts. Michael loved his Da, but he'd always been more at ease with his granda. As a child he loved sitting by the fire on cold winter nights, listening to the old man tell terrifying tales of fairies and banshees. But now, age was taking its toll and lately he was having what Mam called "his moods." When he was in his moods, he didn't recognize anyone. Not even his own wife. He'd forget where he lived and sometimes he couldn't even remember what a spade was used for. These moods, which came without warning and were becoming more and more frequent, frightened Grandmam. When he was like that, she'd scuttle over to the fire and sit with her black shawl thrown over her head, mumbling about evil spirits and banshees. But as quickly as they came, the moods would vanish, and he would become furious when told what he'd said and done.

Grandmam was at her usual place by the fire. A quiet woman, she had little to say and spent most of her time sitting by the fire, staring into the flames, her lips moving in silent prayer.

Mam, rail-thin, lifted the heavy iron pot from the fire and set it on the table. She was only forty-five, but she'd already lost most of her teeth. Her hair, which had once been a strawberry blonde, had turned a mottled gray. The only dress she owned was threadbare and tattered, but Michael had never heard a word of complaint from her lips.

Da came in and shook the water off his hat. "Tis rainin' again. I've never seen anythin' like it."

"Then they'll be no bundlin' the wheat tomorrow," Dermot said hopefully.

"There will," Da said, bringing a scowl back to Dermot's face.

"Is everythin' all right?" Mam asked, looking at her husband intently.

Da nodded. "Aye."

Michael saw his Mam and Da share a knowing look and wondered what that was about.

Supper was a simple affair. There were no plates, knives or forks. Each person took a potato out of the pot, peeled it, and dipped it into a bowl of salted water. A jug of buttermilk was passed around to wash it down. On the rare occasion when a bit of turnip or cabbage was on hand, Mam boiled it with the potatoes. And that was their typical meal—three times a day.

As they ate in silence, Michael began to have second thoughts now that the time had come. *Maybe I'll tell them after Sunday mass,* he told himself. Then, he quickly changed his mind. *No, that won't do. I'll not get a decent night's sleep till then and that's a fact.*

Michael cleared his throat. "I have an announcement to make—"

"And I—" Da said at the same time.

There was a confused silence as the two stared at each other. Finally Mam said, "Let yer Da speak first. I think he has great news."

With the back of his hand Da swept the potato skins in front of him onto the floor. "I spoke to Lord Somerville," he said, rubbing his hands together excitedly. "He'll rent me two more acres. Now, Michael and Dermot, when the time comes for you to get married, you'll have a bit of land for yerselves."

Grandmam clapped her hands. "Saints preserve us. Isn't that grand?"

"Jasus, we're almost landed gentry," Granda muttered.

Michael stared at the tabletop too stunned to speak. He hadn't been expecting this.

"What were you gonna say, Michael?" Grandmam asked. "I don't know if me poor old heart can take any more great news."

"It's nothin'," Michael muttered. "It's not important."

"Come on, Michael," Granda coaxed. "Don't be keepin' us in suspense. Let's see how strong the old girl's heart is."

"I'm goin' to America," he blurted out.

A sudden hush fell over the table.

He might as well have said he was dying of the consumption. To the Irish, emigration was the same as a death in the family. Everyone knew that a son who went out to America would never be seen again, and often a wake was held for him before he left.

Grandmam began keening in the way that old women did at wakes.

Da looked as though he'd been punched in the face. "You'd leave yer land, Michael?" he asked incredulously.

"It isn't my land—or yours, Da. Dermot is right. Everythin' belongs to Somerville and the other landlords."

Grandmam's keening grew louder.

Da waved an impatient hand at her. "For the love of God, Mam, will you hush. Michael, one of the acres is for you."

"Don't you understand? They're not yours to give. If one harvest fails and you can't pay the rent, he'll take the land from you. It's what they've always done."

Da slammed his hand down on the table. "No. I'll manage by Christ. We must keep the family together."

Michael couldn't bear to look into his father's anguished face and fixed his eyes on the table top. "I've made up my mind," he said softly.

Grandmam renewed her keening. Da jumped up and rushed out the door.

The rain was coming down harder than ever. Da stumbled through the potato field, bareheaded, looking at the glistening stalks, but not seeing them. He always went out into the fields when he was angry or frightened. It was the one place where he could clear his head and think without distraction.

And now he was thinking about his son. *How can he abandon the family?* He asked himself over and over again. *Did he not learn anythin'? Did I not teach him proper? Didn't he know that this was a harsh, unforgiving world? A man alone didn't stand a chance. The only way to survive was to be part of a family, to be surrounded by people who would stick with you no matter what. Jasus, how could he not know that?*

From the cottage door Michael watched his father pacing in the field. His mother stood behind him, her arms folded tightly in front of her, as though she were trying to hold herself together.

"I can't live his life, Mam," Michael said.

Her son's announcement had not been a total surprise to her. She'd seen that look in his eyes whenever someone mentioned going out to America. It was, she knew, only a matter of time. "When will you go?" she asked.
"After the harvest."

Michael turned to face his mother. In spite of Da's bluster and bombast, he knew it was she who was the strong one in the family, the glue that held them together. And that is why he was shocked to see, for the first time in his life, tears in her eyes.

"Mam, you understand why I have to go, don't you?"

"Aye, I do. It's just that…" She pushed his unruly hair out of his eyes. "You're my first born, Michael. You've always been special to me."

Michael was surprised to hear that. She'd never said that before. He'd always thought she favored Dermot.

Tears came into his eyes and he turned back to watch his father in the field. "Should I go out and talk to him?"

"No. Leave him be. Tis a terrible blow he's had."

While Da was pacing in the field, Lord Somerville and Emily, sitting at opposite ends of the long dining room table, ate in silence, the only sound, the crackling of a log in the fireplace. Somerville picked at his food, but he had no appetite. Neither, he noticed, did Emily. He put his knife and fork down. "You can clear the dishes, Nora."

He waited until the old housekeeper left the room. "I called you back from London for your own good."

"I can take care of myself."

"Do you call consorting with a married man taking care of yourself?"

"He's married in name only."

"If you believe that, Emily, you're even more naïve than I thought."

"I'll not stay here, Father. I will not live among a bunch of... bog trotters."

"That's a despicable term and I forbid you to ever use it again."

"I intend to live in London."

Somerville picked up his wineglass and swirled the red liquid. "London is very dear."

"I have my allowance."

Somerville said nothing, but Emily saw an unyielding expression in his face and felt a sudden twist in her stomach. "Surely, you wouldn't cut off my allowance?"

He put the wineglass down and said nothing.

Emily jumped up and rushed from the room in tears.

It had been a punishing day that had begun before dawn, and the exhausted Ranahans were ready for their beds as soon as supper was finished. Michael's news had cast a pall over the family. Usually, while they lay in their beds waiting for sleep to overtake them, they shared the news of the day— who was getting married, who was having a baby, who was dying. Then, one by one, they'd drop out of the conversation as they fell asleep. Da was always the last to fade. He was by nature a taciturn man. But there was something about the comforting darkness, the nearness of his family, and knowing that all his family was safely under one roof, that made him uncharacteristically loquacious. The family would often joke about his incessant nocturnal talking, but never to his face.

But there was no conversation tonight. The thought of her family breaking apart kept Mam awake the whole night listening to the rain pounding on the thatched roof. She could tell by the subtle rhythm of his breathing her husband was awake beside her, but she didn't try to speak to him. She knew he would need time to think things through before he'd be ready to talk.

The rains slowed just before dawn and stopped altogether by the time she went out to feed the chickens at dawn. The torrential rains had washed all color from the morning, leaving a dreary, gray landscape blanketed with a thick fog. As she broadcast the feed to the chickens, a puff of wind came up and she was suddenly staggered by a putrid stench that seemed to be coming from the potato field. Curious to see what it was, she started toward the field, thinking it must be a dead animal. As she approached the wall, the fog lifted momentarily and she got a clear view of the field. *"Holy Mother of God..."* She staggered backward, hurriedly blessing herself with the sign of the cross.

Inside the cottage, the rest of the family was finishing their breakfast in strained silence when a wide-eyed Mam burst through the door.

"Come see, John! Somethin' terrible's happened to the praties..."

One by one the men approached the field in stunned disbelief. The stalks that had been thick and green just yesterday were now black and shriveled.

Da stopped at the wall, unable to come any closer to the devastation.

Ignoring the appalling stench, Michael knelt down and examined a plant. The stalk was black and its leaves shriveled as though the devil himself had sucked the life from it. He pulled the plant from the ground. The potatoes looked normal, but when he squeezed them, they dissolved in a mess of black, putrid ooze.

Granda looked at the ruined field in bewilderment. "What's happened? Everything was lovely just yesterday."

Michael's perplexity quickly turned to anger. There could be only one explanation for the ruin. "It's that woman and her damn horse," he said.

Enraged, he threw the plant aside and started out of the field. Da snapped out of his paralysis when he saw the expression on his son's face. "Where do you think you're goin'?"

"The Manor. She caused this and she'll pay for what she's done."

Da blocked his path. "You'll not go there."

"I will."

Father and son faced off. Two stubborn, willful men cut from the same cloth. They might even have come to blows, but at that moment the fog lifted and Grandmam cried out— *"Sweet Jasus ... will ya look!"*

The fog was lifting and now they could see the surrounding fields. Everywhere, as far as the eye could see, were fields of blackened potato stalks. And in every field bewildered farmers wandered among their ruined crop.

Chapter Five

November 1845
London, England

A gentle drizzle fell on the cobblestones in front of 10 Downing. A carriage pulled up and three solemn-faced men, sprouting large black umbrellas, alighted. The first, Dr. Lyon Playfair, clutching a worn leather valise, was a well-known scientist and chemist. Behind him came Dr. John Lindley, editor of the *Gardeners' Chronicle and Horticultural Gazette*. The third man was Professor Robert Kane, a scientist with extensive experience in potato diseases. A constable opened the front door and the three men hurried inside.

Four weeks earlier, as alarming reports on the blight in Ireland started pouring into the Agricultural Ministry, Prime Minister Sir Robert Peel formed a Scientific Commission composed of these three eminent men of science to study the problem. They'd been dispatched to Ireland to study the blight firsthand and now they'd returned to report their findings.

The three men were shown into a large paneled conference room with stained-glass windows. The diffused light coming through the glass gave the room a curiously spiritual ambiance. A moment later, the Prime Minister and his secretary, Anthony Shaw, entered.

Peel was almost fifty-seven, but with his reddish-blond hair, his long aquiline nose, and his large, expressive eyes, he looked much younger. He'd come to prominence in England as Home Secretary after he created London's Metropolitan Police Force, whose constables the press quickly dubbed "Peelers."

Peel sat down at the gleaming conference table and fixed his metal-gray eyes on Dr. Playfair who at sixty was the eldest of the three scientists. "You look tired, sir."

Dr. Playfair nodded in appreciation of the prime minister's concern. "It was a difficult crossing, Prime Minister. I fear I suffer from *mal de mer.*"

"I appreciate your efforts in this most important matter. Now, gentlemen, what have you to tell me?"

"Prime Minister"—Playfair began in a grave tone—"a virulent blight of unknown origin has made its appearance in Ireland. From what we can gather, it attacks the potato plant, literally killing it overnight."

"How much of the country is affected?"

"Half the crop has either been destroyed or is unfit for human consumption. It's most serious in seventeen of the thirty-two counties."

"I see." Peel rose and went to a large globe of the world. He found Ireland, looking tiny and insignificant in proportion to the rest of the world. "What impact will this have on the people?"

"The account is melancholy and cannot be looked upon in other than a most serious light," Playfair responded. "Simply put, the peasants have nothing to eat."

Peel turned away from the globe with a frown. "Surely they can eat something other than potatoes?"

"I'm afraid it's not that simple, Prime Minister," Professor Kane interjected. "For far too long the Irish peasant has relied on the potato as his sole source of food. Indeed, a grown man eats more than fourteen pounds a day."

"Good Lord. Can a man survive on potatoes alone?"

"A diet of potatoes mixed with milk or buttermilk provides a nutritionally satisfying diet," Dr. Lindley explained. "All things considered, the Irish on the whole are a surprisingly healthy people. Still, each year, even in the best of times, the peasants experience hunger. Potatoes don't store well. By May, the previous year's crop has been consumed. Until the harvest in October, the peasants must live through what they call the "hungry months" in which they experience famine-like conditions."

"The potato," Playfair added, "is easy to grow and plentiful. But, alas, it is a double-edged sword. If the crop fails, as it has now, there is nothing to eat until next year's crop is harvested."

Peel clasped his hands behind his back and began to pace the room. "How can that be, man? Ireland exports tons of wheat and barley, among other food stuffs."

"The Irish peasant does not recognize wheat or oats as food per se," Dr. Lindley explained. "To them it's a commodity—like wool or lumber. These crops are grown to pay the rent. And therein lies the peasant's dilemma. If he eats his barley and wheat, he can't pay his rent and he'll be turned off the land. With no place to live and no field to plant his potatoes, he will surely die. Simply put, eating his wheat or barley is tantamount to committing suicide."

Peel returned to the globe and put a long slender finger on Ireland. "How many are we talking about?"

"More than half the population. Close to four million souls."

Peel spun the globe. "Then it would seem to me that there are only two solutions—either we stop exports from the country or we import more grain."

A startled Shaw looked up from his note taking. "But sir, Ireland accounts for more than a million pounds sterling in exports every month. Parliament will never stand for stopping exports."

Peel smiled grimly at his secretary. "Gentlemen, Mr. Shaw is my pragmatic reminder of the realities of the Parliament. Very well, Shaw, then we must act on option two. We'll import grain. We'll need to set up a Relief Commission to oversee relief efforts. Next, a sum of money must be advanced to buy food for the destitute. We'll begin importing Indian corn meal to replace the potatoes—"

"But, Prime Minister," Shaw protested, " Corn Laws—"

Peel waved a dismissive hand. "Those damnable Corn Laws were passed to protect English farmers, but all they've done is create a stagnant economy. I've been after Parliament to repeal them and now maybe they'll listen to me. It's clear the remedy for Ireland's present misfortune is to remove all impediments to the import of food. There must be a total and absolute repeal forever of duties on articles of subsistence."

Shaw nodded noncommittally. The secretary knew better than to disagree with the prime minister when he'd made up his mind about something. But he also knew that any attempt to repeal the Corn Laws would be met with stiff opposition from Parliament, and he didn't relish the coming battle.

Peel put his hand on his secretary's shoulder. "Mr. Shaw," he said to the three seated men, "is worried about what our Whig friends across the aisle will say. Don't fret, Shaw. How can they object? The importation of corn meal will not interfere with private enterprise because no trade in Indian corn exists. What's more, Indian corn has the advantage of being one of the cheapest foods that will keep a man alive."

Peel visibly brightened. He was a man of action and, as far as he was concerned, now that he had a plan, the problem was as good as solved. He sat back down and smiled contentedly. "The troubles in Ireland may be a blessing in disguise, gentlemen."

Dr. Playfair, who did not share Peel's optimism, said, "Prime Minister, will these measures be sufficient?"

"Of course they will, Playfair. Ireland has had crop failures before and she'll have many more, I warrant. But, with a healthy crop next year Ireland will be right as rain."

December, 1845
Somerville Manor

When Lady Eleanor Somerville was still alive, the annual Christmas ball at Somerville Manor had been a much-anticipated event and the highlight of the winter social season. A gracious hostess, she was renowned for her attention to detail. One could count on being served the best food and wine that the continent had to offer. And she always invited interesting people—writers, artists, poets—who could discourse intelligently on the latest in the world of arts and letters. Unlike some of her contemporaries, who held balls and dinners simply to display their wealth and power, she was a person who genuinely liked people, and she made everyone who entered her home feel welcome.

After her death, Lord Somerville stopped the annual tradition and the house remained dark for the next ten seasons. But now that Emily was back, he decided a ball would be the perfect vehicle to reintroduce his daughter to society. He assumed that Emily would take up her mother's duties as mistress of the house. If nothing else it would give her something to do besides sulk.

He was mistaken. When he proposed this idea to her, Emily adamantly refused, claiming that she was a prisoner in her own home and would not make it appear otherwise.

And so, the enormous task of organizing the ball fell on the shoulders of Nora and the house staff. Somerville was, however, able to gain one concession from his daughter: She would come to the ball and assume the duties of hostess just this one time.

The night of the ball was cold with temperatures near freezing, but at least there was no rain. The long road leading up to the house was lined with liverymen and their carriages.

While some drivers stood in small groups, shivering in the cold and sneaking sips of poteen, others crept close to the house to peek through the windows and marvel at the brightly-lit chandeliers, gleaming mirrors, and women in low-cut silk gowns.

Emily, doing her best to look agreeable, stood on the receiving line next to her father and greeted an endless line of guests. She knew none of them, or at least didn't remember any of them, but everyone, it seemed, remembered her.

An octogenarian, wearing an exquisitely detailed silk gown, was next in line. Lord Somerville bent forward and kissed the old woman's bejeweled hand. "Lady Breen, may I introduce you to my daughter, Emily."

"I'm an old family friend," Lady Breen said, brandishing an oriental fan. "I've traveled all the way from Dublin to meet you and I must say, my dear child, you look exactly like your mother. Are you home to assume hostess duties for your father?"

Before Emily could disabuse the old woman of that notion, Somerville hastily led the old woman away to meet the new vicar.

While the guests danced to the music of a string quartet and servants circulated with silver trays filled with flutes of French champagne, Emily was literally backed into a corner, besieged by earnest young men with no other wish than to dance with her or fetch her something to drink. They came in all sizes—tall, short, thin, and fat. And all of them clumsy. One managed to spill champagne on her gown and another to step on her foot before, mercifully, dinner was announced.

The dining room table was set for fifty. Fine English silver and Waterford crystal gleamed in the light of a hundred candles. Lord Somerville sat at one end of the table; Emily at the other.

Seated next to Emily was a tenth-generation landlord, Lord Attwood, a disagreeable old man with small black eyes devoid of emotion. His smile, which he seldom displayed, was more a sneer. His wife, a buxomly woman with a prodigious appetite, was seated opposite him.

Attwood, who had been holding forth about the treachery of the Peel government, intoned, "Mark my words. The government is going to make us pay for this tiresome crop failure."

Lady Breen peered at him through her lorgnette. "I don't think tiresome is the word I would use, Lord Attwood. Without their potatoes, what are the peasants to eat?"

"I am told there is plenty of food stuffs in the market place," Attwood said, popping a medallion of lamb into his mouth.

"My servants tell me that food prices have doubled," Lady Breen persisted.

Attwood shrugged. "That, madam, is not my concern."

Major Robert Wicker, an ill-proportioned man with an oversized head and short legs that gave him a dwarf-like appearance, nodded in agreement. "Eviction," he said, stabbing the air with a fork. "That's what I say. If they can't pay the rents, turn them off the land. It's time these wastrels learned some responsibility."

Emily smiled at the little man's hypocrisy. It was common knowledge that Major Wicker had come to own his estates because his drunken father, a failed grain merchant, had won them in a card game. And if rumors of the son's reckless gambling and drinking were true, Emily was certain the major would lose them just as quickly as his father had acquired them.

"Major Wicker is, as usual, absolutely correct," chimed in the obsequious Mr. Rowe. "Eviction will rid the land of the surplus Irish population."

Unlike the other men at the table, Edward Rowe, a fleshy man in his late fifties, was not a landlord. He was something worse—a property manager. For the past fifteen years he had been managing the estates for a wealthy member of the House of Lords who had never set foot in Ireland.

The arrangement between landlord and property manager was simple and efficient. The property manager was paid a percentage of the profits from the land. Thus, it was in his financial interest to make every patch of dirt pay a dividend. And the landlord, who willingly turned a blind eye to underhanded and brutal practices, cared not how he did it.

Landlords were feared. Property managers were feared *and* despised. Peasants expected to be treated harshly by the upper class, but it was assumed that someone closer to their station would have more compassion. These assumptions were badly misplaced. Rapacious property managers were quicker to eject tenants for late rent payments and more likely to cheat tenants out of monies owed them.

Rowe, a baseborn man who lusted after the good life, was a toady who seized on every opportunity to ingratiate himself with the wealthier landlords. He'd made it his business to find ways to make himself useful to his betters.

And he made it his business to know what they fancied. A gift of a Persian rug to Attwood and a case of fine wine for Wicker had put them in his debt. The only one he had not been able to win over was Somerville, who saw Rowe for the sycophant he was.

Rowe had become frantic when he'd discovered he was not on the guest list for the ball. It was unthinkable that he would not attend the most important social event of the season. He went to Attwood and Wicker and pleaded his case. They in turn entreated with Somerville who, against his better judgment, relented. And now the self-satisfied Rowe sat happily among his betters with grease dripping from his chin and discoursing about eviction.

"Where will the peasants go, Mr. Rowe?" Emily asked. Out of the corner of her eye, she saw her father frown. He thought such topics unsuitable for young ladies.

"Ship them off to America," Rowe said.

Wicker shook his massive head. "Too expensive."

"No more expensive than having them on the land and paying no rent," Rowe countered gently.

"You gentlemen talk about them as though they were cattle," Emily said.

"Would that they were," Rowe mumbled through a mouthful of food. "Then there would be a profit in them."

Attwood stabbed the air with his fork for emphasis. "It is the landlord's right to do as he pleases with his land, madam. If he abstains from harsh treatment of his tenants, he confers a favor, an act of kindness. If, on the other hand, he chooses to stand on his rights, the tenants must be taught that they have no power to oppose or resist. My God, good lady, property would have no value and money would no longer be invested in the cultivation of land if it were not acknowledged that it is the landlord's most sacred right to deal with his property as he wishes."

"Is that how you see it, Father?" Emily saw his uncomfortable expression and was pleased her question had the desired effect.

"It's a very complicated matter, my dear," Somerville said, hoping to end the matter there.

"You mean too complicated for a mere woman to understand?" Emily pressed.

Anger flashed in Somerville's eyes. "Certainly for a *young* woman to understand."

Father and daughter glared at each other across the wide expanse of the table.

"In any event," Lady Breen said, breaking the tense silence, "it's a moot point. Surely next year's harvest will be free of the blight."

Glasses were raised and there was a chorus of "*Hear, hear.*"

At that moment, Emily happened to glance at Nora and the other servants. The old woman's expression was a mask of neutrality. After so many years of servitude and listening to this kind of talk, she was either inured to it or had learned to block it out. But that wasn't true of the younger servants who stood at rigid attention behind the guests, poised to jump to a raised finger. On their faces she saw undisguised anger and hatred. One girl, not much younger than herself, had tears in her eyes.

Suddenly, Emily felt a great shame for herself and for those seated at the table.

Michael lay on his pallet, listening to the sounds of his sleeping family. Earlier in the evening, he'd listened to the thumps and creak of wheels as the carriages made their way down the frost encrusted road from the Manor House. The ball was over and now all was quiet, save for the sounds of breathing.

Suddenly, Dermot whispered in Michael's ear. "Are you awake?"

"Aye."

"Come outside then."

It was a clear, crisp night and the sky was aglow with stars. The milky-white frost crunched under foot as they sat down on the stone wall surrounding the potato field.

For a long time they sat there, content to enjoy the solitude and beauty of the night. Finally, Dermot said abruptly, "Why do you want to leave?"

"I don't want to become Da."

"He has his faults true enough, but he's not a bad sort."

"He's a good man. I just don't want his life."

"What else is there?" Dermot asked, genuinely befuddled.

"America."

"But you know nothin' about it."

"I do. When I went to Dublin to fetch furniture for Lord Attwood, I met two Americans." Michael's eyes lit up at the memory. "One was a captain from Boston who owned his own merchant ship. Dermot, he started out as a cabin boy!

The other owned a printing business in some place called Philadelphia. He started out as an apprentice and fifteen years later managed to earn enough to buy the establishment. Can you believe that? They said they were not unusual, Dermot. They said America is a truly wondrous place. It's place where, if a man works hard, he can own somethin' and once you own it no one can take it away from you."

"That was three years ago you were in Dublin."

"Aye. And it's taken me that long to save the passage money."

"When will you go?"

A gentle gust of wind drove the cold through Michael's threadbare coat. He shivered and pulled it tighter around him. "I was gonna go after this harvest. But there's no leavin' now. With no potatoes, life is gonna be hard and dangerous for the family. I'm needed here."

Dermot clicked his brogues together to knock the frost off them. "Michael, we've no food. We're all gonna die."

Michael saw the fear in his brother's eyes. "Don't be daft. We'll not die. Not if the family sticks together." He said it with conviction, to allay his brother's fears, but he wasn't sure he believed it himself.

He got up and put his arm around Dermot. "Come on. It's cold out here and we need to get some sleep."

The next morning, Mam reached into the bin and took out a handful of potatoes. The family watched, silent, tense.

"That's the last of the lot," she said.

"Lord, what's to become of us?" Grandmam wailed.

"We starve, you foolish woman," Granda said, and added ominously, "When famine comes, we'll die as the birds do when the frost comes."

Michael wondered if his granda was pulling her leg or if he was in one of his moods again.

"Don't be daft," Da said. "I'll buy food."

"With what?" asked Mam.

"The seed money."

There was a stunned silence as they contemplated the unthinkable—spending the seed money meant there would be no seed for next year's planting.

Da looked away from his wife's astonished expression and studied the rough tabletop. "I've got to feed the family, haven't I?" he said quietly. "I've got to keep the family together."

Michael heard his father's words and suddenly knew what he had to do. The blood drained from his face. He felt light-headed, nauseous, claustrophobic. He jumped up from the table and stumbled out the door.

All that morning as Michael worked the fields, he desperately searched his mind for some other way, some other alternative. But by midmorning he had to admit to himself that there was no other way.

Da was in the shed sharpening a plow blade when Michael came in. The old man looked up and continued honing the blade. Since the night Michael had made his announcement about going to America, there had been a strained tension between them that had seen no abatement.

Michael held out a small box covered with dirt.

Da looked at the box. "What's that then?"

"My passage money."

Da stood up and rubbed his hands on his trousers. Unable to look his son in the eye, he stared at the box.

"No, Michael. That's yers. You worked for it."

Michael shoved the box into Da's hand. "You have mouths to feed."

For a long moment father and son faced each other in silence, neither willing to say what they both knew to be a certainty. If Da took the money, Michael's dream of going to America would be lost and gone forever.

Da's eyes glistened as he took the box and gently brushed the dirt from it with a calloused hand. "When times are not so hard," he said quietly, " I'll pay you back."

"Aye. You will."

But both men knew that would never happen

Chapter Six

March 1846
Ballyross, Ireland

They came from near and far—from the valleys, from the bogs, and from the hill country. Desperate men all. They filed into the little village church, an endless stream of silent, sullen men, seeking answers to the misfortune that had befallen them. They filled the pews and, when there was no more room in the pews, they filled the aisles and, when there was no more room in the aisles, they spilled out into the road.

Perched in his pulpit, Father Daniel Rafferty, parish priest and pastor for over fifty years, watched with mounting apprehension as the rising tide of men filled his church. They'd come to him for answers but, dear God, he didn't have any. He was just a simple parish priest. What could he tell them besides what he always told them when he had no answer? *Tis the will of God....*

He pitied them because he knew what their lives were like. In his fifty years as a priest he'd been with them through fever epidemics that had wiped out entire families, crop failures that had spawned starvation, births that gave no joy, and deaths that caused no sadness. But he'd never seen the likes of this. It was as though God in his heaven had cursed the land.

Yes, he pitied them, but he was also angry with them—at least the ones he didn't recognize. With self-righteous indignation he glared down at the sea of fearful, upturned faces, many of whom he'd never seen before. *Who were these strangers?* He asked himself. *Where were these men and their families of a Sunday morning?* Home, no doubt, sleeping late on the one day their God required their presence in his house. They had chosen to defy God, to ignore his commandment, to commit mortal sin Sunday after Sunday, willing to face the fires of eternal damnation. But, now—now that they were frightened and lost, they had discovered their God again. A righteous rage welled up in him, turning his face a deep purple. He gripped the sides of the pulpit with trembling hands, prepared to denounce them. But then he remembered why they were here. He pushed his unworthy thoughts from his mind and asked God to forgive him his anger. *This is not the time for recrimination*, he reminded himself. There would be time for that later on.

"Men," he began in a surprisingly powerful voice for so fragile an old man, "There is good news from England. I am told they are shipping more Indian corn."

Padric Leahy, a red-faced farmer, stood up. "Peel's brimstone," he cried out. "Tis food not fit for pigs."

Pat Doyle stood up a. "Then eat the potatoes in your bin," he shouted.

"I have no potatoes in my bin and you know that full well Pat Doyle."

"Then eat the corn like the rest of us."

"How? Tis like eatin' gravel."

Doyle waved a huge hand in dismissal. "I've eight mouths to feed. I'll take the corn and be glad of it."

Da stood up. "Father, how are we to pay for the corn?"

The priest smiled down at Da benevolently, grateful that Ranahan had interrupted what threatened to turn into a donnybrook right here in his own church. "The new Board of Works will be accepting work applications."

That announcement was met with a wave of frustrated groans. They knew that the Board of Works was the British government's response to the famine. But suspicious of anything British, rumors were already afoot that the Board would not be able to hire all who desired work. And those who got work would receive paltry wages for their efforts.

Sitting in the third row of the old church, John Lacy, an arthritic old man with a head of unruly white hair and a shaggy beard, painfully pulled himself to his feet. "How much will they pay?" he asked.

"Up to ten pence a day," the priest said, trying to sound hopeful.

That remark caused an uproar with dozens of men jumping to their feet and shouting out in protest. Father Rafferty screwed up his face in concentration and cocked a hand behind his mostly deaf ear, but he found it impossible to understand the chaotic babble. Then Pat Doyle's voice boomed over the din clear as a bell. *"Sure a pound of corn is three times that!"*

Michael gripped the back of the pew, enraged. "That's starvation wages," he shouted to the assembled men. "Are we going to stand for that?"

"No…" The crowd roared in unison.

Father Rafferty glared down at the young troublemaker. He knew Michael Ranahan well. Even as a child he'd been too smart for his own good, him always with the questions. "If God loves us," he'd asked when he was preparing for his First Communion, "why does he make us live the way we do?" *And him only seven!*

Father Rafferty surveyed the sea of angry faces beneath him. Sure they were nothing more than a human forest of dried timber in a drought and that young Ranahan was a flaming torch that could set off a conflagration that would do none of them a bit of good.

"Men, men," he shouted over the clamor, "Tis only temporary. God willin', this year's crop will be healthy. Take the work. Just until the next harvest."

That seemed to appease them. There were murmurs of *"God willin',"* as they sat down.

Michael remained standing. *How could they be so docile? How could they think of workin' for starvation wages?* He was about to say as much when Father Rafferty spread his arms out and, looking directly at Michael, intoned, "Kneel for the benediction."

Everyone knelt except Michael. Da reached up, grabbed Michael's sleeve and pulled him down. "Don't be shamin' me before the priest," he hissed. "This is no place to argue."

Michael knelt down, his heart pounding in his chest. *They can do what they want,* he thought, *but by God they'll not starve me without a fight.*

Lord Somerville sat in his favorite wingback chair and a roaring fire bathed the library in soft yellow light. Of the twenty-odd rooms in the house this was his favorite. It was the place he retreated to when the outside world closed in on him. He'd spent a lot of time here after his wife's death. Too much time. He wanted to be alone in his grief forever, content to lose himself in Homer and Cicero. Reading about the misfortunes of those great ancient peoples diverted his attention from his own misery. He might never have come out of the library if it weren't for Nora's gentle, yet persistent, prodding. Still, it had taken months before he was ready to leave the sanctuary of the library and come back into the real world. And by that time he had sent Emily away.

Nora tapped the door and stuck her head in. "Sir, they're here."

"Show them in."

Somerville poured sherry for Wicker, Attwood, and Rowe and sat down at his desk. "I've just received instructions from England," he said. "As members of the Board of Guardians, we have been charged by the Crown to raise taxes to subsidize the Board of Works' projects."

"More taxes?" Attwood growled. "What am I to pay them with? I can't collect the rents due me now."

"I absolutely agree with you, Lord Attwood," Rowe said.

Attwood, ignoring the obsequious Rowe, addressed his question to Somerville. "If we pay our tenants to work on road improvements, when will they have time to tend our fields?"

Major Wicker drained his glass. "I say evict the lot of them. Tumble their damn hovels and good riddance to them."

Rowe nodded his head vigorously. "I quite agree. Perhaps Divine Providence is offering us an opportunity to clear the land of these troublesome cottiers."

Somerville rose to poke at a log that had fallen off the grate. "It's premature to talk of eviction, gentlemen. We must provide the men with public works, pay them, and encourage them to plant their crop." He put the poker down and turned to face the three men with a solemn expression. "Otherwise, there will be no revenues next year for any of us."

That got their attention. The room grew quiet as each man silently tallied up his potential lost profits.

"Very well," Attwood said, breaking the silence. "If we must provide work for them, so be it. But I, for one, will not coddle these shiftless bog trotters."

Rowe downed the rest of his sherry and wiped his mouth with his sleeve. "You are absolutely right, Lord Attwood. If we must offer them employment, let us make sure it's irksome enough so they don't get too comfortable. They can begin by repairing the drainage to my fields below the river."

"That will not be permitted," Somerville said. It was not lost on him that Rowe was quick to volunteer those "troublesome cottiers" to work on his properties first. He picked up the letter of instructions from London and read from it. 'The work is to be of such nature as will not benefit individuals in a greater degree than the rest of the community and therefore not likely to be called for from any motive but the professed one of giving employment.'"

"That's preposterous," Attwood bellowed. "They want us to pay these men for work that will not benefit us?"

Somerville tossed the letter on the desk. "So it would appear."

April 1846
Ballyross, Ireland

The morning the Board of Works was to open was gray and foggy. A chilling rain had been falling steadily since dawn. Inside the gloomy, stone-walled building that was the headquarters of the Board of Works, Alfred Browning, a supervising clerk in the Ministry of Public Works and John Thomas, his assistant, prepared for the opening by having their tea.

The pair had been sent from Dublin Castle to administer the operations of the newly created Board of Works. Both men, country born, but now residents of Dublin city, thought themselves urban sophisticates and believed it beneath their dignity to be posted to this godforsaken village in the wilds of western Ireland. Still, as good civil servants, they had accepted their assignment to Ballyross. And they came prepared to do whatever it took to see to it that every *I* was dotted and every *T* crossed. By God, the government's funds would not be misappropriated or squandered by thieving and shiftless bog trotters as long as they were on the job.

Thomas, rail-thin and lanky, poured tea into two mugs. Alfred Browning, a short, fat man with a bulbous nose, spooned two generous helpings of sugar into his cup. "How many men will we need for this first project?" he asked.

67

Thomas consulted his ledger. "Ten for a drainage ditch and another ten for a bridge repair on the river road, Mr. Browning."

Browning dipped a biscuit in his tea. "Do you think we'll find enough men to fill all twenty positions?"

Thomas sniffed. "With this lot of slackers, I doubt it."

They finished their tea and Browning consulted his pocket watch. It was exactly nine o'clock. "Very well, Thomas. Unlock the door."

Thomas opened the door and staggered backward at the sight before him. His pretentious veneer of sophistication deserted him and he momentarily reverted to his coarse country origins. *"Jasus Christ,"* he blurted out. *"Will you look a' that*?"

Outside, standing in the rain, more than two hundred men stood waiting to sign up for work.

It took three weeks to resolve the Board of Works' first crisis. They had expected no more than twenty men to apply for work. Instead, ten times that number appeared, clamoring for work. After a flurry of letters and dispatches between Dublin Castle and Whitehall, it was decided, however reluctantly, that all applicants should be given work. After all, everyone agreed, it would only be until the next harvest.

The next crisis had to do with *where* the men would work. Rules forbidding work projects that would benefit any one landlord made things difficult because the landlords owned most of the land in the county. In order to find work projects that would not benefit any one of them, the work gangs were consigned to remote corners of the county to build roads to nowhere. These roads became known as—*boithre na mine*— or "meal roads."

To the men, it didn't matter that they were doing useless work. It was still hard work and the rocks were just as heavy, the clay just as tough to spade, and the icy rain just as cold. What did matter was that the work was miles away from the village and the men, weakened from lack of food and freezing in their tattered clothing, exhausted themselves from the sheer effort of just getting to the worksite.

Michael, Dermot, and Da worked alongside one another spading soil made rock-hard by the frost. It was mechanical work. *Spade, lift, toss. Spade, lift, toss.* Under other circumstances Michael would have enjoyed the work, because it would have given him time to think. But, now, that was precisely the problem. He *had* time to think and all he could think of was America.

A whistle blew, mercifully taking him out of his melancholy reverie.

William Tarpy, the barrel-chested road supervisor blew the whistle again. "Time," he called out in a raspy voice.

Tarpy, a beefy man with a thick neck and a mouthful of broken teeth, was a hard taskmaster. It mattered nothing to him that his crew was building a road to nowhere. It mattered nothing to him that his crew was emaciated and weakened by hunger. It mattered nothing to him that the men wore tattered clothing that was pitifully ineffective against the cold and the rain. What mattered to him was that *he* was in charge and by God these slackers would build the finest road to nowhere that had ever been built.

Michael and the others rinsed their spades in the muddy ditch water and lined up for their noon meal of Indian corn. As they filed by, Tarpy measured out a quantity of corn and placed it on their outstretched spades. Then the men went back to the ditch, sprinkled water on the corn to soften it up, and sat down to eat in the rain, using the spade as a plate.

Dermot scooped up a handful of corn, put it in his mouth, and spit it out. "I can't eat this pig slop."

He was about to toss it, but Michael stopped him. "Eat, Dermot. You need to keep up your strength."

Reluctantly, Dermot ate the corn.

The men looked up at the sound of a horse approaching.

Emily came cantering around a bend and brought Shannon up short, surprised to see men here. She'd heard that the Board of Works had road gangs out making repairs, but this was the first time she'd seen one. She walked her horse down the center of the road, pretending to look straight ahead. But she couldn't help notice the pitiful condition of the men. And she couldn't help noticing the young man, the one who'd saddled Shannon the first day of her return, staring at her intently.

A shriveled old man rose from the side of the road. He started to cross in front of her, but he stumbled and collapsed. Shannon reared up, but she quickly got him under control and dismounted. She knelt down beside the unconscious man, put her hand to his chest and was stunned to feel his rib cage beneath his thread worn shirt. No one came forward to help.

"Why are you all cowering like sheep in a ditch? This man needs help."

Michael was suddenly beside her. He put his hand on the man's clammy temple, suddenly and keenly aware of her nearness. Out of the corner of his eye he studied her slender fingers, delicate, pale, against the man's dirty rough jacket. He inhaled the scent of sweet soap. Her skin, clear, almost translucent, was nothing like Moira's coarse skin. Suddenly, he was aware of her staring at him.

"I said, will he be all right?" Emily asked again.

"Oh… yes… He's just passed out from the hunger."

"Then you must get him to the infirmary," Emily said, infuriated by Michael's matter-of-fact tone.

Michael, flustered and still smarting from the sheep comment, jumped up. "Mr. Tarpy, this man needs to go to the infirmary."

Tarpy had his back to the road and was busy eating his own lunch of mutton and beans. He hadn't seen the man fall and he didn't know Emily was there. Without turning around, he said, "Right. I'll carry him to the infirmary on me own back straight away." He chuckled and when no one laughed in response, he turned and saw Lord Somerville's daughter glaring at him.

"Right," he said jumping to his feet. "What's the matter then?"

Michael grinned at Tarpy's discomfort. "This man needs to go to the infirmary." He knew there were no provisions to take care of sick men and he wondered what the thickheaded supervisor would do.

Tarpy glared at Michael and Emily, flustered, angry. No one, especially not a laborer, told *him* what to do. But that woman was watching him. *He had to do something. But*

what? He glanced down at the fallen man. *The man may be
sick, but what has that to do with me?* She was still looking at
him. *Why won't she go away?* He took his cap off, ran his
hands over his bald pate, and put it back on. *I must do
something.* In desperation he turned to two men sitting
nearby and shouted, "The pair of you, get this man to the
infirmary."

The two stunned men rose and went to the fallen man.

Emily remounted her horse and rode off.

Tarpy blew his whistle again. "Right then. Back to work
the lot of you." He pointed a thick finger at Michael. "And
you, Ranahan, you'd do well to mind your own business."

Michael made a move toward him, but Dermot and Da
pulled him away. Michael picked up his spade and watched
Emily canter off into the fog.

Emily rushed into the study and found her father reading
by the fire.

"I passed men working on the cemetery road today," she
said in a voice low-pitched with anger.

Somerville put the book on his lap. "We've put them on
public works."

"Some of those men are so sick they can barely stand.
How do you expect sick men to work?"

"You wouldn't understand."

"For God's sake, Father, I'm not a child. Stop telling me I
don't understand."

"Then understand this," Somerville said sharply.
"Without the public works, these men and their families will
surely starve to death. With the wages they earn, as pitiful as

they are, they can at least buy food and seed for next year's planting."

"You're right about one thing, Father. It is pitiful."

Somerville turned away from her accusing glare, weary of being caught between opposing sides. To his daughter—and most of the members of Parliament, if he was to believe the newspapers—he was an incompetent, merciless landlord bent on squeezing the very lifeblood from of his tenants. To his fellow landlords he was regarded with increasing mistrust. Nothing had been said, but he knew Attwood and the others suspected him of being a reformer; someone whose misguided compassion threatened to destroy their way of life.

"It's only until next year's harvest," he said softly.

"You might want to tell that to the man who fainted from hunger today." Emily turned and walked out of the room.

Somerville rose and stood by the window. The lashing rain was beating on the windowpane and he could hardly see his fields. Since he'd called his daughter home, he'd been waiting for an opportune time to talk to her, to find a way to heal the past. There was so much that he wanted to say; so much he wanted to apologize for. But every time he thought the time right, something like this happened and the gulf between them grew even wider.

Chapter Seven

May 1846
Ballyross, Ireland

Throughout the winter and spring, Board of Works' supervisor Alfred Browning and his assistant, John Thomas, diligently assigned men to work on a succession of useless projects. The rigid rules were carefully enforced by the two men, who were sticklers for protocol. A minimum of a half a day's wages would be paid when the work was called off because it was too cold or there was too much snow. But— there was a caveat. Mr. Browning pointed out that the rules stipulated that every worker had to be present at the morning roll call, which meant that the men had to walk miles in freezing rain or snow just to get to the worksite so they could be told to go home.

During the bitter cold months of January and February, the men built a bridge that spanned nothing. The rains of April found them slogging back and forth across the county, paving roads that led to nowhere. Without questioning the lunacy of it, they did what was asked of them and doggedly kept building the "meal roads." They held their anger when their wages were slow in coming and they went without payment for days, sometimes weeks. And they held their anger when the wages they were paid were scarcely enough to support a family.

As the days turned to weeks and the weeks turned to months, they found it increasingly more difficult to survive. Wages remained the same, but the cost of food was increasing weekly. Desperate men began selling off their belongings. Some thought it foolhardy to sell spades and cooking pots, but what good was a cooking pot if there was no food to put in it? And what good was a spade if there was no crop to dig?

"Just till the harvest..." became the daily prayer of the men who, day after day, bartered away clothing, bedding, tools—whatever would bring a price—just to feed their families for *one more day.* Desperate men take comfort where they find it and they told themselves it would soon be time for the harvest. If they could just hang on a little while longer, the potatoes would save them and then the terrible hunger would be behind them and life would go on as it always had.

And so it would—except for the farmers who had eaten their seed or traded it away. For those who had bartered their future to feed their families, this coming spring would be a time of bitterness and recrimination. Every day they would be forced to face their barren fields, a stark reproach reminding them that there would be no potatoes to harvest this year. With no potatoes they would have to continue laboring for the Board of Works—but even that bleak prospect was uncertain. There were rumors that the Works were going to close as soon as the crops came in—a terrifying prospect for men with no potatoes in their fields.

For those farmers like Da, who did plant, it was a benediction from God to see the fields turn pale green as the small potato plants pushed up through the black soil, promising a harvest and an end to the hunger.

Da slowly crawled along the furrows, carefully examining the plants with their tiny purple flowers and large flat green leaves, while Michael and Dermot followed, looking over his shoulder.

"Well?" Michael asked.

"There's no sign of blight."

"What if it comes back?" Dermot asked.

"Not two years in a row," Da said, as sure as he was of anything. "God would not permit it."

July 1846
London, England

In the summer of 1846, Lord John Russell, Prime Minister Peel's successor, made a fateful decision that would irrevocably alter the course of Irish history. He placed Charles Edward Trevelyan in charge of the "Irish Problem."

Charles Edward Trevelyan came from one of the best and oldest families in England. He was educated at Harrow and went into the Indian Civil Service when he was just twenty. In 1834 he married Hannah More Macaulay, the sister of the poet Macaulay, and together they had three children.

He was tall and strikingly handsome, but beneath that Patrician exterior was a man of rigid beliefs that bordered on the fanatical. He had few hobbies, but he did enjoy reading aloud from the Bible, much to the consternation of those who were forced to listen to his impromptu—and interminable—readings and sermons.

The consummate bureaucrat, he had made himself indispensable and so survived the defeat of the Peel government. His remarkable abilities and tireless effort soon came to the attention of Lord Russell. Under the Peel government, Trevelyan had been the Assistant Secretary of the Treasury and he remained in that title. But now, Lord Russell, trusting in Trevelyan's judgment and stewardship, relinquished full control of the Irish famine relief efforts to him. It was Trevelyan who would have the final say in granting expenses for public works and other requests for relief monies. At the stroke of a pen, he became, in effect, the de facto head of the Treasury and the one man who would most control the destiny of Ireland.

He was thirty-eight-years-old.

In addition to the Bible, which Trevelyan read daily, he believed in two things without question. The first was a fanatical belief in the economic principles of *laissez-faire*—an economic doctrine that opposed governmental regulation of commerce beyond the minimum necessary for a free-enterprise system to operate according to its own economic laws. The second belief, and one that would absolve him of the need for compassion and mercy, was that the famine raging in Ireland was nothing more than Divine Retribution.

Doctors Playfair, Lindley, and Professor Kane hurried down the marble-tiled corridor of the Ministry of the

Treasury. They had been summoned by Trevelyan to report on the latest conditions in Ireland and they were apprehensive. They had not yet met Trevelyan personally, but his reputation for impatience and obsessive attention to detail had preceded him.

"What do you know about this fellow, Trevelyan?" Playfair asked.

"Good family," Kane said. "Ambitious. A favorite of the prime minister."

Lindley opened the door to the Secretary's outer office. "Competent, I hear. But somewhat of a cold fish."

"Well, I can only hope he is more favorably disposed to the Irish problem than Russell," Kane added. "Did either of you read his article in the *Times*?"

"No," Playfair answered. "What did it say?"

"I have it here." Kane slipped the article out of his valise and read: "'It must be thoroughly understood that we cannot feed the Irish people. We can at best keep down prices where there is no regular market and prevent established dealers from raising prices beyond the fair price with ordinary profits.'"

Trevelyan's obsessive neatness was readily apparent in his modest, Spartan-like, office. The only furniture in the room was a simple desk, a chair for him, a row of filing cabinets, and three straight-back chairs for visitors.

Trevelyan sat behind his desk reading a report. Without looking up, he said, "Well, gentlemen, what have you to report?"

Dr. Playfair, who was just about to sit down, raised an eyebrow at the man's ill-mannered abruptness. Was he so busy that there was no time for the exchange of common pleasantries? "Good day, Mr. Trevelyan," he said curtly. He opened a folder and read.

"At the February meeting of the Horticultural Society in London, samples of new potatoes were shown to have unmistakable sign of the blight."

Now Trevelyan looked up and fixed an icy stare on Playfair, which these three men would see often in years to come. "Were not those potatoes grown from sets of potatoes which were already diseased?" he asked sharply.

"Slightly diseased," Playfair said, uncomfortable under Trevelyan's steely gaze. "Nevertheless, we are of the opinion that the blight will return and, if it does, it will be more devastating than ever."

"What is the basis of your assumption?"

"To begin with, we are in receipt of numerous reports from diverse districts in Ireland indicating that people have eaten their seed potatoes. We estimate the acreage of planted potatoes to be one-third less than what it was the year before. Even under the best of circumstances, scarcity is inevitable. If, however, there is a total crop failure..." Playfair shrugged and sat back.

Trevelyan reached for his Bible. "I think Isaiah must have been thinking of Ireland when he wrote"—he found the passage and read—"'And I will punish the world for their evil, and the wicked for their iniquity; and I will cause the arrogance of the proud to cease, and will lay low the haughtiness of the terrible.' Chapter thirteen, verse eleven."

When none of the stunned men responded, he closed the Bible and put it aside. "I, too, have heard reports," he continued. "But unlike yours, I have heard that the weather has been favorable and that the plants look strong and healthy. Indeed, many are predicting an abundant harvest."

"With all due respect," Lindley said, "we believe those reports to be overly optimistic."

"Really." Trevelyan dabbed at a speck of dust on the gleaming table. "Nevertheless, this morning, Parliament voted to shut down the Board of Works."

"When?" a startled Playfair asked.

"In a fortnight." When he saw the stunned expressions on their faces, he added, "Gentlemen, I, too, am a Celt, but I belong to the class of Reformed Cornish Celts, who by long habits of intercourse with the Anglo-Saxons have at least learned to be practical men. Would that all those in Ireland have learned that lesson as well."

Kane fell back in his seat, stunned at the madness of what Trevelyan was proposing. "But what if there is a crop failure? What if you—your reports are wrong?"

Trevelyan folded his hands, as if in prayer. "All the more reason for shutting it down. If we leave the Board of Works in place which, I might add, has become an intolerable burden on the Crown, the people will expect to be fed. The only way to prevent the Irish from becoming habitually dependent on government is to bring the operations to a close. We must stop it now or run the risk of paralyzing all private enterprise and having Ireland on us forever."

August 1846
Ballyross, Ireland

Michael and the other men in his work gang gathered in front of the Board of Works building and eyed the closed door with growing unease. Yesterday, after they'd finished their work, Tarpy had told them to report here this morning for further instructions. And that made the men anxious. They were accustomed to routine and anything that broke that routine was looked upon with suspicion and fear.

In the absence of accurate information rumors and doubts flew through the crowd.

"They're gonna raise our wages..."

"The devil'll fly out your ass before that happens..."

"I heard we're to build new cottages for ourselves..."

"Don't be daft..."

"The Protestants are gonna take our jobs on the work gang..."

"The Prods can have the fecken job ..."

At exactly nine o'clock, the door opened and Supervising Clerk Alfred Browning stepped out. The little man with the bulbous nose looked more sour-faced than usual this morning.

"Will you look at the gub on him?" Scanlon whispered out of the side of his mouth. "Sure he looks like he's eaten a pig's ass for breakfast."

"I have an announcement to read," Browning said. He put his glasses on and looked at the dispatch from London. The announcement itself was brief and there was no need to read it, but he didn't want to be looking at them when he told them. He studied the paper and, clearing his throat, said, "Effective forthwith, the Board of Works is closed. This is to give you time to go home and prepare for the harvest."

For a moment there was absolute silence. Browning took his glasses off and squinted at the crowd, puzzled. *Did they not hear me?*

The anger that the men had been suppressing for so long finally erupted. It started softly, hardly perceptible, like wind moaning through the trees. Then, slowly, it grew in intensity, growing louder and louder, until the collective voice of the crowd became a hair-raising shriek of anger and despair. The crowd became a sea of wild, insane eyes, open-mouthed grimaces of anger and agony.

A terrified Browning took a step back. A huge man with red hair pushed his way to the front of the crowd and came toward him. Others followed. Browning stumbled back toward the safety of his office. He grabbed the doorknob, tried to turn it, but his hand was wet with perspiration and it slipped off.

Suddenly, they were on him, pressing in on him. The big redheaded man spun him around.

"*What do you mean closed?*" he bellowed in the clerk's face. "*How am I to feed me family?*"

Browning was being pushed, jostled by the others. Faces were everywhere. He could smell their sour breaths, feel the heat of their bodies. He began to feel faint.

"*I haven't been paid in three weeks...*"

They poked him... They pulled at his clothing... "*When will I be paid...*"

Faces. Faces everywhere.

Just when Browning thought he was going to faint and be pummeled to death by this unruly mob, a young man pushed his way through the crowd and pulled the angry men away.

"Leave him alone," Michael shouted. "He's only a clerk for Jasus' sake."

Reluctantly, the scowling men backed off.

Browning saw his chance. He yanked on the doorknob. Mercifully, the door opened. He rushed inside, slammed it behind him, and threw the bolt.

Mr. Thomas peeked out from behind a cabinet wide-eyed with fear. "Are you all right, Mr. Browning?"

"A cup of tea I think... Mr. Thomas." Browning fell into a chair, hyperventilating. "A nice cup of tea would be very good indeed..."

"Straight away, Mr. Browning."

Chapter Eight

From his perch in the pulpit, Father Rafferty anxiously watched the streams of men filing into the pews. The last time they were here they'd been reasonably calm and docile. But now they were angry. And hungry. A bad combination that.

Doyle rose to his feet. "I've had no wages in three weeks," his booming voice echoed in the tiny church. "How am I to feed the family?" Others growled their support.

"Now, now, men," Father Rafferty said in a soothing tone. "Let's be calm—"

"*Calm?*" Martin Duane gripped the back of the pew to keep his hands from shaking. "I've a wife and her old Mam to feed."

Others rose to voice their complaints and fears. They all had mouths to feed, people to take care of. Father Rafferty sympathized with them. He knew what they were saying was true, but there was nothing he could do for them. "God will provide," he said, inwardly cringing at the emptiness of his statement. He knew it was not what Martin or the others wanted to hear, but it was all he could offer.

"*Protest!*" Scanlon shouted from the back of the church. Others took up the cry: "*Protest...Protest... Protest...*"

Silently, Father Rafferty thanked God for Scanlon's suggestion. The men needed to act, to do something physical to prove to themselves that they were doing *something*. He held his hands up and the crowd became silent. "I think peaceable protest may be the answer, men. I'll tell you what we'll do. Tomorrow morning, we'll gather in front of the Board of Works building. Now go home to your families, men. They need you."

Father Rafferty breathed a sigh of relief as he watched the men silently file out of the pews. He had no illusions that a protest would change the government's mind one jot, but at least it mollified the men into thinking that they had some control over their destiny. Then, Michael Ranahan, sitting in the back of the church, stood up and Father Rafferty could see all his efforts at pacification suddenly coming to naught.

"I don't know what great fool it was who decided to close the Works," Michael shouted. "But there's unfinished business on the western road. What are we gonna do about that open drainage ditch we dug across the road yesterday?"

The drainage ditch had been yet another useless task. They had been sent to dig a drainage ditch even though there was no possibility of flooding in that area. They'd dug out the ditch, but they had not built a bridge to span it.

"What has that to do with us?" Doyle asked.

"For the love of God, it's five feet wide and at least as deep. We've got to close it before someone gets hurt."

Doyle laughed bitterly. "You're daft. Do you expect us to go all the way out there and fill in a ditch for no wages?"

"I do. Who's with me?"

"Let Lord Russell and the goddamned British Parliament do it," Doyle said, pushing past Michael.

Soon there was no one left in the church except Father Rafferty and the three Ranahans.

From his pulpit Father Rafferty eyed Michael suspiciously. "What is it you're plannin' to do, Michael Ranahan?" He didn't trust this young man. He had the look of a revolutionary about him, and he asked too many questions, and he had entirely too much to say about things that were none of his business.

"Go out there tomorrow and fill in the ditch," Michael said.

The priest smiled. "God bless you. That's a good thing to do." Once again, his prayers had been answered. He didn't need this young troublemaker at the protest, riling up the men. The worksite was miles out of town and, God willin', he'd be gone most of the day.

"Will you ask the men to come with us, Father?"

"Sure I can't ask them to work for no wages."

"No, you couldn't do that, could you."

The priest was stung by the tone of sarcasm, but he let it go.

The next morning, the three Ranahans set out for the worksite. A year ago they could have walked this road for miles and not seen another living soul. But now the road was full of people, entire families on the move. Some had been ejected, others were heading for the larger towns and cities to look for food and shelter. Mixed in with the fleeing homeless were troops of soldiers. Hundreds of them. Some towns had become armed camps as merchants and town officials, fearing the roaming mobs of unemployed men, insisted on military protection.

The Ranahans were on the road for almost an hour and Dermot had been complaining the entire time. "I don't know why we're doin' this."

"For the love of Jasus because it has to be done," Da said. "Haven't you been told that?"

"You want to walk the feet off me and then break me back fillin' in a ditch that shouldn't have been dug in the first place. We're three eejits. That's what we are."

Michael put his arm around his brother. "It's just over the hill, Dermot. For the love of God will you quit your complainin'."

The three turned at the sound of a horse approaching behind them and saw Emily cantering toward them. Michael, remembering the ditch, stepped out into the middle of the roadway to wave her down, and frowned in puzzlement when he saw her suddenly spur Shannon into a gallop. At the last minute he had to jump aside or she would have run him down. A young Cavalry officer was watering his horse by the side of the road. Michael ran over to him.

"Go after her," he said, pointing to Emily. "There's a great ditch in the road up ahead. She must be warned."

The young British officer looked at Michael's tattered clothing with great disdain. "Off with you, beggar."

There was no time to argue. Without a word, Michael jumped on the officer's horse and galloped after Emily. The startled officer fumbled at his holster and finally got his pistol out.

Suddenly, Dermot was standing in front of him brandishing his spade. "You raise that pistol and I'll bash your brains out."

The officer looked at Dermot, the old man standing next to him, who was also carrying a spade, and a handful of rabble who'd stopped to watch the commotion, and decided that for the moment perhaps discretion was indeed the better part of valor.

Shannon was fast, but, fortunately, the Cavalry officer's horse was even faster. Slowly, Michael gained on them. *"Stop."* he shouted. *"Pull up…"*

A mortified Emily dug her spurs into Shannon's flanks to coax even more speed out of him. She hadn't stopped at first because she hadn't recognized Michael. All she saw was a man in the middle of the road waving his arms. With his shapeless hat and tattered clothing, he looked like any one of the dozens of homeless men she passed on the roads every day.

Because there had been reports of robberies and attacks on the road, she'd become frightened and spurred Shannon into a gallop. She was almost upon the man before she recognized who he was. Her initial fear quickly subsided, but then she felt foolish for being so skittish and she'd kept going. As she galloped past him, he shouted something at her, but the wind in her ears made it impossible to hear what he was saying.

Initially, she hadn't stopped because she'd been embarrassed, but now she couldn't stop because her pride was on the line. She'd always been competitive, a trait the nuns had tried unsuccessfully to beat out of her. But in any contest—whether a race or a poetry prize—she would not be bested. She prided herself on being an excellent horsewoman and she would not lose a horse race to some tenant farmer. She spurred Shannon and felt a surge of excitement as the horse's power exploded beneath her.

The uncovered ditch was just a hundred yards beyond the next rise. Michael dug his heels into the horse's flanks. He had no spurs, but the well-trained animal responded to his pressure. Slowly, he closed the distance… *five-hundred yards…three hundred yards…*. The crest was just ahead. He'd given up yelling. Apparently, she wasn't going to stop. He would have to overtake her.

As they thundered up onto the crest and with clay churning up from the horse's hoofs, Michael slowly inched up alongside. Shannon heard the other horse coming, put his ears back, and surged forward. The other horse, answering the same instinct, surged forward as well. And now the two horses, sweating, muscles straining, almost neck and neck, ran full out, side by side, neither horse nor rider willing to yield.

Michael reached out and grabbed Shannon's bridle. But he was no match for Shannon's powerful neck muscles. The two horses, caught up in an instinctive desire to win, bumped together, once, twice; thousands of pounds of flesh, colliding against each other, oblivious to the riders on their backs.

Emily screamed in Michael's ear, *"Let go of my horse, you fool…"*

Michael held on to Shannon's bridle and kept yanking at it. Out of the corner of his eye he saw the gaping ditch just ahead. *It was too late.* They'd run out of room. The four of them were going into the ditch and there was nothing he could do to stop it.

Then his horse spotted it. Trained to recognize and avoid enemy trenches, the horse pulled up abruptly. Michael catapulted over the horse's head, but he hung on to Shannon's bridle and was dragged alone the ground, the thundering hoofs inches from his head. Eventually, the weight of Michael's body caused Shannon to stumble and slow down. With all the effort he had left, Michael yanked on the reins and the horse pulled up just feet from the ditch.

"*Are you mad?*" Emily screamed down at him.

Michael, exhausted, let go of Shannon and fell face down in the middle of the road. Out of breath, all he could do was point to the ditch. Emily looked and, for the first time, saw what he'd been trying to tell her.

"*Oh, my God…*"

Just then, the infuriated Cavalry officer galloped up on a borrowed horse. This time he had his gun drawn and pointed at Michael. "You, there. You're under arrest in the name of the Queen."

"No, wait." Emily pointed at the ditch. "This man saved my life."

The officer glanced at a ditch that straddled the road and shook his head in amazement. Only in Ireland would they dig a ditch across a main road and leave it unattended. He looked at Michael, laying in the dust, bleeding and disheveled. *This beggar may have saved this beautiful woman's life,* he said to himself, *but he'd also stolen my horse and humiliated me in front of pack of Irish rabble. That will not do.*

"I'm glad you're safe, madam," the officer said, bowing slightly to Emily. "Nevertheless, this man has stolen one of Her Majesty's horses and he is under arrest."

"Perhaps you know of my father, Lord Somerville?"

The officer looked at her more closely and noticed for the first time how finely dressed she was. "You're Lord Somerville's daughter?"

"Yes, and I'm sure my father would take kindly to you considering the extenuating circumstances and overlooking this man's theft of your horse," she said sweetly.

"*Theft*?" Michael got to his feet, wiping the blood from his bleeding elbow onto his other sleeve. "What theft? I stole nothin'."

Emily shot him a warning glance to keep silent.

The officer was ambitious, but he was no fool. He might be assigned to this godforsaken country now, but he had a long career ahead of him and it would do him no good to cross someone as powerful as Lord Somerville. He looked down at Michael. *The man deserves a good thrashing, he said to himself, but he's not worth jeopardizing my career.* He turned to Emily, tipped his cap, and smiled obsequiously. "I will be happy to accede to your wishes, Lady Somerville. Captain Haraday at your service."

He remounted his own horse and galloped off, leaving Michael and Emily alone.

Michael tucked his shirt in. Now that they were alone, he felt awkward and painfully aware of the state of his tattered clothing, which was all the worse for being dragged by Shannon.

Emily cleared her throat. "I feel like a great fool."

Michael rubbed his wrist. "I was just tryin' to tell you about..." He nodded toward the ditch.

"Yes, of course. It's just that... well, there have been brigands on the road and..."

"Oh, aye, there have..."

"And, well... anyway, thank you for saving my life..."

Michael didn't know what to say. For the first time, she was looking at him, smiling at him, with beautiful green eyes that held no anger. No hostility. No condescension.

"Oh..." he finally muttered. "It was nothin'."

Emily's eyes twinkled. "Really? My life is nothing?"

"Oh, no... I didn't mean that... I meant... that is..."

He was actually blushing and she found it charming. "That was a witticism," she explained. "A very bad witticism I'm afraid."

Michael stared down at the ground, perplexed. He didn't know what the word meant.

"I was having sport with you," Emily explained further.

"Havin' sport with me?" Michael's eyes flashed. "Why would you be makin' fun of me?"

"No, I wasn't making fun of you. I was just trying to make a laugh. I meant no harm."

"Oh... aye..." Michael looked away in frustration, painfully aware that he was sounding like a tongue-tied buffoon.

Mercifully, at that moment, Da and Dermot came running over the crest toward them.

"Are you all right?" Da called out.

Michael waved.

"Well, I must be going," Emily said.

"Aye." Michael cringed inside. *Aye? Aye? Is that all you can say, you eejit?*

She looked at the ditch again and shuttered involuntarily. "And your name is...?"

"Michael Ranahan."

"You really did save my life, Michael. Thank you."

He slapped Shannon's neck affectionately and nodded.

Emily looked as though she was about to say something else, but she, too, nodded and rode off.

Once Da had satisfied himself that his son hadn't broken any bones, he said, "Well, let's get to work."

For the first time Michael noticed that his hands and knees were shaking. "I think I'll just sit down here for a bit," he said, slumping to the ground.

It took the three of them almost four hours to fill in the ditch. On the way back to the village Dermot made great sport of Michael. Mimicking his brother's voice, he said, "'I think I'll just sit down here for a bit,' he says. And him lookin' like he just shite his pants."

Michael paid no attention to Dermot's ridicule. He was thinking of Emily. *She knows my name,* he kept saying to himself over and over again.

Father Rafferty and the men protested that day in front of the Board of Works. They shouted, shook their fists, made threats, and generally frightened Mr. Browning and Mr. Thomas, who watched the demonstration from behind locked doors and closed curtains. But the order of Charles Trevelyan stood and the Board of Works remained closed. In due time, some would receive the wages owed them. Others would not. And there was nothing that any of them could do about it.

Chapter Nine

August 1846
Ballyross, Ireland

As the time of harvest drew near, it became a ritual for Da and Michael to go into the potato field every day and examine the plants. Crawling on their hands and knees between the rows of stalks, they squinted at leaves, soil, and stems, looking for anything out of the ordinary. But what were they looking for? They had no idea what caused the rot in the potatoes. Yet, so great had their anxiety become that the sight of a common fly or an unrecognized insect was enough to make their hearts pound.

After they finished their examination, Da and Michael completed the ritual by standing in the field and offering to one another dead flies, insects, and blemished leaves for further examination and confirmation.

"Have you ever seen the likes of this?" Michael would ask.

Da would turn the fly over in the palm of his hand. "Aye. It's nothin'."

Then he would hand a leaf with a suspicious spot to his son. "And what do you make of this?"

Michael would examine it carefully. "I've seen it many times."

In this way, they bolstered each other's courage and drove away the doubts and fears. Only after they were satisfied that every plant in the field had been properly inspected, did they go to their supper. At the door, a fearful Da always turned to take one last look at the field, as though he expected it to suddenly turn black before his very eyes.

"Are the plants healthy, John?" Granda would ask when they'd sat down to supper.

"Aye, everythin's lovely," Da would respond. "It's gonna be a wonderful harvest and that's a fact."

It was raining when the family awoke at dawn the next morning. Dermot looked out the tiny window. "Will you look at the downpour? How are we to work in all that rain?"

"Tis only water," Da said. "You'll not melt."

"Tis a deluge I tell you. Look." He yanked open the door to show his father how hard the rain was coming down and, suddenly, a putrid stench filled the tiny cottage.

Da jumped up, knocking his chair over. *"Ah, Jasus, no...no..."*

One by one they went outside into the soaking rain. Silently, they stood staring at the devastation in the potato field. It had happened again.

Then the stillness of the air was shattered by the shrill sound of Grandmam's keening.

September 1846
London, England

"'*And there shall arise after them seven years of famine; and all the plenty shall be forgotten in the land of Egypt; and the famine shall consume the land.*'" Trevelyan closed the Bible and studied the three commission members. "Genesis, Chapter forty-one, verse thirty."

In frustration, Dr. Playfair thumped his fist on Trevelyan's polished conference table. "Sir, may I remind you, Ireland is *not* Egypt. The prospect of the potato crop this year is even more distressing than last. The disease has appeared earlier and its ravages are more extensive. In short, it's total crop failure, Mr. Trevelyan. The peasants have nothing to eat."

Over the past few months, these meetings between Trevelyan and the three members of the Scientific Commission had become more tendentious. Playfair, flanked by Kane and Lindley, sat on one side of the table, Trevelyan on the other, armed only with his Bible, which he freely quoted from, much to the growing irritation of the commission members. Across the width of the table they studied each other like chess players, searching for a weakness, a vulnerability; neither side trusting the other.

It was Trevelyan's move. "Have they no food reserves?"

"Some have a few potatoes from last year, but when they're gone..." Playfair saw no need to finish the sentence.

Trevelyan raised his eyebrows. "When they are gone, what?"

"Famine, Mr. Trevelyan."

"My dear sir, you know how the Irish exaggerate."

"This is no exaggeration, sir," Playfair answered curtly. "This crop failure, falling as it does on the heels of last year's, will be devastating. Even now there are reports of people with nothing to eat but cabbage leaves and nettles."

Dr. Kane interjected. "I must warn you, Mr. Trevelyan. If previous famines are any indication, we can also expect outbreaks of pestilence."

With each meeting, the three scientists were growing more and more frustrated with the obstinate Trevelyan. In the past year, they'd come to learn that Trevelyan would not—or could not—respond with compassion. For some reason known only to him, he refused to acknowledge the plight of these wretched creatures on the other side of the Irish Sea. The only way to get through to him, they'd learned, was to make their case in the most practical terms possible.

Lindley opened a folder and read from his notes. "In the famine of eighty-two, the Irish ports were closed and the homegrown food used for domestic consumption. Under the circumstances, we believe this to be the best course of action."

Trevelyan made a steeple of his fingers and studied the three men with cold gray eyes. Powerful men aren't afraid of silence in conversation because they know no one will interrupt them. He was quiet for a long time. Then, he said, "There will be no closing of Irish ports. This government has no intention of denying merchants a fair and just profit, and we will not interfere with free market trade. You gentlemen do not seem to grasp the essential problem of Ireland. To wit, its overpopulation, which is beyond the power of man to solve. But it is not," he added knowingly, "beyond the power of Divine Providence."

The three men glanced at each other, astonished at Trevelyan's almost mystical belief in God's role in all this. He could invoke the Almighty and free trade all he wanted, but the unassailable truth was that a famine was raging through Ireland and something had to be done.

"I don't think you understand the conditions in Ireland," Playfair said. "Free market trade implies the use of currency. But most of these peasants have no money. Indeed, many of them have never used money. They exist mostly on barter. How are they to buy food without money? How can a free market exist without money?"

"Then they'll have to earn money." Trevelyan said in a tone implying the obvious.

"Prime Minister Peel promised—"

"May I remind you, sir," Trevelyan said, cutting Playfair off, "that Peel is no longer the Prime Minister. As the Assistant Secretary of the Treasury, it is my solemn duty to husband the Crown's purse and that is exactly what I intend to do."

"But, Mr. Trevelyan, the government must provide assistance," Lindley said. "Many sold everything they had to make it through the year—clothing, tools, furniture. I tell you, sir, the people have nothing."

Trevelyan was unmoved by Lindley's words. "I am not surprised. Nor should you be. The deep root of Ireland's ills has been laid bare by Divine Providence. It is God who has ordained this famine and we must trust in God and the operation of natural causes to do its work."

Kane's face reddened in anger. "Are you saying the government will do nothing?"

"On the contrary. I intend to reopen the Board of Works and it will resume on an even larger scale."

The three men sighed in relief. *Finally, he was going to do something.* But their hope that Trevelyan had come to his senses was short-lived when he added, "However, the government will no longer bear half the cost as it did last year. *All* future costs will be borne by the counties in which the works are carried out."

"But that's preposterous," Playfair blurted out. "How can you expect the landlords to carry the financial burden of this famine alone?"

"It is only fair and just that the expense fall entirely on those who own the properties. It's high time the landlords assumed responsibility for their tenants."

"But many of these landlords are near insolvency," Kane said.

"If they are it is because they have chosen to be profligate," Trevelyan snapped. "They erect ostentatious mansions, they fill their stables with costly horseflesh, they acquire hounds for hunting, and they squander kingly sums on balls and such trappings. Are you suggesting we reward their immoral behavior by having the Crown pay for such extravagance?"

"It is not for me to judge the actions of the landlords, as reprehensible as they may be," Kane said patiently. "But the fact is, few were able to collect rents this past year and many are on the verge of bankruptcy."

"Then so be it." Trevelyan's cold eyes swept the three men. "It would be best for the land to fall to someone who will husband it in a proper manner."

Lindley saw no point in continuing this line of argument. "How much food will the government import to Ireland?" he asked.

"None," Trevelyan said.

"None! Sir, last year the government provided corn meal and even then there was not enough food."

"My point exactly," Trevelyan said with a self-satisfied smile. "Free trade was paralyzed because the government interfered with the legitimate pursuit of profits by merchants. Gentlemen, I ask you, how can we expect private enterprise to import grain into Ireland if they feel that at any moment the government will step in and undercut their profits?"

October 1846
Ballyross, Ireland

The thin sound of a lone violin wafting on the night breeze brought back pleasant childhood memories to Emily. She threw open the window to better hear the music. When she was a child, she remembered how the tenants lit huge bonfires to celebrate the end of harvest. All night long they sang and danced around the fire. Emily would sit at this very window and watch the fire's embers shoot up into the starlit sky, wishing she could be part of the festivities. One year she'd asked her mother if she could go and her mother had responded, "You're too young, Emily, and besides, it would make the people uncomfortable." Emily allowed that she might be too young, but she couldn't understand how her mere presence could make anyone uncomfortable.

Nevertheless, she had to be content to sit at the window and listen to the singing and whoops of laughter long into the night until she was so sleepy that she fell asleep with her head resting on the windowsill.

Nora came in to tend the fire and turn down the bed.

"Nora, come hear the music. Is there a wedding?"

The old woman frowned. "I'm sure I don't know." She fluffed the pillows and left without another word.

Emily shrugged off the old woman's curtness as yet another sign of her advancing years. But what Nora knew, and didn't tell Emily, was that the music was not for a wedding. It was for a wake.

A huge bonfire blazed in front of Martin Duane's cottage. Women, holding hands danced around the fire while the men stood to the side passing around a jar of poteen.

"So, it's to Philadelphia you're goin'," an excited Michael asked Martin. "I once spoke with a printer from there. Where is it exactly?"

"Tis near California, I think."

"You're makin' a terrible mistake goin' out to America," Da said.

"He's not," Michael shot back. "It's a grand thing he's doin'."

Da heard the excitement and longing in his son's voice and felt a sting of guilt.

"What choice do I have?" Martin asked. "It's better than bein' beggared here. With no work how am I to feed the family?"

"But America," Da said. "Sure you know nothin' about it."

"It's a wondrous land," Michael said.

Da frowned. There it was again, the excitement in his voice. He'd been hoping Michael would forget his foolish notion of goin' out to America. But apparently he hadn't.

"You should think of goin' yerself," Martin said to Da. "Slowly, but surely, the landlords will strip you of the little you have left."

"I'll never go," Da said and spat on the ground. "This is my land and my home and by God no one will drive me from it."

Granda stepped into the light of the fire and held up his hands for silence. "Martin Duane," he called out. "Time to say yer goodbyes."

Genie stopped fiddling. The dancers stopped. Everything became quiet except for the soft rustling of the wind in the trees.

Martin took a swig of poteen for courage and stepped into the center of the circle. He shot a nervous glance at his sobbing wife. She had her arm around her dazed old mam, who was staring blankly into the fire.

Martin cleared his throat and began in a halting tone, "I've lived my whole life on this land, as did my Da, and his Da before him. I thought my sons would be born here... I thought they would farm the land and then... they would..." He paused and roughly wiped a tear away with his sleeve. "Well... that's not to be..." His voice cracked. "Anyways... thanks for comin' and God bless everyone..."

Grandmam was the first to begin the keening. Soon, the other women joined in.

After the music stopped, a disappointed Emily came away from the window to get ready for bed. As she slipped into her nightgown, a sudden wordless, howling, lament rose into the night air. She rushed to the window to listen. A cry crescendoed into a shrill howl, filling the starlit night. The hair on the back of her neck stood up and an inexplicable sadness came over her. She shut the window, muffling the mournful sounds, and got into bed. But they didn't stop until long after she'd pulled the counterpane over her head.

Chapter Ten

November 1846
Ballyross, Ireland

Charles Trevelyan thought he had solved the "Irish problem," but he had not. At first, only a handful of reports trickled in from counties in the west, the south, and the east about the conditions in Ireland. But soon the trickle became a torrent with every county reporting the same melancholy conclusion: The crop had failed utterly. In the year of our Lord, 1846, there would be no potatoes.

In spite of his personal beliefs, Trevelyan was forced to accept the fact that Ireland was in the throes of a crippling famine. Reluctantly, he authorized funding for additional public works. Within a week, four hundred thousand men applied for thirteen thousand jobs.

The weather during the fall and winter of 1846 was the most severe in recent memory. Weeks went by without a glimpse of the sun. Every day was the same as the day before. Cold and dreary. Then, the snow started falling in early November. A harbinger of the bitter winter to come.

The ones who had employment were the lucky ones. Still, they had to get to the worksite, which was usually some untraveled road far from the village. Some men, weakened by malnutrition and the bone-chilling cold that whipped through their tattered clothing, died on the road trying to reach the worksite. Others, too weak to work once they got there, fell helplessly by the side of the road, shivering and delirious.

The snow had been falling since dawn. Bracing against a bitter wind sweeping off the mountains, the Ranahan men and a work gang of fifteen attacked the frozen earth with picks and spades. Mechanically, as if in a trance, they went about their tasks, hacking at the ground, shoveling the gravelly soil, and prying loose the heavy stones that the frozen earth gave up with only the greatest of struggles. An emaciated man clothed in rags picked up a large stone. As he struggled to carry it out of the ditch, his eyes rolled up in his head and he slumped to the ground.

Michael rushed to the man's side and put his hand on his forehead. "He's burnin' up."

Pat Doyle looked over Michael's shoulder. "In the name of God, will ya look at his face? It's goin' black."

Da grabbed his son's coat collar and dragged him away.

Michael pulled free. "What's got into you?"

Da's eyes were wide with fright. "Come away..."

"Da, the man needs help."

"It's the fever," Da hissed, pulling Michael away from the fallen man. "He's got the fever."

Less than a week later, Lord Somerville called an emergency meeting of the Board of Guardians to discuss what must be done about the alarming outbreak of typhus, which was spreading across the county with virulent speed and deadly results.

The four men sat in the great room close to the fireplace. Despite a roaring fire, it was barely able to keep the damp chill at bay.

Lord Attwood thumped his cane on the flagstone floor. "I will not spend another farthing on these damned Irish. The Crown continues to raise my taxes, my tenants are in arrears with their rents, and I'm paying for them to build bridges that span nothing and roads that lead nowhere. And now we're asked to pay for a damn hospital to take care of them as well? Never, I say. Never."

Somerville was sympathetic to Lord Attwood's anger. He, too, was feeling the burden of these prohibitive costs, but he was also growing weary of dealing with his churlish behavior. Lord Attwood, Wicker, and even Rowe to a lesser extent, were long used to getting their own way. But now that things were not going their way, they had become as peevish and stubborn as children.

"You can complain all you wish about the heavy-handedness of Parliament," Somerville said. "I am not in disagreement with you there. But the fact remains that hundreds are dying of typhus and, if something is not done immediately, I am told, we can expect an even greater outbreak."

"Why can't the British government pay for the hospitals?" Rowe whined.

Somerville, losing his patience with the thickheaded, ignorant property manager, tossed the letter that he'd just received from Whitehall at him. "Read it yourself, man. Trevelyan states quite clearly that his Majesty's government will not pay for fever hospitals that in his view are the responsibility of the landlords. And so gentlemen, it has come to this. Either we set up our own fever hospital or do nothing and let disease ravage our tenants, and"—here he paused dramatically—"our own families as well. Disease respects neither class nor wealth." He looked each of them in the eye. "Well, gentlemen, which will it be?"

Two doctors, who had just shipped in from England, watched workmen erect a hastily written sign that said: *Fever Hospital*. Under the sign, dozens of men, women, and children streamed into the hospital—some under their own power, others carried on backs or in wheelbarrows.

The younger of the doctors stroked his wispy blond mustache. "My God, is there no end to them?"

Dr. McDonald, an older man with bushy eyebrows and an unkempt beard, said, "This is just the beginning. I was in India during a typhus epidemic. Believe me, the worst is yet to come."

The appearance of fever caused panic in the people. Over the span of centuries, the Irish peasant had learned to live with bad weather, drought, and even famine. But they had no understanding of the fever. *What caused it? Where did it come from? How did it suddenly spring up and start its killing?*

Lacking knowledge, they allowed superstition to fill the void. *"Lame men carried the fever..."* it was whispered. *"It comes in on the cold night air..."* others said with certainty. No, none of that. *"Tis somethin' in the soil..."* others said. Though what that somethin' was, no one could say.

The appearance of the "fever" had also changed the culture of the Irish. Irish peasants had always been renowned for their unstinting hospitality. By custom, a passing stranger was always welcome to share whatever meager food was available. It was unthinkable to send a hungry person away from the door without giving the poor soul something, even if it was nothing more than a half a potato and a sup of buttermilk.

But now, as fever spread across the land, the people grew fearful and wary. Strangers thought to be carrying the fever were shunned and, sometimes, stoned if they wouldn't go away. This dread of fever eventually extended to family members as well. When a family member became stricken with the fever, other family members, fearful that the fever would spread to them, took the sick ones from the home and left them to die in a ditch.

Da was especially terrified of the fever. When he was a child, an outbreak of the bloody flux had killed off almost every child in Ballyross and left him near death for weeks. Now he took every opportunity to sternly lecture the family. *"Stay away from strangers,"* he cautioned. *"Stay clear of people lying by the side of the road... Don't drink from streams."*

Da, a man of many superstitions, was convinced that the night air carried the fever, and now he'd taken to standing in the doorway everyday at sunset. As soon as the sun disappeared behind the mountains, he'd bar the door and stuff rags in the cracks.

He was doing just that when Mam said, "What are you doin', John? Dermot's not home yet."

Da forced a rag into the crack under the door. "He knows the rule."

Mam could scarcely believe what she was hearing. "You'll open it when he comes, John."

"I will not."

"Da," Michael said. "It won't hurt to open the door for just a moment."

"Oh, and do you know for a fact how long it takes for the fever to come in on the night air?"

Michael said nothing. When his father was like this there was no talking sense to him. Besides, when the time came, he knew the old man would complain and curse Dermot, but he'd open the door just the same.

Still, for the next hour there was a tense silence in the cottage with everyone's attention riveted on the barred door. Then, finally, the latch shook and Dermot thumped the door. "Open up," he called out.

Mam started for the door, but Da blocked her way. "You'll not open it."

"For the love of God, tis your son out there."

"He knows the rule. I'll not risk the rest of the family."

"John Ranahan, you'll let your son in."

Grandma started to keen.

Granda waved a hand at her. "Whist, woman." But he, too, watched the barred door with growing concern.

Dermot thumped on the door harder. *"Will someone open the door? I'm freezin' out here."*

Michael knew his father was a stubborn man, but he couldn't believe he could be this thickheaded. "Da, you have to let him in."

"I have to do no such thing," Da said with the desperate futility of a drowning man continuing to hold onto a rope even after he knows it's not attached to anything.

Michael moved toward the door, but Da spread his arms wide, blocking him. The thought of striking his father had never entered Michael's mind, not even the time he'd witnessed his father whip a ten-year-old Dermot with a strap until his brother's back was a mass of welts. But he was considering it now.

With a violence Michael had never seen in his mother, she shoved him aside and confronted her husband. "For the love of God, have you gone mad, John Ranahan? Tis your son out there. Get out of the way, you great fool." She shoved her speechless husband aside and undid the bar.

Dermot stood there scowling. "Were you gonna let me stay out here all night and freeze my—"

Michael grabbed him by his coat and yanked him into the room. Da quickly slammed the door and began stuffing the rags back into the cracks.

"Dermot," Michael said through clenched teeth, "the next time you're late, by God you will stay the night outdoors."

All month had seen typical November weather—cold and rainy. But this morning when Emily awoke, she was pleasantly surprised by bright sunlight flooding her room and a gentle breeze rippling the curtains at the open window. Taking advantage of the unusually mild weather and seizing the opportunity to get out of the dreary house, she went to the garden to sit under an oak tree and read her Lord Byron. At thirteen, she'd discovered Byron and had immediately fallen in love with his poetry, even though she had to admit that she didn't understand the half of what he wrote. Still, his words never failed to bring her to tears. Whether they were tears of sadness or melancholy or joy, she was never quite sure.

Now, thru misty eyes, she read:

> *The better days of life were ours;*
> *The worst can be but mine...*

"Oh, so here's where you are."

With a start, Emily shut the book, mildly embarrassed to be caught reading poetry.

Somerville stepped from behind a thick hedge and approached. He feigned surprise at finding her here, but from his bedroom window he'd seen her come into the garden and decided this might be a good time to talk to her.

"I'm sorry. I didn't mean to startle you. Enjoying the garden? It is a lovely day."

"I am going quite mad," she said, irritated that he had intruded into her solitude. "I have nothing to do."

Somerville stiffened at her grating tone, but he was determined not to let her get him angry. "Surely you can find some useful employment."

She glared at him. "Perhaps I could. In London."

Somerville suddenly thought of his wife. If only she were here. *She* was a conciliator with a true gift for bringing people with opposing views together. She was the one who could always handle their headstrong daughter. Then it occurred to him. If she were here, he wouldn't be having this conversation. He would never have sent Emily away and there wouldn't be this gulf between them.

"Emily, there are people on our lands who are dying of fever and starvation. I don't think you need go as far as London to find people who need help." In spite of his promise to himself, his tone dripped with sarcasm.

She rose, tucked her book into her apron pocket, and walked out of the garden without a word.

Somerville sat down heavily on the stone seat and stared at a nearby rose bush. In the spring it would bring forth beautiful red roses, but now there were only thorns on the barren, bare branches and they reminded him of death.

Lady Attwood's sewing room was large, even by the standards of ostentatious landlords. But she'd stuffed it with so much furniture, antiques, and bric-a-brac that she'd collected on her many trips to the continent, that the room seemed positively claustrophobic.

As a *noblesse oblige* gesture, Lady Attwood had sent out invitations to the women in her social circle inviting them to make blankets for "the poor unfortunate wretches."

"I do *not* sew," Mrs. Rowe announced to her husband when she received the invitation.

"*This is not about sewing!*" the property manager had roared in response. "Lady Attwood has invited you to her home and you do not refuse an invitation to visit the Attwood home. Do I make myself clear?"

Mrs. Rowe was the first to arrive in an ill-fitting, vulgar lime-green dress. Now she sat in the sewing room looking bored and put upon, along with a dozen other ladies, including Emily.

When Emily had received her invitation, she'd almost thrown it away. But then she remembered her father's biting admonition and it gave her pause. He was exaggerating of course. Certainly, there were some who were destitute, but had that not always been the case in Ireland? For as long as she could remember, there had always been barefoot, undernourished children and their emaciated parents living in small, dark hovels. What was so different this time? Desperate for something to occupy her time, she decided to accept Lady Attwood's invitation.

The ladies were visibly relieved when after an hour of inept and clumsy effort to sew blankets, the maid arrived with the tea service. As tea was poured, the ladies helped themselves to pastries and commiserated with each other about what a great inconvenience this famine had become.

"My cook tells me it's impossible to get a decent cut of beef," Mrs. Wicker said.

"At least you have a cook," Mrs. Rowe countered. "Mine up and went to America last week and, would you believe it, the ignorant woman gave me absolutely no notice?"

Emily looked out the window at the western mountains shrouded in low hanging clouds. She was so weary of this talk. She'd been hearing it at dinner parties and hound hunts since the crop failed in 1845. At first she found the mutterings of these patronizing women amusing, but now it had become simply tedious.

Lady Attwood put her teacup down and surveyed the output of their handiwork—a handful of badly sewn blankets.

"Well, ladies, I do believe we've done quite enough for today."

There was an audible sigh of relief in the room.

Lady Attwood turned to Emily. "My dear, would you be so kind as to see that these blankets are distributed to the needy?"

Emily smiled weakly. "Of course, Lady Attwood, I should be glad to."

Chapter Eleven

Happy to be away from Lady Attwood and those dreadful women, Emily snapped the whip over the horse's head and the little trap jumped forward. As the horse settled into a comfortable trot, she glanced uneasily at the blankets on the seat next to her, wondering what in the world she was going to do with them.

The trap came over a rise and she saw a man walking toward her. This time she recognized Michael. Since that day when Shannon had run wild, she'd been feeling guilty about not thanking him properly. At first she'd thought of inviting him to the house, but she quickly dismissed that idea. One did not invite a tenant farmer to one's home—even if he did save one's life. Then she thought of bringing something to his cottage. A small gift perhaps. But what? She had no idea what they could use or what they needed. And so she had done nothing. Now, here was a chance to remedy that.

She reined in the horse. "Good day, Michael."

Michael felt a chill course through his body when she said his name. He stopped and took his hat off. "Good day."

There was an awkward silence. Emily bit her lip. *What is the matter with me? I've lived in London for God's sake. I've attended salons and conversed comfortably with intellectuals, poets, and artists. So why am I acting like a flustered schoolgirl in the presence of this tenant farmer?*

Emily avoided looking into his dark blue eyes and handed Michael the blankets. "We ladies made these blankets for the needy. Perhaps you would be good enough to see that they are distributed to the appropriate recipients."

Michael fingered the blankets carefully and his smile faded. "You ladies made these did you? All five of them? It must have taken a fearful amount of time." His tone shifted from mocking to bitter. "Tell me, is it a miracle you expect from me? Like the loaves and the fishes? Do you think I might turn these five blankets into five hundred overnight? Because that's what's needed. Maybe five thousand for all I know. Look around you, woman. People are starvin'. They've no roofs over their heads. They're freezin' in makeshift bog homes, dyin' of the fever. And you give me *five blankets!*"

With each sarcastic jab, Emily literally jumped in her seat. Every time she was about to counter his wild, unfair accusations, he went right on as though she weren't there. *Oh, the impertinence of the man!*

Finally, she found her voice. *"You are an… ingrate!"* she screeched.

"I don't know what that means," he said, looking baffled.

"You have no gratitude."

"Oh, but I do. I'm grateful to anyone who wants to help. But five blankets doesn't count for much, does it?"

Emily fought to catch her breath. She had never been spoken to like this in her entire life.

"At least I'm doing something!" Her voice was at least a half an octave higher than normal. *Dear God, what is going on here?*

Michael shook his head. "*You*, and your ladies, are doin' somethin' for yourselves. No one else."

"You are—*so* wrong."

"Do you remember what you said to me the day that man passed out on the road?"

"Why would I remember anything I said to <u>you</u>?" Emily asked imperiously.

"Oh…" Michael was momentarily stopped by her icy retort, but he quickly regained his momentum. "Well, anyway, you called me a cowerin' sheep in a ditch. I didn't want to admit it to myself at the time, but you were right. Well, I will not be a cowerin' sheep any longer. I will do whatever it takes to save my family, myself, and my people. I suggest you take your own advice. Stop bein' a cowerin' sheep in a ditch and do somethin' useful."

Michael tossed the blankets back in her lap and stomped away.

Emily stood up in the trap, gasping for breath. "*You are*"—she searched for the proper adjective, a word that would cut him to the quick, and had to settle for—"*impertinent!*" As she spoke the last word, the horse took a step forward, flinging her back into her seat and ruining the full effect of her denunciation.

Michael continued down the road, arms stuffed in his pockets, back stiff with indignation. When he was out of sight of the carriage, he yanked his hat off, threw it to the ground, and kicked it into a ditch. "*Eejit!*" he shouted to the surrounding trees.

He climbed down into the ditch, retrieved the hat from a mud puddle, and flopped on the ground completely disgusted with himself. "What's the matter with me?" he muttered aloud. "When I'm around her I either talk like a born eejit or I take off insultin' her. 'Do you remember what you said to me the day the man passed out?' says I to her. 'Why would I remember anythin' I said to *you*?' says she to me. Of course she would not. Who'd remember the rantin' of an eejit?" He flung his hat back into the mud. "*Jasus!*"

Emily trotted down the road in her trap muttering to herself. "That man is *nothing,* A lowly peasant. A tenant farmer. I will not let him upset me."

Ahead, she saw a gaunt man pushing a wheelbarrow. He was stumbling from the load and weaving all over the road. At first she thought he might be drunk but, as she drew closer, she saw what was in the wheelbarrow: It was a young boy no more than ten and he couldn't have weighed more than fifty pounds. His pathetically thin arms and legs hung out of the wheelbarrow like broken sticks, and his lifeless eyes, half open, stared up at the sky.

Emily reined in the horse. "Where are you going, sir?" she asked softly.

The man stopped and looked in her direction, his eyes feverish, unfocused. He hadn't even noticed her until she'd spoken.

"It's to the Fever Hospital... my boy is sick... I must get him help...."

It was clear to Emily that the man himself had the fever. And it was also clear to her that the boy was dead. The man could barely stand, but with superhuman strength, he got the wheelbarrow going again and continued down the road muttering to himself.

Emily watched until the man and his pathetic cargo was out of sight. She picked up the reins, paused, then dropped them in her lap and began to cry uncontrollably.

After a time, she knew not how long, she regained her composure. But now she was puzzled and confused. She felt like an alien in her own land. Something was going on in this country, but she didn't know what. Emily, like most young women of her class, had led a typically sheltered life. She sewed, read poetry, the classics, but not the newspaper— there was nothing in it except politics anyway. She didn't know how the food got onto her table or at what cost. She didn't know how Nora and the house staff were paid or, for that matter, *what* they were paid.

Of course she knew there was a famine, but it was something remote, something that had nothing to do with her; like those endless and tiresome European wars. She'd taken her father and his fellow landlords to task for her own amusement, not out of any deep concern for the plight of the poor. Exactly what impact this famine had on them she had no idea. Certainly the servants who worked in her father's house were well taken care of. They had clothes to wear, food to eat. They looked healthy enough.

It suddenly occurred to her that she had been deluding herself all this time. The truth was, she didn't want to know what was going on. She had gone out of her way to avoid coming into contact with the misery around her. Shocked the first time she'd seen a family of poor wretches on the road, she'd taken to riding only in the fields so she wouldn't have to encounter such sights again. She never rode past the tenant's cottages anymore or stopped to talk to them—something she'd always done as a child. She'd even stopped going into the village because it made her uneasy to see the hordes of displaced people—sometimes whole families—streaming through the village streets, begging for food and shelter.

But the encounter with that man and his dead child had stripped away her self-deluding innocence and she was forced to face the stark reality. People were dying all around her. She must do something. But what? Then she thought of her father. Hadn't he told her to get involved? She thought of Michael. Even that impudent man had thrown her own words back at her. *Well, by God, she would get involved.*

With a newfound resolve she turned the horse toward the village—and within the hour descended into a circle of hell that even Dante had never dreamed of. On the road she passed men, women, and children, apparitions with eyes sunken in their sockets and rags for clothing, mouths stained green from eating grass and nettles. It was a macabre parade of the dead, the dying, and the disenfranchised. She forced herself to look at them, really look at them, for the very first time.

Some had lost their homes, some were carrying their dead, and others were trying to reach the Fever Hospital before they themselves died. She didn't know how it was possible for these people, some of whom were nothing more than flesh hanging from bone, to have the strength to move.

Not all did. She counted a dozen dead bodies lining the sides of the road. She tried not to look, but how could she not? They were everywhere. It was as though God in his Heaven had decided that Ireland, and all who inhabited it, must die. And in his fury he was casting down thunderbolt after thunderbolt to kill all who walked the face of the land.

Emily rode into the village and steered her trap around throngs of specter-like men, women, and pitifully emaciated children aimlessly clogging the roads in search of food and shelter. She reined the horse in and stopped in front of an imposing and forbidding structure with thick gray walls and narrow-slit windows. Six months earlier, it had been her father's granary. But now, he had donated its use to the Public Guardians and it had been turned into a makeshift fever hospital. Even from where Emily sat, more than forty yards from the front door, she could hear the pitiful moans and cries of its wretched inhabitants.

Steeling herself against what she imagined must be behind those imposing iron doors, she marched through them—and stepped into yet another uncharted circle of hell. The sights and smells—as palpable as a slap in the face—overwhelmed her and she had to grab onto a nearby wall to steady herself. The sick and dying were everywhere—on beds, on the floors. The smell of offal, disease, and death assaulted her nostrils. Weakened voices cried out for water; others in pain. Some called out, asking God to let them live;

others to let them die. The individual cries, weak and pitiful, joined with others in a dissonant chorus that rose to a shrieking climax, sounding for all the world like souls dammed to eternal hell.

With a determination that threatened to desert her at any moment, Emily slowly moved through the cacophonous nightmare. A door to a side room opened and Dr. McDonald, the head of the Fever Hospital, came out. His white apron was covered with blood and body fluids.

The doctor's bushy eyebrows rose in astonishment at seeing a lady here. "Can I help you, madam?"

"I would like to offer my services."

McDonald took one look at the dainty, well-dressed *dilettante* before him and scowled. She was young, beautiful, and clearly had never done an honest day's work in her life. More to the point, she certainly had never done the kind of soul-deadening work required in this hospital.

"This is not a fit place for a woman of your sensibilities, madam," he said dismissively. In another time he would have been more solicitous in recognition of her class and standing, but he'd been going nonstop for over twenty hours and he was long since past the stage of politeness and concern for the feelings of her class.

He pushed past her. "Now, if you'll excuse me, I have work to do."

Emily would not be put off that easily. "Dr. McDonald," she said, grabbing his arm firmly. "I want to help. I can do what's required."

McDonald looked into her determined green eyes, then at a patient lying in a nearby bed; an advanced typhoid case. "Tend to that patient," he said.

Emily looked at the sick man and swallowed hard. He was bleeding from his mouth and ears. His eyes, an opaque yellow, stared up at the ceiling, unseeing. Without hesitation she knelt down beside him, rinsed a cloth in a bucket by the bed, and began sponging away the blood.

McDonald looked on with grim satisfaction—and gratification. He needed all the help he could get. If she could deal with this patient, she could probably deal with the others. But only time would tell.

He snapped his fingers at a passing attendant. "Get this woman a clean pail of water," he said.

January 1847
London, England

A reluctant Trevelyan hurried down the corridor for his meeting with the Scientific Commissioners. As usual, he expected to be harangued by those tiresome men who, every day, pleaded with him to do more and more. Before the second crop failure, he'd been adamant about not sending food to Ireland. But conditions had become so appalling by the fall of 1846 that he was forced to reconsider. Playfair and his two colleagues had taken great pains to paint a gruesome picture of starving people subsisting on blackberries and nettles, and hordes of desperate women and children competing with field mice for scraps of overlooked cabbage leaves. But, he had other sources in Ireland who concurred with the Scientific Commission. Their assessment, he was told, was not exaggerated. With nothing to eat, the people, especially the children, were beginning to die in alarming numbers and he was getting pressured by certain members of Parliament to do something. And so he had. He agreed to send Indian corn to Ireland, taking solace in the fact that Indian corn was the cheapest food on the open market and hence not a bone of contention with the ever-watchful merchant class.

Trevelyan came into the conference room and, looking impatiently at his pocket watch, took his usual place across the desk from Playfair, Kane, and Lindley.

"I understand you have a complaint about the Indian corn?" he asked with a pained expression.

"The introduction of corn into the Irish diet has created some difficulties," Kane said.

Trevelyan glanced at his pocket watch again. "What difficulties?"

"The corn is rock-hard. In America, where it's used extensively in the south, it's milled two, sometimes three times. The Irish peasants don't have milling devices at their disposal. They've tried eating it unmilled, but it creates great intestinal discomfort in some, and even death by internal bleeding in others. It's especially hard on the children."

"I have read your reports, your many reports," Trevelyan emphasized the word "many" with a raised eyebrow. It was his way of letting them know that he wasn't pleased with their almost daily reports, all of which implored him and the government to do more.

"I have just the solution," he said with the type of satisfied smile that the three men had come to regard with great suspicion. He only smiled—if, indeed, that grimace could be labeled a smile—when he'd found a solution that cost the government nothing. He went to a cabinet, took out an ancient hand-mill, and placed it on the conference table. "I borrowed this from the India House museum for demonstration purposes. It's really quite simple to operate."

As Trevelyan carefully poured a quantity of Indian corn into the mill, Playfair and his colleagues exchanged questioning glances. Trevelyan tried to crank the handle, but the corn was too hard and it jammed the mechanism. He shook it, turned the handle again. Nothing. Trevelyan was not one to display anger, but clearly he was becoming frustrated. He picked up the mill, held it to his chest, and cranked the handle hard. Corn shot out the top of the mill and the broken handle came off in his hand. Playfair stifled a chuckle into a cough when Trevelyan glared at him.

Trevelyan put the mill down. "In any event, you get the idea." He scooped up the spilled corn from his desk.

Playfair stroked his beard, perplexed. "I'm afraid I don't."

"The solution to grinding the corn, man. I propose to manufacture hand-mills and sell them in Ireland. Of course the new mills will work better than this antique."

Lindley studied the broken mill. "And the cost of these mills will be?"

"I'm told they can be made for only fifteen shillings a piece."

The three men looked at each other in astonishment. To the Irish peasant fifteen shillings was a king's ransom.

Trevelyan was busy scooping random bits of corn kernels from his waistcoat and didn't see their incredulous expressions.

Chapter Twelve

January 1847
Cork Harbor, Ireland

The tall merchant ship, burdened by her heavy cargo, slowly and majestically threaded her way through an armada of ships and fishing curraghs anchored in the bay. Then, seeing a clear shot for the mouth of the harbor, she trimmed her sails and, catching a strong westerly breeze, moved smartly through the rock jetties and out into the wide open sea beyond.

Michael stood on a hill overlooking the harbor intently watching the ship—the fourth one to sail today. For weeks, he'd been hearing unbelievable, if persistent, rumors that ships bound for England were loaded with grain, wheat, and corn and that ships returning were empty. But he didn't believe them. *Ireland was in the grasp of a great hunger*, he told himself. *Surely the British government would not ship food out of a starving country.*

And so he'd come to Cork harbor to see for himself if the rumors were true. To his astonishment, he'd discovered they were. But not just grain, wheat and corn were leaving the country. So, too, were vast quantities of sheep, swine and oxen. For three days he'd kept count of the ships coming and going. Six ships loaded with food cargo sailed out for every ship that came in.

As he watched this latest merchant ship, growing smaller and smaller as it sailed toward the horizon, a thought began to form in his mind. A thought so monstrous in its implication that he didn't want to give life to it. Nevertheless, from what he'd seen with his own eyes, he was forced to admit the unthinkable: The British government was purposely starving the Irish people.

Ballyross, Ireland

Early Sunday morning, as the family was getting ready to go to mass, Michael mentioned to his father that he was going to speak to the men after mass and tell them what he had seen in Cork. The older Ranahan, always careful to steer clear of controversy, was fearful for his son's safety. He took his son by the arm and walked him into the field to talk some sense into him.

"These are treacherous times, Michael," he said. "Sure there's nothin' to be gained by callin' yerself to the attention of the landlords."

A resolute Michael, with his hands stuffed in his coat pockets and his eyes fixed on the ground, said nothing. "Ah, you've the stubbornness of your Mam," Da said in exasperation. "And that's a fact."

When mass was over, the men collected in a field across the road from the church. Michael climbed on a rock and waited for the stragglers to gather round. Behind him, Da paced nervously, head down, muttering to himself.

When the men of the village were all there, Michael began. "I've been to Cork harbor and I can tell you they're takin' the food out of the country while we starve. The ships leave loaded with grain and all manner of food, but they come back empty. I've seen it with my own two eyes."

There was an angry murmur from the crowd. "What can we do about it?" Pat Doyle called out.

"We can stop them," Michael said.

"That's daft." Da shouted, desperate to head off what he knew would come to no good. "How can the likes of us stop those big ships from comin' and goin'? I ask you that."

Da was gratified to see several heads nod in approval, but they were mostly the older men. The younger ones, always sullen and angry these days, didn't want to listen to reason. They glared at him with stone-hard expressions.

"How can we stop them, Michael?" Padric Leahy asked.

"*Guns and bullets!*" a voice cried out over the crowd.

The men fell into stunned silence as Jerry Fowler pushed his way through the crowd. "Guns and bullets will stop them," he repeated.

"No," Michael shouted above a tentative murmur of approval. "It must be a peaceful demonstration."

"Are you afraid, Michael Ranahan?" Fowler was smiling, but his words were a challenge.

It took all of Michael's self control not to go after Fowler, but this issue was too important to let the troublemaker sidetrack him. Ignoring Fowler, he addressed the men. "I say we block the quay gates. I say we not let them put our food on those ships—food that should stay here in Ireland to feed us."

There was an uncertain murmuring among the men as they tried to decide whether Michael or Fowler was right. Then, Bobby Ryan spoke up. "Michael's right. We'll do it the peaceable way." He turned to the men. "What do you say, lads?"

All the pent-up frustration, anger, and fear that had gripped these men for over a year was released in one great howl of support for Michael. For too long they had been shunted aside and treated like dirt by forces they didn't understand. Now, Michael had given them a reason to act like men again.

Jerry Fowler stood with folded arms, watching Michael with a sly smile on his face.

A fearful Da, standing to the side, watched them as well—Michael, Dermot, Doyle and the other young men, joyously thrusting their fists in the air, and an icy hand clutched his heart.

Cork Harbor Quay

The men arrived at the quay in a steady, soaking rain. The sun had been up for an hour, but it couldn't penetrate a thick curtain of metal-gray clouds. The cobble-stoned streets glistened and shadows fell across the hulking gray warehouses surrounding them. It was a cold, forbidding place.

They were fifty strong and they stood hunched against the rain. Michael moved among them offering encouragement to one, sharing a nervous laugh with another.

Pat Doyle, his red hair plastered down by the rain, towered above the crowd. Michael took comfort in his imposing height and brawn. In the past year everyone had lost a fearful amount of weight. So did Pat, but he still looked formidable. Standing beside him, bug-eyed Barry Scanlon looked more terrified than ever. As were they all. Still, they were all here, every last man: Owen Rice, Genie Connor, Tim Finney, newly-wed Bobby Ryan, and old John Lacy, arthritis and all. Even Jerry Fowler was here, still talking guns and violence and revolution with anyone who would listen.

Michael had hoped Fowler would not come. He knew this would have to be a peaceable demonstration if they were to succeed in convincing the government to stop shipping food out of the country. He had never done anything like this before, but he was sure the authorities would listen to reason and he didn't need the likes of Fowler mucking things up. To make sure the hotheaded Fowler stayed in line, Michael had asked Pat Doyle to keep an eye on him. True to his word, the big man was standing right behind Fowler watching his every move.

The only Ballyross man not here this morning was Da. Michael was glad of that—even if it did make him feel like a hypocrite. Hadn't he made it clear that this was their fight and that every man must do his part? But Da didn't see it that way at all. "Tis a reckless thing you, do, Michael Ranahan," Da had told him. "It'll cause nothin' but mischief and I'll have nothin' to do with it."

Michael feigned disapproval, but, secretly, he was glad his father wasn't coming. He didn't know what this day would bring, but if there was going to be violence, he didn't want his father in the middle of it. Besides, he rationalized, he and Dermot were enough to represent the Ranahan clan.

Standing at the front of the crowd and spoiling for a fight was his younger brother and his friends, Billy Moore and Kevin Toomey. The three of them, strutting up and down like bantam cocks, were sharing a laugh about something. Michael shook his head ruefully. To them, this was all just a lark.

The men had made Michael their leader and he'd accepted the role with great reluctance. He believed a leader should be someone who leads, someone who has a plan. But he had no plan except to confront the supply wagons and hopefully, by the sheer force of their numbers, make them turn back. He shivered, partly from the bone-chilling dampness, and partly from the doubts that had kept him awake the whole night.

I'm not up to the task, he'd told himself over and over. Leaders were brave and Michael didn't consider himself a brave man. He wasn't even sure what "brave" was. He'd seen men who called themselves "brave" die needlessly. What most called brave, he called foolish. He'd seen a foolish man disemboweled by a bull when he had no business being in the same field with the crazed beast. He'd seen another foolish man drown trying to show he wasn't afraid to swim a swift flowing river. No, he wasn't here at Cork Harbor and standing in front of these men because he was brave; he was here because it was something that had to be done. It wasn't right that food should be taken away from starving people, and someone had to stand up and say so.

Suddenly, the nervous, idle chatter stopped and everyone strained to listen. In the distance they heard the unmistakable the sound of muffled drums.

"*Jasus, it sounds like there's soldiers with them,*" Dermot whispered hoarsely.

"Spread out, men," Michael said.

The men, doing their best to hide their fear, moved apart until they spanned the entire width of the gate leading onto the quay.

Michael peered down the deserted street, trying to see through a steady wall of rain. There was not a soul in sight. When the local tradesmen had seen the men gathering, they'd locked up their shops and pulled down the shades. And now the street was as quiet as a Sunday morning.

The drums grew louder, echoing off the stone-walled buildings. Michael moved up and down the line. "Hold your ground, lads," he said, trying to sound confident and praying his voice wouldn't crack. "We have a right to a peaceable demonstration. Remember that."

"*Look—*!" Tim Finney pointed toward the top of the street.

Michael turned and saw the first line of soldiers come into view around a corner; their bayonets glistening in the gray light. A stiff-backed army captain led the column from atop a prancing brown gelding. As they drew closer, Michael recognized him. He was the same officer whose horse he'd taken to catch Emily.

Next came the wagons loaded with the food bound for England—one, two—a total of fifteen wagons in all. More soldiers with fixed bayonets flanked the wagons on either side. Two drummers—who couldn't have been more than sixteen—tapped out a slow-tempo cadence that beat a tattoo of dread in Michael's heart.

Closer and closer they came. Michael, shivering with excitement and tension, was suddenly and acutely aware of the smallest sound—the nervous shuffling of feet behind him, the creaking of wagon wheels, the hollow *clop-clop* of the horse's hooves on the cobblestone. His mouth went dry and he found it hard to swallow. *Please God, let me be able to speak when the time comes.*

The soldiers were closing with no sign of slowing. For one terrible moment Michael thought they would march right through them without stopping, bayoneting and shooting as they went.

But, then, when the column was just fifty feet away, the captain held up his hand and shouted, *"Column, halt!"*

He coaxed his horse forward and looked down at Michael with contempt in his eyes. At first he didn't recognize him, but then he looked more closely and smiled. "Ah, if it isn't the beggar who stole my horse. You'll not hide behind a woman's skirt today, lad."

A line of soldiers had followed the captain and now stood less than twenty feet in front of Michael and the men. Michael looked into their faces. Most were no older than he. Many were younger and they all looked as frightened as he was.

"Stand aside, hooligans," the captain said with great distain.

"We will not," Michael answered, surprised at the forcefulness in his voice. "You'll not ship food out of Ireland while there are people starvin'."

The captain put his hand on the hilt of his saber. "This is your last warning. Cease and desist or—"

A rock flew from behind Michael and caught the captain on the cheek. His horse reared, throwing him to the ground.

Michael, stunned by this unexpected turn of events, stepped forward to help the fallen captain. As he did so, a frightened soldier, seeing his captain on the ground bleeding, panicked and fired his musket. The round struck a farmer standing between Pat Doyle and Jerry Fowler. The man went down, blood spurting from a gaping wound in his chest.

"*No...*" Michael yanked the rifle from the soldier's hands.

Another soldier slammed the butt of his rifle into the side of Michael's head, driving him to his knees.

Suddenly, a hail of rocks flew into the rank of soldiers. Another shot was fired. Another farmer went down.

The captain, blood flowing down his cheek, was on his feet, saber drawn, yelling, "*Cease fire! Cease fire...!*"

But the terrified young troops lacked the discipline of seasoned soldiers and another volley of shots exploded into the farmers.

By now the men of Ballyross were in full-scale flight, running and tripping over their fallen comrades. Amidst the chaos, Michael reached down, grabbed a wounded man, and dragged him into an alley as shots whined about his head.

Out of the line of fire, he propped the man up against a wall and tore open the man's bloody shirt.

"You'll be all right, lad, you'll be—"

He stopped talking when he saw the gaping, bloody hole in the man's chest.

Then, he looked into the man's face for the first time. *Oh, Jasus....*

Bobby Ryan stared at Michael with lifeless eyes.

Numbly, Michael crawled to the edge of the alley and stuck his head out. Men he'd known all his life lay dead and dying in the middle of the road. A handful of soldiers moved among the fallen, calling out— *"This one's dead..." "This one's alive..."*

The captain, astride his horse, moved back and forth in front of the gate, directing the wagons as they moved single file onto the quay.

Michael slumped against the wall. *"My God..."* he whispered to the dead Bobby Ryan. *"What have I done? In the name of Christ, what have I done...?"*

Chapter Thirteen

February 1847
The Reform Club
London, England

The elite Reform Club of London boasted members of the highest rank in English society. Although Doctors Playfair, Lindley, and Professor Kane were eminent men of science, their middle-class backgrounds precluded their eligibility for membership in such an august club. And that is why they were puzzled—and not a little pleased—when Trevelyan invited them to "a special luncheon." A cryptic message sprawled on the invitation mentioned "an alternative to the corn that appears to be too hard for delicate Irish stomachs." The three men were shown to a private dining room where several high-ranking members of the Ministry of the Interior and the Foreign Office were already present. Trevelyan greeted them, looking uncharacteristically cheerful.

A long table with two large cooking pots had been set up in front of the room. At Trevelyan's urging, the group took their seats and, a moment later, a man, dressed in the uniform of a chef, made a dramatic entrance, followed by a bustling entourage of minions.

Dr. Lindley, a man who fancied himself something of a gourmet, immediately recognized Alexis Soyer, who was not only the club's chef, but also one of the most famous chefs in all of Europe. Lindley leaned close to Kane and whispered excitedly, "The man is a culinary genius. I do believe we are in for a treat."

"Gentlemen," Soyer began in a thick French accent, "today I am going to demonstrate for you my new creation—a soup for the poor that will cost but three farthings a quart."

Dr. Lindley turned to Kane with a glum expression. "It would appear I was mistaken."

"This soup," Soyer continued, "has been tasted by noblemen and members of Parliament. And one and all have declared it to be wholesome and delicious."

Soyer described the soup's unappetizing ingredients as his assistants added them to the pot. "We begin with one-quarter pound of leg of beef, two gallons of water, two ounces of drippings, two onions, one-half pound of flour, one-half pound of barley, add a pinch of salt, some brown sugar and—*voilà*!"

Trevelyan was the only one in the mystified audience to applaud. "Well, gentlemen," he said, rubbing his hands together, "shall we sample the soup?"

One by one the reluctant guests stepped up to a second pot of soup that has been previously prepared. With a self-satisfied smile Soyer ladled the thin mixture into the club's eighteen-carat gold-rimmed soup bowls.

Playfair took a cautious sip and made a face. "Swill," he muttered.

That was enough for Lindley, who put his bowl down without tasting it.

Trevelyan took a taste from his bowl. "Hot and nourishing," he announced. "Certainly a suitable repast for the destitute."

Kane tasted the soup and found it thin, tasteless and, he suspected, of little nutritional value. "Mr. Trevelyan, what do you plan to do with this—soup?" he asked.

"Send the recipe to Ireland, man. It will feed thousands at very little cost."

"Do you think the Irish can survive on this—soup?" Kane had difficulty calling the tasteless slop, soup.

Trevelyan's eyebrow arched at the tone of sarcasm in Kane's voice. "If they will not eat the corn, perhaps they will eat the soup. One does what one can, Mr. Kane. The rest is in God's hands."

"Mr. Trevelyan, I beg you to come to grips with what is going on in Ireland," Kane pleaded. "Just last week the coroner of Cork City declared that he would no longer hold inquests on the bodies of persons found dead in the streets in order to avoid the great expense, which the innumerable inquests from these causes would surely bring upon the city."

"Mr. Kane, may I remind you that Her Majesty's government has to date spent more than five million pounds and employed more than three-quarters of a million men. In fact, so many are employed that they have neglected to plant seed. I am reluctant to give away cooked food to the Irish lest they fall into total idleness. So we will offer Monsieur Soyer's recipe to the Irish and hope that they will take it upon themselves to at least cook their own food."

He put his bowl down. "And now, gentlemen," he said, "shall we retire to the dining room for lunch?" He took Dr. Lindley's arm. "I understand you are something of a gourmet. I think you will enjoy what Monsieur Soyer has prepared for us."

Dr. Lindley, appalled that Trevelyan could think of eating a gourmet meal after suggesting that the starving Irish eat inedible swill, pulled away from Trevelyan. "I think not, sir," he said. "I seem to have lost my appetite."

Trevelyan stepped back. "As you wish," he said coldly, and moved off toward the dining room with the others.

March 1847
Ballyross, Ireland

Trevelyan's unremitting policy of *laissez-faire* was wreaking havoc in Ireland. Merchants who could not afford the inflated wholesale price of goods went bankrupt. Those who had the money to buy goods, raised prices to usurious levels. Now, although there was a great supply of food in Ireland, ironically, the poor couldn't afford to buy it.

Within sight of food purveyor shops, whose windows were crammed with foodstuffs, starving women and children combed harvested fields, competing with dogs and rodents in hopes of gleaning an overlooked piece of turnip or a half-ear of corn.

The main roads had become clogged with ever increasing numbers as more and more tenants were being ejected from their homes. The specter of dead bodies alongside the road was now a common sight. Entire families, carrying their paltry possessions in bundles, swarmed over the countryside with no discernible destination, save some place where they might get a bite of food and a roof to put over their heads. Starvation and disease were killing so many that harried gravediggers had begun burying the dead in mass graves because they'd run out of wood to build caskets. There was not enough time in the day to bury all the dead and lanterns could be seen glowing in cemeteries as gravediggers worked through the night.

On their way home from a Works project, Michael and Dermot, who had grown hardened to the sight of dead bodies along the road, stepped around a bloated body covered by a cloud of furious flies. Further up the road, a dog was tearing at a corpse and Dermot hurled a rock at it. "Go away with you, you damned cur," Dermot shouted.

"Do you notice somethin' different now?" Michael asked, watching the dog backing away, stripping its teeth at Dermot.

"What's that?"

"It used to be the dogs would scurry away from the bodies when they saw us comin'. Now, they're defiant and stand their ground and only a rock or a stick will turn them away."

"Do you think they might attack us as well?" Dermot asked, warily eying the dog who was still baring its fangs at him.

"I don't know, Dermot. I don't know."

"Somethin's got to be done." Dermot saw the dog inching towards the corpse and flung another stone at it.

Michael didn't respond. He agreed with his brother, but he didn't want to encourage yet another shrill harangue. Dermot was becoming more militant with each passing day and it was getting on Michael's nerves.

"I think we should demand the Board of Works pay decent wages," Dermot said.

"We did that and they cut our wages."

"Then Jerry Fowler's right. Tis time to make our demands with guns."

Michael, his eyes blazing with anger, spun his brother around. "In the name of Jasus, didn't what happened in Cork teach you anythin'?"

"It was bad, I know. But Jerry says—"

"Jerry Fowler is a great fool and you'll stay away from him."

"Just because you don't like him doesn't mean he's not right about fightin'."

"Fight with what? Are we to fight the Brit's musket and cannon with spade and pitchfork? Use your head, man."

Michael continued walking in silence, furious at his brother for reopening a wound that refused to heal. Since that disastrous morning at the Cork quay, Michael had thought about nothing else. He couldn't sleep at night without seeing in his dreams the faces of Bobby Ryan and those dead farmers. He'd been wrong to think they could stand up to the might of the British Empire. Good men had died because of him and that was something he would have to live with for the rest of his life. There was, however, one thing he could do, and that was to make sure that hotheads like Jerry Fowler didn't do anything to cause the shedding of more Irish blood.

An old man with a shapeless hat pulled down in front of his face stumbled toward them. Suddenly, he pitched forward onto the ground. The dazed crowd, lost in its own misery, stepped around him and paid him no mind.

Michael knelt down beside the man and rolled him over. The face was so bloated Michael almost didn't recognize John Lacy, the feisty old-timer who'd stood with him at the Cork quay.

Dermot looked over Michael's shoulder and his eyes widened when he saw the telltale blackening of the face. "Get away, Michael. He's got the fever."

"It's John Lacy. He needs help."

Dermot grabbed Michael's arm and pulled him away violently. "For Jasus' sake, do you want to kill the lot of us?"

Michael pulled away from Dermot. "We can't leave him to die on the road."

As he lifted the comatose man and slung him over his shoulder, Dermot backed away in horror. "What are you doin?"

Michael waved his brother off. "Go home, Dermot. And mind, don't you be tellin' Da about this."

Michael started back down the road carrying the unconscious John Lacy. Dozens of people streamed past them, but no one gave them so much as a glance.

Michael kicked open the doors of the Fever Hospital, carried Lacy to a bed, and put him down gently. A nurse was tending a patient with her back to him. Michael called out to her. "Nurse, this man needs help."

The nurse turned and Michael and Emily came face to face. For a moment they stood there, silent, neither knowing what to say.

Emily was the first to find her voice. "Is it your father?"

"No, no... A friend."

At that moment, Dr. McDonald came by. He glanced down at Lacy and called to an attendant. "Get this man out of here."

Michael turned on the doctor in fury. "I don't care if he's poor. He's sick and by God you'll treat him."

"He's dead." The doctor shook his head and walked away.

Michael looked down at the dead man and backed away in confusion. "But, I spoke to him not a moment ago."

For the first time he looked at the people in the beds around him—frightening skulls covered by gaunt, yellow-skin, hardly human. Then it sunk in what he'd done. *He'd carried a fevered man!* He rubbed his hands on his coat, as though that could rid him of the contamination.

"I spoke to him not a moment ago..." he repeated to Emily.

Emily's heart went out to him. Michael Ranahan might be impertinent. He was certainly infuriating, but—he was also a man of compassion.

"I'm sorry," she said, not knowing what else to say.

She'd seen this reaction before. People brought sick relatives in. One minute they were alive, the next they were dead. It was something that was hard to reconcile—unless you've seen too much of it.

Michael continued to back away, bumping into beds. Then, panicked, he turned and bolted through the doors.

He ran and ran, as though the sheer act of running would itself wash the fever from him. He ran and everywhere he ran he saw death. He bumped into a man carrying his dead wife on his back…. He jumped into a ditch and almost stepped on a rat gnawing on a dead baby's face….

Bodies everywhere. Bodies and more bodies….

Blindly, he ran across an open field toward the river. *Toward cleansing waters!* Without slowing, he plunged headlong into the frigid water. The cold stabbed at him with a thousand daggers. Involuntarily, he cried out in pain, but he gritted his teeth. *Good comes from pain.* Isn't that what the priests had told him? Pain was good for his soul. Good for his body. He imagined that every stab of pain meant that the fever was being ripped from his body and it consoled him.

In the water he stripped off his clothing and, naked, dove underwater. The cold took his breath away. He gasped, came to the surface, took another breath, and dove under again.

It was like a baptism. He would be renewed. Given new life. A second chance. *Please God,* he prayed, *give me a second chance.* He dove under the frigid water a third time.

He came to the surface, but more slowly this time. The cold had begun to sap his strength. The riverbank was only twenty yards away but, somewhere in the recesses of his cold-benumbed mind, it occurred to him that he didn't have the strength to reach it.

He was suddenly very tired. Hypothermia was taking control of his body, leeching power from his muscles. He was losing sensation in his legs. His arms were leaden and refused to tread water any longer. He felt himself sinking down, down into the black abyss of the river. His entire body resonated with a painful and wondrous tingling.

The water was suddenly—*warm.*

Warm as in—*birth.* He was eight years old again, helping his father birth a calf for the first time. It was winter and the barn was cold. He blew on his little hands to keep warm, but it did no good.

The cow lay on her side, lowing, wide-eyed with fright and anticipation; her flanks heaving in and out like a giant bellows. Then, inexplicably, a small head appeared under her tail. Michael looked at it in wide-eyed fascination. How did it get *there?*

"Go ahead," Da said. "Take hold of the head and pull gently."

Michael did as he was told. There was resistance, but he pulled harder, harder, and suddenly, the calf, fully formed with a head, a body, and four spindly legs, gushed forth in a cascade of warm, sticky liquid.

"Watch him," Da whispered. "He'll be on his feet in a minute."

But Michael wasn't watching the calf. He was looking at his hands covered in the warm, sticky substance. He rubbed his hands together. *They were warm. The cold was gone.*

Now, as he sank deeper and deeper into the river, he became detached from his body. Without alarm, he watched his body sinking down into the darkness and he was not only unafraid, he welcomed it. Down there in the darkness was peace. Down there was no more hunger. No more death. No more guilt.

As he slowly spiraled down, bubbles rushed against his ears playing the most fantastic music. The water, soft as a mother's breast, embraced his body. If this was death, it was nothing to be afraid of. He let his body go, giving himself up to the river, offering himself in expiation for those men who'd died at the quay....

Then, something bumped him. Slowly, he turned and came face to face with a bloated, grinning maw, black eyeless sockets, and hair waving in the current like seaweed. A dead body claimed by the fever and it was *here* in his comforting waters. *The waters that were to be his home for all eternity!*

No! He could not be with death and disease for all eternity!

Jolted out of his lethargy, he looked up toward the light. *Toward life.* With every ounce of strength he willed his body to go back up. Despite lungs spent of air and burning as though he'd swallowed lye, despite arms and legs that had lost all feeling, he began to go up, up...

He broke the surface gasping for precious, sweet air. He flailed toward the shoreline, clawed his way up the muddy bank, and lay there naked, shivering and exhausted.

Then, he began to laugh uncontrollably. *The river had spit him out. Given him life. He was a new man. Reborn of the river.*

He rolled over on his side, gasping for breath, and watched the cadaver float face down on the gentle current with arms stretched wide, as though embracing the river.

Chapter Fourteen

April 1847
Ballyross, Ireland

For days afterward, Michael washed his hands incessantly—much to the amusement of Dermot, whose idea of washing his hands was to spit on them and rub them briskly on his trousers. Da noticed the excessive hand washing as well, but said nothing. There was a lot going on lately that he didn't understand.

Michael became obsessed with the thought that he might pass the fever to his family. Ever vigilant, he watched them for early signs.

Once, Granda, who was in his moods, caught Michael staring at him. "And what are yer lookin' at?"

"Nothin'."

"Then stop gawkin' as though you expect the devil to fly out me arse."

Michael avoided touching members of his family, which wasn't difficult. The Ranahans were not a demonstrative family and there was little touching between them. Finally, after three weeks and no symptoms he decided he and his family were clear of the fever.

Michael had taken to accompanying Mam when she went to the village to shop. There were more strangers on the road now and while most of them were harmless, pitiful souls, there were some who had mischief on their minds and others who were so crazed by hunger that they were capable of doing terrible things.

O'Mally's bakeshop was just down the road from the church. Mam had heard that Frank O'Mally had gotten hold of some grain and was selling bread. By the time Michael and Mam arrived, there was a long line outside the bakeshop.

As they slowly shuffled closer to the front door, Michael looked at the empty window and remembered how in the old days it used to be full of every manner of baked goods. As a child he would stand in front of that window, wide-eyed, dreaming of eating those fantastic cakes and buns sculptured with mouthwatering creams and icings. When a customer entered the shop, he'd run to the door so he could smell the delicious aromas coming from inside.

He never did get to taste a cake or bun. On the rare occasion when there was a bit of money, Mam bought a loaf of bread as a treat. *Hot bread, dipped in buttermilk.* He was certain no fancy cake or bun could taste better than that.

Now the window that had tempted him with so many lovely treats was vacant. Gone were the fancy cakes and buns. In its place just a sad, empty space with faded rings where the dishes had once sat on the oilcloth cover.

Finally, it was their turn and they squeezed inside the crowded little shop. The portly, red-faced O'Mally stood behind the counter, wiping his hands in his apron as he transacted his business. Michael envied him. There was a rumor that the baker was going to shut his shop and go out to America.

O'Mally held up a tiny loaf of bread.

"Tis the last one," he announced.

"Give it here," a desperate woman with wild red hair shouted.

A gaunt woman about Mam's age elbowed the redhead aside. "Never mind her, I have seven mouths to feed."

Bug-eyed Barry Scanlon pushed the two women aside.

"I'll give you half a shillin'," he said to O'Mally.

"Sure that's ten times what it's worth!" the redheaded woman said.

There was silence as O'Mally pursed his lips and considered his options.

"Done," he said.

As he reached across the counter to hand the loaf of bread to Scanlon, the redheaded woman snatched the bread. The gaunt woman, grabbed at the redheaded woman's arm and the bread flew into the air. Dozens of desperate hands reached for it. The loaf bounced off the tips of their outstretched, clutching hands. For a moment, the loaf seemed to defy gravity. Then, suddenly, it vanished. There was a mad scramble as the loaf hit the floor. Frenzied hands tore at the tiny loaf until it was reduced to mere crumbs. The redheaded woman pushed the gaunt woman. A man punched another man who'd bumped into him, and all hell broke

loose. Punches flew. Hair was pulled. Screams and shouts
filled the tiny shop.

Men and women who had been neighbors and friends
before the famine thrashed about on the floor in a tangle of
arms and legs. Someone pushed Mam. She lost her balance
and fell on top of the pile. Michael reached for her and caught
two punches to the head before he was able to disentangle
her from the pile. In wide-eyed horror Mam pulled her shawl
around herself protectively, watching her neighbors brawling
over crumbs. "In the name of God what's got into them?"

Michael took her by the arm and rushed her toward the
door. He didn't know what had gotten into them, but he was
certain they would see this kind of behavior more and more.

Michael stood across the road from the Fever Hospital,
hoping to get a glimpse of Emily. He'd been doing this every
day since he'd brought John Lacy here over a month ago. He'd
seen her only three times—once standing outside talking to a
young doctor with a wispy yellow mustache, another time
going home, and another time when she opened the front
door to let someone in. She didn't see him and he didn't try to
approach her.

*Why do I come here day after day? Why do I waste my
time here?* He didn't know the answer to those questions and
it left him feeling confused and foolish. Da was right. She was
not for the likes of him. The few times he did talk to her he'd
made a proper eejit of himself. But, still, here he was.

He was about to leave when the door opened and she
came out. Before he could duck behind a tree, she spotted

him and waved. Embarrassed that she'd seen him, he waved back and started to hurry away.

"Michael. Wait."

He turned and was mortified to see her coming across the road toward him.

"How have you been?" she asked when she caught up with him.

"Fine."

"And your family?"

"Fine." *Jasus, can I not put more than two words together when I talk to her?*

"I'm so sorry about your friend. The one you brought in."

"Oh, aye. So many are dyin'."

He turned away from her intense green eyes. She looked tired. There were rings under her eyes and she looked alarmingly thinner. But she was as beautiful as ever. He wanted to tell her that she should get more rest, but instead, he nodded toward the hospital and said, "It's a good thing you're doin' there."

"Thank you. I don't know, sometimes it just doesn't seem enough."

"I'm sorry," he blurted out.

She looked puzzled. "About what?"

"What I said to you about the blankets and all."

"Oh, that. After I calmed down I realized you were right. Five badly sewn blankets. My God."

She laughed and he realized it was the first time he'd ever heard her laugh. It sounded like the most beautiful music he'd ever heard.

"What are you staring at?"

"What? Oh..." He was staring at her. Disconcerted, he turned away, toward the west. The sun was almost touching the mountain tops.

"Well, I'd best be goin'."

He couldn't tell her that his Da would be standing at the door waiting to lock and bolt it as soon as the sun set. She'd think they were a family of eejits.

"Michael, do you know my name?"

"What—? Oh, Mistress Somerville."

"Mistress is not my first name. It's Emily."

Michael nodded, not sure where this was going.

"Please call me Emily."

"All right, ...Emily."

"So"—now she was beginning to look as uncomfortable as he felt—"I'm glad your family is well."

"Aye. Thank you."

"Well, goodbye then."

"Aye. Goodbye."

He ran all the way home to beat the setting sun. As he trotted along the River Road, he thought about their conversation, savoring every word she'd said. Then, something suddenly occurred to him—*he should have asked about her family.*

Eejit.

As he trotted up the road toward the cottage, he heard his Grandmam keening. That could mean only one thing— someone in the family was dead or dying. With a pounding heart he rushed inside to find the family huddled against one wall.

"What's the matter?" he asked.

"Tis himself," Da said. "He's got the fever."

Granda was lying in his bed. Even in the gloomy light, Michael could see that the old man had the near-dead look of those poor souls he'd seen in the Fever Hospital.

There was a rushing in his ears and he felt hot with guilt. *I thought enough time had passed! I thought the family was out of danger!* "We'll keep him warm," Michael said in desperation. "He'll be all right." He started toward the old man. Da yanked him back.

"He can't stay here, Michael."

"It's his home. Where is he to go?"

"For the love of God, will ya listen to me? He can't stay here. He's got the fever."

"All this talk about keepin' the family together and you won't help your own Da?"

"What good is the family if we're all dead?"

Father and son stood face to face.

Once again, they might have come to blows, but then Granda spoke. "Listen to your Da, Michael," he said in a small, weak voice. "I'm a dead man and I know it."

Grandmam began to keen louder.

"Ah, will you whist, woman. All that caterwaulin' will only hasten me demise."

Sadly, Michael realized his da was right. There was nothing they could do for the old man except watch him die. At least in the Fever Hospital there were doctors and medicines. There he at least had a chance.

Michael picked the old man up, stunned at how light he was. He could feel the old man's bones through the rag blanket.

"I'll take you to the Fever Hospital, Granda."

The old man shook his head. "You'll do no such thing. You'll dig me a scalp."

Michael was appalled at his granda's suggestion. A "scalp" was nothing more than a hole in the ground, two or three feet deep, covered over with sticks and pieces of turf. It had become the only shelter available to families who had been turned out of their cottages and left homeless.

"I'll not leave you in a ditch," Michael said.

"And I'll not go to the Fever Hospital to die among strangers."

Michael looked from his frightened Da to his stubborn Granda and realized he had no choice but to do as the old man asked.

Michael would dig a scalp for his Granda, but he would stay with him and take care of him until the end. He searched for a ditch on Somerville's property. He knew that Somerville, unlike other heartless landlords, never sent men and dogs to drive families from their scalps. He found a suitable spot less than a mile away from the cottage. It hadn't rained in awhile and the ground was dry. With his hands he scooped out a hollow and covered the top with sticks. He gently placed the old man in the hole.

He tried one more time. "Granda, please let me take you to the hospital."

The old man shook his head. "I've spent me whole life in these fields. Tis here I'll die. When I'm dead, just spade the soil over me."

Michael studied the old man's face, wondering if the moods had come on him. Then the old man winked. "You're too serious, Michael."

Michael grinned. It's what the old man always said to him when he was upset about something. At least he was himself, and Michael was grateful for that. He didn't want him to die in one of his queer moods. "Did you eat, Granda?"

He shook his head and grabbed his grandson's arm with a weak, bony hand. "You were right to want to go out to America. This place is not for the likes of you. You're a dreamer. You've always been different from the rest of us. You go there and make me proud, Michael." His breathing was becoming shallower. He stopped to catch his breath. "I think you'll do somethin' grand with your life, but you'll not do it here."

Michael tucked the blanket around the old man's legs and blinked back tears. He'd always been close to his granda, but the old man had never spoken to him like this before.

"You rest. I'm gonna get you somethin' to eat."

The old man tightened his grip on Michael's arm and his eyes widened. "Michael, when I was just a lad we had so many potatoes one year I went into the village with me Da to sell them. Sure we couldn't give them away. They weren't worth the bother to bring home so on the way back we tossed the lot in a ditch. I wonder if the hunger is God's punishment for the great waste of food."

Michael patted the old man's bony hand. "I don't know why God sent the hunger, Granda. But I'm sure it wasn't because of you."

When he got back to the cottage, Da was outside burning the old man's bedding. Mam stood in the door, her arms tightly wrapped around her, watching.

"Have you supper for me?" Michael asked his mother.

"Aye."

"Give it to me out here, will you?"

Da squinted through the heavy smoke. "What is it you're gonna do?"

"Bring it to the old man."

Da jabbed a finger at Michael. "That's foolishness. He's as good as dead. You need to keep up your own strength."

"It's my fault he got the fever," Michael said quietly.

Da stepped away from the fire, waving the smoke out of his eyes. "What is it you're sayin'?"

"I carried John Lacy to the Fever Hospital."

Da staggered back, his mouth open, hardly able to comprehend the enormity of what his son had done. *"In the name of God did I not warn ya?"*

"You did. I'll stay away from the house."

"You'll not," Mam said firmly.

Both men looked at her, taken aback by the unexpected steel in her voice.

"We're family, John Ranahan, and I'll not have one of my sons wanderin' about the countryside."

"But the fever—"

"The fever be damned. I'd rather we all die together."

Da, stunned by the vehemence in her tone, stared at his wife, not knowing what to make of her. His jaw worked, but nothing came out. He took his cap off and ran his hand through his unruly hair, thoroughly confused. He loved his family. More than anything he wanted them to stay together. Isn't that what he'd been saying all along? But…. *What if Michael is carryin' the fever?* His mind was a muddle and he couldn't sort it out. He was a simple man, not used to all the change and upheaval that had been going on around him since his fields had turned black. He just wanted things to be the way they were. God knows it had never been an easy life, but at least he understood it and he knew his place in it. Not like now.

He looked into Michael's stubborn blue eyes—he was his mother's son all right—and knew he couldn't send his son away. Maybe Mary was right. Maybe it was better if they all died together. "Go fetch yer Granda," he said.

"The door will be open when you get back." Mam spoke to Michael, but she was looking at Da.

"Aye," Da said quietly. "The door will be open."

Michael, carrying a plate of Indian corn, slid into the ditch and ducked into the scalp. "I'm back, Granda. You're wanted at home. You'll eat this and then I'll bring you home and—"

Granda lay on his back looking up at the stick roof with sightless eyes. His mouth was open as though he'd just seen something wondrous.

Michael reached out and closed the old man's eyes.

Chapter Fifteen

While Michael was in the scalp praying over his granda, a small dinner party was underway at Lord Attwood's estate. It was no special occasion, but events had been so dreary of late that Lady Attwood thought it a good way to liven up an otherwise less than stellar social season. Still, no matter how hard she tried, she couldn't get the men off the subject of eviction.

Major Wicker sawed at his mutton chop, elbows akimbo. "I understand the great man, Trevelyan, himself, is coming to Dublin Castle next week."

Lord Somerville, who was about to say something to Lady Attwood, turned toward him. "I didn't know that."

Wicker grinned. "There are rumors that some Board of Works' accounts are in confusion."

Lord Attwood tapped his wineglass with his knife. "Somerville, as the chairman of the Board of Guardians, I do believe this would be an excellent opportunity for you to meet with Trevelyan and tell him face to face the problems we have here."

Somerville immediately saw the merit in Attwood's suggestion. He had been writing to the Treasury Ministry almost daily, but his entreaties for additional money and assistance had gone unanswered. "I believe you are right. I will go and see him."

"Meanwhile, the evictions are coming along splendidly," Wicker announced to the table. "I've tumbled over a hundred cottages so far."

"Tumbling" was the term used to describe the Draconian method landlords employed to make sure an evicted tenant left the property and didn't return. If a tenant was in arrears with the rent, the bailiff served a notice to clear off the land. Next, the bailiff's "crowbar brigade"—hired men who were willing to tear down a man's home for a few shillings—moved in. The technique was simple enough. First they torched the thatched roof to destroy the roof beams. Then, armed with crowbars and sledgehammers, they attacked the walls, smashing them until they tumbled into a pile of rubble.

"I've heard there are landlords who are chartering entire ships and offering free passage to their tenants, provided they tumble their own cottages," Rowe said.

"That sounds prohibitively expensive," Wicker said, intrigued by the idea nevertheless.

"Not in the long run," Rowe explained. "Once you clear the land of the rabble, you can open it to grazing sheep and cattle. A much more profitable enterprise."

The men's cold, indifference tone infuriated Emily. "Major Wicker," she asked, barely able to control her anger, "where do you think your hundred tenants went?"

He looked at her as though she had asked the price of the wine he'd been consuming in great quantities all evening.

"I have no idea, madam."

"Many of them end up in the Fever Hospital to die."

Lord Somerville cleared his throat. "Emily is volunteering at the Fever Hospital." He shot his daughter a warning glance that said she was going too far.

"My dear," Lady Attwood said, "is that wise, exposing yourself to those dreadful diseases?"

"You should join me, Lady Attwood. You, too, ladies." She smiled at Mrs. Wicker and Mrs. Rowe. "It's really quite gratifying. Much better than sewing blankets."

"Yes, quite." Lady Attwood said, ending that discussion.

Emily had cast a decided pall over the dinner and the dining room sank into gloomy silence, save for the scrapes and clunks of Major Wicker attacking his mutton chop.

Billy Moore was short. Barely five foot. Genetics played a role—all the Moores were short. But so did his bent legs—the result of a childhood bout with rickets. In spite of his diminutive stature—or because of it—he was a ferocious fighter and men twice his size stayed clear of him. He was the same age as Dermot but he already had a well-deserved reputation in the village as a troublemaker.

Billy's father had died before he was born, leaving his mother to raise Billy and four brothers and sisters. She'd done a tolerable job with the others, considering the circumstances, but Billy had been a lost cause from the very beginning. He'd been an unruly child then and he was a wild man now. Billy Moore possessed the one essential ingredient necessary to be truly fearless: he had absolutely no fear of dying.

Billy's explosive anger and dangerous recklessness attracted Dermot like a crow to a corn field. The only thing that kept Dermot from becoming another Billy was the certainty of Da's wrath and, more importantly, Michael's disapproval. Dermot tolerated his Da, but he adored his older brother.

Hulking eighteen-year-old Kevin Toomey, the third member of the trio, towered over Dermot and Billy. He possessed prodigious strength and had once lifted a capsized wagon off a man all by himself. He, too, was in awe of Billy and wanted to be just like him, but he lacked Billy's cocky self-assuredness.

The three had been at the Cork quay that morning, and it had been Billy who had thrown the first stone that unhorsed the captain.

Now, the three stood on a riverbank skipping flat rocks into the river.

Kevin let loose a perfectly flat rock. It bounced six times and stuck in the mud of the far riverbank. "I'm starvin'," he said.

"So am I," Dermot said. "Soon they'll be no food in the country a'tall."

"I know where there's food," Billy said.

Dermot kicked at a pile of stones with his well-worn brogue, looking for a good skimmer. "Where's that?"

"Clancy's Market. There's a delivery every Tuesday mornin'. It'd be easy takin'."

"You're daft," Dermot said. "Fancy Clancy's? Where the landlords shop? I hear a peeler goes with the driver for Jasus' sake."

"There's only one peeler and three of us." Dermot recognized that unfocused, wild look in Billy's eyes and knew it meant trouble. "Don't be daft."

"Tomorrow's Tuesday," Billy said. "Are you with me, Kevin?"

The big man let fly a rock that hopped four times before sinking. "Aye, Billy, I'm with you."

Dermot saw the flicker of fear in Kevin's eyes, but he knew the big glom would agree to kick the devil himself in the arse if Billy asked him to. It was a stupid idea. If they were caught, they'd be put in prison for sure and that was a fact.

Dermot stared at the ground, pretending to look for a rock, but he was desperately trying to think of a way out of this. He knew Billy was watching him with his small squinty eyes. Billy loved this, he did. Getting them to do things that were daft. Egging them on, always egging them on. Sometimes Dermot was able to talk Billy out of his wild notions. But that wasn't possible now, was it? He looked at Kevin with disgust. *Not after this big lummox said "yes" when he really wanted to say "no."*

Billy punched Dermot's arm. "Well, are you with us or not?"

Dermot shrugged in resignation. "Aye, Billy. I'm with you."

It was just after dawn and a white, wispy fog rose up from the road. Dermot, Billy, and Kevin stood behind a stand of trees at the edge of the village, waiting. They heard the crunch of wheels and the creak of wood before they saw Clancy's provision wagon lumber out of the fog.

Dermot licked his lips in fear—and anticipation. He knew the wagon would be loaded with food. Fantastic foods that he'd heard about but never tasted—beef, lamb, veal, tomatoes, vegetables he didn't even know the names of, and all manner of pastries and cakes.

As the wagon came into view, the driver leaned over and said something to the constable sitting next to him. The constable shifted in his seat and Dermot saw his buttons gleam in the hazy light. Muffled laughter floated on the thick air.

Billy put a rag over his face. Dermot and Kevin did the same. "All right, lads," Billy whispered. "You know what to do."

Gripping stout branches as clubs, the three materialized out of the fog. The startled driver tried to whip the old horse into a gallop, but Kevin grabbed the bridle with his strong hands and restrained it.

"All right, now. Be calm," Billy shouted. "We only want the food."

The constable stood up. "This is robbery, you hooligans."

"Shut your gub, peeler."

As Billy started toward the back of the wagon, the constable blew his whistle. Dermot looked at the man in open-mouthed astonishment. *Now why would he do that?* The high-pitched whistle pierced the quiet morning air loud enough to wake the dead. Certainly loud enough to alert every constable for miles around.

"*You bastard—*" Billy dragged the constable off the wagon and both men went down, wrestling in the muddy road. In the struggle, the constable ripped off Billy's mask and got a look at his face. Enraged, Billy clubbed the man into unconsciousness.

Dermot pulled Billy off. "*Jasus, you've killed him!*" he said, looking down at the bleeding and unconscious man.

Billy rushed to the back of the wagon and threw open the doors. He and Dermot took a step back. The wagon was stacked to the roof with boxes, crates, bags of meats, cheeses, breads… They had never seen this much food in all their lives.

"*Will you look at that?*" Billy whispered.

Dermot jumped at the sound of a shrill whistle in the distance. He spun, half-expecting to see a squad of constables rushing out of the fog toward them.

"*Come on,*" he whispered. "*It's the peelers comin'.*"

Billy looked at the food and tears of frustration welled up in his eyes. He wanted to carry it all off. He wanted to go somewhere where no one would find him and eat and eat until he vomited, and then eat some more, until he devoured every last morsel of food in that wagon.

The shrill whistle sounded again. This time much nearer.

Kevin let go of the horse's bridle and ran to the back of the wagon. "Let's go."

Billy stood, transfixed, staring at the boxes of food. Dermot heard the muffled voices of the constables and pulled at his sleeve. "For the love of God, Billy, will you come away."

Billy turned and snarled at Dermot. His eyes darted about with the furtive, maniacal look of a starving animal denied food.

Kevin looked up the road and started backing away. Shapes were emerging out of the fog. Indistinguishable at first, but then he saw the caps, gold buttons. Four men, running.

Billy's eyes glistened with hatred. Then, with a howl of frustration, he scooped up an armful of bread and, followed by Kevin and Dermot, ran into the open field.

They ran until they were sure they'd outrun the constables and then they collapsed in a clearing near a stream. Billy threw the bread on the ground. Kevin, gasping for breath, snatched a loaf, bit off a piece and, glancing around nervously, stuffed it in his mouth.

Billy ripped a piece off a loaf. "Don't worry," he said, his mouth crammed with bread. "They'll not find us here."

Dermot picked up a loaf with a trembling hand. He, too, was starving. He, too, wanted to devour the warm, soft, delicious-smelling bread, but he couldn't. He couldn't get the image of the bleeding constable out of his mind.

Billy, watching Dermot, said, "What's the matter? Is it too stale for your taste?"

"Do you think you killed him, Billy?"

"Peelers got thick skulls." Billy stuffed the last of the bread into his mouth and stood up. "Go on home lads. Stay out of the village for a time. Everythin' will be right in a day or so."

Kevin grabbed the last loaf and stood up. "I'll bring this home to the family."

Dermot looked at his loaf. "I can't bring this home. Me Da will kill me."

Billy's crooked teeth bared in a malevolent grin. "Then shove it up your arse for all I care."

A perplexed Dermot stood in the clearing long after Billy and Kevin had gone, trying to decide what to do. He couldn't eat the bread and that was a fact. His stomach was in turmoil and he knew he'd just chuck it back up. But he couldn't throw it away either. Sure it would be a mortal sin to waste good food what with there being hunger everywhere. He surely couldn't bring it into the house. He might be able to make up a story that Da would believe, but he'd never fool his brother. Unable to decide what he should do, he tucked the loaf under his arm and started for home.

Back at the cottage, he snuck into the tool shed and covered the bread with rags. *I'll think about it tomorrow,* he told himself. *When I'm thinkin' better.*

The next morning Michael opened the shed door and saw mice scurrying from under a rag. He picked up the rag and when he saw the half-gnawed loaf his heart sunk. The robbery of Clancy's food wagon was the talk of the valley, especially since the "unknown miscreants" had assaulted a constable in the bargain. Reinforcements had been called in from neighboring counties and there were constables everywhere, shooting hard, suspicious looks at the locals and poking about the countryside with a grim determination. It was one thing to rob a wealthy food purveyor, but, by God, no one was going to assault a constable and get away with it.

Michael knew they would not give up until they found the scoundrels.

Michael dragged Dermot into the shed and threw the half-eaten loaf at him.

"What's this then?"

"How should I know?"

Michael shoved Dermot against the wall. "Don't lie to me, Dermot. Where did it come from?"

Dermot pulled away. "Leave off. You know full well Clancy can well afford it."

It was what Michael expected to hear, but still, hearing his brother admit to taking part in the robbery and assault stunned him. "Dermot, don't you know they're lookin' for any excuse to throw the lot of us in jail? Use your head, man."

"Well, someone has to stand up to these bastards."

"A grand gesture that. You risked your freedom to feed a handful of mice."

Michael picked up what was left of the bread and waved it in front of Dermot's face. "Is your life worth this? If you won't think of yourself, think of Mam. You know she dotes on you. What would it do to her if you were tossed in jail?"

"It's done, Michael. They didn't catch us. It's done." Dermot repeated the phrase as though merely saying it would make it so.

"Who was with you?"

"Don't ask me that. I'll not inform."

"Honor among thieves is it? Well, little brother, you'd better hope that the others are as honorable as you when the constables get hold of them."

Chapter Sixteen

April 1847
Dublin Castle

Lord Somerville arrived in Dublin city at dusk. As his carriage passed St. Stephen's Green on the way to his hotel on Cuffe Street, he consulted his pocket watch and realized he would have less than three hours to dress for the gala dinner being held at Dublin Castle to honor Charles Trevelyan.

Somerville reflected on his great good fortune in obtaining what had turned out to be the most sought after invitation of the season. Everyone in the government—and Dublin society it appeared—wanted to meet Charles Trevelyan, who, everyone knew, was a favorite of the prime minister. Obtaining his own invitation had not been easy given who he was or, more precisely, *what* he was. Over the past two years, the British government had mounted a campaign to vilify the landlords and indict them as the sole villains in the "Irish Problem," and it had been hugely successful. Now, almost everyone agreed that it was the rapaciousness of the landlords that was at the core of the troubles in Ireland. In the end, the only reason Somerville was able to secure an invitation was because of his family name.

As night fell across the ancient city of Dublin, Lord Somerville's brougham took its place outside Cork Hill Gate behind dozens of carriages waiting to disgorge the best and the brightest in Dublin society. While he waited for his carriage to reach the front doors of St. Patrick's Hall, he studied the eclectic architecture of the castle with fond admiration. Over the past six centuries, succeeding generations of monarchs had added buildings and towers to the castle and now it was a magnificent, sprawling fusion of Norse, Norman, and Georgian architecture.

He had not been here since his wife's death, but when she was alive they looked forward to the six festive weeks of balls and social events, which began in January and culminated with the highlight of the season—the Saint Patrick's Day Ball.

As he stepped out of his carriage and made his way into St. Patrick's Hall with the others, he was taken aback at the ostentatious display of wealth. Men in white tie and tails strolled imperiously beside women glittering in diamond earrings and necklaces. He found it unseemly that the Dublin social season should continue in the face of the devastating famine that was gripping the country. Could these men and women who flocked to the season's balls and parties be that oblivious to what was happening in the country? Somerville knew that was not possible. There were too many reminders all around them. As he'd come through the gate earlier, he'd caught sight of a throng of shivering, emaciated people and his driver had told him that in the last year they'd been streaming into the city from the countryside in alarming numbers. Dublin society, obscenely arrayed in all their finery, knew about the famine. They just didn't care. He was ashamed to be among such company and under other circumstances he would not. But, he reminded himself, he was here for a reason—to plead his case before Charles Trevelyan.

St. Patrick's Hall with its high ceilings, painted frescos, and fine tapestries adorning the walls was just as he remembered it. A long table, set for a hundred guests, was aglow with gleaming tableware, sparkling crystal, and enormous flower centerpieces, all of which had been set with the meticulous detail of a military formation. Under other circumstances, Somerville would have enjoyed the music— played by a string quartet from the Royal Irish Dragoon Guards—and the delightful women in their colorful silk gowns. But he was here to discuss famine conditions in Ballyross and anything else was a frivolous waste of time.

Somerville found his place at the table and patiently endured the tedious conversation of his contiguous tablemates—a half-deaf elderly duchess to his right, and to his left, an enormously obese banker who couldn't refrain from eating with his fingers.

Finally, as dinner concluded, a servant in a bright crimson uniform appeared at his side and discretely whispered in his ear, "Sir, the Lord Lieutenant Governor wishes your company for brandy and cigars in his private rooms. If you'll please follow me."

Somerville, glad to be getting away from his tiresome tablemates, excused himself and followed the servant.

Lieutenant Governor of Ireland George William Frederick Villiers, 4th Earl of Clarendon, was the head of Britain's administration in Ireland. Earlier in the year, Prime Minister Russell had prevailed upon him to accept the office of Lieutenant Governor. In the few months that he'd been here, he'd already demonstrated his ineptness by resorting to coercive legislation to prevent what he perceived to be mutinous outbreaks of violence. In addition, he'd hastily sponsored several relief projects, which all proved to be completely ineffective.

Now, resplendent in his ceremonial uniform, the Lieutenant Governor greeted Somerville at the door with less than great enthusiasm. And Somerville knew why. When Villiers had discovered that Somerville was a landlord from the west, he'd tried to rescind the invitation, but he was too late. It had already gone out.

"Lord Somerville," Villiers inclined his head ever so slightly. "So glad you could come."

"Thank you, sir," Somerville responded, ignoring Villiers coolness. "The pleasure is all mine."

Somerville moved into the smoke-filled room already crowded with men anxious to meet Trevelyan, or at least be seen in his company. Two servants in scarlet and gold uniforms appeared before him. One offered a glass of brandy from a silver tray and the other cigars from a finely crafted mahogany humidor. Somerville accepted the brandy and waved off the cigar.

Suddenly, there was a buzz in the room. Somerville turned toward the door as Charles Trevelyan came in. At dinner he'd had gotten a glimpse of the secretary of the treasury, but he was seated at the opposite end of the long table. Now, seeing him up close, Somerville was surprised at how tall he was and how youthful he appeared. Then he reminded himself that the secretary was only forty-years-old.

Villiers, accompanying Trevelyan, circulated about the room introducing him to selected guests. When it became apparent to Somerville that Villiers had no intention of introducing him, he stepped forward and said, "Mr. Trevelyan, Lord Somerville of Ballyross."

Trevelyan bowed slightly. "Your servant, sir."

An agitated Villiers took Trevelyan's arm. "Yes, quite. Mr. Trevelyan, there is someone you must meet," he said.

"Mr. Trevelyan," Somerville said in a voice loud enough to turn heads, "I've come here to discuss the famine and the monstrous conditions in the country."

The room went suddenly silent and the Lieutenant Governor shot Somerville a furious look. Apparently, in these circles, it was bad form to bring up so distasteful a topic as the famine.

Trevelyan studied Somerville with cold, grey eyes. "I understand you are a landlord."

"I am," Somerville answered, ignoring the dripping distain in the secretary's voice. "And I represent the Board of Guardians in Ballyross Union. I must tell you, Mr. Trevelyan, the aid from England is not nearly enough. We must do more to stop the starving and dying."

An elderly, balding gentleman with the musty, unkempt look of an academic, stepped forward and addressed Trevelyan. "I am led to believe that the famine will not kill more than a million people and that will scarcely be enough to do much good."

Trevelyan's tight lips parted in a slight smile. "And you are, sir?"

"Nassau Senior, economics professor at Oxford. At your service."

"What an extraordinary thing to say," Somerville said, stunned by the man's callousness.

"Why? I only speak the truth. My good man, the heart of the problem in Ireland is simply too many people. The Irish breed like rabbits and the only way to right the economy is for the surplus to die. And, as I said, I'm afraid a million will not be nearly enough."

"How many would you suggest," Somerville asked sarcastically.

"At least a million and a half."

"I will give you the benefit of the doubt that you are jesting," Somerville said, fighting to control his anger. "But I must say that, given the number of dead and dying and the misery spreading through this tortured country, it is a poor jest indeed."

Senior looked at him over his wire-rimmed glasses. "I assure you, sir, I am not jesting."

Ignoring the contemptable little man, Somerville turned to Trevelyan. "Sir, the accumulated evils of misgovernment and mismanagement are now coming to a crisis and something must be done."

"The British government is doing all that it can do," Trevelyan said in a wearisome tone. "I would offer that too much has already been done for the Irish. They grow worse instead of better."

"The British government is expending only *one* pound to keep *one* person alive for thirty-four weeks," Somerville countered. "I have heard a member of the House of Commons say that these figures should not be made public for fear that the government would be accused of slowly murdering the peasantry by the scantiness of its relief."

A self-important young man with a large mutton chop whiskers stepped forward. "James Wilson, editor of the *Economist*, at your service. I think it is an absolute tenet of *laissez faire* that it is no man's business to provide for another. If left to the natural law of distribution, those who deserve more will obtain it."

"Quite so," Trevelyan interjected, recognizing a fellow traveler. "You echo the sound observation of Thomas Malthus who said, 'If a man cannot get sustenance from his parents, on whom he has a just demand, and if society does not want his labor, he has no claim of right to the smallest portion of food and, in fact, has no business to be where he is.'"

"*Balderdash.*"

Trevelyan stepped back as though a pan of cold water had been hurled in his face. He pursed his lips and narrowed his eyes at the combative, ruddy-faced man who had shouted the word. Trevelyan had been in Ireland only two days, but, nevertheless, his suspicions had been confirmed. The Irish, even the supposedly intellectual class, were a nation of louts and boors.

"What is being allowed to happen in this country is nothing short of genocide," the ruddy-faced man said.

"And you are, sir?" Trevelyan snapped, no longer trying to mask his displeasure.

"George Berkeley, and, for want of a better description of my employment, philosopher. Last year I had reason to be in America. On that journey I had the occasion to observe Negro slaves on American plantations. It's quite extraordinary, really. The Negroes have a saying: 'If a Negro was not a Negro, Irishmen would be the Negro.'"

Trevelyan turned to the Lieutenant Governor. "It's getting quite late and I have much to do tomorrow."

"Yes, of course," Villiers said, relieved to see an end to this discordant and troubling conversation.

As Trevelyan started to move away, Somerville made one last plea. "Mr. Trevelyan, I beg you, sir. Come to Ballyross. See with your own eyes what is happening."

Trevelyan turned and the coldness in his eyes stunned Somerville. "There is no need of that, sir. I receive detailed reports daily. Rest assured, I know what is going on in Ireland. Besides, no matter what you or I say or do, it is, in the end, all in God's hands, is it not?"

Somerville was too taken aback to respond. He'd heard that Trevelyan was a zealous believer in *laissez faire*, and he'd heard rumors that Trevelyan firmly believed that the famine was divine retribution. But he found it incredible that the man would not avail himself of the opportunity to see, first hand, the extent of the famine.

A crestfallen Somerville watched Trevelyan leave the room to polite applause and realized the only man who could solve the problems of the famine would not do it.

Chapter Seventeen

Three days after the bungled attack on Clancy's provisions wagon, Dermot, Billy, and Kevin were part of a road gang working on a drainage project far from the village. Billy was in a foul mood and everyone, even Tarpy, the road supervisor, stayed clear of him.

"I hate this fecken county," Billy muttered, jabbing the spade into the hard ground. "I hate being hungry. I hate diggin' ditches like a dog. I wish I could get out of this cursed place!"

Dermot was the first to see them coming. He moved close to Billy and nudged him. In the distance, a black constable wagon, drawn by two horses, was approaching.

Billy kept digging, but his mood became more subdued. "Pay them no mind," he muttered. "There's peelers all over the countryside. They're just passin' by."

But they weren't just passing by. The covered wagon— black and ominous in the swirling dust—slowed and came to a stop in front of the group.

The men stopped working and stood silent, leaning on their spades.

They couldn't see what was behind the opaque window curtains, but they knew the constables were inside, looking out at them. Michael had been watching Dermot as the wagon approach. He'd seen him say something to Billy. Then, he'd seen Dermot shoot a worried glance at Kevin. And now he knew who else had robbed Clancy's wagon.

The back door opened and they came out—one, two, three—eight in all; tall, stern, thick-necked men with truncheons. They spread out without saying a word. The last one to come out was the constable who'd been attacked by Billy. His head was swathed in bandages.

Silently, the injured constable walked through the road gang, studying each face intently. Billy slipped behind Dermot and Kevin. The constable moved along the line of men. He stopped and studied Kevin's face. Kevin stared at the ground, his face as pale as the underbelly of a dead alewife. After what seemed to Kevin like an eternity, the constable moved on.

He stopped and studied Dermot's face for a moment and moved on. Dermot breathed a sigh of relief. Then the constable stopped, turned, and came back to take a closer look at Billy, who was standing behind Kevin, trying to be inconspicuous.

Another eternity passed. *He can't remember him*, Dermot told himself. *He saw him for just a moment...*

"*That's him!*" the constable shouted.

The other constables formed a circle around Billy and moved in. Billy swung his spade, knocking one man to the ground. He swung again, staggering another. For just a moment, for one wild moment, Dermot thought he would fight them off. *All by himself. Skinny, daft, Billy with his crooked legs.*

But there were too many of them. Like wolves bringing down a wounded deer, they swarmed over him in their black uniforms and their shinny gold buttons, truncheons flailing like so many windmills run amuck.

Billy threw up his arms in a futile effort to ward off the blows raining down on him. He fought like a wild man, but there were too many constables, too many truncheons. Billy's knees buckled and he went down under the onslaught of thudding clubs.

Michael's body shook with fury. One part of him wanted to jump into the melee, grab one of those clubs and show them what it felt like to be beaten like an animal. But another part of him knew it was futile. The constables were like a force of nature and nothing he could do would stop them.

Then it was over. Billy lay twitching in the dirt, unconscious and bleeding. Four constables picked him up, carried him to the wagon and threw him into the back.

The injured constable, breathing heavily from his exertions, turned to the sullen, watching men. "We'll be back for the other two as soon as he tells us who they are."

That night neither Dermot nor Michael slept.

Sometime after midnight, Dermot leaned close and whispered in Michael's ear. "Will I be arrested do you think?"

Michael couldn't see his brother in the darkness, but he could hear the fear in his voice. There was no point in lying to him. "If they make Billy inform."

"*Oh, Jasus...*"

"Go to sleep, little brother. Billy's a tough old bugger. There isn't a peeler alive who'll make him inform on his friends."

"Do you think so?"

"Aye. Go to sleep now."

But Michael didn't believe that. He'd seen how the constables had beaten Billy. They were crazed. Billy had attacked one of their own and that made it personal. Billy might be as tough as the local granite rocks that blunted plow blades, but even he wouldn't be able to withstand the wrath of the constables.

Michael listened to his mam's soft breathing. *She'll die if Dermot is arrested.* He's always been her favorite, though Michael never understood why. Dermot caused her more grief than Michael ever did. But for as long as he could remember, it had been his job to rescue Dermot when he got into trouble. Every time they went out his mother would say, "Now, Michael, mind you watch out for your little brother."

Michael couldn't count the number of fights he'd gotten into because of Dermot. He couldn't remember the number of lies he'd told on his brother's behalf. He kept telling himself Dermot would get better as he got older, but he never did. And now, he was in the biggest trouble of his life.

Michael sat up and slipped on his brogues.

"Where you goin'?" Dermot whispered.

"Never you mind. Go back to sleep."

The constables' barracks, a squat, menacing two-story building of gray fieldstone, was on a lonely road a mile outside the village. Michael stood in a field on the other side of the road studying a barred window on the second floor. He knew that's where Billy was.

He could see silhouettes moving behind a shade in the downstairs window. He waited until he was certain no one was going to come out. Then he slipped across the road and shimmied up a drainpipe.

He was almost to the roof when he heard footsteps below him. He stepped onto a narrow ledge and looked down. A sergeant in shirtsleeves came around the side of the building. Michael wasn't used to being this high off the ground and he suddenly felt dizzy. He grabbed at a roof shingle and—it came loose. In slow motion, he watched the shingle sail out into the thin air, and... Michael's hand shot out and grabbed it. He hugged the side of the building, his face pressed against the coarse stone, his heart pounding.

The sergeant stopped beneath him. It was a moonless night, but there was enough light that if he looked up, he would see Michael.

Michael dared not look down. He dared not move.

He heard a match flare. The sergeant lit his pipe. Michael heard puffing, and a moment later the sweet aroma of tobacco smoke engulfed him.

My God, he's gonna smoke his pipe out here!

Michael was hanging on by his fingertips. They began to cramp, shooting excruciating ribbons of pain up his fingers and into his arms. He didn't know how much longer he could hold on.

From inside the building, a voice called out. "Sergeant Lafferty, come have your tea."

The sergeant spat and went back inside.

Michael finally let himself breathe, as pinwheels floated before his eyes.

"Have you come to get me out?"

The disembodied voice startled Michael and he almost let go of the roof tiles. He slid along the ledge toward the window. The voice didn't sound like Billy. Then he saw Billy's face squeezed between the bars on the window and knew why. The few teeth Billy had were gone and his gums were crusted with blood. The small, squinty eyes were almost swollen shut. The skinny face lumpy with bruises.

"Have you come to get me out, Michael?"

"No, Billy. I did not."

"Then that's all the worse for me, isn't it?" he said without rancor. He glanced over his shoulder. "They said they were goin' for tea, but they'll be back."

"Billy, did you tell them anythin'?"

"Never," Billy hissed. A spittle of blood splattered the bars. "They'll not make me inform."

In spite of Billy's bravado, Michael heard fear in his voice. He knew the only way for Billy to withstand a beating was to give him hope. And Michael prayed he could offer the hope that Billy needed.

"Billy, today you said you wanted out of the country."

The young man's face pressed against the bars. "Aye."

"If you don't tell them about Dermot, I'll tell you how to get out."

Billy's grin was a horrible leer. "You do, and I swear I'll not inform. They'll have to kill me first."

Michael leaned close and whispered in Billy's ear.

Billy's head bobbed excitedly. "Thanks, Michael. You've saved me life."

He pulled back from the bars. "I hear footsteps on the stairs." Fear flickered in his eyes. "They've finished their tea."

Michael shimmied down the drainpipe and raced across the road into the safety of the field. As he moved toward the tree line, an inhuman howl of pain pierced the damp night.

Michael shivered, thinking of his brother. *Please God,* he prayed. *Give Billy the strength not to inform....*

The rural courts of western Ireland were almost a parody of the majestic courts of London. There were no imposing buildings, no "Old Bailey," no marbled corridors filled with wigged barristers and solicitors, no great orators to mesmerize a galley packed with idle rich matrons.

Court was held in the first floor of the constables' barracks. A resident magistrate, generally an outcast or incompetent, presided over a docket of sheep stealers and perpetrators of assorted misdemeanors in a cramped room that smelled of cow manure and musty wool.

Michael and Dermot were among a handful in the gallery. The resident magistrate, a ruddy-faced alcoholic with an ill-fitting wig, banged his gavel.

"Bailiff, bring out the next prisoner."

Two constables, holding up Billy's broken body, dragged the shackled little man into the court. Michael winced when he saw Billy's face. He looked even worse than he did last night. His eyes were mere slits and his hair was matted with dried blood.

There was a cursory trial of sorts. The assaulted constable stood in the dock and identified Billy as his assailant. Billy was asked if he had anything to say in his defense. When he shook his head no, the magistrate banged his gavel and said, "Guilty." The magistrate peered down at Billy with merciless, bloodshot eyes. "Billy Moore," he intoned in a gravelly voice, "you have been found guilty of robbery and felonious assault upon a constable in her Majesty's constabulary. Before I pass judgment on you, know that this court will show leniency and mercy if you name your accomplices. What say you?"

Billy's swollen eyes darted about the room and he saw Michael. The toothless mouth formed a blood-caked grin. He looked up at the magistrate.

"What do I say?"

His voice was a hoarse whisper and the magistrate leaned forward to hear him better. "Speak up, man."

In a louder voice, Billy said, "I say you're a dirty British bastard and you have no right to be in my country."

The gallery erupted in stunned laughter and cheers.

The enraged magistrate slammed his gavel down so hard it shattered. *"Silence!"* he sputtered. *"Silence, I say!"*

When order was restored, the enraged magistrate glared down on Billy. *This may only be a godforsaken court in a godforsaken land,* he thought. *But I am the magistrate here. This is my court and by God I will teach them respect.*

"I sentence this defendant to seven years transportation to Australia."

As they dragged Billy away, he looked up at Michael, grinned, and mouthed a silent *thank you.*

Michael and Dermot walked home, each lost in thought. Dermot was thinking of how close he'd come to being transported to Australia. Michael was thinking of Billy and what his life would be like. He'd heard Australia was harsh and dangerous. But so was Billy. If anyone could survive seven years in an Australia penal colony, Billy could.

"Thanks, Michael," Dermot said.

Brought out of his reverie, Michael studied his brother. Dermot was tough in his own way. Despite all his complaining, he was capable of hard work. Still, he was no Billy. Seven years in an Australian penal colony would kill him and that was a fact.

"You can thank me by stayin' out of trouble."

"I will, Michael. I swear. That Billy was a bad influence. I know that now. But he's gone now and...." He trailed off, thinking of little skinny Billy in far away Australia. It was as though he were already dead.

After a long silence, Dermot blurted out, "Michael, when you go out to America, take me with you."

Michael's stomach tightened. Since he'd given his passage money to Da, he'd not allowed himself to think of America. It was too painful remembering how hard it had been to earn the money and knowing he'd never be able to do it again, especially in the midst of this great hunger.

"I'll not be goin' out to America."

"You will. You always do what you set your mind to. Will you take me with you?"

Michael heard his brother's pleading tone and for the first time it occurred to him what the impact of his going would have meant to Dermot. If he'd gone out to America, Mam would have been sad and Da would have been angry. But they'd have gotten on with their lives just like they did when their other children died.

But, Dermot—he'd given no serious thought to him. He assumed it wouldn't have mattered to his younger brother what he did. But he was wrong. He knew now that Dermot would be lost without him. His younger brother was almost twenty-one, but he was still a child with a childlike inability to make the right decisions.

The thought of taking care of Dermot for the rest of his life was not something that Michael contemplated with a light heart. On the other hand, it was a moot point wasn't it? He was never going to America.

"All right," Michael said. "*If* I go, I'll take you."

Chapter Eighteen

May 1847
Ballyross, Ireland

As the spring of 1847 and the time for planting approached, there were those who had already mortgaged their future by eating the seed that was meant for this year's crop. For those who had seed to plant, a great debate ensued over whether the blight would return yet again. Those who were convinced it would, didn't plant. Others, like Da, were determined to be ready. They had suffered for two long years and, surely, God would not let them suffer yet another.

The harvest was months away and families scrambled to find food until then. With no potatoes in the bin, food had to be purchase with money; an alien notion to most of these poor people. There was of course the Board Of Works' projects, but the wages—paltry and infrequent—were not nearly enough to feed an entire family.

The Ranahans had been more fortunate than most. Michael's passage money had helped them through the first difficult year and they had three healthy wage earners in the family. But when Trevelyan closed down the Board Of Works, they, too, found themselves struggling to survive. Even after the Board Of Works reopened, there was less work available and the wages had been cut yet again.

"I've no money to pay the rent," Da announced to the startled family, just as they finished a meager meal of corn and water.

"What'll we do?" Mam asked.

Da stared into his empty bowl. "We'll have to sell off our things."

"You'll not sell my chest?" an alarmed Grandmam asked.

The chest, the only possession she owned in the world, had been a wedding present from her husband. He'd made it from the finest oak and had lovingly sanded the wood and varnished it until it was as smooth as a baby's cheek. He'd used the best lock and hinges he could afford and the result was a well-crafted chest that was a thing of beauty. But the years had taken their toll. In its time, the chest had been used as a seat, a table, a storage bin and a stepping tool, and now the varnish had worn off, the smooth wood was gouged and dented, and the lock no longer worked. But to Grandmam it was still as bright and shiny as it was the day her husband gave it to her.

"I've got to sell it, Mam. And anythin' else that will fetch a price."

"Who has money to buy?" Michael asked.

"The gombeen man."

Mam's hand shot to her mouth. "Oh, dear God, John. You'll not deal with the likes of him."

"And why not?" Da said defensively. "Isn't he the only one with money?"

If the famine benefited anyone, it was the "gombeen man"—a corruption of the Gaelic word for usury, *gaimbin*. Found in every city and village in Ireland, the gombeen man was universally hated and despised. He was the last resort in times of financial trouble, and to the people in need of him it was like dealing with the devil himself. When a man needed money to buy seed, he went to the gombeen man. When a man needed money for a down payment on land, he went to the gombeen man. When the crop failed and a man needed money to pay the rent, he went to the gombeen man.

Like a leech, the gombeen man fed off the misery of others and got fat on their misfortunes. He bought desperate men's possessions at a pittance of their value and charged usurious rates to borrow money. In any transaction, great or small, the gombeen man always made a profit.

Fergus Kincaid was Ballyross' gombeen man. Thin, with the small piercing eyes of a raven and hair the same color, he'd appeared one day twenty years ago in the valley with a wagonload of goods and never left. A loner, he was well suited for his work. He was forty-five, but he'd never married because he couldn't see the economic sense in sharing his hard-earned wealth with someone else. He'd never had a permanent home, preferring to stay at an occasional inn, but often sleeping in the back of his wagon nestled among his treasures of broken tools and threadbare dresses and coats. But now that he was growing wealthy, he had been thinking about securing a permanent home, one that would be as grand as any in the county—no, the entire country.

If compassion was ever in his makeup, it had long since atrophied. He went about his business with quiet efficiency, picking through clothing, jewelry, and livestock, while his mind calculated cost and profit. He carted away people's precious possessions and paid no mind to the bewildered expressions of the children, the rage in the faces of the men, or the tears in the eyes of the women. Their misfortune was his good fortune. It was simply a matter of opportunity and profit.

To the casual observer, it was inconceivable that the gombeen man could earn a living buying and selling worthless junk and making loans to poor farmers. But the casual observer didn't know what Fergus Kincaid knew: Large or small, there was a profit to be made in any transaction. He knew well the verities of his trade: What was one man's junk was another man's necessity... When it came to land, a man's judgment was sure to be clouded... A desperate man about to lose his land would not quibble over a hundred-percent interest rate or more... Kincaid was a shrewd judge of human nature and lived by one simple formula: A desperate man will always pay the price.

When the crop failed in '45, Fergus Kincaid could scarcely believe his good fortune. He'd always made a comfortable living, but the famine presented him with opportunity beyond his wildest imagining. In the past two years, he'd been able to buy land, goods, and livestock at absurdly low prices. He'd invested in corn futures and had realized a tidy sum for his efforts. He'd bought corn and grain and resold it at twice the price. Every shilling invested was returned two-fold, five-fold—and more. It was a heady experience for a man who had once measured his success in ha'pennies.

He'd even taken a profit from the haughty landlords who regarded him with such great distain. They were the wastrels and alcoholics who gambled and drank away their inheritance. Yet they treated him as though he were lower than the filthy peasants who tilled their fields. But Kincaid smiled through his seething anger and humiliation because he knew that one day he would be their equal—*nay their superior.* In the meantime, he profusely thanked Lord Attwood for the privilege of carting away paintings of his ancestors. He fawned over Major Wicker's gun collection for which he paid a fraction of its value. And he commiserated with Mr. Rowe over the loss of his Waterford goblets.

Who was the master and who was the servant now? When all was said and done it was he, the gombeen man, who owned their precious possessions. Most he sold for a handsome profit, but others, like the Waterford crystal, he kept for himself, knowing that one day, he would own one of those great mansions and he would need the proper accoutrements.

And now, as he came out of the Ranahan cottage, huffing from the exertion of carrying Grandmam's chest, he paid no mind to Da, Michael, and Dermot sullenly watching him carry away the few pathetic possessions that represented their lives. A couple of picture frames, a milk churn, their last good blanket, were all flung onto a wagon already heaped high with the possessions of other unfortunates.

Dermot, who was standing by Kincaid's wagon, saw something wrapped in a blanket sticking out from under a pile of clothing and chairs. He pushed the blanket aside and saw a fiddle.

"Look, Michael. He's got old Genie's fiddle."

"Get away from that you," Kincaid growled.

In his haste to make sure Dermot didn't steal anything from his wagon, he stumbled and fell down. The lid popped off Grandmam's chest.

"For the love of God," he said, looking at Da accusingly. "Tis junk you sold me, Ranahan."

Michael lunged for Kincaid. "Don't you be callin' my Grandmam's chest junk, gombeen man—"

Dermot threw his arms around Michael and wrestled him away.

"Oh, it's heirlooms, is it?" Kincaid said mockingly.

With a great show of distain he tossed Grandmam's precious chest onto the pile in his wagon and climbed aboard. He looked down at the three men with a smile colder than a winter night.

"No one likes the gombeen man until they need him," he said. "And I'm thinkin' you'll have need of me again." He tipped his hat and smiled at Michael. "Good day to you all."

It was late afternoon and Lord Somerville was tending Clara's roses. His wife had always loved roses and he'd planted these bushes as a wedding present to her twenty-two years ago. She'd cared for them as though they were her children. Every day without fail she watered them, picked aphids off them, pruned them, nurtured and coaxed them until they were producing the most magnificent roses in the valley.

After she died he couldn't bear to look at them. They were everything she wasn't—full of life, color, and beauty; a reproachful reminder of what their lives should have been. He wanted them to die as she had died.

Then, after he came out of his library to rejoin the world, he went into the garden and saw the roses choked with weeds. He'd never been a gardener, nor had he any desire to be one. But when he saw those bushes, the bushes that his wife had nurtured so lovingly, he resolved to make them flourish again. He would do it for her. And now Somerville roses were once again the pride of the valley.

He was studying a specimen when a shadow crossed his light. He looked up and saw John Ranahan standing over him.

"Sir, I've come with the rent."

Somerville brushed the dirt from his knees and stood up abruptly. He enjoyed working with the roses because it made him feel close to his wife, but he always felt foolish when someone, especially another man, found him thus engaged.

"Ranahan... Yes, well, where did you get the money—? No, never mind. Put it away. You'll need it to feed your family."

Da stood there, awkwardly holding a handful of coins in the palm of his calloused hand. He hadn't been expecting this response and wasn't sure what to say. "Your Lordship," he began hesitantly, "I pay my debts..."

"Of course you do, Ranahan. When things are right again, you'll pay me. Now off with you."

Da tried to speak, but the lump in his throat wouldn't let him. He turned and retreated in confusion—and gratitude. The money would feed the family until the next harvest. *Thanks be to God. We're saved.*

Somerville watched him go with an expression of sadness and—concern.

Grandmam had not been the same since her husband's death, but since her prized chest had been sold off to the gombeen man, she had retreated into herself even more. Always an early riser, she started getting up later and later. Soon she was spending most of her time in bed unable—or unwilling—to take her customary place by the fire. The family didn't know what to make of it. She didn't have the fever, but clearly she was dying.

One night, as the rest of the family was getting ready for bed, Grandmam announced, "I want to go to the Workhouse tomorrow."

"You'll not," Da said. "No Ranahan will ever go there as long as I've a breath in me."

Da was appalled that his mother would even consider such a thing. The Workhouse was a place of shame and dread, a place for the destitute who had no one else to look after them. Workhouse rules were harsh and designed to discourage less than industrious people from taking advantage of the good will of the government.

"I'm dyin'," Grandmam said. There was no fear or regret in her voice. It was simply a statement of fact.

"Then all the more reason you'll stay right here with your family around you," Da said.

"I'll go to the Workhouse, John Ranahan," she said more emphatically.

Michael knelt down beside her. "Why, Grandmam?"

"I'll get the coffin, Michael."

Michael looked at her, puzzled.

"It's God's own truth. I saw it with me own eyes. The Workhouse in Ballyross gives a proper Christian burial with a coffin and all. I've seen those mass graves and I'll not be thrown into the ground like a sack of rotten lumpers."

"You'll not go to that place," Da shouted. "And that's final. The family is stayin' together."

The next morning, before dawn, Michael felt a cold, frail hand on his arm. He came awake with a start. He was still having nightmares about the body in the river. But it was only Grandmam, sitting on the floor next to him.

"Michael, take me to the Workhouse."

Da awoke and came to kneel beside her. "Mam, we want you to stay here with us," he said softly.

She looked at her son with sad, rheumy eyes. "John, can you give me a coffin?"

Da picked a piece of straw out of her gray hair. "No, I cannot."

Later that morning, Michael carried the frail old woman to the Workhouse, an inhospitable, long gray brick building with all the charm of a penitentiary. He rang the bell and a heavy-bosomed matron in a severe gray uniform opened the door. She glared at Grandmam. "Has she the fever?"

"No, she does not."

"Do I get the coffin when I die?" Grandmam asked.

The matron stepped back. "Bring her in."

Michael had never been inside the Workhouse, but he'd heard the terrible rumors about what went on behind these thick gray walls. *They poison you with a little black bottle... No one ever comes out of the Workhouse alive... They feed the bodies to the pigs...*

He didn't know if those stories were true or not, but the Workhouse, itself, was a bleak, inhospitable place. In a great room, just off the vestibule, Michael saw dozens of pale, sickly women, all dressed in the same drab gray dresses, sitting at tables knitting in forced silence and lost in their own despair.

Michael put his Grandmam down on a chair while the matron went off to find the attendants. "Grandmam, are you sure you want to stay here?"

"Aye." She squeezed his arm with a bony hand. "Michael, you were right to want to go out to America. Save yerself. Sure this country is doomed."

The matron came back with two attendants. "You can go now," she said to Michael.

Michael kissed his Grandmam. "I'll come see you tomorrow."

At the front door, he turned and saw his Grandmam being carried away by the two attendants. She looked so small and frail. The women continued their knitting. No one looked up. They were not permitted to speak. There was no sound save the soft *click, click* of the knitting needles.

Michael stepped outside and filled his lungs with cold, clean air.

They put Grandmam in a ward crowded with the sick and dying. Discordant, pitiful moans filled an air reeking of death and decay. She lay on a bed that was nothing more than a board covered with a tattered stained rag. She paid no mind to the hard wood against her bony shoulder blades, the smells, the moans. She knew she wouldn't be here long.

She'd tenaciously clung to life, refusing to die, until she was certain she'd be buried in a coffin. *How could a decent Christian woman go meet her maker without a coffin?* Now that that matter was settled, she allowed herself to slip away. She felt at peace. The arthritic pain that had twisted her hands into useless claws subsided. The chronic gnawing hunger in her stomach abated. She closed her eyes, content to dream of her coffin. She didn't know how long she lay like that, but when she opened her eyes, Granda was standing at the foot of the bed, smiling at her.

"Woman, are you gonna sleep away the whole long day?"

Grandmam squinted at her husband. "Are you in one of your queer moods, Hugh?"

"I am not. Come on, Aileen"—his eyes twinkled—"it's a grand day outside. Let's take a walk down by the river like we used to."

"I don't know if I can get out of this bed, Hugh."

"Of course you can." He offered his hand and to her surprise she floated out of the bed effortlessly. Then she turned and saw why. There, still in the bed, lay her frail body. But she wasn't frightened—or surprised. "I'll be back," she said to her body. "I'm just goin' for a walk with my Hugh."

And together, holding hands like they did when they courted, they walked out the door.

An hour later, the matron stopped by Grandmam's bed. "This one's dead," she said to an attendant. "Move her out."

The attendant wrapped Grandmam's body in the rag that had covered the board. Then he carried the body to a window. Outside a wooden slide had been built from the windowsill to the ground below.

He placed the body on the slide. "Here comes another one," he shouted. The old woman's body went down the slide and bounced onto the ground. Two attendants picked it up and stacked it alongside five other corpses.

The next morning, while the family was having their breakfast of cornmeal and water, there was a knock at the door.

Da opened the door to one of Pat Doyle's sons. "I was told to tell you the old woman's dead." The lad turned and ran off.

That afternoon the family came to the Workhouse to claim the body of Aileen Ranahan. The heavy-bosomed matron who'd accepted Grandma the day before, stuck a piece of paper in front of Da.

"Sign here to authorize the burial and return of the body to you," she said gruffly.

Da stared at the paper. "I don't know how to read or write."

"Claimant illiterate," she muttered as she scrawled the words across the paper. "Wait outside."

Minutes later, two attendants came out carrying Grandmam's coffin. They followed the men into the cemetery. The ground was pockmarked with freshly dug graves, so close to each other that Michael wondered how they didn't collapse in on each other.

The men stopped and placed the coffin down by a freshly dug grave. Michael peered into the hole, surprised at how deep it was.

"Where's Father Rafferty?" Mam asked.

"Called away to the next parish," the older attendant said. "The priest there died of the fever last night. God rest his soul."

"Then there's no one to say a prayer over the grave?" Da asked, appalled that his mother would not have this final ritual.

"Ah, no. But I've been doin' it all day. Would you like me to?"

Da nodded, perplexed.

The attendants took off their caps. The older attendant began, "Dear Lord, here is the recently departed soul—?" He looked at Da.

Da had always called her Mam. He wasn't sure what her real name was.

"Aileen Ranahan," Mam said.

"Are you sure?" Da asked.

"Of course I'm sure. Could I forget your own Mam's name?"

"Aileen Ranahan," Da confirmed.

The attendant nodded. "Just so. Here is the recently departed soul, Aileen Ranahan. Dust we are and to dust shall we return." He put his cap on and looked at the family apologetically. "That's all I usually say."

Da nodded. The attendants stood on one side of the hole, the Ranahans on the other. The two groups looked at each other in awkward silence.

"Are you not goin' to lower the coffin into the ground then?" Da asked.

"Ah, no," the older attendant said. "Not just yet. We have certain preparations to attend to."

Michael could see that whatever the "certain preparations" were, they weren't going to do them as long as the family was there.

"Come on, Da." Michael took his father's arm. "Let's go home."

As they started back on the road to the cottage, Mam said, "It's so sad, her dyin' in the Workhouse and all."

"Aye," Da said. "Well, at least she got her coffin. Oh…" He reached into his pocket and took out a coin. "Here, Michael, I forgot to give this to the men."

"Have we so much money we can afford to give it away to grave diggers?" Dermot said.

Michael shot Dermot a warning look. "You go on, I'll catch up."

Michael made his way back to the gravesite, stepping carefully to avoid falling into an open grave. As he neared his Grandmam's burial site, he saw the two attendants awkwardly maneuver the coffin over the open grave. Puzzled by their odd behavior, he stepped behind a tombstone to watch. When they had positioned the casket over the open hole, the older attendant reached under the coffin and yanked a lever. Suddenly, the hinged bottom of the coffin snapped open and Grandmam's body dropped into the hole.

For an agonizing instant, Michael was too stunned to react. Then, in a blind rage, he hurled himself on the startled attendants, punching, kicking, flailing at them like a wild man.

The older attendant scrambled away, shouting, "In the name of God, what's got into you?"

Michael straddle the younger attendant's chest, "I saw what you did you dirty bastards. Are you gonna sell her coffin to someone else then?" he bellowed, raining down blows on the hapless man.

"For the love of God, we've only the one coffin," the older attendant shouted.

Michael stopped punching the man. "What are you sayin'?"

"We do it for the family. Sure we've no money to buy coffins, and even if we did, there's no wood to be had. They're dyin' too fast."

Michael rolled off the man and slumped against a headstone, trying to comprehend what the attendant was saying. He looked into the deep hole and now he understood. "You put more than one in a grave."

The younger attendant wiped blood from his nose with his sleeve. "We have to. There's not enough ground to give them all their own place."

Michael looked at the two frightened men. "I'm sorry... I didn't know."

He stood up and started to walk away. Then, he remembered the coin in his pocket. He fished it out and handed it to the older attendant. "I'm sorry," he said again and stumbled away.

Chapter Nineteen

June 1847
Ballyross, Ireland

Emily sat at her dressing table getting ready for yet another tedious afternoon tea at Lord Attwood's estate. She'd done her best to be as obnoxious and unpleasant as possible, but in spite of her efforts she was still being invited to these interminable teas and dinners. No doubt Lord Attwood's forbearance had more to do with her father's position than any desire to entertain an ill-mannered young girl.

The door opened and Nora came in. "I've some fresh bed linens, Miss Emily."

"Thank you, Nora. Oh, would you please fetch my mother's emerald earrings?"

"Ah, the emerald earrings. They're me favorites. Your mother, God rest her soul, used to wear them all the time. Why she looked like a—" Nora wiped her hands on her apron, suddenly realizing she was talking about Emily's dead mam. "Oh, I am sorry, Miss Emily..."

"No, that's all right. I like hearing about her. Did my mother really look beautiful in them?"

"Aye. That she did. A queen she was. I'll go fetch them."
Emily picked up the photo of her mother and her
thoughts went back ten years. A lifetime ago. The weeks
before her mother's death had been a time of stomach-
churning anxiety and loneliness. She knew her mother was
sick, but no one would tell her the nature of the illness. The
servants moved about the house quietly, speaking in hushed
tones. When she asked them what was the matter with her
mother, she was told to "ask the master." When she asked
her father, he brushed her off and retreated to his library.
Every day teams of doctors came and went. They would
examine her mother and then disappear into the library.
She'd put her ear to the closed doors, but all she'd hear was
her father and the doctors speaking in muffled,
incomprehensible voices.

Then one morning her father came to her room and
woke her. His eyes, red-rimmed and lifeless, frightened her.
"Your mother is dead," was all he said.

The next two weeks were a blur. She had a vague
recollection of a gleaming casket in the grand entrance hall,
surrounded by dozens of people, all dressed in black,
mumbling in hushed tones. Then she was standing at the
hillside family cemetery in the rain next to her father
watching the casket being lowered into the dark, forbidding
earth.

The first thing she clearly remembered about that time
was climbing into the carriage, seeing her father standing rigid
in the doorway and not waving as she was driven off to the
train station. At her London boarding school, she would
sometimes awake in the middle of the night in a panic, unable

to remember what her mother's face looked like. She'd light a candle with a trembling hand and stare at her mother's photo until, comforted that she would never forget what she looked like, she'd fall back asleep.

Nora came rushing back into the bedroom. *"Holy Mother of God...!"*

Emily put the photograph down. "What is it, Nora?"

The old woman held up the empty jewelry box. *"They're gone, Miss Emily! The earrings, the necklaces, everything! All gone!"*

Emily barged into the library where her father was sitting by the fire reading Horace. "Father, there's a thief in the house," she announced. "You must send for the constabulary immediately."

Somerville put his book down, took off his reading glasses, and rubbed his eyes. "Emily, what are you talking about?"

She held up the empty jewelry box. "Mother's jewelry. Everything's been stolen."

"Nothing's been stolen," he said quietly.

"But—"

"They've been sold."

Emily slumped against the door. *"Sold...?"*

Somerville went to the fireplace, picked up a poker and stabbed at a smoldering log. "That fool Trevelyan expects the landlords to shoulder this burden alone. Parliament keeps raising our taxes while at the same time pushing the responsibility of feeding the people on to us. But where am I to get the money? The tenants can't pay their rent. They have

nothing left. Many have eaten the seed for next year's crop."
He put the poker down and sat down heavily in his chair. "I
can't say I blame them."

Emily, hardly listening to his excuses, was desperately
trying to make sense of what she'd just heard. *They've been
sold.* Her mother's jewelry. Jewelry that was her birthright. It
suddenly occurred to her that more than just her mother's
jewelry had been sold. In the last several months, she'd
noticed paintings missing from the walls. She hadn't seen the
good silver in months. Tapestries had been removed from the
great room. But she'd paid no attention, assuming that they'd
been sent out for cleaning or repair. But now she knew
where they'd gone. *He'd sold them.*

A thought came to her, a thought so unthinkable that she
could barely speak it. "Are we penniless?"

He turned away from her. "No, no. We'll be fine. As
soon as—"

Emily heard the uncertainty in her father's voice. *"My
God, how could you squander everything, Father!"*

Somerville's head snapped back as though he'd been
struck.

"Emily—"

"This estate has been in the family for more than six
generations. In the name of God, are you so incompetent
that you've lost it all?"

"Emily, I will not permit you to speak to me in that
manner. You don't understand—"

"I understand perfectly." Hot tears coursed down her
cheeks. "You're a *hypocrite.* You lecture me about

responsibility and accountability, but clearly *you* were not responsible. *You* were not accountable."

Somerville, looking very tired, stared into the fire.

"Emily, there are things you don't understand. I've done my best to—"

"I don't want to hear any more excuses."

She turned and ran from the room.

Astride Shannon, Emily galloped blindly across the fields, jumping hedges, stone walls, fallen tree stumps—anything that stood in her way. She spurred Shannon to make him go faster and faster, almost hoping she'd fall or Shannon would trip and she'd break her neck. Even death would be preferable to being impoverished. But the horse gave out before she could kill either of them. He pulled up short in front of a five-foot stone wall, snorting in protest. She felt his massive chest heaving beneath her and smelled the pungent sweat steaming from his glistening body.

"I'm sorry, Shannon," she said, patting his pulsing neck. "I'm sorry...."

She led him to a stream and, while he drank, she sat under a tree. And the tears came. She wasn't sure if the tears were for her lost mother or the family's lost fortunes or for herself. Whatever the reason, the cry had a cathartic effect and when she'd cried herself out, she felt much better. All was not lost, she told herself as she brushed the grass from her dress and remounted Shannon. Her father said they weren't penniless and she hoped he wasn't lying to her. But clearly, the estate was in serious financial trouble. In any event, there was nothing she could do about it. And with that realization she felt the unexpected peace of one who has been dreading bad news only to discover that the news is not as bad as not knowing.

On the way home, she rode across the bleak landscape of Lord Attwood's fields and counted dozens of tumbled cottages. Farther up the road, she crossed over onto Major Wicker's land and saw more of the same— barren land, unattended, untilled, and even more abandoned cottages. Attwood and Wicker had talked so causally of tumbled cottages, but now, seeing them, like so many scars on the landscape, she suddenly realized that each of these ruined cottages represented ruined families, ruined lives.

When she crossed over to the fields of the Somerville estates, there was a marked difference. Not one cottage had been tumbled. She steered Shannon toward a cluster of cottages where a handful of men were quietly talking. When they saw her approaching they scurried away and disappeared into their cottages like so many frightened rabbits.

Emily stopped in front of one of the cottages that was not much more than a mud hut. "Hello, is anyone home?"

No one answered, but she could see someone looking out at her from the partially opened door. "Hello! May I ask you a question?"

"They won't come out."

Emily turned and Michael was standing there.

"Why not?"

"They're afraid of you."

"Why should they be afraid of me?"

"You're the ruling class."

Emily, stung by the sarcasm in his voice, said, "I meant no harm. I just wanted to ask a question."

Michael called out, "It's all right, Pat."

The door opened and a big man with flaming red hair stepped out. Six children, no more than a year apart in age, squirted out behind him and pressed against the cottage wall, watching Emily with big shy eyes. Emily was stunned at their emaciated appearance and their clothing, which was literally rags.

"Ask away," Michael said.

Pat Doyle swept the cap off his head and stood silent, apprehensive.

"The question I had... that is...." With Michael staring at her, and this big man cowering before her as though she held the power of life and death, she suddenly felt like a great fool. "Are you in arrears with your rent?" she blurted out.

Doyle shot a glance at Michael. Emily saw the look of genuine terror in the man's eyes and realized she shouldn't have asked that question. "It's quite all right," she said quickly. "I'm not here to collect the rent or anything. I just want to know."

"He is," Michael said. "And so am I. And so is every tenant on your Da's lands."

"I see."

The other men had come out of their cottages and one by one had come to stand silent, watching her. The abject fear in their eyes was painful to see. She wanted to run away, but she held her ground. She had to know.

Pat Doyle said, "Your Da, God bless him, has told us the rent is forgiven till the great hunger is gone."

"I see." He'd answered the question she'd come to ask, but now she wished she'd never asked it. She wished she'd never stopped. She didn't belong here. She was an intruder-- an unwelcomed witness to their misery and degradation.

"Every day we pray for his long life," another man added.

Emily studied the man's face for a sign of mockery, but saw only genuineness.

A red-faced farmer stepped out of the group. "The others have not been so kind, young mistress," he said.

"And you are, sir?"

"Padric Leahy."

"Who do you mean by the others, Mr. Leahy?"

"The other landlords," Michael said. "Rowe, Wicker, Attwood—they've all been tumblin' cottages."

Things were beginning to sort themselves out in her head.

"Thank you." She nodded to the men and turned Shannon around.

Michael was suddenly beside her. "Did you get the answers to your questions?"

"I did," she answered, stung by the harshness in his tone.

She started to spur Shannon, but Michael grabbed the bridle. "Can I ask you a question?"

"What is it?"

"I was just wonderin'. Why would you shame a man by askin' if he owed rent?"

Emily felt herself redden. "I didn't mean to shame anyone."

"Well you did all the same. You shamed them and scared the life out of them in the bargain. These men owe two years' rent. They're not proud of that. They may be poor, but they have their pride and they don't like to be reminded that they've not paid their just debts."

Emily felt the anger rising at his supercilious tone, "I didn't mean to imply—"

"My God, woman. Do you not know the power you have over them? Your Da can turn them off the land with a scratch of a pen. And a man without a bit of land is a dead man."

There he was, being a patronizing fool again. "You don't seem afraid or shamed," she snapped.

"I don't scare easily and besides, I'm doing the best I can. What else can I do?"

"You can let go of my horse," she said evenly.

Michael released the reins and patted Shannon's neck. He looked up at her and the blue sky reflecting off his eyes made them even bluer. He knew he was acting the fool again. How could she know the power she had over them, real or imagined? He had no right to talk to her like that. "Your Da is a good man," he said, trying in his own way to make amends.

"I'll be sure and tell him you approve."

Emily spurred Shannon and galloped off.

Michael stood in the clearing, silently cursing himself. *He'd done it again.* He'd wanted to tell her what it was like for him and the others. How they were truly grateful to Lord Somerville for what he was doing. But it didn't come out the way he meant it to and once again he was left feeling the proper eejit.

As Emily rode home, she couldn't get the sight of those tumbled cottages out of her mind. And she kept hearing what Doyle and Leahy—and even that maddening Michael had said. *They loved her father.* No, love was too strong a word. They didn't love him. But they certainly respected him.

To Emily, her father had always been—at least since he'd sent her away—an unfeeling autocrat who even now was trying to control her life. But perhaps he hadn't always been that way. From time to time she recalled dim memories of a man who smiled a lot, a man who played with her, a man who read her bedtime stories. But she could never be sure if those memories were real or just memories she wanted to believe were real. Nevertheless, she had learned something about him today that she'd not known—or perhaps not permitted herself to know. Her father was a generous, compassionate man.

Emily found him working in the rose garden. He stood up abruptly when he saw her approaching and wiped his hands on his apron.

Emily stood there, silent, awkward. Then, she took off her sapphire ring and held it out to her father. "I want to help."

Somerville took the ring and examined it. "Your mother gave you this ring just before she died. It was her grandmother's. He took her hand and slipped it back on her finger. "You keep it, Emily. To remind you of your mother."

Emily felt a constriction in her throat. When she could finally speak, she said, "Will we be all right, Father?"

Somerville nodded. "We will. Once the next harvest is in, the country will be right as rain."

"Good. I'm glad."

Emily studied the ring, sparkling in the bright sun. She looked up at her father. She hadn't permitted herself to really look at him since she'd come back. His face was scored with deep lines. He looked old, tired. But beneath that weariness was the man she remembered. The bushy eyebrows, now gray; the long aquiline nose, the firm chin.

And suddenly she knew. Those childhood memories were real.

Emily threw her arms around her father, buried her face in his chest and wept.

"I'm so sorry, Father..."

Somerville blinked back tears and swallowed hard. "Welcome home, Emily."

Chapter Twenty

August 1847
Ministry of the Treasury

"I have seen women and children covered in filthy rags gleaning fields in a futile search for a bit of turnip," Dr. Playfair said, his voice quaking with emotion. "I have seen dead bodies in various states of decay along the roadside. I have seen with my own eyes, Mr. Trevelyan, barren and untilled fields because there is no money to buy seed. The country, I tell you, is all lost and gone. This famine is an evil upon the land."

Dr. Playfair, weary from an arduous three-day journey from Dublin, sat across the conference table from Trevelyan. He hadn't had a proper night's sleep in a fortnight, his face was pale and drawn, and he'd lost weight. The strain of working day and night and trying to get through to the merciless Trevelyan was taking its toll on his old body.

Dr. Kane and Mr. Lindley sat to either side of Playfair in silence. By tacit agreement Playfair had become their spokesman. At this moment both men were glad they were not the recipients of that cold stare which Trevelyan was bringing to bear on Playfair. Dr. Playfair had tried to give Trevelyan a sense of the horrific conditions in Ireland, but judging from Trevelyan's implacable expression, he hadn't succeeded.

Trevelyan studied a well-manicured fingernail. "The real evil with which we have to content, my dear Playfair, is not the physical evil of the famine, but the moral evil of the selfish, perverse and turbulent character of the people. Dependency on charity," he continued in his irritating, clipped voice, "must not be made an agreeable mode of life. Quite frankly, I find it astonishing that the Irish haven't discovered an alternative to their potato crop. Instead, they have become even more ungrateful and rebellious."

Playfair, reddening at the intransigency of the man, rummaged through a stack of papers in his briefcase and pulled out a folder.

"This is a report from the Surgeon General at Dublin Castle." The paper shook in his hand as he read from it. "Reports are coming in from the west of Ireland that the people are eating nettles and weeds and—"

"My dear Playfair, I cannot and will not undercut the grain merchants and upset all their calculations."

"In the name of God how can you talk of profit when so many are starving?"

"I have told you more than once, Dr. Playfair, the Irish exaggerate. And exaggeration is apparently contagious. Even clear-thinking men such as yourselves appear to be prone to the disease."

Playfair trembled with rage. "I do not exaggerate, sir. It is well for some to sit here in England, well fed and secure in their homes, and judge an impoverished people across the Irish Sea."

Kane put a restraining hand on Playfair's arm and shot him a warning glace. It would not do to insult the secretary. "Mr. Trevelyan," Kane said, in a more conciliatory tone, "we have just come from Ireland. Believe me, no words can describe the horrors that are being visited upon that godforsaken country."

Trevelyan shifted to a more conciliatory tone as well. "Things are not right in Ireland, I know. Nevertheless, we must take care not to create in the peasant a habit of dependence on government. I remind you again, gentlemen, it is the landlord's responsibility to provide relief to the poor, not the Crown's. It is the landlords who must accept their responsibility to feed the poor and destitute."

Playfair waved the document in the air. "Mr. Trevelyan, if you will just listen to what the Surgeon General says about—"

Trevelyan stopped him with a wave of the hand. "I have a meeting with Lord Russell this afternoon. I believe we may have an answer to the Irish question once and for all."

"But the report—"

"Be so kind as to put your findings in writing and submit them to me." Trevelyan stood up. "Thank you, gentlemen."

He walked out, leaving the three men sitting in stunned frustration.

September 1847
Somerville Manor

Lord Attwood's pink jowls shook with fury. *"Are they mad?"*

Wicker pounded his fist into his open palm. "The government expects us to pay the *entire* cost of running the Public Works?"

Rowe, pale and sweating profusely, gulped his sherry, too stunned to speak.

Lord Somerville studied the document that he'd just received from the Treasury Office outlining the provisions of the new Labor Rate Act. In the dry language of the bureaucracy it spelled out how the government—or more precisely the landlords—would deal with the continuing famine.

"I don't understand," Rowe said, when he was finally able to catch his breath. "The government paid the entire cost of administrating the Board Of Works the first year."

"But they only paid half the second year," Attwood said in disgust. "We should have seen this coming."

Somerville tossed the document onto his desk. "According to the *London Times*, Parliament has rebelled at the huge sums expended—*squandered* said the editorial page. The editorial also questions why Parliament should continue to subsidize profligate landlords and lazy Irish peasants when they will not lift a finger to help themselves."

"And so," Attwood concluded, "the upshot is that the entire cost of maintaining the Public Works will be shifted from the government to us."

"The expense of maintaining these Public Works without government assistance will be enormous," Rowe whispered, eyes wide with fright as he contemplated the specter of bankruptcy. "Where in the name of God are we to get the money?"

"There are provisions for loans," Somerville said.

"*At three and a half percent,*" Attwood snapped.

Without asking permission, Wicker poured himself another sherry with a shaking hand. "It's usurious, I say."

"It's preposterous," Rowe agreed. "I'm on the verge of ruin."

"It is preposterous," Attwood agreed. Then his eyes narrowed and what passed for a smile crossed his thin lips. "But there is a provision in the law that may be to our advantage."

"And what provision is that?" Rowe asked, hoping for some respite from this draconian edict.

"The law states that any tenant working more than a quarter of an acre of land is not eligible for relief from the Workhouse." When he saw the puzzled expression on Rowe's face, he explained further. "Don't you get it, man? If he can't get relief from the Workhouse and he can't pay his rent, what is he to do?"

Rowe nodded, finally getting Lord Attwood's drift. "I see. We use this provision as a wedge to drive the tenants off the land."

"Exactly."

"Then the answer is to step up evictions," Wicker said with great conviction.

Somerville slammed his glass down on the table. He'd been listening to these fools patiently, but his forbearance was at an end. "For God's sake, we have some responsibility to our tenants. We can't just drive them off the land like so many crows."

"The only responsibility I have is to my own estates," Lord Attwood said, thrusting a bony finger at Somerville. "These people occupy my land at my pleasure. As long as they produce, I confer a favor upon them. If they can no longer produce, they go. It's as simple as that."

"But where are they to go?" Somerville asked in frustration.

"To hell or Connaught," Attwood shouted, echoing the words of Oliver Cromwell, 17th century England's most infamous persecutor of the Irish.

Wicker and Rowe nodded in vigorous agreement.

Shannon reared up, nostrils flaring, eyes wide, and kicked at Kincaid. The gombeen man dropped the reins and half ran, half fell out of the stall. Enraged, he looked for something he could use to punish the impudent animal and found an axe handle. "I'll show you who's master here, me boyo—"

Suddenly, the axe handle was wrenched from his grasp. As he turned to see who would dare do such a thing, Michael rammed the handle into Kincaid's stomach. The gombeen man sunk to his knees gasping for air.

"How dare you assault my person," he hissed. "That horse is my property and I'll do with it as I please."

Michael, standing over him, waved the handle at him menacingly. "If I ever find out you've hurt this animal—" Michael raised the axe handle over his head and came down with all his might. Kincaid saw the handle coming, but he was too paralyzed with fear to move. He closed his eyes and felt the handle whistle past his ear and shatter against a tree stump next to his head. Michael leaned down and whispered in his ear. "The next time it'll be your useless skull that breaks."

Kincaid scrambled to his feet, trembling. "That horse is mad—"

"That horse is a good judge of character."

Kincaid backed away from Michael and the horse. They were both quite mad. For a moment he considered not buying the animal, but his gombeen mind overruled him. The horse was worth far more than the pittance he'd paid for it and there would be a handsome profit to be made. "Bring him along with the others," he growled at Michael. "And be quick about it."

Outside, Lord Somerville and Emily watched Dermot and Da tie the set of Chestnuts to Kincaid's wagon.

Kincaid hurried out of the barn and climbed up onto his wagon. Michael came behind, leading Shannon. "Hurry up, man," Kincaid said, "I haven't all day."

Michael tied Shannon to the back of the wagon.

The gombeen man studied Michael with small black eyes, glistening with hatred. "You're a Ranahan, aren't you?"

"Michael Ranahan."

"I'll remember you, Michael Ranahan."

Kincaid turned to Somerville and gave him a syrupy smile. "That's the lot your lordship. If I can be of any further service?"

Somerville waved him away dismissively.

As the gombeen man's wagon rolled down the road with yet another wagonload of the Somerville estate's property, Emily, fighting back tears, rushed into the barn. She stood in front of Shannon's empty stall, lost in melancholy thoughts, recalling all the wonderful, glorious rides the two had shared.

"He was a cranky old horse," Michael said from the doorway.

Emily whirled, about to erupt in anger. Then, she saw his sad smile and she smiled through her tears.

"He was a cranky old horse."

The two stood looking at each other. They were no more than ten feet apart, but she was the landlord's daughter and he was the tenant farmer's son. Those ten feet might as well have been the width of a great ocean.

Emily studied Michael. His clothing was in tatters, his black, wavy hair was a wild mess, and he was alarmingly thin. But there was something about him. She sensed an inner strength, a man who would not be bowed. She thought of the dreadful way he and the other tenant farmers lived.

"How do you survive?" she asked.

"You do," Michael said. "You just do."

Chapter Twenty One

It was after dawn and the three Ranahan men were just finishing up a breakfast of a small pitcher of buttermilk and a gruel of watery corn meal.

Dermot shoved his empty bowl aside in disgust. "Tis not enough. Sure the worksite's a good five-mile walk. I'll die of the hunger before I even lift a spade."

"Here, son. Take mine. I'm not hungry."

Mam tried to give Dermot her bowl, but Da pushed it away. "He's had as much as the rest of us. Come on," he said, reaching for his coat. "We'll all die of the hunger if we don't collect our wages from the public works and that's a fact."

Michael tossed Dermot his coat. "Save your strength. We've a long walk."

Suddenly, there was an urgent pounding on the door. Michael opened it and Barry Scanlon's eldest son was standing there with tears streaming down his cheeks. "My Da says come quick. They're tumblin' our cottage."

By the time Michael, Da, and Dermot arrived, a crowd had gathered outside Barry Scanlon's cottage. An impatient Major Wicker, standing with a bailiff and three constables, watched Scanlon and his wife carry the last of what few possessions they owned out of the cottage.

Scanlon, the man who had bought the last loaf of bread in O'Mally's bakery, looked about in fright, his eyes bulging more than ever. His four children, too terrified to even cry, crouched under a nearby bush. Standing to the side, a group of sullen farmers muttered among themselves.

Wicker looked at his pocket watch. "All right," he shouted. "Tumble it and be quick about it."

Michael looked around, puzzled. *Who was he talking to? Surely there was no man here who would do the black work of the crowbar brigade against one of their own?*

A tall, hulking figure pushed through the crowd. Michael saw a flash of red hair and Pat Doyle, carrying a crowbar, stepped into the clearing. Before Michael could utter a word, Padric Leahy and Tim Finney, their eyes downcast, came behind him.

Michael shoved his way through the crowd. "Pat... Padric... Tim... for the love of God, you can't tumble Barry's home."

Wicker pointed his riding crop at Michael. "Remove this man," he said to the constables.

A constable started moving toward Michael. Ignoring him, Michael jumped in front of Doyle. The big redheaded man refused to make eye contact. Michael grabbed his frayed coat. "Pat, will you listen to me?"

Doyle stared straight ahead, eyes unfocused. "Stay out of this," he snarled. "I have mouths to feed."

"So does Barry—"

The constable cracked Michael over the head with his truncheon. Suddenly, the landscape tilted and went blurry. A loud buzzing erupted in his ears, blocking out the shouting around him. Michael stumbled and fell to the ground. He tried to get to his feet, but the constable hit him again. He dropped to his knees and the buzzing grew louder. Warm, sticky blood flowed into his eyes. Through a red haze he saw a blur pass him and heard a curse as the constable went down under the weight of Dermot's charge.

In a flash, the other two constables were on Dermot, clubs flailing. Then, Da was there, pulling at a constable's arm. The man spun around and jammed his club into Da's stomach. As Da sunk to the ground, the constable delivered a savage blow to the top of Da's head.

Michael tried to rise, but the ground was tilting at a crazy angle and he couldn't get his feet under him. He wiped the blood from his eyes with his sleeve, but it kept coming, obscuring his vision. He had to get up. He had to help Da and Dermot...

Then another blow to the back of his head and he fell face down in the soil.

Darkness. From a great distance he heard a voice. The voice grew louder, shouting in his ear. He finally understood what the voice was saying. *"Stay down for the love of God or they'll kill you for sure..."* Michael blinked the blood out of his eyes. Through his blurred vision he saw the frightened face of

Father Rafferty, inches from his. "*Stay down, Michael. Will you stay down*."

Pat Doyle stood frozen, watching the Ranahans being beaten, uncertain of what he should do next. Then he heard a great swooshing sound and a roar. He turned and saw the thatched roof engulfed in flames. Then a short man with a big head was standing in front of him, jabbing him with his riding crop. "*I'm not paying you to stand idle, man,*" Wicker shouted over the roar of the fire. "*Get to it.*"

Doyle stared at the crowbar in his huge hands. For a moment he couldn't remember why he was here. Then, slowly, the reasons came back to him. Reasons he'd used to convince himself that he was doing the right thing. *I've six mouths to feed...* When that didn't fully allay his feeling of shame, he added, *If I don't do it, someone else will...*

With a primal grunt he turned and attacked the walls of Scanlon's cottage. With each swing of the crowbar he repeated to himself over and over again: *I've six mouths to feed...*

Michael, sprawled in the dirt and surrounded by wary constables with their truncheons at the ready, watched Doyle and the others bash at the walls with their crowbars in disbelief and sadness. It didn't take much effort to bring the cottage down. It was nothing more than a windowless hut with cracked walls and a roof badly in need of new thatch.

Finally, it was done. Doyle and the others stepped back, panting from their exertions, as the walls fell in on themselves in one final, sad sigh.

Then silence. The men looked at the rubble of Scanlon's cottage and thought of their own homes. Pat Doyle dropped his crowbar, tears flowing down the big man's cheeks.

"Give the warning," Wicker said to the bailiff.

The bailiff took a sheet of paper from inside his coat and read. "All here be advised that one Barry Scanlon, tenant, having failed to pay rent and being in arrears, is evicted this day. He, and his family, will remove themselves from the land forthwith under penalty of criminal trespass—"

"*That's a sentence of death!*" Michael shouted.

The bailiff glanced at Michael and stopped reading, uncertain.

"Go on, man," Wicker said. "Read the rest."

The bailiff cleared his throat. "Anyone giving refuge and shelter to this family will themselves be subject to immediate eviction."

And it was over. What had been Barry Scanlon's home—such as it was—for three generations had been reduced to a pile of smoldering rubble. One by one the farmers turned and silently went back to their homes.

A constable jabbed Michael with his club. "On your feet the lot of you. You're under arrest."

Father Rafferty pulled the sergeant constable aside. "Sure you can be merciful and let them go. They caused you no harm and haven't they been punished enough?"

The constable looked down at the three bleeding men. Perhaps the old priest was right. Taking this lot into custody would only create more paperwork. Besides, a cracked head served as a better warning not to interfere with the work of the constabulary than a day or two in jail ever would.

He poked Michael with the tip of his truncheon. Michael recognized him. He was the same sergeant who'd smoked his pipe outside the barracks while he'd clung to the roof twenty feet above.

"You've come to my attention and now I know who you are, bucko. Stay out of trouble or you'll answer to me. And the next time I won't let you off so easy."

Scanlon and his family gathered their belongings—an old mattress, a cooking pot, and a worn horse blanket—and started down the road. Michael ran to catch up with them.

"Where will you go, Barry?"

"The Workhouse."

"Ah, you can't go there, man."

"Where else then? The family is without sup or home."

Michael saw the anguish in Barry's eyes. "Aye, you're right. Where else can you go?"

Mary Scanlon, Barry's ten-year-old daughter, threw her arms around Michael's legs. "Michael, I'm afraid... I hear tell people die in the Workhouse."

He picked her up, shocked by the feel of bones under her rags. He wiped the tears from her dirty face. He had often told his Granda's scary stories to the young ones and it was always Mary, squealing the loudest in self-induced terror, who could never get enough of them.

"Sure that's just rumor, Mary."

"It's not. Didn't your own grandmam die there?"

"She was dyin' anyway. She went there for the coffin."

"Will you come to the Workhouse with us, Michael? Will you tell me scary stories there?"

"I can't, Mary." Tears welled up in her eyes. "But, I'll tell you what I'll do. I'll walk to the Workhouse with you. Would that be all right?"

She buried her face in his chest. "Aye."

As Michael and the Scanlon family started down the road toward the Workhouse, he saw Emily standing by a grove of trees. She looked at him for a moment, her lovely face ashen, her eyes glistening, and then she turned and disappeared into the trees.

The Workhouse was just as intimidating as it had been when Michael brought his grandmam there. Only this time, now that famine conditions were worsening, there was a long line of forlorn souls queued alongside the gray walls, waiting for their turn to get in.

Michael shook hands with Barry and kissed his wife. He hugged Mary. "You'll be all right here. They'll feed you and give you a nice place to sleep. And then, when the bad times are over, you'll come home and everythin' will be grand again."

"But we've no cottage to come to, Michael. They tumbled it down."

"Your Da and I will build another. Bigger and better. You'll see."

Michael waited with them in line until it was time for the family to enter through the massive oaken doors. As they disappeared into that terrible place, Michael knew that in spite of what he'd told Mary, he would never see them again.

Chapter Twenty Two

October 1847
Ballyross, Ireland

Despite Emily's brave promise to Dr. McDonald, she
almost didn't make it through her first week in the Fever
Hospital. Every morning, without fail, she became physically ill
as soon as she walked into the building and was assaulted by
the stomach-turning stench of offal and death. At the end of
the day, she'd rush home, soak in a hot tub, and scrub herself
until her skin was rubbed raw. But no matter how hard she
scrubbed, she couldn't get the smell out of her skin. It was as
though the stench of death had permeated the very cells of
her body. But, somehow, she made it through that first week.
And then a second week. And then, one day—as Dr.
McDonald had predicted—she no longer noticed the smell.

The smells were one thing. Tending the pitiful victims
was another. When she'd first arrived, they were trickling
into the hospital five or six a day. Now, the trickle had
become a torrent of sick and dying, threatening to overwhelm
the hospital and staff. The beds quickly filled. Blankets were
spread on the floor and the floor became beds. When the

rooms were full, patients were put in the corridors. As soon as one died, another was put in the bed. Even if there had been bed linens available, there would have been no time to change them. The hospital had become a hopeless, sad assembly line of death.

The patients were already emaciated by starvation. But once the fever took hold, the inexorable, downward spiral of death began in earnest. At first Emily had been stunned and outraged by Dr. McDonald's callous form of triage. Every morning he would walk up and down a narrow aisle between beds that held the new patients. He would give them a cursory examination—sometimes nothing more than a mere glance—and consign the patient to either a treatment bed or the dying room.

Emily protested. "You are not God, Dr. McDonald. How can you say this one will live or that one will die without giving them a proper examination?"

The doctor wiped his hands on his bloodstained apron, too weary to take offense at having his authority challenged by a mere girl. "When you've seen as many fever victims as I have, you don't need to examine them."

She was offended by his God-like arrogance, but she soon discovered he was right. After a week, even she was able to predict with just a glance who would live and who would die. It wasn't hard. Almost all who came to the hospital died eventually.

Emily put a spoonful of water to a little boy's parched lips. "Here, Thomas, try to drink just a little."

The father had brought the six-year-old in two days earlier. He, himself, died that night, but Emily was determined to keep his son alive. In spite of the telltale signs—he'd begun to develop rose-colored spots on his chest—Emily refused to accept the fact that this child was dying. He had become a personal crusade. *This child will live.* If she could keep just one child alive, she reasoned, it would ease the pain of watching so many others die.

The water dribbled out of the side of his mouth. Emily patiently dipped the spoon in a bucket of water and tried again. "Come on, Thomas, I know you can do it."

She looked into his yellow-hued eyes. They looked back at her, but there was no spark of life in them.

Two attendants rushed into the room carrying a man on a stretcher. As soon as they placed him on a bed, he started to convulse.

Dr. McDonald appeared. "Emily, give a hand here."

Emily and the two attendants held the man down while the doctor jammed a wooden stick into the patient's mouth to keep him from biting his tongue. In a matter of minutes the convulsion passed. The man's ruddy skin turned the color of yellowed parchment. Emily wasn't surprised when Dr. McDonald told the attendants to take the man to the dying room.

Emily returned to her patient. The youngster's eyes were closed. "Please, Thomas. You really must drink something." She forced the spoon into his mouth. The water trickled down his chin. She tried again. "'All right. One more time."

"He's gone, Emily."

Emily stiffened. "No, Dr. McDonald. He just needs to get some fluids in him. As soon as he gets some—"

Dr. McDonald gently took the spoon out of Emily's hand and held her by the shoulders. "Emily, listen to me," he said quietly. "The boy is dead."

Tears welled up in her eyes. "He can't be dead. I promised him he wouldn't die."

"Never promise such foolishness. Not here."

"He's too young to die…"

"Go home, Emily. You've had enough for one day."

Emily looked around her and it was as though she were seeing the hospital for the first time. And in a sense she was. From the beginning, she had not permitted herself to register the misery and devastation around her. At some level, she knew that she would not be able to function if she allowed herself to grasp the true horror of what was happening. But now, *the little boy was dead.* She could no longer maintain that pretense.

And it suddenly occurred to her what her true role was in this living hell. It was not to make these poor creatures well, it was to simply make their last hours as comfortable as possible.

"*They're all going to die…*" she sobbed. "*They're all going to die…*"

Dr. McDonald led her outside and sat her down on the steps.

"Will you be all right?"

"Yes, I'll be fine. I'll just rest here a bit."

To take her mind off the child's death, she concentrated on trying to sort out what was going on. *How did this happen? Why were so many people dying?* In her less lucid moments, she imagined that all this was some kind of giant, cosmic puzzle—that there had to be an answer somewhere. If she could only discover it, she could stop the dying and the misery. But then reality returned and she knew that there was no answer to what was going on here in Ireland. There were so many things for which she had no answer. But one thing she did know for certain. She could not go back into the hospital again. Ever.

A shadow passed in front of her face and a pleasant voice said, "Perhaps thee can help me?"

Startled, Emily looked up. A young man dressed all in black and wearing a wide flat-brimmed hat was standing before her. He had straight, longish blond hair, cobalt blue eyes, and an honest smile that seemed immune to misery.

"My name is Marcus Goodbody, good lady. Perhaps thee can help me?"

Looking askance at the stranger in the queer costume, Nora brought the tea service into the library.

As she poured, Emily said, "Mr. Goodbody, please explain your mission to my father."

Goodbody took a cup from Nora. "I thank thee."

Thee? Nora shot him a perplexed look, but said nothing.

"The Society of Friends—most know us as Quakers—is desirous of opening soup kitchens throughout Ireland."

Somerville stirred his tea. "An admirable undertaking, sir. What can I do to help?"

"Mr. Goodbody needs a place to set up his kitchen, Father."

"I have a barn and an empty stable. God knows they're of no use now. You are welcome to them, Mr. Goodbody."

"I thank thee. There is one more thing. Thy daughter has volunteered to assist me, but I will require the services of a few men as well. Dost thee know where I might find such men?"

"Yes, I do. Nora, would you fetch John Ranahan and his sons?"

Five minutes later Nora was back with the Ranahan men.

Hat in hand, Da stood rigidly at attention as Mr. Goodbody explained his mission. Dermot, who'd never been inside the Somerville Manor, couldn't stop gawking at the books and paintings. Michael couldn't stop looking at Emily, who couldn't stop stirring her tea even after the cup was half empty.

"I will not be able to pay thee wages," Goodbody explained. "But I can provide food for thee and thy family."

Da's heart thumped in his chest. Feeding his family was all he thought about day and night. The little money he and his sons earned on the Public Works was not enough to keep up with the rising cost of food. And now this man, who dressed so oddly and spoke so queer, was offering food. No, more than food. He was offering *survival*. Yet, in spite of his joy, his pride intervened and he heard himself say, "I cannot accept charity, sir."

"It will not be charity, Mr. Ranahan. Rest assured, the hours will be long and the work arduous for thee and thy sons."

Da exhaled in relief. "A Ranahan has never been afraid of hard work, sir."

Somerville stood up. "Good. Then that's settled. Is there anything else we can do for you Mr. Goodbody?"

Goodbody turned to Da. "Mr. Ranahan, perhaps one of thy sons could show me what conditions are like in the countryside?"

Emily put her cup on the silver tray. "I'll be glad to show you, Mr. Goodbody."

Michael saw her smile at this strange man and felt a sting of jealousy. "I'd better go, too," he said quickly.

"That won't be necessary," Emily said coolly.

She was still angry at Michael, whose behavior, in her opinion, seesawed maddeningly from a certain rustic charm to infuriating condescension.

That day she'd spotted him across the road from the Fever Hospital, she knew he'd been watching her. She'd seen him on three prior occasions, but not once did he approach her. Was he shy? Indifferent? That's why she'd crossed the road and approached him. To find out for herself. They'd had a pleasant enough conversation, even if all he could manage to say was "aye."

Then there was that scene in front of that redheaded man's cottage where he deigned to lecture her on the evils of the class system. The insufferable, patronizing fool.

"There are desperate men afoot on the roads these days your lordship," Michael said.

"I do believe he's right," Somerville said. "Young Ranahan will go with you."

"Very well." Emily didn't look at all happy. "Please get the trap ready."

Michael bridled at the dismissive tone in her voice, but he held his tongue.

Inside the barn, Michael harnessed the only horse left in the stable. She was so old even the gombeen man wouldn't buy her. As he led the horse out of the barn, he saw Emily and Goodbody came out of the manor house. They seemed to be having a grand time together.

After Goodbody inspected the barn, Emily said, "Will the barn serve your purpose, Mr. Goodbody?"

"It will indeed, Mistress Somerville. I would be pleased if thee would call me by my Christian name, Marcus."

"Very well. But only if you call me Emily."

Michael yanked at the harness straps, getting angrier by the minute. He studied the man in his queer hat and long black coat. He was almost as tall as Michael and judging from the breath of his back and the way he moved he was used to hard work. He had a ready smile and he didn't put on airs like most of the young sons of the gentry. In short, he was the kind of man Michael could take a liking to. So why, he asked himself, was he feeling this great dislike for a man he barely knew?

His eyes went to Emily. *Will you look at her? She can't take her eyes off the man. She's shameless.*

"So you live in London, Marcus?"

"I do."

"Oh, do tell me, what's playing in the theaters? It's been so long."

"I would not know, Emily. We are a plain people and do not go in for entertainments and such."

"Oh, really? Why—"

"The trap is ready," Michael said brusquely.

They looked at him as though they'd forgotten he was there, and that made him even angrier.

Emily handed him a hamper filled with bread. "Please take care of this."

There was that dismissive tone again. Michael slammed the hamper under the seat and climbed up onto the trap.

Emily climbed into the trap and sat between Goodbody and Michael.

In a foul, black humor, Michael guided the horse through back roads that only the tenant farmers used. Emily, pointing to a field of ripened corn, said, "I don't understand. Why don't the farmers eat the corn?"

"Because it's the crop that pays the rent," Michael snapped. "They eat that and they'll be thrown off the land for sure."

"There's no need to take that tone," Emily said, irritated by his petulance. "You asked and I told you." Michael knew he'd gone too far and that made his black humor even blacker.

They traveled in tense silence for a while and then, as they came around a bend, they saw five men chasing a cow across a field. One of the men threw a rope around the animal's neck. Then, while two men held the terrified animal still, another made a quick incision in the cow's neck. The fourth man held a bowl under the incision to catch the blood. When the bowl was filled, the third man stuffed a clump of grass in the wound and they released the animal.

"What in the world are they doing?" Emily asked, horrified.

"Collectin' the blood," Michael said. "They'll mix it with a bit of corn meal and fry it. It's not very tasty, but it does fill the belly. Of course it's not somethin' you'd have at one of your grand dinners."

Emily, thoroughly exasperated by Michael's irritable behavior, turned in her seat to face him. "Mr. Ranahan, if it is your purpose to be uncivil you are succeeding admirably."

Michael pulled his cap down over his eyes and snapped the reins. The trap lurched forward. *Eejit*, he said to himself. *Can you not shut your gub for one minute?*

A mile up the road they passed a cluster of cottages that were in such a state of disrepair that Goodbody assumed they must surely be abandoned. But then they saw thin plumes of smoke rising from several chimneys.

"Do people still live there do you think?" Goodbody asked.

Michael reined in the horse. "It would seem so."

The Quaker pointed at the most dilapidated of the cottages. "Might we speak to the people inside, do you think?"

Michael noted the cracked walls, the sagging roof. No self-respecting tenant would allow his home be in such disrepair, even in these times. If anyone lived there, they had to be sick. Maybe even dead. He'd heard stories of entire families being found dead in their cottages. Weakened by the fever, they died one by one until the whole family was gone.

"I don't think you'll be wantin' to do that. It won't be a pretty sight."

"Mr. Ranahan, that is why I am here. How else am I to know what must be done?"

Michael studied Goodbody's honest face and saw anxiety flicker in those blue eyes. Clearly, he didn't want to go into the cottage, but he was prepared to do his duty. Despite his own conflicted feeling about the man, Michael had to grudgingly admire that kind of courage.

"Right. Let's go."

Emily started to get out of the trap. "It's best you stay here," Michael said.

"*Please* don't tell me what to do, Mr. Ranahan."

"I think Mr. Ranahan is right, Emily. Perhaps you should remain in the trap."

Emily stood up and put her hands on her hips, now infuriated with both men. "I want you both to stop treating me like a child. I've worked in the Fever Hospital. Surely there is nothing that I have not already seen. Michael, get the hamper."

Still fuming at her superior tone—*get the hamper*—Michael knocked on the door and listened. There was no sound inside. He pushed the door open and he and Goodbody involuntarily stepped back, staggered by the overwhelming, putrid stench of decaying flesh. To their astonishment, Emily pushed past them and stepped through the door as though it were the most natural thing in the world. They put their hands to their noses and followed her inside.

The only source of light inside the gloomy cabin came from a smoldering turf fire. In a corner Michael saw three heads half-hidden by a tattered horse blanket. He pulled the blanket aside and saw the cause of the stench—a man's decomposing body. To either side of the body, two skeleton-thin children gazed up at him with dull, rheumy eyes.

"Their Da must have died," Michael said. "And these little ones are too sick to even get out of the bed."

Emily let out a gasp and Michael turned to see what she was looking at. There, by the fire, sitting on the floor, was a figure, hardly human. It was a half-naked woman, her eyes wild with madness, rocking back and forth.

Emily knelt down beside her and offered her a loaf of bread. The woman stared at it but didn't move.

"Her mind's gone," Michael said. "She doesn't even recognize food."

Emily put the bread in her lap and Michael led Emily and Goodbody outside. Goodbody staggered a step and vomited against the cottage wall.

Suddenly, they were surrounded by a cluster of gaunt men, women, and children. Scrawny hands clutched at them feebly.

"*Somethin' for the hunger, your honor, before I perish from want...*"

"*A bit of bread please...*"

"*Some food to keep the life in me...*"

Michael pulled Emily and Goodbody away from the groping hands and pushed them into the trap. Then he distributed the bread to outstretched hands, saving the last two loaves.

He pulled aside two of the healthier men and gave them the loaves. To the first man he said, "See that the man inside is given a decent burial." To the other he said, "Get the wife and the little ones to the Fever Hospital. Will you do that for me?"

The men took the loaves. "We will, your honor. God bless you."

For a long time while they rode back to the Manor, no one spoke. Finally, Goodbody broke the strained silence. "If we did not happen upon those people in that hovel what would have become of them?"

"They'd have died," Michael said. "Then the neighbors, if they had the strength, would have tumbled the cottage down on them. Their home would become their grave. That's how we bury people nowadays."

They rode into the village of Ballyross. In the two years since the first blight, there had been dramatic changes. O'Mally's bakeshop, along with several other shops, stood abandoned and boarded up. Today was Saturday, market day. In better times the road would have been crowded with farmers bringing animals and produce to market. But now it was deserted, except for a solitary dog padding up the center of the dirt road.

Emily watched the dog coming towards them. "Well at least he looks well fed."

She saw Michael and Goodbody exchange a quick glance. Then she remembered all the dead bodies that they'd seen lining the sides of the road.

"*Stop!*"

Even before Michael could bring the trap to a halt, Emily jumped off. She staggered to the side of the road and retched. As she crouched by the ditch, her head swimming and her stomach clenching, she realized she'd been wrong. *There were still some things that she had not seen.*

Chapter Twenty Three

When Emily and the Ranahan men came into Somerville's barn at first light the next morning, Mr. Goodbody was already at work. He'd already unloaded his kitchen utensils and was in the process of lighting a fire under one of several large cauldrons.

Emily, not used to rising at this hour, stifled a yawn. "What do you want us to do?" she asked.

Not accustomed to giving orders, especially to a beautiful young woman, he looked at her flustered, almost shy. "Oh, perhaps thee could tend the fire?"

"And what do you want us to do?" Michael asked.

"Well... Mr. Ranahan, perhaps thee would take charge of washing the soup bowls."

The three Ranahan men stared at each other. "Which Ranahan are you talkin' to?" Michael asked.

Goodbody rubbed his hand together, perplexed. "This is most difficult. I do not know thee well enough to call thee by thy Christian names."

Michael took Goodbody's hand and shook it. "Marcus, I'm Michael." He nodded to his father and brother. "And this is Da and this is Dermot. Do you think now you know us well enough to call us by our Christian names?"

Goodbody grinned shyly. "Very well. Perhaps Da will wash the bowls and Dermot could hand out and collect the bowls. Michael, perhaps thee and Emily will help me dispense the soup. If"—he added apologetically—"none of thee would object."

Emily answered for all of them. "This is your soup kitchen, Marcus. We will do whatever you ask."

With not a little concern, Michael watched Goodbody stirring a huge cauldron that contained enough soup to feed the entire village of Ballyross. "What if no one comes?" he asked, wondering what they would do with all that soup if no one came. "Do you think we should go on to the roads and into the village and tell people we've soup for them."

"There's no need," Goodbody said with great certainty. "They'll know."

Michael thought he was daft. *How would they know there was soup here if no one told them?* He went outside, intent on going into the village himself—but then he saw them coming. Trudging up the road in groups of twos and threes—indeed, whole families—they appeared out of the fog like ghostly apparitions. And Michael wondered, *how did they know?* Later, when Michael put that question to Goodbody, the Quaker responded, "I do not know. But I've seen it happen many, many times. I don't know how they know. They just do. Perhaps God speaks to them."

Michael recognized some of the people standing in line waiting for the soup. They lived in the valley and attended the same old church he did. Others were strangers, passing through and going God knows where. The sight filled him with an overwhelming sadness. These men, at least the ones he knew, had once been strong men of the land. They'd withstood rain, blight, hunger, death, and the wrath of capricious landlords. But now, these tough, proud men shuffled into their place in the line, standing silent, docile, beaten, their eyes fixed on the muddy road at their feet.

All day long they came. And the sights were pitiful. One man was so weak he couldn't hold the bread he'd been given. Leaning against a tree, he put the piece between his knees and, as he leaned forward to take a bite, he let out a small cry and fell over dead. Later that day, an incident occurred that convinced Michael, if he ever needed more convincing, that the growing famine was causing otherwise sane men to do insane things. He had just taken a boiling cauldron of soup off the fire and placed it on the serving table. A man about his father's age, so weakened by hunger that he could barely stand, lunged at the cauldron. Before Michael could stop him, he plunged his hands into the scalding soup. He was so crazed with hunger that he felt no pain as he scooped handfuls of boiling soup into his mouth. There was nothing they could do for the man who died within minutes. After that horrific event, Dermot's job was to stand in front of the soup cauldron to prevent anyone one else from doing the same thing.

Finally, at sunset, they fed the last of them and Goodbody announced that they were done for the day. Now it was time to clean up. At Goodbody's gentle direction, they went about their assigned tasks. Michael scrubbed the tables. Emily and Goodbody washed the bowls. Da, determined to earn his keep for the food he'd gotten this day, wanted to do everything. But, Emily, concerned for the old man's health, insisted that he go home after the last feeding. As soon as Da left, Dermot saw his opportunity and slipped out of the barn and went off to find his friends.

Doing as he was told, a perplexed Michael scrubbed the tables with scalding hot water and brown soap. As far as he was concerned, brushing the odd crumb of bread onto the ground and wiping up the odd spill was enough, but Goodbody had this peculiar notion that the fever was spread by contact and he insisted that everything be scrubbed clean. Michael thought it a daft idea, but he did it nevertheless, unable to resist Goodbody's sincerity. In spite of himself, he'd begun to like this man who dressed and spoke so queer.

He liked Goodbody well enough, but he didn't like seeing the Quaker and Emily together. Michael attacked the tables with the scrub brush, furtively watching them laughing and talking about things he knew nothing about. *Probably some foolishness about London.*

When he'd finished the last table, he announced, "I'm done now."

They didn't even respond. And that made him even angrier. *I might as well be invisible.*

He threw the brush into bucket, walked out of the barn, and sat down on a stone wall by the side of the barn.

It was a glorious early fall night. The sky, lit with a million stars, soothed his bruised ego. He forced himself to think of something other than Emily. He thought of the coming harvest. Soon it would be time to bring in the potatoes. And, God willing, everything would be right in the world again.

Working in the soup kitchen was the right thing to do, but he had no liking for it. Truth told, he preferred to be out in the fields in God's own fresh air.

For weeks now, he and Da had been going into the fields morning and evening to check the plants. So far there had been no sign of the blight. But there had been no sign of the blight in the past and it had come anyway. He could hardly remember what it was like before the blight and the great hunger. His plans to go to America seemed like something that had happened in a dream a very long time ago.

"A ha'penny for your thoughts."

Michael looked up in surprise. He'd been so deep in thought that he hadn't heard Emily approach. In spite of his irritation with her, he was happy to see her. She sat down next to him and he smelled a sweet fragrance coming from her hair. The air was chilly, but he felt himself growing warmer.

Remembering his past oversight, he blurted out, "How's your family?"

"What—?"

"Your Da, and…" he didn't know if she had more family."

"Oh, my father is fine. Thank you for asking."

After an awkward silence, she said, "Why are you out here sitting in the dark?"

"In the dark it's easier to remember the way things used to be—when children weren't starvin', and men had their work, and women had food for their pots."

She studied him for a long while. "Dermot told me you were planning on going to America."

He thought he detected a note of disappointment in her voice. But perhaps that was just wishful thinking. He glanced at her, but he couldn't see her expression in the darkness.

"Aye."

"Why didn't you go?"

"Oh, lots of reasons." He couldn't bring himself to tell her about the spent passage money and that his dream of going out to America was lost and gone forever. "Where's Mr. Goodbody?" he asked, changing the subject.

"He went off to pray."

"Do you like him then?" Michael blurted out. He cringed, glad that the darkness hid his embarrassment.

Fortunately, she misunderstood the intent of his question. "Oh, yes. He's a fine, good man. I don't know much about the Quakers, or as he calls it, the Religious Society of Friends, but we can all be grateful that these fine people are here to help us."

"Aye, he is a good man," Michael added grudgingly.

"When does the harvest begin?"

"In a fortnight."

"Could the blight come a third year do you think?"

Michael took a moment to answer. "I said no the last time. I'll say nothin' this time." To his chagrin, it suddenly occurred to him—some of his Da's superstitions were rubbing off on him as well.

Neither spoke for a long time. Finally, Emily said, "Well, I'm exhausted. I think I'll retire. Goodnight, Michael."

"Aye. Goodnight."

He sat there a long time after she'd gone, regretting another lost chance to talk to her. There was so much he wanted to say to her, but when she was near him, he simply couldn't find the words. He sat there until the last lingering scent of her blew off in the evening breeze. Then he went home.

In spite of Goodbody's best intentions, not everything ran smoothly that first week. The next day sixty starving people showed up and they ran out of hot water to wash the bowls. On the fifth day over a hundred showed up and there wasn't enough seating for them. But with the help of Emily and the Ranahans, Goodbody addressed these problems with good humor and dispatch and soon the soup kitchen was feeding over a hundred a day with little difficulty.

The second week the soup kitchen was open, an especially emaciated old man came through the line and Emily handed him a piece of bread. "Do you think I might have another, miss?" he asked in a soft, hoarse voice. "I haven't had a bite to me mouth in five days."

"Of course." Emily gave him another piece.

"I wouldn't do that," Michael cautioned.

"The man is starving," she said, pointedly.

"Still, he's not used to eatin'. He'll get sick and—"

"Mr. Ranahan, if you don't mind, I'll be the judge of what the man can and cannot have."

The half-starved old man didn't wait to sit down. While he was still in line, he stuffed the bread into his mouth and gulped at the soup as thought at any moment someone might snatch it away from him. Within minutes his stomach rebelled at the unaccustomed quantity of food and he vomited up the entire meal. Michael shot an I-told-you-so look at Emily. She pretended not to notice, but she stopped giving extra portions.

As he did every day, Lord Somerville came into the barn to see how the feedings were going. He moved about the tables nodding and stopping occasionally to speak to the grateful people who filled his barn. But today he only half-listened to what the poor wretches were saying because he was intent on watching his daughter. The stress of working long hours, first in the Fever Hospital and now in the soup kitchen, was beginning to show. He knew she wasn't sleeping well. Sometimes in the early morning hours when he himself couldn't sleep, he'd heard her pacing in her room. Her skin, which had always been an ivory white, was sallow and there were deep smudges under her eyes.

And I am responsible. He had told her to get involved and now he was having serious doubts about the wisdom of that advice. He'd wanted her to do something to take her mind off the tedious boredom of country life, but he'd never meant for her to work herself into a state of exhaustion. Still, in spite of everything, he had to admit there was a glow, an inner strength, a competence about her that he'd never seen before. Still.

I've put it off long enough, he said to himself as he watched her ladling soup into bowls. *Tonight I must tell her.*

The dining room in Somerville Manor had taken on a shabby appearance since the removal of the wall tapestries and the Waterford chandelier. Somerville didn't tell Emily, but he was still doing business with Kincaid. When bills came due and there were no funds in the accounts, he called in the gombeen man and sold off yet another piece of the Somerville family legacy.

Emily's legacy.

Lord Somerville picked at his food, waiting for an opportune time to speak.

"We fed a hundred and thirty today, Father."

"Most commendable. What you and Mr. Goodbody are doing is admirable."

"I'm just so grateful to Marcus for giving me the opportunity to do something worthwhile. I felt so guilty about not being able to go back to the Fever Hospital, but…I just couldn't."

"I for one am glad to see you out of that dreadful place. Besides, it's more gratifying keeping people alive than watching them die, is it not?"

"Oh, yes. I only wish I could do more."

Somerville studied his beautiful daughter and felt tremendous pride—and gratitude. Just two short years ago she'd come back from London a petulant, spoiled girl. And he had been at a loss as what to do with her. But, in that time, she'd turned into a responsible, caring young woman.

He put his fork down. He could put it off no longer. "Emily, I'm sending you off to London to stay with Aunt Sarah." He tried to make his tone sound casual, but he failed. "I think it best that—"

Emily shook her head. "I'm not leaving, Father."

In spite of his resolve—and concern—Somerville felt a surge of joy. He was concerned for her health. For her own good it was best that she leave this desolate country as soon as possible, even though he knew he would miss her terribly.

"You would have jumped at the chance two years ago."

"*Two years!* It seems like another life. So much has happened. I can't go, Father. Did you see the article in this morning's *London Times?* Calcutta has sent fourteen thousand pounds to Ireland to help in the relief effort. *Calcutta!* My God. How could I possibly leave?"

"How could you indeed?" Somerville answered, feeling pleased—and apprehensive.

Chapter Twenty Four

October 1847
Ballyross, Ireland

It was just before sunset when Michael and his father, as was their custom, went into the field to painstakingly check every plant. When they were done, Michael stood up and stretched his aching back. "Well, there's no sign of the blight."

Da squinted at his small field with a look of distrust, as though he expected the leaves to turn black before his very eyes.

"They're ready, Da." Michael said, sensing his father's indecisiveness. "We should dig them up tomorrow."

"*Hush your tongue!*" an alarmed Da hissed. "We'll do no such a thing," he shouted into the field.

Michael shook his head at his father's foolish superstitious notions. Since that first morning when the blight destroyed his potatoes, Da had gotten into his head the notion that the little people had heard him say he was going to dig up the potatoes and they'd punished him for his presumptuousness. Since then, he'd become convinced that it was bad luck to say anything about future plans.

To pacify his anxious Da, Michael shouted into the field. "You're right. We'll not dig them up tomorrow."

But they both knew they would.

No one slept that night in the Ranahan cottage. Lost in their own thoughts, no one talked either. Each had their own special prayer. Da prayed that the terrible black rot would not come in the night. Mam prayed for an end to the great hunger that was threatening to destroy what was left of her family. Dermot dreamed about getting away from this place.

And Michael dreamed of Emily.

An hour before dawn, Da sat abruptly upright in bed. "Oh, Lord God in heaven. Do you smell it?"

"Smell what?" Dermot asked.

"The rot."

Dermot sniffed. "I don't."

"Me neither," Michael said.

"I can smell it, I tell ya."

"Go back to sleep," Mam said. "You're imaginin' it."

"I'm not. Tis the blight. Can you not smell it, woman?"

"I cannot," Dermot said. "Go have a look outside and see for yourself."

"I will not. Tis bad luck to get up before the dawn."

Michael got out of bed. He knew better, but all this talk of blight and rot was making even him jittery. Cautiously, he opened the door, half-expecting to be overwhelmed by that unforgettable stench of decay. Instead, he inhaled the damp, sweet smell of early morning air.

"Everything's lovely," he said.

"Didn't I tell you?" Dermot said.

"Give it up," Mam said.

"Well didn't he scare the life out of me with his talk of the rot?"

Michael crawled back onto his pallet. "Dermot, for the love of God, go back to sleep."

"How am I to sleep now?"

He didn't. Nor did anyone else. They lay in their beds silent and tense until they heard the crow of a distant rooster. Then, as one, they got up and, trying to be appear calm, hurriedly dressed. Then, as a group, they cautiously stepped out into the thin light of dawn.

Da sniffed the air suspiciously.

Michael walked into the field, knelt down and touched a leaf. It was thick and soft with life. He pulled a plant out of the ground and squeezed a potato. *Solid.* He brushed away the dirt and bit into it. *Firm.*

He sat back on his haunches and his voice cracked with emotion. "The potatoes are lovely."

Cautiously, Da came into the field. He knelt down next to Michael and pulled up a plant to see for himself. He examined it. Bit into it and waited a moment, as though he expected the potato to turn putrid in his mouth. Then he cautiously chewed. "Aye. Tis good."

Mam and Dermot were next. As Michael and Da had done, each of them pulled up a plant and bit into the raw potato.

"Well?" Da asked.

"It's lovely," Mam said.

"Aye, it's lovely," Dermot echoed.

The four Ranahans sat on the ground in the field, surrounded by the healthy potatoes that would feed them till next year. *The great hunger was over.*

They were too stoic to cry and too reserved to express their elation, but no one was able to speak for a very long time.

Chapter Twenty Five

Lord Somerville held up his glass in a toast. "To a bountiful harvest."

Sitting next to her father Emily, clinked her glass against his. "Here, here." Since that day in the garden when they'd reestablished contact with each other, she'd instructed Nora to set her place beside her father instead of the opposite end of the great dining room table.

"And to the end of the famine," she added cheerfully.

Somerville frowned. "I fear the famine is not yet over."

"But there's no blight. The potato crop is healthy."

"Yes, but only Ranahan and a handful of others had the good sense—or seed—to plant a crop. The rest..." he shook his head.

"What will happen to them?"

"I'm afraid that depends on Charles Trevelyan and the government."

November 1847
Ministry of the Treasury

"One *fifth*?" Trevelyan glared across the table at the three scientific commission members as though they were personally responsible for the dismal figures. "Are you telling me that only twenty percent of the farmers planted a potato crop?"

"We warned you, Mr. Trevelyan," Playfair said patiently. "All year we've been saying this calamity would occur."

Trevelyan slammed his hand down on the gleaming tabletop, furious at the gross irresponsibility of these thick Irish tenant farmers. "In the name of God, why did they not plant?"

"Many ate their seed. Others couldn't afford to buy seed. The sum and total of it is that eighty percent of the fields weren't planted and now these farmers sit on barren acres."

Irritated with himself for his momentary loss of self control, Trevelyan quickly regained his composure. Straightening his cuffs, he said, "Well, no matter. In any event the famine is over. Now perhaps I'll be able to go on holiday with my family."

"But it's not over," Dr. Lindley said, amazed that Trevelyan still did not grasp the import of what they were trying to tell him. "There are severe food shortages and, surely, matters will worsen. Disease is rampant in the countryside. People will continue to starve and die. The destitution and misery in some districts cannot be exaggerated. Mr. Trevelyan, you are the British government's voice in matters of the Irish famine. What do you propose to do about this calamity?"

Trevelyan glared at Playfair. "The government proposes to do nothing. "

Summoning every ounce of self-control at his possession, Playfair said, "Mr. Trevelyan, history will not look kindly on a nation that treats its subjects so harshly."

"There are whispers of genocide," Dr. Lindley added.

Trevelyan sat back and made a steeple of his fingers, his gray eyes colder than ever. "I do not credit rumors, Dr. Lindley. And as for history, Dr. Playfair, I believe it will show that the British government has displayed an admirable forbearance toward a nation that refuses to heal herself. Rumor and innuendo aside, one fact remains: The famine is over. Tomorrow I will sign an order closing the Board of Works."

November 1847
Ballyross, Ireland

A steady rain fell upon the shapeless, colorless knot of men gathered outside the Board Of Works office. They stood with the posture of defeated men—silent and passive, heads bowed, knowing that another blow was about to fall. Yesterday, after they'd done their work, Tarpy, the road supervisor, had told them to report to the Board Of Works office this morning. The last time they'd been summoned here rumors born of fear and uncertainty had surged through the crowd like an out-of-control brush fire. But that was last year, when they still had spirit, when they still had hope. Now they were too weary, too beaten to listen to even rumors. They stood in the rain, silent, watching the door, awaiting their fate.

At precisely nine o'clock a shadowed figure appeared behind the curtained door. The sound of chains being undone and bars being slid echoed in the hushed stillness. The door opened and a jittery Alfred Browning poked his head out. He remained behind the door, prepared to slam and bar it at the first sign of insurrection. He'd learned his lesson the last time. He would not expose his person to this mob again.

"The famine has been declared over," he shouted from the doorway. "The Board Of Works is forthwith shut down."

Anticipating a rush of angry men, he slammed the door and with a trembling hand did the chains and bars as quickly as he could. But, unlike last time, there was no reaction from the men. No anger. No shouting. No fist waving.

"Did you inform them, Mr. Browning?" Thomas asked from his hiding place behind a record cabinet.

"I did."

"And what was their reaction?"

Browning pushed the curtain aside and peeked out. "There was no reaction, Mr. Thomas. Why they're just standing there. Silent. In the rain."

"How strange."

"How strange indeed."

As the Ranahans walked back to their home, Dermot muttered, "They're killin' us all. They're killin' us all, I tell ya."

A year ago, Da would have told him to mind his tongue, but now he said nothing because he was beginning to think his son was right. He squinted up at the black clouds scudding across the gray sky and saw it as a mark of God's anger toward them. *But what had they done?*

"You're right, Dermot. They are killin' us all." Jerry Fowler handed him the jar of poteen.

Dermot took a sip and shuddered as the harsh alcohol burned its way down into his stomach. "I haven't seen a jar in over a year. Where'd you get this?"

Fowler took the jar and passed it to Kevin. "Let's just say I liberated it from a very careless man."

It was almost midnight and the three men were sitting in the ruins of Barry Scanlon's tumbled cottage. No one in the village had seen Jerry Fowler in almost a year. One rumor was that he'd married a rich widow and had gone to America. Another rumor, perhaps wishful thinking on the part of those who disliked him, was that he'd sailed on a coffin ship and had gone down in the north Atlantic.

Then, yesterday, he appeared just as suddenly as he disappeared. As only Jerry Fowler could, he entranced some and angered others with amazing tales of his travels that might have been true—or, knowing Fowler's penchant for embellishment and exaggeration—just stories conjured up from his vivid imagination.

Dermot and Kevin had agreed to meet Fowler here tonight, partly because of the promise of poteen, and partly because they were curious to hear about his "great plan." But for Dermot, the real reason he was here was because Jerry Fowler had asked him to come. Dermot had always had a need to attach himself to someone he perceived to be strong and powerful. In the past, it had been Billy Moore. But Billy was now either alive or dead in an Australian penal colony and in any event very far away. And so, he turned to the handsome, tough talking Jerry Fowler for salvation.

"So where have you been?" Dermot asked.

"Traveling the roads, lads. Let me tell ya, unlike the lot of you, I've seen some things."

"And so have we," Kevin said defensively.

Fowler slapped the big man's knee. "Is that right? You old blatherskite, you've not set foot out of this godforsaken place since the hunger started. So, what could you have seen? Will you tell me that?"

Kevin shrugged, not knowing what to say.

"I've been to Dublin and back again," Fowler said. "I've gone north and south. And I've seen a thing or two."

Dermot took a swig of the poteen and passed it to Kevin. "And what did you see, Jerry?"

Fowler's wide grin vanished. "I've seen enough to know the Brits are doin' their best to starve us all to death."

"Why do you say that?" Dermot asked.

"They've closed the Public Works again, haven't they? And why do you think they did that? Because they want to starve us to death and that's a fact."

For the next half hour Fowler harangued them with example after example of the harsh and unfair treatment they were getting at the hands of the landlords and the British government. And with each sip of the poteen, Dermot and Kevin slowly became more and more enraged.

"They know full well most of us have no potatoes," Fowler said. Then he repeated Dermot's oft spoken fear. "I tell ya, they're killin' us."

Kevin took a sip and wiped his mouth with a ragged sleeve. "Me Da says we'll soon have to leave here. I hear Rowe's offerin' passage to America to anyone who'll quit the land."

"I'd go tomorrow," Dermot said, "but me Da will never leave."

"Will you listen to the pair of you?" Fowler's voice dripped with sarcasm. "All this talk of runnin' away. I ask you, why should *we* leave the land that's rightfully ours?"

"What else can we do?" Dermot asked.

"We can make them leave."

Dermot grinned at Fowler. "Me brother's right. You are daft."

"'Tis your brother who's daft, thinking he could fight armed troops with rocks and sticks. Sure there's too many of them. They have all the guns in the world."

"So how do we fight them then?" Kevin asked.

"Not head-on like at Cork quay for Jasus' sake. Not man-to-man. We hit and run. Hit and run. Tonight here. Tomorrow there."

Kevin's eyes glistened from the potent drink and the excitement of what the confident Fowler was saying. "Just who is it you plan on hittin', Jerry?"

Even though they were sitting in the ruins of an old cottage and miles from prying ears, Fowler leaned into the two men and whispered, "The landlords."

Dermot and Kevin were struck speechless. Attacking the peelers and soldiers was one thing. But to go after the powerful landlords—well, it *was* daft. There was no other way to think it.

"If we're caught, they'll tumble our homes down on us," Dermot said. "We'll be transported for life and that's a fact."

"We won't get caught. Not if we're careful."

"But why the landlords?" Kevin asked.

"Because *they* are at the heart of my plan. We make them so afraid they'll want to leave the country forever."

"How does the likes of you propose to make the landlords afraid?" Dermot asked.

"We burn their barns. We kill their livestock. We set fire to their fields."

In spite of his apprehension, Dermot was stirred by Fowler's words. Here was a man of action. Here was a man who would no longer bow his head to the landlords. Something began to burn inside him and it felt terrifying and exhilarating at the same time. He was tired of doing nothing. And nothing was all anyone was doing. Da, he knew, had no stomach for a fight, but he'd thought Michael was different. Dermot had been so proud of his brother that morning at the Cork quay. Some had died to be sure, but wasn't that to be expected in a revolution?

At the quay, Dermot had felt the same terror and exhilaration he was feeling now. When he saw the soldiers fire their rifles and saw his friends fall, he was sure that this was the beginning of an uprising with his brother as the leader. But to his great disappointment, there was no uprising. Something happened to Michael that morning. Dermot was ashamed to admit it, but his brother had become a coward.

But Jerry Fowler was no coward, and everything he said was God's own truth. Dermot was tired of being beaten down, tired of working day and night for wages that could barely put a bite of food in his mouth. It was time to strike back, to make someone else afraid for a change.

Fowler saw Dermot's hardening expression and knew he had him. "Are you with me?" he asked, slapping his hands on Dermot's shoulders.

"I am," Dermot said without hesitation.

"And you, Kevin?"

"I don't know, Jerry…"

Fowler leaned forward and put his face close to Kevin's. "Poor Billy Moore's probably dead by now. But let me ask you, Kevin, if he was here what would he do?"

For a moment Kevin's face screwed up in concentration as he tried to recall the man he'd worshipped all his life. *What would Billy do?* He thought for a moment and then pounded his big fists on his thighs as the answer came to him. "He'd be with you, Jerry, and so will I."

The thought that he was at a crucial crossroad in his life, made Dermot's stomach tightened. He took a deep slug of the poteen and the burning liquid brought tears to his eyes. The potent brew drove away the fear and he felt strong. Indestructible.

Kevin reached out a massive hand. "Give me the jar here."

Dermot gave it to him and Kevin emptied what was left. Then he hurled the jar and it shattered against the rubble of the ruined cottage. "That's what'll become of the cursed landlords," he roared.

Fowler slapped the big man's back. "That's the spirit, Kevin."

Dermot grinned along with the others, but he was watching Kevin's face and despite the great show of bravado Dermot still saw fear in the big man's eyes.

"When do we act?" Kevin asked.

Fowler winked at the two men. "Soon, lads. Very soon."

Michael's eyes snapped open, unsure if the sound he heard was real or something he'd dreamed. For weeks now, he'd been having alternating nightmares almost nightly. One night it was the dead man from the river, chasing him across the fields, beckoning him to return to the black waters. Another night it was the men who'd died at the Cork quay. They never spoke. They just pointed fingers at him.

Now he lay in bed, holding his breath and listening. He heard nothing but the sound of his family breathing. He closed his eyes, deciding he'd been dreaming. Then he heard it again. *The sound of a creaky door opening.*

He shook Dermot awake. "Someone's in the shed," he whispered. He leaned over and poked his father. "Da, someone's in the shed."

The three men slipped on their brogues. Da lit a torch from the smoldering turf fire and they silently slipped outside.

The air was cold and sharp. The frost crunched under their feet as they moved toward the shed. There was no moon, but the dome of stars above cast enough light so they could see that the door to the shed was partially opened. Michael and Dermot picked up heavy sticks and they came to stand on either side of the door. At a nod from Da, the three rushed inside.

Five shapeless forms crouched on the floor gnawing on raw potatoes. At the unexpected appearance of the Ranahan men, they scurried into a corner. At first Michael thought it was a pack of animals, but then Da thrust the torch above his head to illuminate the tiny room and took a step back in shock. "*Jasus God...*"

The flickering torchlight cast shadows across the sunken faces. With their matted hair and tattered rags they looked more animal than human.

A man, a woman, and three children clutched raw potatoes in their claw-like hands and stared back at Da with hollowed, frightened eyes. Da lowered the torch toward the three children and squinted. At first he thought the light was playing tricks with his eyes, but it was no trick. The children's faces were covered with hair, giving them a monkey-like visage. Da had no way of knowing it, but doctors would later confirm that the condition, which affected only children, was caused by *marasmus*—a debilitating and bizarre side effect of starvation.

Dermot was the first to react. He raised the stick over his head. "You thieving bastards—"

He was about to bring the stick down on the man's head when Michael yanked it out of his hand. "Dermot, for the love of God—"

"They're stealin' our food—"

Da shoved him away. "Go back in the house, eejit."

Dermot glared at the five creatures on the floor for a moment, then his father, and stomped out of the shed.

The man spoke in a soft voice, raspy from hunger. "Sirs, we've not had a mouthful of food in five days. Have pity..."

If the fever weren't still raging through the countryside, Da would have taken them in, but he dared not put his family at risk. Without taking his eyes off the skeletal, pathetic children, he muttered, "Take what you want..."

"God bless you, sirs," the man said.

They gathered up as many potatoes as they could carry and without another word scurried out of the shed. They had come and gone so quickly that Michael almost wondered if this was yet another bad dream.

A bewildered Da, still holding the torch above his head, said, "The hunger's not over yet, is it?"

Michael put the lid back on the potato bin. "No, it is not."

Chapter Twenty Six

Emily was getting ready for bed when she heard the sound of music coming from somewhere in the distance. She opened the window and the rasping sound of a fiddle floated on the clear night air. She returned to her bed, pulled down the comforter, and started to untie her robe. Then, intrigued by the music, she went back to the window and listened as the fiddler started in on a jig. She danced a little step, paused, looked out the window, as though trying to make up her mind about something, and then rushed to the closet and slipped into a dress.

The night air was cold and crisp. A full moon illuminated the night sky, but the stars would not be outdone and they glistened in bright rivalry. Emily pulled her cloak tightly around her to ward off the chill and moved through the trees in the direction of the music.

Approaching a clearing, she saw a dozen or more young men and women dancing around a bonfire. Off to the side, a diminutive, oddly shaped figure of a man played a fiddle. Emily watched, fascinated. Smoke swirled around him, cloaking him in a shroud of mist. The light of the flames flickered off him, giving him an unworldly, almost mystical visage. Emily shivered, suddenly reminded of the leprechauns and the wee people that Nora was always talking about.

A figure materialized out of the smoke and came toward her. He was backlit by the fire and she couldn't see his face. Suddenly afraid, she realized that she shouldn't have come here. Now that tenants were being ejected in greater numbers, she'd been hearing stories of displaced, bitter men burning down barns, killing livestock, and even assaulting landlords.

She was just about to turn and run, when the figure spoke. "Why have you come here?"

She recognized Michael's voice. In the darkness she couldn't see his face and without that visual cue she couldn't tell if he was being accusatory—or just curious.

"I heard the music."

He put his hand out and to her surprise she took it. Perhaps it was the darkness, or the music, or the woods, but it seemed like the most natural thing in the world to do. His rough hand was calloused, but it was strong and warm.

He led her into the clearing by the fire. But now that they were in the light, Michael thought it unseemly to be holding her hand and reluctantly let her go.

Emily faced him, feeling as awkward as a schoolgirl at her first cotillion. "It's been so long since I danced," she said. "Do you think it would be all right…?"

A stern voice inside her was telling her that she shouldn't be doing this. But it was a soft voice and she allowed it to be drowned out by the sound of the fiddle and the merry shouts of the dancers. Michael put his hands out. She raised hers to his. Suddenly, a group of dancers, whooping and shouting, came by and grabbed her outstretched hands. Michael could only shrug helplessly as Emily was swept away in an exuberant swirl of bodies.

He stood to the side with his arms folded, content to watch her as she and the other dancers disappeared behind the bonfire and reappeared through flying sparks. Her long auburn hair swayed with the movement of the dance and the fire cast a soft yellow glow on her smooth skin. And Michael thought he had never seen anyone so beautiful in all his life.

The third time she came around, he stepped out and gently pulled her away. She was laughing and he thought he could go on listening to the sound of her laughter forever. Her eyes sparkled and her skin glistened from the exertion of dancing. He took her hands in his and together they danced around the fire, bumping into others, laughing, whooping. He whirled her faster and faster. She put her head back and gave way to the music and the moment. Glimpses of faces and shooting flames spun around her in a dizzying blur. She was light-headed, intoxicated by the music and the exuberance of the other dancers, the nearness of Michael. She wanted it to go on forever.

Then the fiddle stopped.

Emily looked around in surprise, but the others seemed to be expecting it.

Pat Doyle, the man she'd questioned about his rent, stepped into the clearing and intoned, "Padric Leahy, tis time to say your goodbyes."

The mood was suddenly somber. The light of the fire flickered in the tear-filled eyes of the women. Grim-faced men shuffled in place with their arms folded across their chests.

"What's happening?" Emily whispered.

"Padric's agreed to have his cottage tumbled. Mr. Rowe's payin' their passage out to America."

She heard a longing in his tone when he mentioned America. But before she could think further on that, Leahy began to speak.

"Tis with a heavy heart I leave my home, my friends, and my land. Tomorrow we set sail across the great thunderin' ocean to a better life. God willin'."

He stepped back and, as the old women began to keen, people lined up to say their last goodbyes to Leahy, his wife, and children. Having done that sad duty, they moved off into the darkness to return to their own homes, wondering, each in turn, when their time would come.

"Where's everyone going? Emily asked. "Is the party over?"

"They're goin' home," Michael said. "The wake's over."

"*Wake*? Oh, my." She felt like a complete fool. How could she mistake a wake for a party?

"When people leave Ireland we think of them as dyin'," Michael explained. "In Padric's case it's probably true. They'll be sailin' on a coffin ship."

"A coffin ship? I don't understand."

"They're called coffin ships because so many die in them. Rowe won't pay passage on a decent ship, so Padric and his family are sailin' on a derelict vessel not fit for the journey.

Even if the ship doesn't sink, they'll be more than a month at sea, cramped below in sleepin' spaces with scarcely enough room to turn around. What little food they have will quickly spoil. The drinking water will become brackish. There'll be all manner of disease. Those who die will be tossed over the side without a decent burial or the word of a priest."

As Emily listened to Michael, she recalled with a sudden fury the self-satisfied expression on Rowe's face as he sat at Lord Attwood's dining room table proudly telling everyone how he'd been ridding his land of useless farmers by packing them off in ships.

Michael fell silent. He was looking into the fading fire with eyes unfocused, as though he were looking at something very far away.

She knew what he was thinking.   "In spite of the danger and hardship, you wish you were going, don't you?" she asked.

"Aye."

"If my father offered you and your family passage to leave your home, would you do it?"

"By God I would."

Emily felt a sudden clenching of her heart at his quick and unflinching response. She had hoped that he might have at least hesitated.

"But my Da will never leave the land," he added.

"But you could go," she pressed. "Why would you stay?"

"These are desperate times and my family needs me."

He said it without a trace of rancor and Emily was astonished that he would put his own future second to his family's. She was also disappointed, because in some crazy way, she'd hoped that he would have mentioned her as another reason for staying.

She assured him that she could walk back to the house alone, but Michael insisted on walking with her. He mumbled something about dangerous men afoot at this hour and how she might be in need of protection. They both pretended to believe that.

When they got to the courtyard, Emily glanced up at the moon, standing motionless in the sky as though it had been snagged by the craggy peaks of the western mountains. "It's such a beautiful moon, isn't it?

Michael wanted to say *she* was beautiful. He wanted to say that compared to her, the moon was nothing. But all he could say was, "Aye."

Emily wanted to ask Michael why he had so little to say to her. She wanted to hear about this intriguing man's dreams. She wanted to know where he would live in America. How he would earn a living. Instead, all she said was, "Well, I must go inside. It's very chilly."

"Aye. Tis."

Later that night, while Emily lay in her comfortable four-poster bed and Michael on his straw pallet, each savored the time they'd spent together. And yet, as sweet as it was, they each felt a certain regret because they knew that they'd been given a very special moment and they had not seized it.

Chapter Twenty Seven

March 1848
Ballyross, Ireland

It was late in the evening and Lord Somerville was sitting by a roaring fire in the library reading. The door opened and Emily came in carrying a tray.

"What's this?" he said, removing his reading glasses.

"I brought you hot milk."

"Why thank you, Emily," Somerville said, genuinely touched. "You know your mother used to do that."

"I know. Nora told me."

She handed him a well-worn mug that the servants used. It had a chip on the rim and it was discolored from a lifetime of use, but it was the best one she could find in the cupboard. Emily was no longer shocked when she looked into a cupboard or a sideboard and saw empty shelves and drawers where the good china and silver service used to be kept. She assumed her father was still selling off the household goods to that dreadful man, Kincaid, but she said nothing. She knew it was difficult enough for him without her commenting on it as well.

She sat on the arm of his chair while he sipped his milk and they stared silently into the fire. "Do you remember much about your mother?" Somerville asked suddenly.

Emily was taken aback. Since they'd made their peace in the garden that afternoon, there had been no mention of the past. By tacit agreement it was understood that their lives had begun anew that day and there was nothing to be gained by dredging up the past.

"Sometimes I think I do," she answered tentatively. "I'll remember a story she read to me or a picnic down by the lake. But then I think I may have imagined these memories. I'm never sure."

Somerville studied the fire and a great sadness filled his eyes.

"Do you miss her terribly, Father?"

"Every hour of every day. I should never have sent you away," he said suddenly.

"Don't reproach yourself. You weren't equipped to care for a rebellious child all alone."

Somerville smiled at the memory. "You were that. Do you remember the time you galloped Shannon through Lord Attwood's garden party and interrupted the croquet game? I thought the man would have apoplexy."

Emily laughed. "I thought *you* would have apoplexy."

Somerville sipped his milk and a smile played about his lips. "We did have some good times here at Somerville Manor, didn't we?"

She patted his hand. "We did and we shall have many more when all this is over."

Somerville touched his daughter's cheek and his eyes were filled with melancholy. "When I'm gone I hope you can stay on here."

The tone of desolation in his voice alarmed her. "Of course I will. And so will you. For many and many years to come."

She'd answered instinctively, but in so doing she'd also answered the question that had been on her mind for quite some time. She'd assumed she would eventually go back to London when this great strife was over. But now, she'd just heard herself say she would stay on and she realized she meant it. When she had come to that decision, she couldn't say.

The past two years had certainly been difficult, watching her world slowly come apart. It saddened her to walk into a room and see an empty space on a wall where a painting or a tapestry had been. It infuriated her knowing that that horrible man Kincaid now owned her property and could do with it what he would. And she still hadn't gotten used to the drastic changes in their eating habits. Nora had always prided herself on her cooking, and delighted in outdoing herself by creating new and different dishes. Over the years, she'd taken advantage of every opportunity to charm secrets out of visiting chefs from Paris, London, and Milan and, in the process, had become something of a gourmet cook in her own right. But even the greatest cook is at a disadvantage when the ingredients are limited to tough mutton and stringy chicken—when Nora could get even that. Emily also lamented the loss of Shannon and felt a great emptiness in her heart every time she went into the barn and saw his vacant stall.

And it upset her to see how her father was deteriorating. Since she'd been back, she's seen him visibly age from the burden of trying to maintain the estate in the face of famine and economic disaster.

Yet, paradoxically, in spite of all these difficulties, the past two years had been the most rewarding period of her life. For the first time, she felt as though she was doing something useful. To take some of the weight off her father's shoulders, she'd assumed responsibility for running the house. She supervised Nora and the dwindling staff, teaching them to cut corners where they could. In the evenings she sat in the kitchen with Nora and the maids mending and sewing worn linens. By day she poured over the household accounts and, to her surprise—and Nora's amazement—she'd learned to haggle with the food purveyors like the rest of the old crones.

In the past two years she'd learned how much the servants earned and how much food cost. In the process, she'd been astonished to learn how much money it took to run an estate the size of Somerville Manor. In short, she'd learned more in the past year than the ten years she'd spent in those fancy European finishing schools.

There was a knock at the door. They both looked at the clock on the mantle that had just chimed eight. "Who could it be at this hour?" Emily asked.

She rose to go to the door, but, Somerville put a restraining hand on her. "No, Emily, I'll get it."

He tried not to alarm Emily, but she detected the note of unease in his tone. And she thought she knew why. Lately, there had been an disquieting increase in the number of reports concerning vagabonds attacking landlords and burning their homes and possessions.

Somerville took a pistol from the desk drawer. "Just a precaution," he said, looking embarrassed as he tucked it into his dressing gown pocket.

Somerville opened the door and one of Lord Attwood's young male servants, hat in hand, was standing there. "Sir, his Lordship asks that you come to the village church on an urgent matter."

"Very well. Tell his Lordship I'll be along presently.

Jerry Fowler, Dermot, and Kevin stood in the shadows across the road from the old village church. They'd been waiting there since they'd followed Lord Attwood. When they'd met earlier this evening, Fowler had taken them to Lord Attwood's estates with the intention of burning down the old lord's barn to the ground. He hadn't told his young recruits that this was his opening gambit in the war against the landlords, because he wasn't sure they'd have the sand for it.

But, just as they'd arrived at the estates, they saw Attwood's carriage coming down the road, and Fowler, taking advantage of the situation, changed his plans and they'd followed him to the church.

Now, hiding in a stand of trees across the road from the old church, Fowler hatched an improvised plan: they would waylay Attwood on his way home and give him a sound beating.

As they anxiously waited in the shadows, Fowler couldn't believe his good fortune when, minutes later, Major Wicker, and Mr. Rowe arrived in a carriage and went inside. Now he had three of them.

"What do you think's goin' on?" Dermot asked.

"Must be some kind of big meetin'," Fowler said. Now if only—" He stopped when he saw Lord Somerville on horseback canter up to the church and dismount. Jerry Fowler had long since lost his faith in God, but at times like this he was tempted to doubt his faithlessness. It was as if God himself had intervened to deliver all four landlords into his hands at the same time. For a moment, as he watched Somerville tie the reins of his horse to the back of Wicker's carriage and hurry into the church, he considered torching the church and killing all four at once. But remnants of his earlier religious upbringing, which he couldn't totally excise, remained with him. *If there is a God*, he told himself uneasily, *I'll surely burn in hell for all eternity if I set fire to His house.*

Dismissing that plan from his mind and, knowing that he would come up with another, Fowler rubbed his hands together. "Lads, this is it. At last, our time has come."

"What are we to do?" Kevin asked.

"What have I been tellin' ya, for Jasus sake? Haven't I been sayin' we've got to teach the landlords a lesson? Well, now's our chance, me buckos."

Dermot saw the wild expression in Fowler's eyes and a knot formed in his stomach. He glanced at Kevin and saw that he, too, was afraid. Still, as afraid as Kevin was, Dermot knew Kevin would never admit it. *Well, I'll be damned to hell if I'll admit I'm afraid,* Dermot told himself. And so, he had no choice but to go along with whatever plan Fowler had in his daft mind.

At the sound of a knock, Father Rafferty shuffled over to the door and unbolted the lock. In all his fifty years as a priest, he'd never locked a church door, but now, things were different. In these hard times, he'd been hearing of miscreants breaking into churches and stealing candleholders, poor boxes and even, God forgive them, tabernacles.

He opened the door. "Thank you for coming on such short notice, Lord Somerville."

"Yes, yes," Somerville muttered, irritated that he'd been called away from his home at this hour of the night. He glanced at the other three. "What's this all about?"

"It's my fault, I'm afraid," Father Rafferty said. "I've been hearing rumors that the Board of Works will reopen again, and I just want to get the facts so I can reassure the men that they will have their work."

"It is a rumor," Attwood said. "And an unfounded one at that. Trevelyan has shut down the Works and good riddance I say."

"But sure the men need work," Father Rafferty protested.

Attwood thumped his silver cane on the floor. "*Damn* the men. Get it into your head, man. We have no more money to pay them. We've been bled dry."

"Perhaps, you could petition the government—"

"Petition? Petition who?" Major Wicker asked sarcastically. "Trevelyan? The bloody bastard thinks this famine is our fault."

"There is something we can do," Somerville said, trying to restore a note of civility into the conversation. He wasn't a

Catholic, nor were the others, but that was no excuse for their rude tone to the old priest. "I suggest we forgive the past due rents and provide the tenants with seed so they'll plant next year."

"*Never!*" Wicker shouted. "I'll evict every last man on my properties first."

"Major Wicker," Father Rafferty said, stunned that a good Christian, even if he was a Protestant, could say such a thing. "Eviction is sure death."

"Then perhaps that is the will of God," Lord Attwood said.

And on that discouraging note, the meeting was over before it started.

When Fowler saw the four men coming out of the church, he slipped a rag over his face and motioned for Kevin and Dermot to do the same.

As the men approached the carriages, the three masked figures materialized out of the darkness.

"Who are you?" Lord Attwood asked sharply. "State your business."

"We seek justice and retribution," Fowler said.

"Off with you buggers before I put the constables on you."

Attwood's dismissive tone enraged Fowler. All his life he'd been hearing that tone of voice and he would have no more of it. He stepped up to Attwood and jabbed his finger into the old lord's chest. "You'll not kill us off, landlord. They'll be no more tumblin's, no more—"

Before he could finish the sentence, Lord Attwood, enraged that a filthy bog trotter would dare touch his person, stepped back and slashed Fowler across the face with his cane.

Fowler, more stunned than hurt, stumbled back, blood gushing from a gash across his cheek.

Unlike the others, when Somerville had seen the three men approach them, he felt no fear. Since he'd allowed Goodbody to open the soup kitchen in his barn, he'd gotten to know some of these people, including John Ranahan and his boys. Over time, he'd begun to feel empathy for these poor wretches. Lord knows, they were not a bad sort. But they had their troubles. He, and his fellow landlords, stood to lose money to be sure. But it was only money. These poor beggars stood to lose everything they had—as little as it was—including their lives.

He was in the act of reaching into his vest pocket for a few coins when he saw Attwood strike one of them across the face. Stunned by Attwood's violent action, Somerville stepped forward and grabbed Attwood's upraised arm. "For God's sake, man…"

At the same time, Fowler, reeling from the humiliation of the blow, yanked a pistol from his waistband.

A terrified Dermot saw Fowler raise the pistol towards Attwood. *Oh, my God, no…* He lunged at Fowler and grabbed his arm, hoping to deflect his aim. Instantaneously, a deafening explosion ruptured the quiet night.

The six men, standing no more than six feet apart, stared at each other through a cloud of blue gunpowder smoke now mingling with a white mist rising from the ground frost. For a moment there was complete silence, as though no one could believe what had just occurred.

Then Lord Somerville slumped to the ground.

As Attwood, Wicker, and Rowe rushed to his aid, Fowler, Kevin and Dermot turned and ran off into to the darkness.

"Scatter, men. Scatter," Fowler shouted as he jumped over a ditch and ran off toward a grove of trees just outside the village.

Dermot, going the opposite way, ran and ran until his legs ached so that he stumbled and fell headfirst into a mud puddle. Too exhausted to get up, he lay there, covered in mud, half-expecting at any moment to hear the piercing whistles of the constables and the thump of boots on the road. But all he heard was the wind gently rustling the leaves in the trees over his head. A vision of Somerville slumping to the ground brought hot tears to his eyes. For a long as he lived, he would never forget the terrible sight of him laying on the ground, gasping for air, as a dark stain spread across his white silk shirt.

"Jasus, Jerry"—Dermot pounded the mud with his fists— "You've killed him. And you've killed us all as well."

After they'd finished cleaning up the soup kitchen for the night, Goodbody had excused himself and gone off to his room behind the barn, leaving Michael and Emily alone. And leaving Michael in a great state of confusion.

All day long, as he watched her ladle out soup or tend to a sick child, he longed to be alone with her. In his mind he thought of all kinds of wonderful and clever things to say. But now that they were alone, his mind was a blank.

Finally, Emily broke the awkward silence. "Michael, would you like to come to the house for a cup of tea?"

She tried to make her question sound casual, but Michael immediately understood the enormity of what she had just said. In spite of their tentative relationship—often derailed by mutual misunderstandings and irritations—it was tacitly understood, at least by him, that there would always be a distinct difference between them. After all, she was the landlord's daughter and he was just the tenant farmer's son. It has not escaped Michael's attention that Goodbody had been to dinner in the house often, but in all the time that he'd known her, she'd never once invited him.

He heard her words again. *"Would you like to come to the house for a cup of tea?"*

My God, of course he would. He wanted nothing more than to have tea with her—in her house or on the moon, as far as he was concerned. He was about to say yes, when the little voice in his head spoke to him. *"Tea in the Manor House? And what do you know about drinking tea out of a real teacup? You wouldn't know where to sit or what to do. If you go, Michael Ranahan, you'll make a proper eejit of yourself.*

"Oh, I don't think so, Emily. I'd best be gettin' home and—"

"Nonsense." She took his hand. "I need a cup of tea and so do you."

Delighted, but at the same time, apprehensive—Michael allowed himself to be led to the house.

To Somerville Manor. Michael had been there several times, but always because he's been summoned to do some odd chore. But now, he was coming here as a guest of the lady of the house. The thought filled him with joy and terror at the same time. Just as they reached the front door, they heard the frantic clatter of hoof beats and turned to see Major Wicker's carriage thundering up the drive.

"Lord Somerville's been shot," Wicker called out, reining in the horse. "Give a hand here."

Michael rushed to the carriage and threw open the door. A pale Lord Attwood sat stiffly against the far side of the carriage, as though whatever had happened to Lord Somerville was contagious. Michael could see that Somerville, who was laying across the seat, was unconscious and bleeding profusely. He and Wicker carried the limp body into the great room.

As they gently laid him on a couch, Emily followed them into the room. Michael expected her to be hysterical, but, although she was ghost white, she was absolutely calm and in control. "What happened?" she asked.

Three scoundrels waylaid us outside the village church," Attwood said, wiping perspiration from his brow with a silk handkerchief. "One had a pistol and shot your father without warning."

Emily ripped away the front of her father's bloody shirt, exposing a gaping wound in the center of his chest from which blood spurted forth. "Nora," she said calmly, "hot water and plenty of linens. Quickly."

The old woman, who was standing in the doorway paralyzed by fear, snapped out of her lethargy and hurried down the hall toward the kitchen.

Emily tried to wipe the blood from the wound opening, but the blood kept spurting out. Attwood, looking as though he were about to be ill, turned away. "We sent Rowe to fetch the doctor," he muttered into his handkerchief. "I'll go see if he's coming," he said, hurrying from the room.

Wicker, petrified by the thought that that could have been him on the couch, was panicked at the notion that there might be more assassins out there waiting for him. He poured himself a large glass of port with trembling hands and drank it down in one swallow.

Michael took a large towel and, gently pushing Emily aside, pressed the cloth on the wound. "I've seen this before," he explained. "When it keeps gushin', there's nothin' to do but keep pressure on it till the doctor comes."

And he stayed like that, arms straight out, leaning over Somerville, and applying the weight of his body. In spite of his efforts, blood seeped through the thick towel and ran through his fingers. Through his hands, Michael could feel Somerville's pulse grow weaker and weaker.

His arms began to ache from the strain of holding the unnaturally straight-armed position. He looked around to see if there were anyone who could spell him. Emily wasn't strong enough. Attwood was gone. That left Major Wicker. But he'd be no help. The cowardly major, with one hand holding the port decanter and the other a glass, stared at the floor in a terrified stupor.

Just when he thought he couldn't hold the position a second longer, the doctor rushed into the room. He pushed Michael aside and examined the wound. Then he put his fingers on Somerville's neck checking for a pulse. He turned to Emily and shook his head. "It's no use, he's lost too much blood. I'm afraid there's nothing to be done."

Before Emily could protest that there must be something he could do, a terrible rattling sound emanated from Somerville's throat. His whole body shook, and then he was still. The doctor felt for a pulse again.

Michael knew what the doctor would say. The blood that had been spurting from the wound had slowed to a trickle.

"He's gone," the doctor said to Emily. "May almighty God have mercy on his soul."

The next morning, a cold rain whipped the men gathered in front of the Board of Works. News of Somerville's murder had quickly spread across the valley.

"Sure it had to be a stranger," Da said. "There's no one in these parts who would do such a terrible thing."

Pat Doyle pulled his collar up against the driving rain. "Aye. And I don't mind tellin' ya that it's a damn shame that if one of the landlords had to be murdered, it had to be himself."

The other men nodded in agreement.

"Sure there's not a man here who can say he's ever been mistreated by his Lordship," Da said.

"Aye," Pat Doyle agreed. "And that's a lot more than could be said of the others."

Again, more heads nodded in silent agreement.

The door to the Public Works opened. They expected to see Mr. Browning. Instead, the stern looking chief constable of the region came out and stood with arms on his hips, facing the crowd.

"There have been rumors that the Board of Works will reopen. I have been authorized to tell you that those rumors are false. And I am also authorized to tell you that the Board of Works will never open in Ballyross until the murderers of Lord Somerville are apprehended." He glared down at the men with undisguised loathing. "If any of you lot knows who these miscreants are, you would do well to tell me now."

"We'll not be informers," someone shouted out from the crowd.

"Then you'll not be workers either," the constable shot back. "While you listen to the growl of your bellies, you might want to think of who it was that has brought you to this sorry state."

And on those words, he turned and went back inside, slamming the door behind him.

Chapter Twenty Eight

In the days following the murder of Lord Somerville, a steady stream of gleaming black carriages—some from as far away as Dublin—climbed the long road to the manor house. Solemn men and tearful women, arrayed in well-tailored black suits and gowns, had come from far and wide to pay their last respects.

From the pantry window, Nora watched the growing number of visitors with increasing distress. She'd been a servant in the Somerville house, girl and woman, for over fifty years. She felt deeply the loss of her beloved master, but she had had no time to mourn properly because she'd been too busy trying to accommodate the wants and needs of the dozens of visitors—some of whom said they would require sleeping accommodations—and all of whom would require food and drink.

In the old days—the days before the great hunger—Nora would have thought nothing of sending the Ranahan boys off to Cork, or even Dublin, to fetch the proper provisioning for such an august group of guests. She would have had the services of the house's half-dozen servants, and more from the village if necessary. With her customary efficiency, she would have supervised the scrubbing of the entire house from attic to root cellar, as well as the polishing of the silver service and the Waterford crystal. And while that was going on, she would have marshaled additional forces in the kitchen to prepare any number of sumptuous meals on demand.

But all that was in the past. Now, she and Rose were the only servants left. And Nora could hardly count on Rose, her half-witted niece, who was kept on by the family more out of charity than for her usefulness. And worse, there was no money in the household accounts to pay even the local victualers.

It was going on four in the afternoon when Emily came into the kitchen and found Nora, her head on the table, sobbing bitterly. Emily felt for the old woman. She knew she had taken Lord Somerville's death hard—in some ways, perhaps harder than she herself had. She also knew that the old woman was working day and night trying to deal with the burden of so many unexpected guests.

She put her hand on the old woman's shoulder. "Nora, what is it?"

Nora jumped to her feet, startled and embarrassed to be caught crying. Since a child she'd been told that *servants were never to display emotion in front of their betters.*

She wiped her tears with her apron. "I don't know what to do, Miss Emily. There's twelve people upstairs waiting to be fed and six of them have told me they intend to stay the night. How am I to feed them and prepare the rooms with only Rose to help?"

Emily put her arms around the old woman. "You let me worry about that. What do we have in the larder?"

"Just flour, Miss."

"Have we any preserves left?"

"Aye."

"Then that is what we will feed them."

Nora stepped back, aghast. *"Bread and jam?"*

In spite of her own feelings of overwhelming sadness, Emily had to smile at the horrified expression on the old woman's face. "It's bread and jam, Nora. Not arsenic.

"But—"

"Never mind. Have Rose help. When you're ready, bring it up to the drawing room."

Upstairs in the drawing room, a small cluster of wide-eyed landlords from adjoining counties surrounded Lord Attwood as he recounted the scene in front of the village church that night.

The old lord, who had finally gotten over the fear of that night, growled, "Had I known the scoundrel was armed, I'd have horsewhipped him to within an inch of his life."

"You describe the murderer as a common bog trotter," one rotund man with a few strands of black hair plastered across his shining pate asked. "Where in the world would he get a firearm?"

"They've been robbing houses all across the land," a reed-thin landlord from Skiberdeen whispered. "Just last week they stole a brace of shotguns from my property manager's cottage."

"All the more reason to tumble their damn houses," Major Wicker, said, pouring himself another port. "Better yet, pack them off to America. It's worth the few pounds to get them out of the county."

The other landlords nodded vigorously at this sensible solution.

When Emily came into the drawing room, there were more than a dozen men and women engaged in hushed conversation. There was Lord and Lady Attwood by the fireplace, talking to Mrs. Wicker. And there was Major Wicker, as usual, hovering about the port bottle, like a hungry crow waiting to devour a dead field mouse. But as for the rest, she had no idea who they were. In a fog since her father's death, she'd dutifully received each guest and nodded as they introduced themselves and offered their expressions of bereavement, but for the life of her she couldn't remember one name.

"May I have your attention," she said softly.

All conversation came to an abrupt halt. She knew they were all anxiously awaiting the banquet that was customary laid out for wakes. It was uncharitable she knew, but she suspected that some of them were here for only that reason. Two years ago, she would have been mortified to say what she was about to say. But she had done a lot of growing up in these last two years and she no longer possessed the genteel and foolish sensibilities of the young girl who had been summoned back from London.

"I know you all must be famished. In a little while, my housekeeper, Nora, will be serving bread and jam with tea."

A stunned murmur swept the room and sideward glances were exchanged. Times were difficult of course, but still, they had expected to be served the usual courses of good meats, cheeses, and sweets.

Emily went on. "I understand some of you have traveled a great distance to be here for the funeral tomorrow and wish to remain the night. You're most welcome. You'll find fresh linens on the beds, but I'm afraid I'll have to ask you to make your own beds. I just don't have staff to do it for you. I'm sure you understand."

From the stunned expressions on their faces, it was clear they didn't.

The next morning, the guests assembled in the drawing room for the burial service. There were less than the previous day—apparently the thought of making one's own bed was more than some could bear and several had departed in the night.

After one last private viewing with Emily and Nora, the casket was closed and she and the others followed the cortège to the hilltop family graveyard.

A gentle rain, little more than a mist, fell on the hill where Lord Somerville was to be buried alongside his wife and six generations of Somervilles.

Michael had not been invited to the funeral—whether by neglect or design he didn't know—but he went nevertheless. Standing a respectful distance from the group surrounding the grave, he hoped to get a glimpse of Emily, but her face was hidden beneath a black veil. He hadn't seen her since the night her father died and he wondered how she was holding up. He was ashamed of himself, given the tragic circumstances, but since that night all he could think about was the way she'd taken his hand. And how angry he was that that wonderful moment had been taken away from them so abruptly.

Concerned about the future of his soup kitchen, Mr. Goodbody had asked Michael if he thought Emily would be disposed to continue its good works. Michael had assured him that she would. Of that he had no doubt. What troubled him was that she might go back to London and leave the estate in the hands of a property manager—or worse, sell everything off.

In any event, it would be her decision and her decision alone. Now that Lord Somerville was dead, she was the mistress of Somerville Manor and it was for her to decide whether to continue or shut down the kitchen. At first, Michael found it hard to reconcile that the young, impetuous girl who had been recalled from London was now mistress of Somerville Manor. But the truth was, she wasn't impetuous any more. She had matured into a thoughtful, determined young woman.

As Michael watched the cortège slowly ascend the hill, he couldn't help but compare this fine, elaborate funeral with his grandmam's. He was certain the gleaming mahogany coffin with its golden handles had no hinged trapdoor at the bottom to pitch his lordship's body into a grave that would soon be filled with strange corpses. Instead of a gravedigger to mutter a pathetic little prayer, a bishop, arrayed in his splendid finery, had come all the way from the cathedral in Dublin to conduct the services.

Michael studied the crowd around the grave site. Clothed in black, in the mist of the rain, they reminded him of a flock of crows in a corn field. Of course he recognized Attwood and neighboring landlords, but the others were all strangers—except for Mr. Goodbody. *He* had been invited the funeral, much to Michael's great annoyance. Michael glared at the Quaker, standing with hat in hand and staring at the ground as the rain plastered down his fine, yellow hair. But as much as he tried, Michael couldn't be angry at the pleasant, congenial man who never seemed to get ruffled or angry. In his more reasoned moments, Michael had to admit that Goodbody had so much more in common with Emily, than he, a simple landless farmer. He couldn't be angry at Goodbody, but he could be jealous and he was that. It hadn't escaped him that Goodbody and Emily spent a lot of time together

Michael was brought out of his thoughts by the abrupt sound of silence. The praying had stopped. Emily stepped forward, scooped up a handful of dirt, and tossed it into the grave. Slowly, others followed.

Michael turned and went back down the hill. It was time to open the soup kitchen.

Chapter Twenty Nine

It had been nearly a week since Lord Somerville's burial and in that time Dermot had gone missing. Lately, he'd been disappearing for long periods of time, but not for such an extended period of time as this. His absence created an atmosphere of tension in the Ranahan cottage and, although no one mentioned him, he was all that anyone thought about. Da, already in a black mood since the Board of Works had been shut down, and knowing that it would not reopen until the murderers of Lord Somerville were caught, sat by the fire muttering about his worthless son. Mam moved about the cottage, her lips moving in silent prayer, hoping for his safe return. She'd taken to going to the door every morning and peering down the road in the vain hope that she'd see her youngest son coming up the road through the mist. Michael watched all this and cursed his brother's thoughtlessness. *Wasn't there enough worry in the house without this? And wasn't the harvest due in less than a fortnight? And shouldn't he be here to help in the gathering?*

Just before dawn, Michael and Da, after a breakfast of corn meal and a shared cup of buttermilk, were about to leave for the soup kitchen, when the door swung open and Dermot came in as thought nothing was amiss.

Mam rushed to him and threw her arms around him. "Thank God, you're all right, son. Sure I was afraid you were dead and lyin' in some ditch."

Dermot pulled away. "I'm all right, Mam."

"And where is it you've been all this time?" Da glared at his wayward son "You've had you Mam worried sick."

"I was lookin' for work. Me and Kevin went all the way to Knockmare."

Michael studied his brother and his initial anger gave way to a growing sense of unease. He could always tell when Dermot was lying and he was lying now. Dermot was the laziest man he'd ever known. There was no way he, of all people, would walk all the way to Knockmare, more than fifty miles, to find work. And then there was another sure sign he was lying—his brother wouldn't look him in the eye.

"And there was no work?" Mam asked, brushing the wild, straw-like hair out of Dermot's eyes.

Dermot pushed her hand away and sat down at the table. "None. I'm hungry. Is there anythin' to eat?"

Mam slid her small bowl of cornmeal toward him. "Here, son. I saved this for you."

It was too much for Michael. It had not escaped his notice that lately his Mam always took the smallest portion of food for herself. When he protested, she said it was more important that he and his Da had the food in their bellies so they could do the hard work. She had always been thin, but now she had become gaunt and her one raggedy dress hung from her boney frame.

Michael grabbed Dermot by the collar and yanked him out of his seat. "You'll not eat your Mam's food."

"But I haven't eaten in—"

Michael shoved him toward the door. "We're goin' to work in the soup kitchen, Dermot. While you've been off gallivantin', we've had to do your job as well."

Dermot was about to say he wouldn't go, but he saw the unaccustomed fury in his big brother's eyes and wisely decided not to challenge him.

Over time, Michael had become aware that the lines at the soup kitchen were growing longer and longer every day. As the hunger spread across the land, more and more families were being evicted from their cottages and turned into refugees in their own land. Increasing numbers of emaciated men, women, and children wandered the countryside in a pitiful effort to find a bit of food and shelter from the weather.

Now, as Michael ladled out bowls of soup, he studied his brother who was washing stacks of bowls in a huge cauldron of boiling water. He'd been back two days, but he'd yet to speak a word to anyone, including Michael. From the moment Dermot walked into the cottage that morning, Michael had been harboring a nagging suspicion that he dared not give life to. But in spite of himself, the questions kept coming. *Why did he disappear without a word to anyone? Was it just a coincidence that he went missing the day after Lord Somerville was murdered?*

The day after Dermot had disappeared, Michael had gone to find Kevin, hoping that his friend would know of Dermot's whereabouts. But no one had seen Kevin either. He recalled Dermot's daft story about him and Kevin going to Knockmare to look for work. A lie for sure. If there was anyone lazier than Dermot, it was big Kevin.

Even more troubling, Michael had overheard the constables talking. They said it was three masked men who had attacked the landlords. An overwhelming sense of dread washed over him. Everything pointed to one inescapable conclusion: Somehow his brother had something to do with Lord Somerville's murder.

That evening, Michael and Dermot were left to clean up and make preparations for the morning's feeding. Mr. Goodbody had been invited to the manor house for dinner. He wanted to stay and help clean up, but Michael insisted that he go because he wanted to be alone with Dermot. When the two brothers were finished with their chores, Michael shoved Dermot into the tack room and slammed the door behind him.

"Did you have anythin' to do with Lord Somerville's death?"

"Don't be daft."

"Don't lie to me, Dermot."

"I'm not lyin'."

Michael backhanded his brother, sending him crashing against the tool table. "You'll not leave here till I know the truth."

Dermot snatched a scythe off the table and spun toward Michael. "You keep away from me, Michael or…"

"Or what? You'll kill me, too."

Dermot stood for a long moment, the scythe raised above his head, glaring at the brother he loved more than anything in the world. Then he dropped the scythe and slumped to the floor, sobbing. "I didn't know he had a pistol, Michael. I swear to Jasus, I didn't know. Then, when… that is, after… we just ran and ran. I couldn't go home… I didn't know what to do…"

Michael felt a great emptiness inside him. By Dermot's reckless actions, he had killed himself. Maybe all of them. "Where did you go?" His voice sounded hollow in his ears.

"I lived in the hills. God forgive me, Michael, I stole food from people's homes."

"Was Kevin there that night?"

"Aye."

Michael could barely make himself ask the next question. "Dermot, was it you who fired the pistol?"

Dermot took a deep breath and wiped his eyes on his tattered sleeve. "No. It was Jerry Fowler."

Jerry Fowler, Kevin, and a handful of men were digging in a peat bog when Kevin looked up and saw Michael coming. "Oh, oh. Here comes trouble."

Fowler looked up and saw Michael jump a fence and come toward them in a determined half-run. Fowler leaned on his spade, watching Michael approach, trying to decide if he should run or fight. "I have no quarrel with you, Michael Ranahan," he called out.

Michael kept coming. When he was just steps away, Fowler, without warning, took a vicious cut at Michael's head with the spade. Michael ducked and drove his head into Fowler's stomach. Both men went down, rolling in the recently dug peat. Fowler tried to use the spade as a weapon, but Michael wrenched it out of his hand and threw it aside.

He straddled Fowler's chest and, releasing all his pent up fury at Fowler for abusing Moira and putting his brother in mortal peril, rained down blows on him. He might have killed him had Kevin not dragged him off the half-conscious man.

His chest heaving from exhaustion, Michael grabbed Fowler's collar and started to drag him toward the road.

"*What are ya doin'*?" Fowler gasped.

"I'm takin' you to the peelers, you murderin' bastard."

"Then you'd better take your brother as well."

Michael let go his grip and Fowler sagged to the ground.

"What are you sayin'?"

"It was your own brother that hit my arm. Sure I was only goin' to scare the bejasus out of the man, but Dermot hit my arm and the pistol went off. It was him responsible for killin' Somerville, not me."

Michael looked at Kevin. "Is what he says true?"

The young man stared at the ground, unable to look Michael in the eye. "Aye. Dermot was only tryin' to stop Jerry from firin', but still..."

Michael stared at the man at his feet. In his rage and frustration at Fowler for visiting this terrible peril on his family, he would have gladly strangled the worthless bastard, but that, he knew, would solve nothing. He didn't believe Fowler's story about only wanting to scare the landlords, but it didn't matter what he thought. What mattered was what the constables thought. One thing was for certain: the landlords wanted blood. If he handed Fowler over to the peelers, all was lost. Fowler was no Billy Moore. He would inform and Dermot would surely hang with him.

Michael yanked the bleeding man to his feet. "Clear out, Fowler." He shoved the man toward the road. "And don't ever come back or, by God, I'll kill you myself."

Chapter Thirty

September 1848
Ministry of the Treasury
London, England

It didn't seem possible. It ran contrary to the laws of probability. And it sorely tested the beliefs of those who believed in a merciful God. But in 1848, the blight struck yet again and two-thirds of the crop failed. And this year—coming on the heels of three previous years of blight, famine, and disease—was the worst of all. After the successful crop of '47, farmers were convinced that the blight was over and they gambled everything on this crop, selling clothing, furniture, and livestock to buy seed. And now, having expended everything they had, all was lost.

At Trevelyan's office in the Ministry of the Treasury, Trevelyan, once again, sat across the table from Playfair, Kane, and Lindley. For almost three years, these men of the Scientific Commission had been meeting with Trevelyan and every time they met, they did their utmost to report factually and objectively on what was happening in Ireland. But in all that time, not once had Trevelyan taken their advice on how to relieve the suffering and death that continued to plague that godforsaken country. In their first meetings, there had been guarded suspicion of Trevelyan. But then, as time went, the suspicions turned to bewilderment at the secretary's unrealistic and calculating pronouncements. And now, as they sat across the gleaming conference table from Trevelyan, there was a feeling of acrimony that was almost palpable in the air of Trevelyan's chilly office.

Playfair spoke first. "Mr. Trevelyan, last year Parliament decreed that the landlords would be responsible for the entire cost of the Public Works and—"

"That is correct," Trevelyan interjected. "As I have reminded you time and time again, it is their responsibility to solve the Irish problem."

"But the landlords are on the brink of financial ruin," Lindley said.

"And whose fault is that?" Trevelyan snapped. "My God, the government offered them loans did it not? And what did the landlords do? They defaulted, leaving her Majesty's government with millions of pounds of unsecured loans that will never be repaid."

"But that's because you offered the loans at three and a half percent," Playfair answered, his voice rising in frustration. "Terms which were most favorable to the government, but ruinous to landlords on the brink of bankruptcy."

Trevelyan put his hands up. "Enough, gentlemen. I am firm in my resolve to stop the hemorrhaging of the government's treasury to finance what I consider to be a lost cause."

Dr. Kane shot forward in his seat. "A lost cause? Mr. Trevelyan how in the name of God can you describe a county of four million souls, many of whom are starving and dying, a lost cause. Is there no charity in your heart, sir?"

"I have recommended to Parliament," Trevelyan went on as thought he hadn't heard Dr. Kane, "that it issue a proclamation that henceforth, the government will no longer grant loans to the Boards of Guardians."

Playfair jumped up. "But this will place the total cost of financing the famine on the backs of the landlords alone."

"Exactly where it should be."

Playfair furiously stuffed his reports back into his valise "Mark my words, Mr. Trevelyan, this unconscionable response of the government will wipe out hundreds of landlords who were on the verge of bankruptcy. Those who are still solvent, will step up the evictions and clear their lands of the last remaining tenants."

Trevelyan stood up, signaling that the meeting was over. "It's in God's hands, gentlemen."

Ballyross, Ireland

In addition to the loss of the crop and no sign that the Board of Works would open, Michael continued to worry that sooner or later the peelers would discover Dermot's role in the murder of Lord Somerville. Leaving his sullen Da to sit by the fire, Michael set off into the village to talk to Father Rafferty about an idea he had. It was a daft idea, he knew, but it just might work.

Ballyross had never been a thriving village, but now it was almost completely deserted. Michael passed O'Malley's shuttered pastry shop and had envious visions of the fat, prosperous baker living a wonderful life somewhere in America. The general store where he and his Da came to fetch the supplies for Somerville Manor was gone as well. He glanced down the road toward the train station remembering that first glimpse of Emily as she rode by in the carriage. He had never seen anyone so beautiful in his life and he still thought so. *So much has happened since then.* He continued down the street and stopped in front of Father Rafferty's old church. He looked down at the mud in the road in front of the church and imagined he could see the stains of Lord Somerville's blood there. *My God, Dermot, what were you thinkin'?*

He studied the little church that he'd attended all his life. It, like everything else in the village, looked broken and shrunken into insignificance.

Inside the church, a faint scent of sweet incense permeated the air. Michael slid into the last pew and the old wood creaked in protest under his weight. When his eyes grew accustomed to the gloom, he realized that the altar was bare. Father Rafferty had sensibly removed all the candle holders, the tabernacle, and even the few faded religious paintings that had adorned the plaster-peeling walls. *There's no sign of God here,* Michael thought bitterly. *Maybe it's because God has abandoned us.*

Still, there was something peaceful about the space and Michael recalled Mr. Goodbody's description of a Quaker meetinghouse. *"It's a plain and simple room with facing benches. There's no adornment. We do not allow outward signs of religion. The simplicity of the surroundings allows us to mediate without distraction."*

Michael thought that this stripped-down church must be the way a Quaker meetinghouse looked. He slumped in the pew, suddenly very tired. The weight of all that had happened began to press on him like a huge stone. For the first time since the crop had failed, he began to feel that everything was hopeless. If Fowler was caught, he would surely inform on Dermot and his little brother would hang. *And that would surely kill Mam.* There was no work and there would be none the constable had said until Lord Somerville's murderer was apprehended. *Lord Somerville dead.* Would Emily go away? *What's the difference, you eejit?* his inner voice chided. *Do you think she would ever have anythin' to do with the likes of you?*

The sound of a door opening focused his mind on the present. Father Rafferty came out of the sacristy and genuflected in front of the bare altar. Even the old priest looked worn and broken, just like everything else in the forlorn land.

"Hello, Father."

The little priest jumped at the unexpected sound of a voice. "Jasus, Mary and Joseph... who is that scared the life out of me?" he asked, squinting into gloom.

"It's Michael Ranahan."

"Ranahan. And what would you be doin' here?"

"It's my own church, isn't it?"

"Neither your church nor me has seen hide nor hair of you in a month of Sundays."

The priest came down the aisle. "Have you come to take the confession?" he asked hopefully. Then he saw the expression on Michael's face, and added, "No, I didn't think so. What do you want?"

"You've got to get the landlords to open up the Board of Works."

"Don't you think I've tried? Sure they have hearts of stone. And now after the murder of Lord Somerville, they'll never open the Works until the murderer, God forgive him, is caught."

"He's not goin' to be caught."

The little priest peered into Michael face. "And how do you know that?" He saw a hardness in Michael's eyes that told him he should ask no more about it.

Father Rafferty turned to look toward his bare altar and his tears welled up in his eyes. The world that he'd known was changing and he didn't know how much more he could abide. Who would have believed that a priest would have to strip his altar bare to protect the tabernacle—God's very house—from thieving Catholics, no less? He asked himself. My parish is dwindling. Most have died or been driven off the land and gone away. Those that are left, like young Michael Ranahan here, have lost their faith and have stopped attending Mass. And now, here was young Ranahan, sitting before me, knowing something about the murder of a landlord and him not telling me, and me afraid to ask. The words that Christ cried out on the cross flashed into the priest's mind. *"My God, my God, why hast thou forsaken me?"*

Why indeed.

"You've got to get the landlords to open up the Board of Works," Michael repeated.

The old priest glared at Michael. "And how am I goin' to do that, may I ask?"

Father Rafferty shivered. In the gloom, Michael's evil smile looked like the grimace of a devil.

Chapter Thirty One

Major Robert Wicker licked his lips and eyed the almost full bottle of port on Lord Attwood's side table. He, Lord Attwood, and Edward Rowe had been sitting in Attwood's library for over an hour tediously arguing about whether the Board of Guardians should appoint someone to replace Somerville. *Now there was a gentlemen,* Wicker thought. *Somerville always poured a glass of port when they met in his home and never stinted in the refilling.* He shot a sideward glance at the scrawny Lord Attwood. *Unlike this miserly old skinflint who has yet to offer either of us a drink.*

"Do you think we should add another member," the obsequious Mr. Rowe asked Lord Attwood.

"Damn it, man. Isn't that the question we've been bandying about for the last hour? That's what we're here to decide."

"I believe we should," Wicker said, tearing his eyes away from the bottle. "There is safety in numbers," he added cryptically.

"Meaning?" Attwood asked.

"I don't mind telling you, since Lord Somerville was shot dead before our very eyes, I've become increasingly concerned for my...*our* safety. Since we've closed down the Works the cottiers have been in an ugly mood."

"Are you suggesting we reopen the Works?" Rowe asked.

"*Never.*" Attwood pounded his skinny fist on his polished desk. "There'll be no work until the knave who murdered Lord Somerville is caught and hanged. We agreed to that."

"I know, but..."

"But what, man?"

Wicker shrugged and stole a glance at the port bottle. If only he could have a drink, it would be so much easier to deal with all this. He wanted to tell them that his accounts were in shambles. But he could never admit to Attwood or Rowe that he was on the verge of financial ruin. As things had gotten worse, he'd convinced himself that his predicament was due to the famine and the crop failures. But mostly to that blackguard, Charles Trevelyan. But the truth, which he could not admit to himself, was that the fault lay with his reckless gambling and drinking. Wicker rung his hands. *It was all well and good for his lordship to dismiss the loss of income as though it were nothing*, he thought bitterly. Indeed, to the old lord it was nothing. With his family's wealth he could afford to go on like this forever. But, sadly, that was not the case with Wicker's estates where, daily, unpaid bills mounted at an alarming rate.

"Perhaps we could invite Miss Somerville to take her father's place on the Board?" Rowe offered.

Attwood squinted at him over his reading glasses. "A *woman*? Have you taken leave of your senses?"

"Yes, of course, you're absolutely correct," Rowe said, backpedaling quickly. "It's quite unthinkable, really."

Wicker was convinced that the only way to salvage his estates was to put the men back to work. "I don't want to be an alarmist, but I am of the firm belief that if we don't put the men back to work, we may be endangering ourselves."

There was silence in the room as Attwood considered Wicker's comment. For all his bravado, Attwood, too, was growing more and more concerned for his safety. Every day brought more reports of violent confrontations between landlord and tenant. Wicker had a point, but Attwood was too proud a man to admit that he, too, was afraid. He studied Rowe, confident that the little toady, with his hands nervously clenched in front of him like a chastised school boy, would agree with whatever he said. In Wicker's eyes, Attwood saw naked fear. No gentleman that. A true gentleman never reveals his emotions. For a moment, Attwood longed to have Somerville back. He'd always been too liberal for Attwood's taste, but at least he was a gentleman, unlike these two low-borns.

Attwood stood up, signaling the meeting was over. "For the time being, we'll hold off on appointing another member to the Board."

"What about putting the men back to work?" Wicker had meant the question to sound like a simple query, but it came out like a plea.

"No," Attwood said emphatically. "Not until someone hangs."

The elderly butler knocked on the door and entered. "Lord Attwood, a Father Rafferty is here to see you and your guests."

"How did he know we were here?," Wicker asked, suddenly alarmed.

"There's nothing we do that the villagers don't know about," Rowe said.

"Exactly my point," Wicker said. "There are spies everywhere. They know too much about us, I tell you.

Attwood waved a dismissive hand at the hysterical Wicker. "Get a grip, man. Very well," he said to the butler. "Show the priest in."

On his way to the Attwood estates, Father Rafferty had been rehearsing over and over again in his mind what Michael had told him to say. When the devious Ranahan had first told him about his plan, he'd indignantly refused to be part of so dishonest a scheme. He would not use fear as a tool of intimidation. He would not lie, nor by prevarication let others believe what was not true. But then the more he thought about it, the more it occurred to him that it just might be worth the sin if it would get the men back to work.

He was shown into the library. Attwood behind a huge antique desk, Wicker and Rowe in large, high-backed chairs. None of the men rose, which didn't surprise the old priest. *What could you expect from a pack of black protestants?*

"What can I do for you?" Attwood asked brusquely.

"Thank you for your time, gentlemen. I'll get right to the point. I've come to ask, nay beg, you to reconsider opening the Works."

"Why we were just talking about—"

"I believe I've made our position clear the last time we spoke," Attwood said, cutting off Rowe and giving him a sharp look. There was no reason for this priest to know what they had been discussing. "Not until the murderer is found. And I suspect some of the men in this village—or for that matter, all of them—know who that person is."

"All I'm sayin' is, let the constabulary do their work and let the men do theirs." Father Rafferty studied their cold, heartless expressions and knew he wasn't getting through to them. Then he remembered what young Ranahan had coached him to say. "Gentlemen," he whispered gravely, "my priestly concern is with the souls of these men, destitute and out of work. And because of that great concern"—he paused for effect—"I also have a great fear."

"Which is?" asked Wicker, who knew something about fear.

The old priest took a deep breath. *How can I tell such a bold lie? May God forgive me.* "I fear that some desperate soul may rise up and smite those who are tryin' to destroy them."

He saw the three men exchange nervous glances and knew he'd gotten their attention.

"Is that a threat?" Attwood asked gruffly.

"Oh, no, no, your Lordship. Not at all. What I'm sayin' is that murder is a heinous, grievous sin in the eyes of God." He drew himself up, stern and righteous and indignant. "And any man who would dare *take the life of another*"—he paused here again to let them consider who that "another" might be—"will be cast down into the everlasting fires of hell for all

317

eternity." He was gratified to see that he had their total and undivided attention. "So you see," he said in a very reasonable tone, "I wouldn't want that to happen to anyone in my parish."

Attwood cleared his throat. "If you would please wait outside while we discuss this?"

"Certainly."

A moment later, Attwood came out. "The Works will open tomorrow." Without another word, he turned and went back into the library.

Thanks be to God, Father Rafferty muttered, almost dancing down the great corridor. Then he remembered his lie. *And may God forgive me—and Michael Ranahan.*

It had been a month since Lord Somerville's funeral. In that time Emily had been busy first with the funeral arrangements, and then with the endless onslaught of guests who meant well, but who took up an inordinate amount of her time. Once the last of the guests had departed, her next priority was to assume total control of all the particulars involved in running Somerville Manor. In the past year, she'd learned a great deal about the running of the house, but now, it was her intention to know everything there was to know about running the estate and all that that entailed.

Just discovering where the voluminous number of necessary records, documents, and receipts were kept had become a daunting task. She still hadn't collected everything, but, what she's seen so far alarmed her. The accounts were in arrears and there was practically no income. She would get to the bottom of it all in due time, but right now, she needed a respite from the bills, the accounts, and the pervasive sadness in the house.

Almost everything she came across—from handwritten notes to the sight of the rose garden—reminded her of her father and how much she missed him. She also missed Michael and she felt terrible about the way she'd treated him—or more precisely, ignored him. She'd meant to invite him to the funeral service, but with one thing and another she hadn't done it. The morning of the funeral, when she caught a glimpse of him standing halfway down the hill, she was touched that he'd come. Then, later, she'd considered inviting him to the house for supper, but in the end she didn't because she thought it might have made him uncomfortable. Instead, she invited Mr. Goodbody and spent most of the evening pumping him for news about Michael.

Her plan for today was to spend the morning with the accounts, and then go to the barn and help Mr. Goodbody and Michael with the midday feeding. She heard a knock at the door and was about to go downstairs and answer it, but she saw Nora was already there.

The old housekeeper opened the door to Fergus Kincaid, the gombeen man, looking like a fop in an ill-fitting green silk suit with yellow stripes and gold-buckled shoes.

"Be so kind as to inform the mistress of the house that one Fergus Kincaid is here and wishes to speak with her," he announced in what he imagined to be a cultured tone.

Nora looked him up and down, unimpressed. "Since when does the likes of you knock at the front door? Go round to the back—"

"I think not," Kincaid said. He stepped aside and for the first time she saw the bailiff standing behind him at the foot of the stairs.

"I think you'd best get the mistress of the house," the bailiff said gravely.

Making no attempt to hide his curiosity, Kincaid took in everything in the great room as though he were doing a mental inventory. And, in fact, he was. The bailiff stood near the door, looking decidedly uncomfortable, with his hands clasped behind his back.

Emily, still in shock, read the notice a second time. "I don't understand..."

Kincaid snatched the notice from her hand. "It's quite clear..." he studied the note and then, remembering he didn't know how to read, thrust it into the bailiff's hand. "Tell her what it says, man."

The bailiff handed the notice back to Kincaid. "I believe Miss Somerville understands the import of the notice."

"Well, there you have it," Kincaid said. "I am now the owner of the Somerville Estates including all goods and chattels."

"A combination of back taxes and outstanding loans, I'm afraid," an embarrassed bailiff explained to a stunned Emily. "According to this notice, the property has been in arrears for over two years."

"And *I* have given a considerable number of loans to your father," Kincaid said smugly. "Which have not been paid in accordance with lawful and signed agreements. And as the notice points out, he used the estates as collateral."

"Which means, *you* own Somerville Manor?" she said more to herself than to him.

"Lock, stock, and barrel."

After Emily got over her initial shock, she sprang into action. She immediately sent off a letter to the family solicitor in London to find out what could be done to overturn this travesty of justice. A week later, she received the bad news. There was nothing to be done. The property was indeed in default of properly executed loans. The fact that she had not received a timely notice of default, the solicitor went on to explain, may have been due to the circumstances surrounding Lord Somerville's untimely death. Perhaps he received the notice, but died before he could respond to it. He also offered another, more nefarious, possibility—that Kincaid, himself, may have bribed someone to see to it that the notices did not go out. In any event, the solicitor concluded, there was nothing to be done. The property was now in the hands of Fergus Kincaid.

With a heavy heart, Emily set about packing her belongings. There wasn't much to pack. Almost everything in the house belonged to gombeen man now.

She was in the dining room, packing a few figurines that her mother had given her. Suddenly, the door swung open and Kincaid strode in with Nora close behind. This time he was dressed in a garish purple silk suit with broad white stripes.

"I tried to stop him," Nora said, puffing from the exertion of chasing Kincaid down the hall, "but he wouldn't mind."

"This *is* my house," Kincaid said imperiously, "and I will come and go as I please."

"Thank you, Nora. That will be all."

Nora, holding back tears, fled from the room.

"I only have a few more things to pack, Mr. Kincaid. I'll be out of the house by the end of the week if that is agreeable to you."

Kincaid picked up one of the figurines and examined it with a practiced eye. "There's no hurry, madam." According to the decree, technically he owned everything in the house, but these figurines wouldn't fetch more than a couple of pounds. They certainly weren't worth incurring the wrath of this lovely young woman.

Emily had her back to him and didn't see him approach. Suddenly, his arms were around her waist. "Why don't you stay here and be my mistress?" he whispered in her ear.

She pulled away. "*Are you mad?*"

Kincaid wouldn't take no for an answer. He pinned her arms and tried to kiss her. He was much stronger, and she was easily overpowered. Slowly, the oily face came closer and closer. She could smell his foul breath and his rheumy eyes glistened with lust. Suddenly, and inexplicably, he was yanked away from her, as if by some unseen force. But it was no unseen force. It was Michael.

Michael had been shocked when he'd heard that Kincaid was now the master of the estates. He'd wanted to go to Emily and tell her how very sorry he was, but his stubbornness got in the way. *Why should I go to see her,* he told himself, *when she has made no effort to see me*? It had been over a month since the night he'd tried to staunch the flow of blood from Lord Somerville's fatal wound and in that time she had not spoken to him. In the beginning he made excuses—she was in mourning, there was so much to do... But eventually, he'd come to the conclusion that she'd made no effort to see him because he didn't mean anything to her. *Of course you don't mean anythin' to her, you eejit,* his inner voice mocked. *"Shut your gub,"* Michael had shouted out loud, startling an old man he was serving soup to.

After several sleepless nights, he decided to swallow his pride and go see her.

And now, as he walked up the road toward the Manor house, he told himself, *"It's just a condolence call. After all, it's the Christian thing to do. I'll tell her I'm sorry for her loss, and the loss of her fortune, and that'll be that. And I'll be on my way.*

Suddenly, he saw Nora running toward him, yelling something about Kincaid and Miss Emily.

When he barged into the dining room, he saw that Kincaid had Emily backed over the dining room table, about to kiss her. He lunged for the man, grabbed the back of his collar, and flung him across the room. In a rage, he threw himself on the gombeen man and would have gladly strangled the life out of him, but hands were around his neck. *Her* hands, pulling him away and shouting, "No, Michael, that's enough. That's enough..."

Michael climbed off the terror-stricken man. "This is my house," Kincaid rasped, clutching his throat. "You can't—"

Michael started toward him again and the gombeen man scurried under the dining room table, cringing like a whipped dog. "Kincaid, this is not your house until she's gone from here." He grabbed the shaking man by the back of his silk coat, dragged him to the French doors, put his brogue to Kincaid's backside and sent him sprawling.

Tripping over the fieldstones and ripping the knees out of his new trousers, Kincaid scrambled to his feet. "I'll not forget this, Ranahan," he said, pointing a trembling, bejeweled finger at Michael.

When Michael made a move towards him, the gombeen man darted off the terrace with such alacrity that Michael had to smile.

He went back inside and Emily was standing rigidly by the table. "Thank you for..."

"It's nothin'."

Emily carefully wrapped a figurine in paper. "Fortunately, I don't have much to pack. Almost everything here belongs to him."

Not knowing what to say, Michael said nothing.

Then Emily began to weep and Michael went to her. And suddenly, she was in his arms. Her hair, smelling of scented flowers, brushed his cheek and the feel of her soft body made his knees weak

"It's all gone," she mumbled into his chest. "It's all gone..."

Michael held her tight, saying nothing. His heart broke for her, but he never wanted this moment to end.

Chapter Thirty Two

In the past, mealtimes in the Ranahan cottage had always offered a pleasant respite from the harsh day-to-day toils of the outside world. Away from the watchful eyes of landlords and overseers, they could be themselves— laughing, joking, and doing all the things that free men and women took for granted. It was a time for Granda to tell his tall tales, for Mam to talk of deaths and births in the valley, and for Michael and Dermot to learn more about what it was to be a Ranahan in Ballyross. But in the past few years, as the great hunger increased its stranglehold, deprivation, and dread of what the future held, had driven them more and more into their own private, silent worlds.

Tonight, supper at the Ranahan cottage was a quiet affair and hardly a word was spoken. Mam, stealing glances at her husband and sons, knew why. She'd lived with her husband long enough to know that he always retreated into himself when he was frightened. And God knows he had every reason to be frightened now with no food in the larder and wondering what was to become of all of them now that Somerville estates were in the hands of Fergus Kincaid.

Her youngest son's silence was more puzzling. Dermot had never been much of a talker, preferring to rage inwardly. But lately, he barely spoke at all. And when he did speak it was only to quarrel with someone in the family. She'd noticed it started right after Lord Somerville's murder. With a mother's intuition she suspected that Dermot was somehow involved in that terrible tragedy, but she dared not ask him about it. Once, when she'd broached the subject with Michael, he'd cut her off saying that he didn't know anything about it. She suspected he was lying, but she decided not to pursue it further.

She watched Michael pick at his food. At least she knew the reason for his silence. He was thinking about *her*. Just the thought of Emily made Mam's stomach tighten. She was a lovely girl to be sure, but she was far above Michael's station and Mam didn't want to see her son's heartbroken over something that could never be. She knew her husband had tried to warn him off her, but it did no good. Whenever her name was mentioned, he looked like a love-starved calf. For the life of her, Mam couldn't understand his unreasonable longing for this girl. In many ways, Michael had always been the most responsible one in the family. Didn't he have more common sense than all of us put together? So how could he possibly think he could win the love of this cultured woman of class?

"When does Miss Emily leave?" Mam heard herself ask Michael.

"Tomorrow. On the afternoon train."

Da stared at the rough-hewn table top. "The gombeen man," he said, the despondency dulling his eyes. "Our new landlord. God help us all."

Michael jumped up from the table and rushed out the door.

Mam watched her broken hearted son go and thought that her own heart would break.

The lives of tenant farmers and their wives were lonely. The men worked long hours in the fields, often alone, while the women, isolated in their cottages, tended the animals, mended the clothes, and did the other countless tasks required of them. Market day was a pleasant respite from this loneliness and the women—and the men, though they would never admit it—looked forward to it.

In addition to the opportunity to buy any manner of goods from a pig to a cauliflower, market days offered an opportunity to just talk and share a bit of gossip. The men would congregate around the cow pens, hotly recounting the latest outrages of the landlords and, in between harangues, argue over the true value of a cow or horse that was for sale, while the women, clustered around the vegetable stands, discussed deaths, births, and the merits of white eggs over brown.

Saturday was market day in Ballyross and Mam, as she'd done every Saturday since she was a new bride, went into the village. But market days now were a pale comparison to market days of the past. Where it had once been possible to buy every necessity, this morning there were only two farmers selling their limited wares.

In spite of the bad times, Mam, like most of the women, still came into the village on market day more out of habit than need. After all, she, like everyone else, had no money to buy. But Mam had a special reason for coming today. She knew Nora would be there and she had to talk to her. As Mam turned into the market area, she saw the old woman haggling with a farmer over a cabbage. She waited until the transaction was done before she approached.

"Nora, I've heard the news. I'm so sorry."

"Aye. Tis terrible."

"Where will you stay?"

"I have a wee cottage the master deeded to me years ago." She leaned close to Mam and whispered, " I've been assured that that damned scoundrel, Kincaid, can't touch it."

"Oh, that's grand."

Mam acted surprised, but she knew all about the little cottage.

"Aye, but it's been a terrible time. First it's losin' the master, now the estate. But to tell you the truth, the only thing I really care about is Miss Emily. She's goin' away today, ya know." Tears welled up in the old lady's eyes. "I've raised that child since she was just a wee one."

Mam shook her head sympathetically and silently prayed for the courage to do what she's come here to do. Seeing Michael's unhappiness, she'd lain awake the entire night trying to think of some way to help him. She knew what it had meant to him to give up the passage money. It meant giving up his dream of going to America. But the truth was, without that money, the family might have starved the first winter. She'd always felt guilty about the way she'd lavished her love on Dermot, sometimes at the expense of Michael. But Dermot needed her more than her eldest son did. Michael had always been independent and self-reliant, unlike his younger brother. While Mam instinctively knew that it was sometimes necessary to give more love to one child than another, it didn't make her feel any better. And so, sometime in the dark of last night, she'd made up her mind. She would make this one daft attempt to make it up to her son. And now she prayed that what she was about to do would not break his heart even more.

"Tis a shame Miss Emily has to leave," Mam said, carefully watching the old woman.

"Aye, tis. But what can she do? Sure there's no place for her to stay."

"Well," Mam said tentatively, "maybe there is."

That afternoon, Emily, carrying the few possessions she owned, climbed into the waiting carriage. As an act of kindness—or to assuage his guilt—Lord Attwood had sent his carriage to fetch her to the train station. Kincaid, the new lord and master of Somerville estates, stood in the doorway smirking as Emily and the carriage rolled down the road for the last time.

The carriage was almost half way to town when a man stepped into the road and flagged it down. Emily was alarmed at first, thinking it might be a highwayman—just last week there was s report of a brazen robbery in the next village. But then she chuckled to herself. What self-respecting highwayman would waste his time stealing her paltry possessions? As the carriage drew nearer, she saw that it was Michael and her heart raced. She'd wanted to say goodbye to him, but she couldn't bring herself to go to his cottage. She'd told herself that she didn't want to embarrass him and his family, but the truth was, she didn't think she could have done it without breaking down and embarrassing herself.

She tapped the roof of the carriage. "Driver, please stop."

Michael approached the door, cap in hand.

"So you're goin' then?"

"Yes, I am."

"I just wanted to say thanks for helpin' us and all. In the soup kitchen, I mean. I didn't expect it of you... I mean, I did, but..." Michael stopped talking and cursed himself. *Why must I always be so tongue-tied when I speak to this woman?* "It's best you leave here," he continued. "There's nothin' for you here now and..." He stopped again, not believing a word of what he was saying. "Well, anyway," he tried one more time, "goodbye and Godspeed."

"Thank you, Michael." Emily was greatly disappointed. Somehow she'd expected him to say more. But what? That she should stay? Lord knows she desperately wanted to. Reluctantly, she'd made arrangements to live with a distantly-related aunt in England, but it was clear from the tone of the exchange of letters that the aunt was not happy with the arrangement. And the feeling was mutual. But she had to go. There was no place else for her.

Michael stood back. "Well, then... your train..."

"Yes." She tapped the roof. "You may go on now, driver."

As the carriage turned at a bend in the road, Emily glanced out the back window. Michael was still standing in the middle of the road, cap in hand, watching her.

Emily, the only one at the train station, was near to tears, thinking of Michael. She was also bitterly disappointed that Nora had not come to see her off. In the distance, she heard a train whistle. In spite of all that had befallen this godforsaken country, at least the trains still ran on time. As the train grew nearer she could hear the whoosh, whoosh of the engine as it sent hot burning embers up the coal stack.

"Miss Emily…"

Emily turned and saw Nora approaching.

Emily put her hands out to the old woman. "Oh, Nora, I'm so glad you've come to see me off."

"I've somethin' to say to you, Miss Emily." Nora said, looking uncharacteristically indecisive. "I hope you won't take offense, because none is intended."

"Nothing you could say would offend me," Emily said, puzzled by the old woman's uneasiness. "You know that, Nora."

"Well then, here goes." In her high state of anxiety the words that she'd so carefully rehearsed came out in a great torrent. "God forgive me. You could stay with me if you like. I know it's a cheeky thing for me to say what with your being a lady and all and you probably have some wonderful place to go and you would never consider livin' in such miserable accommodations as I have and besides I couldn't offer you half of what you're accustomed to and…"

As Nora gushed through her rambling, non-ending sentence, the train pulled into the station with a great hiss of steam and screeching brakes. The conductor jumped down from a car and tipped his cap at Emily. "Are you boarding, Miss?"

Nora stopped babbling and stared at Emily open-mouthed.

"No, thank you, sir." Emily picked up her bag. "I'm going to live with this wonderful woman."

Marcus Goodbody was alone in the barn cleaning a soup cauldron when Fergus Kincaid came in. With mounting apprehension, Goodbody had been expecting a visit from Kincaid now that he was the new owner of the Somerville estates. From Michael's description of the man, he feared that one so parsimonious would not be amenable to allowing the soup kitchen to remain on his property. So he'd taken it as a good sign that he had not yet come. Hopefully, Mr. Kincaid had more important things to think about than a trifling soup kitchen operating out of his barn.

But now, here he was dressed in a garish cream-colored silk suit. Goodbody smiled, trying to put the best face on it. "Good morning, Mr. Kincaid. I trust thee is well?"

Kincaid, unaccustomed to Quaker speech and not trusting anything he didn't understand, squinted at the Quaker through narrow, suspicious eyes. "I'm well enough." He studied the piles of bowls laid out on the table to dry. "How many come here a day?"

Goodbody wiped his brow with his sleeve. "Oh, I have never counted, but I would speculate that nearly a hundred poor souls come here every day."

Kincaid was silent for a moment, as though he were doing some internal calculation. Then he announced, "I think it best you pay me by the head."

"*Head*? I don't understand."

"Rent, man. Rent. You don't expect to stay on here for free."

"*Rent...?* But, sir, surely thee must know that we are a charitable institution. And as such, everything we have we put into providing soup and bread for the poor souls who are landless and homeless. Thee can take great pride, as Lord Somerville did before thee, in helping us assist those who are more unfortunate than thee or me. God will look down favorably on all those who provide succor and comfort to the poor and homeless." Goodbody could see that he wasn't getting through to the stone-faced gombeen man. He made one final appeal. "Surely as a good Christian gentleman thee understands the great importance and need of a soup kitchen here in your barn."

Michael was walking the road to Somerville Manor on his way to help Marcus set up for tomorrow's meal. When he came over a rise he was surprised to see the Quaker coming toward him, leading his donkey and cart overburdened with cauldrons, utensils, and sacks of soup bowls.

"Marcus, what's happened?"

The Quaker threw up his hands, befuddled. "Michael," he blurted out, "I'm kitchenless."

"In *my* church?" Father Rafferty's thundering voice echoed throughout the little church.

"Sure he has no place else to go."

Michael's reasonable tone only made the old priest's face a darker shade of purple. "But... but..." he sputtered. "He's a... *Quaker*."

Michael started for the door.

"And where are you goin', Michael Ranahan?"

"To bring Marcus in. It's time you two met."

Father Rafferty, his arms folded stubbornly across his chest, stood defiantly guarding the altar as though at any moment he expected Beelzebub, himself, and his legions of demons to storm his little church. Instead of the devil, a tall, blond haired man came in. He swept his black hat off and, giving a tentative look around the church, came down the aisle. Father Rafferty squinted in the gloom to get a better look at him. *He doesn't look like a Quaker,* he muttered to himself. Then he realized that he didn't know what a Quaker looked like. The man was young, with a broad brow and fine yellow hair and his eyes were the color of a summer sky. All in all, Father Rafferty conceded, he could be taken for a Catholic if you didn't know better.

Marcus offered his hand. "I thank thee for permitting me to use your church for my soup kitchen."

Thee? Sure the man talks like he's just stepped off the pages of the scriptures. Father Rafferty took Marcus' hand and shook it firmly. "Let me warn you now, Mr. Goodbody, they'll be no proselytizing under the roof of this church. I'll have no triflin' with the souls in my parish. Is that clear?"

"I just want to feed the hungry, Father Rafferty."

Before Father Rafferty could add any more admonitions, the door opened and Emily came in.

Michael blinked, hardly believing his eyes.

When he'd watched Lord Attwood's carriage disappear around the bend on the way to the train station, he thought his heart would break. It had been his last chance to speak to her and he, as usual, babbled nonsense. He'd actually run after the carriage for a while, determined to talk to her one last time. But then he stopped. What would he say to her? That he loved her? That he wanted her to stay? Such foolishness. He had nothing to offer her and that was a fact.

"A change of plans. I'll be staying with Nora," she announced. "I heard Kincaid turned you out. Is there still work for me?"

Goodbody rushed to her and took her hands in his. "Emily, I am most pleased thou art staying. Yes, there is work. Father Rafferty has consented to allow the soup kitchen to be set up here."

Michael stood motionless, staring at her, certain that she must hear his heart pounding in the stillness of the church. He said nothing, because emotions that he didn't understand and had never experienced before threatened to overwhelm him and he couldn't trust what might come out of his mouth.

"And will you be working with us, Michael?" Emily asked.

"Aye," Michael said, a little too quickly.

"You'll be doin' no such thing," Father Rafferty said. "Have you forgotten? The Works are openin' tomorrow mornin'."

In his excitement at seeing Emily again, Michael had indeed forgotten all about the Works opening. For a brief second, he considered telling the priest that he would not be going to the Works, that he would stay here and work in the kitchen. But, he knew that wasn't possible. The family needed the money, as trifling as it was. He couldn't count on Da, who in recent weeks had turned into a wizened, frail old man before his very eyes. The terrible times were finally taking their toll on him and Michael doubted that his father would be able to do the grueling work much longer. He couldn't count on Dermot, who was behaving more queer with every passing day. Lately, he'd been disappearing for days on end and when he came home he would not say where he had gone or with whom he was with. Michael suspected that his brother was running with Jerry Fowler, but he couldn't get his brother to admit it. So, with one member of the family unable to work and the other unwilling, it fell to him to earn money for the family.

"I forgot," he said reluctantly. "I'll be goin' to the Works tomorrow."

Was that an expression of disappointment in her eyes? he wondered. Then his inner voice set him straight. *No, ya eejit. It's your own foolish mind playin' tricks on you.*

Chapter Thirty Three

For the next three weeks, Michael, along with more than a dozen men, worked on an abandoned road two miles outside the village. As before, they had been assigned yet another useless task—widening a little-used back road that, unlike the busy road leading to the village, saw little traffic. But the men were glad for the work and didn't complain.

At the beginning of the second week, Tarpy, the road work supervisor, pulled Da aside to talk to him. Michael didn't trust the supervisor and joined them.

"This doesn't concern you, Ranahan. Go back to work."

"If it concerns my Da, it concerns me. What is it?"

"All right then, I'll tell you as well. I'm lettin' your brother go."

"Oh, Jasus, no," Da cried out. "Sure we need the money, Mr. Tarpy."

"And he should be paid for what? Sure the man doesn't show up for work half the time. If he's too good for the work, there's many a man who will gladly do it."

Michael had seen this coming, but he'd been powerless to stop it. When the Works had reopened, Dermot had gone to work the first three days. Then he disappeared for two. For the next two weeks he was gone more days than he worked. In turn, Michael and Da tried talking to him, but Dermot wouldn't listen. Even the heartless Tarpy didn't want to see Dermot lose his job in these desperate times. He'd warned him repeatedly that he'd be sacked if he missed another day.

And now that day had come. Michael studied his father, pale and shaken. He wondered how much more the old man could take. On top of everything else that had befallen him, he had a defiant son who refused to obey him and now there was one less Ranahan to earn money.

"I warned him," Tarpy growled. "You know I did."

"Aye, you did," Michael said. "It's not your fault."

The following day, Michael and Da went to the worksite together. Dermot had still not come home. The weather was cold, and a light misting rain had begun to fall. Around midmorning, Michael began to feel lightheaded and decided it must be because he had not eaten anything yet. At breakfast, over the objections of Mam, he'd insisted on giving his meager portion of cornmeal to his Da, who looked as though he barely had the strength to walk out to the worksite. It was a measure of the old man's weakness that he took the food without argument.

Michael bent down to pick up a large stone and everything began to blur. His field of vision narrowed to a tiny circle and all he could see was the stone. The clank and thump of the men attacking the road with picks and shovels was blotted out by a loud whooshing in his ears. He grabbed the stone with his two hands and tried to lift it, but it wouldn't budge. He stared at it, puzzled. He'd lifted hundreds of stones like this—even bigger—but this one seemed to hold the weight of the world. He tried again, but he was as weak as a child. He gave one last great heave.

Then everything went black.

"Man down," someone shouted.

Da turned, saw Michael sprawled in the middle of the road, and ran to him. Michael's face was white and when Da touched his son's forehead, it was clammy with sweat.

"Give a hand here," he cried out.

As the men rushed to help, Tarpy took a close look at Michael and backed away. "Jasus, he's got the fever..."

When Da, Pat Doyle and Matt Flanagan carried the unconscious Michael into the cottage, Mam crossed herself and knew her worst fears were realized. Since the start of the troubles, she had prayed every night without fail, asking God to protect her family from disease and death. So far, her prayers had been answered—at least for her husband and two sons—and for that she was most grateful. But when the men brought Michael in, she took one look at her son and knew that her time of grace was over.

Mam stayed at his side day and night. There was nothing to do but bathe his feverish head with rags soaked in water and change the soiled straw bedding almost hourly. Semi-conscious most of the time, he writhed on the straw, muttering and crying out. She couldn't understand most of what he was saying, but she did understand one word, which he repeated over and over again. *Emily*...

She tried to get a bit of food into him, but it was no use. He was vomiting constantly and could hold nothing down. After four days, she was exhausted from lack of sleep, but she had no one to spell her. Dermot still hadn't come home and Da had to go to the worksite. But no matter. She shook off the fatigue, grimly determined that death would not take her first born son. *She* would die first.

Weakened from lack of sleep and little food, she was nodding off after having just replaced the soiled straw when she heard footsteps outside the cottage. She stiffened. Every day she listened for the sounds of footsteps outside, praying it was Dermot, and yet dreading that it might be someone to tell her that Dermot was dead, or someone carrying her husband home with the fever.

The door swung open and Emily ducked into the cottage.

"Mrs. Ranahan, I'm Emily Somerville."

"Yes, I know you are," Mam said, stunned to see Lord Somerville's daughter actually here in her cottage.

"I just heard Michael was sick and I've come to help."

"Oh, this is not the work for a fine young lady such as yourself."

Emily knelt down and touched Michael's feverish forehead. She was shocked at his appearance. He'd been thin for a long time, but now he was positively gaunt. But at least he didn't have that certain look of death, the kind of look that would have caused Dr. McDonald to send him to the dying room.

"Has he been vomiting?"

"Yes. Constantly."

"Has he been conscious?"

340

"Not really."

Emily could see that the woman was on the verge of collapse. Gently, she helped her to her feet and made her lie down on her own pallet. "You get some rest. Let me tend to things here." The exhausted woman was asleep before Emily could spread a threadbare blanket over her.

Emily turned her attention to Michael. He was deathly pale and his shirt was soaked through with perspiration. Recalling her experiences in the Fever Hospital, she realized that Michael could have any number of diseases. Typhus—or as the Irish called it, the "Black Fever"—caused the face to swell and the skin to turn a dark congested hue. Fortunately, it was usually not fatal. Then there was "Relapsing Fever," which caused high temperatures and vomiting. She prayed he didn't have that. Those afflicted with Relapsing Fever seemed to recover after several days, but there was always a relapse, and the whole cycle of fever and vomiting was repeated again. Emily had seen the cycle repeat itself as much as four times, but most patients, exhausted and debilitated, died well before that. She prayed it was only dysentery, whose symptoms were fever, vomiting, and violent evacuations. If she could keep plenty of fluids in him, he would survive. In the Fever Hospital, Dr. McDonald's main concern with dysentery was that it often turned into bacillary dysentery. Almost everyone who contracted bacillary dysentery died.

Oh, what's the difference what he has, she chided herself as she dipped a rag into a bucket of cool water. *I'm going to make him well and that's that.*

For the next ten days, Emily and Mam took turns tending to Michael and it seemed as though the fever would never break. At the end of the day, an exhausted Da would straggle in from the worksite, gaze at Michael, his brow knitted with worry, and ask how he was doing. He'd stopped asking Mam if Dermot had come home. Looking more haggard and thin with each passing day, he would then go sit by the fire and stare at it in silence until it was time to eat.

Sometime into the third week, Michael's fever broke. He opened his eyes, saw Emily staring down at him, and thought that he'd died and gone to heaven. Then Da peered over her shoulder. "Well, I guess you didn't die."

Michael rubbed his throbbing head. "I think I may be wishin' I had."

Michael fell into a deep sleep and slept peacefully well into the next evening. When he awoke he was lightheaded and every part of his body ached, but at least the fever was gone.

"Did Emily go?" he asked Mam.

"No, she's outside."

Overjoyed that she was still here, Michael pulled on his trousers and a shirt and went outside. She was sitting on the stone wall bordering the potato field.

"Why do you always sit in the dark?" he asked, echoing her question to him.

He could see her smile in the moonlight. "It's easier to remember the way things used to be."

He wanted to take her in his arms and bury his face in her sweet-smelling hair and tell her he loved her. Instead, he said, "Thanks for takin' care of me."

"I'm glad you're well again, Michael."

In the moonlight they studied each other in silence. When Emily had come into the cottage that first day and saw him lying on the bed, pale, feverish, and close to death, she thought *she* would die. Her only thought was to make him well. To make him live. Now, as she looked at him, she wished that he would say what she, herself, was longing to say. *That she loved him.* But he stood with his hands thrust into his trouser pockets, silently studying the trees in the distance.

Well, she thought, *if he won't say something, I will.* "Michael, I—"

"Hello..."

When Michael turned and saw Dermot coming up the road swaying on his short, bandy legs, a great anger rose in him. He wasn't sure if was because Dermot's absence had worried Mam sick or because he had spoiled this wonderful moment alone with Emily.

"Where have you been?" he said, trying, and failing, to keep the anger out of his voice.

"Lookin' for work."

"You had work here."

"Bustin' rocks for old Tarpy? I wanted somethin' more than that."

"And did you get it?" Michael asked, already knowing the answer.

"No."

Mam and Da heard Dermot's voice and came of the cottage. Mam rushed to her son and wrapped her arms around him. "Dermot, thank God you're alive. You've worried the life out of me."

Dermot pushed her away. "Sure I can take care of meself, Mam."

Da, standing rigidly in the doorway, made no attempt to approach his son. "So, you're home, is it?" he said in a voice constricted with rage.

"Aye. And I'm ready to go back to work with you and Michael."

"You've been sacked."

"Old Tarpy sacked me?"

"Don't act surprised, Dermot," Michael said. "He warned you. We all warned you."

Emily stood up. "Well, I think I'll be going," she said, not wanting to witness a family fight.

"I'll walk with you," Michael said.

"No, you need to rest up and get your strength back. The fever can return if the body is not strong."

He didn't protest. He was still feeling lightheaded and weak and wasn't sure he'd be able to walk her to Nora's cabin and make it back. "Well, thank you again, Emily. For everything."

"It's nuthin'," she said with a sly smile.

Michael watched her go down the road and it suddenly occurred to him that when she'd said "It's nuthin'," she was repeating what he'd said to her when he'd saved her from going into the ditch with Shannon.

When Michael went into the cottage, Da and Dermot were still arguing.

"Well, what am I to do now?" Dermot asked.

"You'll work in the soup kitchen with Mr. Goodbody and Miss Emily," Da said. "They need the help. Since the Works opened your brother and me have not been able to help out."

Dermot stomped out the door and went to sit on the same wall Emily had been sitting on. *Work in the soup kitchen.* The only thing he hated more than working with the road gang was working in the soup kitchen. He resented washing the endless pile of soup bowls and he detested the pathetic stream of beggars who came every day for their soup and a bite of bread.

After the life he'd been living for the past three weeks, the thought of working in the soup kitchen was unbearable. He, Jerry Fowler, and a few other lads had roamed the countryside near the town of Innismorn, twenty-five miles from Ballyross. At first they only stole from homes and barns. But when that didn't yield enough money, they moved up to stopping carriages on the road and relieving the wealthy passengers of their money and jewels. The risks were higher, but so were the rewards. In the beginning, he'd been terrified that he'd be shot or arrested, but the fear soon gave way to a surge of great excitement every time they stepped out into the roadway and stopped a carriage.

With more money to spend than he'd ever seen in his life, he and Jerry and the others lived and ate well. But then, two nights ago, something went terribly wrong. Dermot shook his head at the memory of it. They'd followed their usual plan —posting someone to stand across the street from the town's hotel. As soon as he saw a carriage being loaded with fancy dressed men and women, he'd run off to tell Fowler and the others. Then the whole group would wait two miles down the road for the arrival of the carriage. It was so easy, it was like snatching chickens in a hen house. Until that night.

Dermot couldn't get the images out of his mind. The carriage came around the bend. Following a prearranged plan, they jumped out into the roadway just as the carriage was upon them. Dermot's job was to grab the bridle and hold the horses still while Jerry and the others surrounded the carriage and robbed the passengers. As he usually did, Jerry stepped up to the carriage waving a firearm and announced, "I have a pistol. Don't resist and there'll be no trouble."

Usually, the sight of the pistol was enough to start the passengers throwing their valuables into the roadway. But this time, he'd barely gotten the words out of his mouth, when a shot rang out. At first, Dermot thought Fowler had fired the shot, but then one of the lads standing behind Fowler fell backward into the dirt. Frightened and confused by the sudden turn of events, Fowler fired wildly into the air and raced for the trees. "Run lads," he shouted. "Tis a trap."

Later, when Dermot met up with Fowler, he found out that one of the passengers had a firearm and had killed young Terry Wall, a sixteen-year-old runaway who had just joined up with them a week earlier. Jerry told Dermot to go home and lay low and promised he'd meet up with him later.

On the long walk home, Dermot comforted himself that at least he still had some money. He put his hand into his pocket and was stunned to discovered there was nothing left. Not a farthing. *My God, where did it all go?*

Like most men unaccustomed to using currency, he'd spent his ill-gotten gains with reckless abandon on women, drink, and food. He'd just assumed that there would always be more money. But those days were over. At least for now.

As Dermot sat on the wall, staring at the cottage—which to his eye was nothing more than a sorry pile of mud and thatch—the rage in him grew. It was a rage fueled by his knowledge that there was a better life out there than breaking rocks, or washing soup bowls, or farming another man's land.

In his travels with Jerry Fowler, he'd experienced that better life. And if it meant stealing and robbing to have that life, so be it. Anything was better than this miserable existence.

"All right," he muttered into the night. "I'll work in the soup kitchen. But just until Jerry Fowler comes back."

Chapter Thirty Four

It had been almost a week since Dermot returned home. And every day, prodded by Da's threat of banishment from the house, he went to the soup kitchen in the old village church. Conditions, he noted with disgust, were even worse than before he'd left. More and more starving people were coming for the food, and he was kept so busy that he hadn't a minute to himself. Worse, now that the soup kitchen had been relocated to the church, he also had nosy old Father Rafferty looking over his shoulder all day long, watching his every move.

It was toward the end of the day when Dermot, surrounded by a mountain of dirty soup bowls, saw his brother slip into the church. It amused him to see his big, serious brother so addle-headed over a woman. Even with Moira he was never like this. Michael always found some lame excuse for coming to the church after his work on the roads, but he didn't fool Dermot. Still, Dermot couldn't understand how his brother could be sweet on Emily Somerville. True, she was the most beautiful girl Dermot had ever seen, but she was the landlord's daughter for Jasus' sake—or was it ex-landlord's daughter? Whatever. His brother had no chance of winnin' her and Dermot thought him daft for moonin' over somethin' he could never have.

Michael was helping Emily move a cauldron over the fire when an uncharacteristically animated Marcus Goodbody barged in waving a newspaper. He thrust the newspaper at Michael. "Read this, Michael, and tell me what thee thinks."

Michael backed away. "I... I can't read," he mumbled, glancing at Emily.

"Oh." Embarrassed for Michael, Goodbody slipped the newspaper behind his back. "I am so sorry. I didn't know."

Emily broke the embarrassed silence. "What does it say, Marcus?"

Goodbody waved the paper in the air. "Queen Victoria is coming to Ireland next week."

Emily wiped her hands on her apron. "Well, I for one am glad. Perhaps when the queen sees how bad things are here, she'll make Mr. Trevelyan do more."

"That was my thought," Goodbody agreed. "When she sees conditions here, I am sure she will—"

"She'll not do anythin'," Dermot snarled. "She's a bloody Brit, just like the rest of them. They all want us dead and that's a fact."

"Mind your tongue," Michael said, stunned by the vehemence in Dermot's tone. "You're in the house of God."

Dermot threw his rag down. "Am I done here?" he asked Emily.

"Yes, Dermot." There was still a pile of bowls to be washed, but she knew that if she didn't give him permission to go, he would only slip out anyway. "You're free to go."

Dermot stomped out of the church without another word.

Once outside, his scowl quickly turned to a smile when he saw Jerry Fowler across the road, standing under a tree.

"Jerry, where have you been?" Dermot asked, happy to see the man he considered his best friend.

"Back in the soup kitchen are ya?"

"Aye. And they're killin' me with the endless washin' and dryin'."

"What about the Works?"

"That's gone. Old Tarpy sacked me."

"Ah, to hell with Tarpy. Dermot, I want you and Kevin to meet me at Scanlon's cottage tonight."

"Why?"

He pulled Dermot close and whispered, "I'm plannin' somethin' big. Very big."

After supper that night, while Mam and Da were getting ready for bed, Dermot slipped outside. Michael followed. "Dermot, don't you be goin' off again, you hear? Da has told you. You go away again, you're not to come back."

"For Jasus' sake, I'm just goin' to see Kevin. Can't I do even that without you getting' on me?"

Dermot met Kevin at the crossroads and the two men tracked across a barren field to the ruins of Scanlon's tumbled cottage. It was a dark night with no moon and they could barely make out the jagged edges of the cottage walls against the dark sky.

Kevin listened for a moment. "He's not here," he said, sounding almost relieved. "Let's go."

In the past year Dermot had come to realize that for all his great size Kevin was a bit of a mollycoddle—especially after Billy had been transported to Australia. For weeks after, Kevin would jump like a frightened field mouse every time he caught sight of a wagon coming down the road, thinking it might be the peelers again. When they were kids everyone was afraid of Kevin because he towered over them all. But, now, Dermot realized, Kevin was nothing but a coward who hid his fear behind his great size.

They were about to leave when a voice came out of the darkness, frightening the life out of both of them. *"Over here."*

Fowler appeared from behind a shattered wall holding a candle. "Over here. I've somethin' to show the pair of you."

They followed Fowler behind the wall and Dermot was surprised to see the two lads he'd recently run with, and another man he'd never seen before.

"Dermot, you know Sean and William. And this"—he pointed to the stranger—"is Frankie. And this big lad here, is Kevin."

Fowler pulled a bottle of poteen out of his coat pocket and handed it to Dermot. "Take a pull and pass it." He rubbed his hands together. "Tonight, lads, we're about to do something that will strike a blow for freedom. It'll be one for the history books, I promise ya."

Dermot's stomach tighten in fear—the same way it had when Fowler first proposed robbing houses and barns, and then carriages. Still, there was something in Fowler's tone—a certain smoothness, a confidence—that had a way of allaying all fear and doubt. Whatever it was, Dermot knew that Jerry Fowler could talk him into going anywhere and doing anything.

While the other men took their swigs, Fowler put the candle on a flat rock and unfolded a map. "Gather round."

He stuck his finger on a point on the map. "Right here. She'll be landing in Cork Harbor this Friday night."

"Who?" Dermot asked.

In the flickering candle light, Fowler's grin was malignant. "Queen Victoria. Who else?"

He moved his finger to another point. "And right here is Black Rock Castle, where she's to have lunch on Saturday next."

"How do you know that?" Kevin asked.

Fowler nodded toward the stranger. "Frankie, here, works in Dublin Castle. He's our eyes and ears."

Fowler's dirty finger traced a road from the harbor going toward the castle. "And right here in this bend in the road is where we'll do it."

"Do what?" Dermot asked, almost afraid of the answer.

"Assassinate her. What else?"

Until now, the others had been silent. They knew the kind of man Fowler was and sensed that he was planning something dangerous. But at Fowler's announcement, everyone gasped at the audacity of it.

"You're mad," Sean sputtered.

William shook his head. "We'd never get away with it..."

"Anyone else have anything to say?" Fowler asked, unfazed by their objections.

Dermot and Kevin shook their heads.

"Have you forgotten what the Brits have done to us?" Fowler went on. "They've starved us, they've taken our crops out of the country, and they've stood by and watched us die of famine and disease. Lads, this is a chance of a lifetime. A chance to strike a blow for freedom. We must let the bastards know we're not a bunch of sheep to be slaughtered in meek silence."

Dermot took another deep swig of the poteen and felt his head starting to go all queer and light. He was stunned by Fowler's foolhardy plan, but he had to admit there was truth in what he said. They were starvin' us. Didn't he see that every day at the soup kitchen? And didn't the fever take his own Granda and Grandmam, and very nearly his brother? If things went on the way they were goin', they would all die and that was a fact. "I'm in," he said.

"Good lad. Who else is with us?"

Reluctantly, the others nodded their assent.

"Good. Now, gather around and I'll explain the plan."

On the way home Dermot and Kevin walked the road in silence, thinking of the outrageous scheme Fowler had laid out . At the crossroads, Dermot said, "Will you do it, Kevin?"

"Aye. You?"

Dermot heard the hesitation in Kevin's voice. "Aye," he replied without hesitation. But he wondered if it was the poteen talking.

Dublin Castle

August 1849

In a small, damp room in the bowels of Dublin Castle, Scotland Yard Inspector Thomas Cronin, faced a room full of veteran police detectives brought in from London for a special detail. He was a cheerless man in his early fifties and with a broken nose that made his constant scowl even more fierce. And now he was scowling at the men seated before him.

"We must be ever vigilant, men. As you well know, there's a great deal of unrest in the country. And it is our mission to ensure the safety of the Queen. As you mingle with the populace, I want you to keep your eyes open and your ears sharp."

The door opened and an assistant hurried up to the inspector and whispered something in his ear.

"Sgt. Cunningham," the inspector said to a barrel-chested man with ruddy cheeks, "give them their assignments. And remember, men. Vigilance."

As he hurried down the corridor, the inspector asked the assistant, "Who is this man?"

"One of our informants, Inspector."

"Reliable?"

"He is, sir."

The assistant opened the door marked "Interrogation Room," and there, sitting in a chair, shrunken with nervousness, sat Frankie—Jerry Fowler's eyes and ears in Dublin Castle.

Just before dawn, Dermot, nervous and excited, quietly slipped out of the cottage. He waited at the crossroads for

Kevin for almost a half hour, stomping his brogues on the hard ground to ward off the early morning chill. When there was still no sight of Kevin, he went up the road to his cottage and tossed a stone against the side of the house. A moment later, Kevin came out.

"Come on, Kevin. We'll be late."

The big man kicked at a stone with his huge brogue. "I'm not goin'."

"And why not?"

"Sure it's a daft idea. We'll all be killed."

Dermot was furious with the big man. Fortified by the poteen, he'd been all for Fowler's plan that night. But the more he thought about it, the more he realized how impossible and dangerous it was. *Assassinate Queen Victoria*? Sure that was not possible. If only Kevin had expressed doubt or, better yet, said he wouldn't do it, Dermot and the others might have done the same. Now it was too late.

"Are you goin'?" Kevin asked.

"I am," Dermot said, trying to sound fearless.

Kevin stuck his big hand out. "Well, then, good luck to you."

Dermot shook Kevin's hand and, shivering—not sure if it was from the cold or fear—set off in the darkness to meet with Fowler and the others.

Michael had always been a light sleeper and, if he'd been healthy, he would surely have awakened when Dermot got up. But since his bout with the fever he was exhausted all the time and when he put his head down at night, he slept like a dead man.

Da woke him with a poke. "Where is he?"

Michael rubbed his eyes and it took him a second to realize he was talking about Dermot. "I don't know."

"I warned him. Didn't I tell him that if he runs off again, he'll not come back into this house?"

Mam, awake now, tried to sooth her husband. "Now, John—"

"*No*. I'll not listen to you this time. I've warned him."

Mam shot Michael a pleading look.

Michael pulled his boots on. "I'll go find him, Mam. Don't you worry."

While Da set off for the worksite, Michael hurried to the church. He prayed he would find Dermot there, preparing the morning's feed. But deep down he knew there was no way his lazy brother would have gotten up early to go to work.

Michael came into the church through the back door and found Emily alone, adding ingredients to a large soup cauldron. It never failed. Every time he saw her face, his heart pounded in his chest.

"Is Dermot here?" he asked.

Emily shook her head. "No. Not yet." She saw his troubled expression. "Is something the matter?"

"I'm not sure."

Just then Goodbody came in with a newspaper in his hand. "Good morning, Michael," he said with his usual, cheerful manner. "Emily, has thee seen this morning's newspaper? It says the queen is lunching at Black Rock Castle today. Is that far from here?"

"About five miles," Emily said.

Michael felt his stomach knot, suddenly remembering Dermot's vehement outburst of the other day: *She's a bloody Brit, just like the rest of them...*

Without a word Michael turned and ran out, leaving a puzzled Emily and Mr. Goodbody to shrug at each other.

Michael hurried to the worksite, praying that he'd find Kevin there. If anyone knew where his brother was, it would be Kevin. He breathed a sigh of relief when he saw the big man shoveling gravel onto the roadbed.

He pulled Kevin aside, ignoring Tarpy's flinty stare. "Kevin, where is he?"

"Who?"

"My brother, for Jasus' sake."

"Sure I don't know."

Michael could tell he was lying. Enraged, he grabbed the front of Kevin's ragged coat. "Kevin, you're bigger than I am. But by God, if you don't tell me where Dermot is I'll beat the livin' shite out of you."

Tears welled up in Kevin's eyes. "They're all gonna be killed," he blurted out. "Michael, I tried to warn him."

Michael sprinted down the road as fast as he could. Mulrooney's Inn, almost six miles away, was where Kevin said Dermot and the others were to meet. He'd run just over a mile, but already he was at the point of exhaustion. He staggered to a stop, bent over and put his hands on his knees and dry wretched.

Before the fever he could have run five times this distance without even breathing hard. But now he was as weak as a calf and he still had five more miles to go. What was he to do? There was no way he could run the entire distance and there was no time to walk. In a field to his left—Kincaid's fields now—he saw a horse grazing. Horse thievery, he knew, was a very serious offense. If he was caught, he would surely be transported to Australia. But what choice did he have?

Without a second thought, he climbed the fence, grabbed a clump of grass, and slowly approached the horse. "Here, boy," he said softly. "Look what I've got for you."

The wary horse backed away, but Michael, careful not to make any sudden moves, continued to move toward him with the clump of grass extended in his hand. Finally, he got within arm's reach of the horse. He put the grass under the horse's nose. As the horse tentatively nibbled at the offering, Michael slipped his hand around the bridle and quickly climbed onto the horse's back.

Used to riding without a saddle, Michael dug the heels of his brogues into the horse's flanks and felt a powerful surge burst beneath him. This was no plow horse. It was probably some landlord's expensive hunter, sold off to Kincaid to pay debts. Whatever the reason, Michael was grateful for a horse that would get him to Mulrooney's quickly.

With every step he took along the road, Dermot became more and more convinced that he was making a terrible mistake. But it was too late to turn back now. What would

Fowler think if he backed out now? Suppressing his doubts, he continued on down the road.

When Dermot met up with Fowler, Sean and William at the ruins of Scanlon's cottage, he was secretly pleased that Frankie wasn't with them. Perhaps Frankie, like Kevin, had changed his mind.

"Where's Frankie?" Dermot asked hopefully. If the man wasn't coming, Fowler might call the whole thing off.

"He'll meet us at Mulrooney's. Where's Kevin?"

"He's not comin'."

"I'm not surprised," Sean said. "I knew the big glom didn't have the sand for this."

"This changes nothing," Fowler said, much to Dermot's disappointment. "Let's get a move on. We've no time to lose."

Chapter Thirty Five

Mulrooney's Inn had been a fixture on the Cork Road for over a hundred years. It had seen good times and bad, but now it was seeing the worst times in all its history. The Inn, situated on the only major road that led to the west and south of Ireland, was usually bustling with the comings and goings of men of commerce, farmers, and bankers of every stripe. But since the hunger, fewer and fewer people needed a reason to pass this way and the Inn, experiencing a sharp decline in business, was on the verge of financial ruin.

When Jerry Fowler and the others walked into the Inn's pub room, there was no one there except the proprietor, who was standing behind the bar cleaning glasses.

The four men sat at a corner table. "How about a round of pints?" Fowler called out.

Mulrooney, an angular man with a shock of white hair, brought the mugs. He looked frightened and his hands were shaking so badly, he spilled half the ale onto the rough-hewn table top.

"Have one yourself," Fowler said, winking at the others. "It'll calm your nerves."

The proprietor, grim as a mortician, wiped up the spill and quickly retreated to his place behind the bar.

Michael didn't want to call attention to himself and resisted the temptation to bring the horse to a full gallop. But even at a canter, the superbly conditioned animal covered the ground with ease. He was making good time. Still, mindful that the sight of a raggedy-dressed farmer on a sleek hunter was bound to attract attention, whenever he saw another horseman or carriage approach, he led his horse off the road and waited in the hedges until they passed.

Back on the road, he rounded a turn and there—barely a hundred yards ahead—was Mulrooney's Inn. He was about to dig his heels into the horse's flanks and cover the last hundred yards at a gallop, when suddenly his eye caught a glimpse of something shiny in the hedgerow across the road from the Inn. He dismounted and tied the horse to a tree. Concealed by the hedge line on the Inn side of the road, he crept closer. And then he saw him. A small, wiry man with a broken nose standing next to a tree, directing the placement of several men armed with rifles.

My God! He's setting up an ambush. Michael was still fifty yards from the Inn and on the same side of the road, but he was afraid that if he continued, he might be spotted by the men. He got down on his hands and knees and set off crawling the last fifty yards.

Inside the Inn, the men sitting at the table had become very quiet. There was no more laughter or banter. The long, tense wait had drained the false bravado from everyone, even Jerry Fowler. Frankie, the man who was supposed to bring the rifles, was over an hour late.

Dermot shot a sideways glance at Sean and William. *They're as uneasy as me*, he said to himself. *Why don't they say somethin'*?

Finally, he couldn't take the tension any longer. "So where is he?" Dermot blurted out.

"Don't worry. He'll be here." Fowler tried to sound confident, but Dermot noticed that he was nervously tapping his empty glass on the table. "Innkeeper, how about another—" Fowler turned toward the bar, but the owner wasn't there.

Suddenly, Jerry Fowler was conscious of a great stillness. He cocked an ear. Not a bird was singing outside, not even the ever-present cawing of crows. Fowler felt the hair on the back of his neck rise.

"Dermot," he said softly, "be a good lad and take a look outside and see if you see Frankie comin'."

Exhausted and covered with mud, Michael had crawled to within twenty yards of the Inn when the back door opened and a man with a shock of white hair slipped out and ran off into the woods. Ignoring his burning lungs and the pain of scraped-raw elbows, Michael quickened his pace. Finally, when he was sure the building blocked him from the view of the gunmen across the road, he stood up and raced the last ten yards for the open back door.

Michael barged into the pub room just as Dermot was opening the front door.

"*No, Dermot,*" Michael shouted. "*Don't—*"

But he was too late.

Dermot had already swung the door open. At the sound of Michael's voice, Dermot turned with a puzzled expression at seeing his brother here. At the same time, there was an explosion of gunfire from the hedges across the road. Dermot, framed in the doorway, was struck by a hail of bullets and blown back into the room. He crashed to the oak-beamed floor, screaming and writhing in agony.

In the next instant, the pub room became the center of a terrifying maelstrom of sound and fury. Bullets crashed through windows, exploding shattered glass across the room. Bullets thunked into hundred-year-old walls, crumbling plaster and knocking faded paintings off the wall. Behind the bar, bottles and pots exploded, spraying spirits everywhere.

Ducking behind the thick oak bar, Michael glanced across the room and saw a petrified Fowler and another man cowered behind an overturned table. Behind them, a third man was slumped against the wall with half of his face blown away.

It took every bit of self-control for Michael to keep himself from rushing across the room and strangling Fowler, the cause of all this. But he had to help his brother. With bullets whining all around him and shattered glass raining down on him, Michael crawled toward Dermot. Shards of glass tore at his clothing, lacerating his arms and legs. Dermot had stopped screaming, but now, sprawled on the floor, he lay ominously still. A rivulet of blood oozing from his chest snaked its way across the planked floor and pooled by the leg of an overturned chair.

Michael reached out and grabbed Dermot's collar. "Dermot can you hear me?" he shouted over the gunfire.

Dermot tried to turn his head, but he couldn't. "Michael, they're killin' us…"

"We're gettin' out of here. Can you help me?"

Dermot started to sob. "Michael, I can't feel my legs…"

"It's all right. I've got you."

Slowly, Michael started pulling his brother toward the back of the room. There was no letup in the fusillade of bullets, but Michael felt a small measure of comfort in that because he knew that once the bullets stopped, they would be coming. Michael's chest heaved with the effort and he was beginning to feel lightheaded, but he had to get Dermot out of the Inn and into the fields before the men came. It was their only chance. He'd pulled Dermot about half the distance when his strength gave out. He could pull his brother no farther.

"For the love of God, give a hand here," an exhausted Michael called out to Fowler.

The man hiding next to Fowler, tears streaming down his face and holding his hands over his ears, kept screaming, *"We've got to give up… For Jasus' sake… We've got to give it up…"*

From his position behind the upturned table, Fowler glanced at Dermot and shook his head. "Tis too dangerous. It's every man for himself."

Fowler's response didn't surprise Michael. That's what Fowler was—a coward. Michael had planned to lead Fowler and the other man out the back door and to possible safety. But now, it would be as Fowler said: *Every man for himself.*

All I have to do is get Dermot outside, Michael told himself. *From there I can carry him to the horse and then we're free and clear.*

Calling on every ounce of strength he had left, Michael yanked on the back of Dermot's collar and, slowly, Dermot began to slide across the floor. Tugging and pulling, Michael finally got his brother to the back door and pulled him through.

Outside, Michael, gasping for air, took a quick look around. Thank God they had not sent anyone around to cover the back. He looked down at Dermot. His brother's face was drained of color and the front of his shirt was covered with blood.

"I'm gonna die," Dermot whispered through parched lips.

"You're not gonna die, Dermot. Didn't I promise I'd take you to America with me?"

A little spark came into Dermot's eyes. "Aye, you did. When can we go…"

Michael lifted his brother up and carefully slid him over his shoulder. "Soon, Dermot. We'll go soon."

"That's good, Michael. Ireland is cursed…"

Taking a chance that the gunmen would be too busy firing into the Inn to notice them, Michael ran along the hedgerow with his brother over his shoulder until he came to where he'd tied the horse.

Carefully, Michael slid his brother across the horse's back. Suddenly, the shooting stopped. After the constant din of gunfire the sudden stillness was unnerving.

Michael moved to the edge of the clearing and watched. Someone was shouting from inside the Inn, but he was too far away to hear what he said. Then, someone in the hedges shouted a response, but, again, he couldn't make out what was said. A moment later, the Inn's front door opened and the man who had been screaming about surrendering came out with his hands high over his head.

"It's just like Jerry Fowler," Michael muttered. "Let someone else do the dangerous work."

Cautiously, several men carrying rifles came out of the woods. The man with the broken nose seemed to be in charge. He walked up to the man who'd surrendered. There was an exchange of words and then, to Michael's horror, the man took a revolver out of his waistband and shot Fowler's friend in the head. The man dropped to the ground like a sack of wheat. Stepping over the body, the broken nosed man led the others into the Inn. Seconds later, there was another shot. And a minute after that, two of the gunmen came out dragging a dead Jerry Fowler by his feet, leaving a trail of blood on the graveled driveway.

Michael ran back to his brother. "Dermot we're got to get out of here before—" He stopped talking when he saw Dermot's lifeless eyes staring at the ground.

Wordlessly, Michael closed his brother's eyes, turned the horse around, and headed for home.

It was almost dark by the time Michael got back to the cottage. As he came up the road, Da was outside tending the potato field. When he saw Dermot laid across the horse's back, he called out to his wife, "Mary, you'd better come out here."

Mam came out of the cottage just as Michael pulled the horse up to the door.

Michael hung his head, unwilling to look into his mother's anguished face. "Mam, I'm sorry..."

It took a moment for it all to sink in, then Mam, shrieking in grief, rushed to the lifeless body of her youngest son.

Inside the cottage, Dermot's bloody body lay stretched out on the table. Mam, sitting beside him, stroked his hair. "We'll have to make arrangements for a proper burial," she said.

Michael looked to his father to say something. Outside, he'd explained to his father that it would not be possible to bury Dermot properly. But now, Da stared into the fire unable—or unwilling—to deliver this final blow to his wife.

"Mam," Michael said gently. "We can't have a proper burial for Dermot."

She looked at him, baffled. "What are you sayin', Michael Ranahan? Of course we must have a proper burial for your brother. You'll go and fetch Father Rafferty. He'll do the service."

Michael shot a pleading glance at his father, but the old man would not look up from the fire. "Mam, listen to me. The peelers will be crawlin' all over the countryside lookin' for someone dead or wounded. If they find out that Dermot has been shot dead, they'll arrest me for sure, and probably Da. For certain they'll tumble the cottage."

When the full import of what Michael was saying finally set in, she collapsed to the floor, screaming, "Oh, Jasus, in Heaven… No….no… Please dear God… tis my son… my son…"

Michael helped her up and gently put her down on her pallet. Soon, she stopped crying and stared up at the ceiling with a terrible resignation in her eyes that broke Michael's heart. She had always been a strong woman, but Michael wondered how much more of this she could take.

"In the bog?"

Michael and Da were standing in the potato field and Michael had just told him where they would have to bury Dermot.

A grief-stricken Da stared at Michael with red rimmed eyes. "Sure the bog is a place of evil things, terrible things, unspeakable things. My son cannot be buried in such a place as that."

"The peelers will be lookin' everywhere. If they find a fresh grave, they'll dig it up. It has to be the bog. Dermot's body must never be found. If it is, we're all lost. Do you understand?"

Da stared at Michael, unwilling to accept what he was being told. Then he blinked in resignation. "When must it be done?"

"Tonight."

Gruffly wiping a tear with his sleeve, Da turned from Michael and went back into the cottage.

Inside, Mam was preparing the body. She'd washed away the blood as best she could. There was no clean shirt for him, so she had to leave the bloodstained one on. She wet the tips of her fingers and smoothed down his unruly, straw-like hair. Then she lovingly wrapped the body in a threadbare sheet.

When she was done, Michael carried the body outside and laid it on a length of charred roof beam he'd secured from Scanlon's tumbled cottage. He tied the body to the plank with lengths of rope. Then he added rocks to Dermot's pockets until he was sure the body would sink. When all was finished, he hitched the plank to the horse and called his Mam and Da out for their final goodbye.

In silence, the three Ranahans stood by the body. Mam knelt and placed a trembling hand on the shroud. Da stood rigid, his shapeless hat in his hands. He said nothing, but his lips were moving and Michael assumed he was praying for his dead son.

For his part, Michael didn't know what to think about his dead brother. He'd always been a handful, but, he was after all his brother. Something had gotten into Dermot in the past year and it had changed him for the worst. He'd become moodier, angrier, shunning even his own family. Was it the strain of trying to survive the famine that made him that way? Or was it just something that had always been inside him? Whatever it was, Michael suspected Jerry Fowler had something to do with the change in his brother and was glad that Fowler, too, was dead.

It was time to get on with it. Michael helped his mother to her feet. "Da, you stay with Mam. I can manage this myself."

As he led the horse away in the darkness toward the bog, a shrill sound ripped the still night. The hair on the back of Michael's neck stood up. It was the first time he'd ever heard his Mam keen.

At the edge of a bog pool, Michael unhitched the horse from the roof beam. He upended the plank into the bank and pushed. The roof beam, weighted down with Dermot's body, easily slid down the slippery slope. Gurgling and sucking, the bog claimed the body of Dermot Ranahan and it sunk into the ancient black ooze.

The last thing Michael did before he went home was to free the horse. Knowing how Kincaid treated animals, he couldn't bring himself to take the horse back to the field. As he smacked the horse's rump and watched it trot off into the darkness, he envied the horse's freedom—as short-lived as it might be—and hoped that he would find someone worthy to take care of him.

It was late when Michael got back to the cottage. Sorrow had acted like a sedative on Da and Mam and, mercifully, they were asleep. Michael was glad of that. He didn't think he could take any more of his mother's sorrow just now.

Exhausted, he lay on his pallet staring up at the thatched ceiling, suddenly mindful of the extra room in the bed. No more would he have to shove Dermot back to his side. Never again would he have to reclaim his share of the blanket or ward off the kicks of his restless brother.

In the darkness, hot tears stung his eyes and Michael was finally able to weep.

Chapter Thirty Six

Just after dawn, Michael awoke with a start. He thought he'd heard muffled voices. *Was it a dream?* Suddenly, there was a loud crack and the front door came crashing down. A half-dozen men armed with rifles rushed into the cottage. A dazed Michael looked up at them and thought he must be dreaming. It had to be another one of his nightmares. But then the small, wiry man with the broken nose ducked through the door.

Michael tried to get up, but one of the men smashed the butt of his rifle into Michael's neck and he fell back down.

Two other men trained rifles on Mam and Da, who huddled together, terrified.

"I'm looking for Dermot Ranahan," Chief Inspector Cronin announced. "Where is he?"

"Gone from here," Michael said.

"Gone where?"

"I think he said he was gonna join the British army. You might look for him there."

At a nod from Cronin, the man standing behind Michael smashed the rifle butt down on the back of Michael's neck again.

"And what's your name?" Cronin asked.

"Michael Ranahan."

"Where were you yesterday, Michael Ranahan? A man fitting your description was seen riding a horse on the Cork Road."

"I don't own a horse."

"One was reported stolen near here."

"Probably for food," Michael said.

That response got Michael another crack of the rifle butt.

"Take him outside," Cronin said.

Two men dragged Michael to his feet and shoved him through the door.

There was a black constabulary wagon in the yard. Inspector Cronin went to the wagon and pulled a curtain aside. Frankie peeked out the window nervously.

"Well?" Cronin asked, pointing at Michael. "Is this one of them?"

Michael held his breath. He didn't recognize the man, but obviously he was an informer and informers were never to particular about who they fingered, especially if there was a shilling reward in the bargain. But to Michael's relief, the man shook his head.

Cronin looked disappointed. "All right, he said to the men holding Michael, let him go."

As soon as the men let go of Michael's arms, Michael charged at the man who had smashed him with the rifle butt and slammed him to the ground. He rolled on top of him and, grabbing the man's hair with both hands, smashed his head into the ground.

Suddenly, Michael felt cold steel as Cronin pressed his revolver into Michael's neck. "That will be enough of that. Get up."

Reluctantly, Michael rolled off the half-unconscious man and stood up.

Cronin put his face so close that Michael could smell cigar smoke on the man's breath. "If your brother's alive, we'll find him," Cronin said softly. "If he's dead, then that's one less bog trotter to worry about, isn't it?"

It was days before Michael could bring himself to go back to the church. He wanted desperately to see Emily, but he knew she would ask him about Dermot's whereabouts and he didn't know what to say. Finally, he couldn't keep away any longer and he went to the church after his work on the road gang.

By the time he got there, it was late and all those seeking food had gone to seek shelter for the night. Emily and Goodbody were having a cup of tea when Michael came in. And once again, seeing them together like this, a devil's brew of jealously, anger, and sadness welled up within him. But, as usual, Marcus Goodbody, with his good cheer and warmth, quickly dispelled any notions that there might be anything going on between him and Emily—at least on his part.

"Michael," Goodbody said, coming forward to shake Michael's hand. "My friend, where has thou been? We have been most worried about thee."

Michael mumbled about being busy working on the road gang and tending the crops.

Emily offered Michael a cup of tea. Tea was something he had never drunk before working in the soup kitchen. At first, he disliked the bitter and weak brew and wondered why Emily and Goodbody insisted on drinking it every afternoon. But as foul as it was, he drank it anyway, because it was one way of reaching into the mysterious and wonderful world of Emily and Goodbody. But, over time, he found that he actually liked it, and looked forward to taking afternoon tea with them.

Michael took his cup. "Thank you, Emily."

"We missed you," she said, turning away from his intense gaze to stir her tea.

"Aye."

Aye? Is that all you have to say, you eejit? All the way here you've been practicin' what you would say to her and now all you can say is—Aye?

Then she asked the question he'd been dreading. "Where's Dermot?"

"Gone," he mumbled.

"Gone? Gone where?"

"Just gone."

Emily looked at him with a puzzled expression. "Gone off to be with his friends or gone for good?"

"He won't be comin' back." Michael felt tears welling up and quickly turned away.

Goodbody saw there was something wrong and came to Michael's rescue. "Emily, I think that Michael does not want to talk about his brother just now."

"Oh. I'm sorry."

Michael, stirring his tea furiously, said nothing.

"I pray the harvest is bountiful this year," Goodbody said. "Does thee pray for the same, Michael?"

"Michael?" Emily tugged at his sleeve.

"What? Oh, aye."

Chapter Thirty Seven

September 1849
Ballyross, Ireland

The summer wore on and the weather, wet and gray, was a fitting reflection of the way the men of Ballyross felt. As the time for the harvest approached, those who had planted a crop—and there were fewer and fewer of them— took to visiting their fields every day. They walked the rows, carefully examining every stalk, praying that the shoots would remain green, and trying not to think of what they would do if the potatoes turned black, as they had done for the past three out of four years.

Da, growing more lethargic each day, had given up checking his crop. Michael was disturbed by the changes taking place in the old man. Until now, there had been no one more diligent about inspecting his fields than Da. But since Dermot's death, something had gone out of him. He continued to go to the worksite every day, but he barely spoke to anyone, not even Michael. When he came home, instead of inspecting the field as he had in years past, he went directly into the cottage where he waited for his dinner by the fire in brooding silence.

It was left to Michael to do the job alone. Every day, he got down on hands and knees and examined the tiny shoots. But one day toward the end of July he realized the futility of what he was doing. *What in God's name am I looking for?* he asked himself. *And if I find something, what am I to do about it?* He stood up, dusted the soil from his trousers, and never checked the plants again.

Michael also worried about his Mam. Dermot's death seemed to suck the very life out of her and the light had gone out of her eyes. Mechanically, she went about her work—mending and cooking. But her heart wasn't in it. She had always been thin, but now she was positively skeletal. She barely ate and Michael wondered where she found the strength to rise from her bed every day. Again, he asked himself the question that he'd been asking himself since Dermot's death: *How much more can she take?*

One late September morning Michael awoke at dawn and knew it had happened again. During the night, the now familiar stench of decaying potatoes had seeped through the cracks and crevices of the old cottage. Like a harbinger of death, it permeated the very air, announcing to one and all that more death lay ahead... more famine... more sickness.

"Oh, God, no..." Da cried out in despair.

Michael turned toward his Mam. She lay in the bed, staring up at the ceiling, unable—or unwilling—to say anything.

October 1849
Ministry of the Treasury
London, England

As soon as Mr. Playfair received word of the crop failure, he scheduled an emergency meeting with Trevelyan. He, and his fellow commissioners, Dr. Lindley and Mr. Kane, were in total agreement—something had to be done immediately.

Now they sat across the conference table in Trevelyan's office, once again stunned by the man's intransigence.

"For God's sake, Mr. Trevelyan," Playfair exclaimed, trying mightily to control his temper. "The entire country is starving. Disease is rampant. What food there is, is too dear for the peasants to afford. In the name of all that is just, you must do something to alleviate the misery at once. For five years now, these poor souls have been pounded with unceasing starvation, disease, and death."

Trevelyan, still steadfast in his righteous beliefs, was unruffled by the pleadings of the three men seated before him. He made a steeple of his fingers and studied the oak-beamed ceiling. "I believe it was Thomas Malthus who said: 'If society does not want a man's labor, he has no claim of right to the smallest portion of food and, in fact, has no business to be where he is.'"

"Well, it would appear that Mr. Malthus is having his way," an exasperated Mr. Kane spluttered. "Thousands are leaving the land and migrating to America. Entire families are breaking up."

"Unlike you, Mr. Kane, I do not see that as a deficit. Now the landlords will be forced to sell their estates to persons who know how to run a proper business enterprise."

Playfair, giving way to the pent-up fury that had been building since 1845, slammed his fist on the table. "Year after year, we have pleaded and begged you to help this destitute country. Each time you have done something, but it has never been nearly enough. And now, sir, I ask you, in the name of God, is the British government to stand by and watch an entire nation starve to death?"

Trevelyan shrugged in a manner that never failed to infuriate the three commissioners. It was a movement that said: *Whatever you say is of no consequence.* "We are in the hands of Providence, Dr. Playfair. Without a possibility of averting the catastrophe, we can only await the results."

A red-faced Playfair tossed an envelope to Trevelyan and slowly rose to his feet. "Mr. Trevelyan,"—his voice trembled with rage—"the destitution in Ireland is so horrible and the indifference of you and the government to it is so manifest that I am an unfit agent of a policy which, I can only conclude, must be one of extermination. I have been placed in a position which no man of honor or humanity can endure."

"Very well, Dr. Playfair," Trevelyan said. I accept your resignation."

October 1849
Ballyross, Ireland

It had been a month since the crop failed. The farmers had burned every scrap of putrid potato and decaying plant, but the smell continued to hang in the air like a malignant presence. Not even three days of soaking rain was able to scour the stench from the stricken countryside.

On the way home from the worksite, Da, sniffing the air, broke his usual silence. "It's God's reminder that he's taken away our food." He turned to Michael with eyes clouded with fear. "What have we done to displease God so?"

Michael wanted to tell his father that there was no sense in making things worse by blaming himself for this disaster. Michael doubted there was a God, but if there was, why, he reasoned, would he waste his efforts on this forlorn country? That's what he wanted to say, instead, he said, "We've done nothin' to displease God, Da." Then he remembered the words of a Father Rafferty sermon, words that meant nothing to him, but might be a comfort to his Da. "It's as Father Rafferty says, the Lord works in mysterious ways."

As they approached the cottage, Michael knew immediately something was amiss. The front door was shut, which it never was during the day, and there was no usual wisp of smoke rising from the chimney. Fearing the worse, he handed his shovel to his father. "Would you put this in the shed for me?"

Da gave Michael a curious look, but he was so unaccustomed to Michael asking him to do anything, that he took the shovel without protest and went on to the shed.

Michael pushed the cottage door open and stepped inside. With the turf fire out, the interior of the cottage was even darker than usual. It took a moment for Michael's eyes to adjust to the dim light and it was then that he saw his Mam.

She was lying on her pallet, as though she had decided to lie down for a bit of a sleep. But her eyes were open, staring up at the ceiling. He knelt down beside her and touched her cold cheek, and wondered how he was going tell his Da.

"*Oh, Jasus, Michael... What is it?*" Da was standing in the doorway, grasping the doorframe to steady himself. "Why is your Mam lying there like that? Is it the fever, Michael? Does she have the fever?" He shuffled forward. "Sure she'll be all right. We'll take care of her. She'll be right as rain in no time, won't she, Michael?" Da stared down at his wife and tears streamed down his face. "She'll be all right, won't she, Michael?"

Michael stood up. He wanted to put his arms around the frightened old man, but his father had never been one for displays of affection. It suddenly occurred to Michael that he had never hugged his father. Not once.

"She's gone, Da. Gone to a better place." Michael fervently hoped that was true.

Da dropped to his knees and threw himself across her body. "No, Mary... You can't leave me... You mustn't leave me... For the love of God, please don't leave me...."

It was the first time Michael had ever seen his father cry.

Mam's burial was a simple affair. Earlier that morning, Michael had gone to the cemetery to dig the grave himself because there were no gravediggers left. They'd all died or fled the countryside.

While a gentle rain fell, Father Rafferty recited the prayers for the dead while Da, Michael, Emily, and Goodbody looked on. When he was done, Michael lowered his Mam, wrapped in a threadbare sheet, into the ground. He waited for everyone to leave before he filled in the hole.

Emily insisted they all go back to the church where she made sure Da ate something. When she was satisfied that he'd eaten, she went outside and found Michael sitting on a stone wall. She sat down next to him.

"Your father isn't taking it well."

"All he ever wanted was to keep the family together. And now, there's just the two of us."

"What will you do?" she asked, almost afraid of the answer.

"I asked him if he wanted to go to Cork or maybe Dublin. Perhaps there I might be able to earn enough for passage for the two us to go out to America."

At the mention of him going to America, Emily felt a sinking feeling in her heart. "What did he say?" she asked bleakly.

"He's a stubborn old man. He said he'll never leave his land." Michael chuckled mirthlessly. "*His* land. He still thinks he owns that miserable bit of dirt."

Emily bit her lip in relief, eternally grateful for the stubbornness of an old man.

November 1849
Ballyross, Ireland

It was midmorning and Da should have been at the worksite, but he sat by the fire, all alone in the cottage. It was a bitter, cold day and Michael, concerned for his father's health, had insisted that the old man stay home. Uncharacteristically, he had given Michael no argument.

He was still sitting by the hearth, staring into the glowing turf fire, when there was a knock at the door. It was a small boy. "I'm to tell you Squire Kincaid wants you up at the big house straightaway," he announced before running away.

Da was shown into the great room and memories came flooding back. He remembered how joyful he'd been when Lord Somerville had agreed to sell him the acres that would support his two sons. That seemed ages ago. And then, when that dream was lost and gone in the shambles of the famine, his overwhelming gratitude when Somerville offered him and his sons the opportunity to work with Mr. Goodbody in the soup kitchen, knowing that no matter what, the family would always have a bite to eat.

The great room looked very much the same as the last time Da saw it, only it was more cluttered than it used to be. There seemed to be more furniture and bric-a-brac about, more things to break, but, now, Da didn't care if he broke anything or not.

It saddened him to see the gombeen man, all puffed up and trying to look important, sitting behind Lord Somerville's big desk. Across the room, a clerk, a little wisp of a man with sneaky black eyes, sat at a small writing table.

"You wanted to see me, Mr. Kincaid?"

Kincaid, looking outlandish in a cream-colored long coat, straightened his cravat. "That's *Squire* Kincaid to you, Ranahan."

"Yes, sir."

"How much, Stanley?"

The obsequious clerk leafed through a thick ledger on his desk and squinted at the tiny, neat rows of numbers. "That'd be forty pounds, Squire."

"There it is," Kincaid said. "You're forty pounds in arrears. When can I expect full payment?"

"Mr. Kin—I mean, *Squire* Kincaid. For the love of God, I don't have that kind of money."

"But you do have a son who likes to meddle in other people's affairs, do you not? Perhaps he can advance you the sum."

"Sure he doesn't have—"

"Then I'll say good day to you, Ranahan. You have till Saturday next to pay or suffer the consequences."

Every chance he got, Michael continued to go to the soup kitchen just so he could be near Emily. By the end of the day, he was tired to the point of exhaustion, but he went to the church just the same. He blamed his constant fatigue on his bout with the fever, but he was only partly right. The chronic lethargy, which Michael shared with all the other men on the work gang, was also due to a combination of a diet bordering on starvation and the impossibly hard work on the road gangs. Indeed, as the famine worsened, more and more men were dying on the roads just from the effort to get to the worksite.

The day before, an official inspector from England had come to the worksite to inspect it. Michael overheard him say to Tarpy, "As a Royal engineer, I'm ashamed to be paying these men for so little work. As a man, I'm ashamed of requiring so much from them."

Michael was drying a pile of soup bowls when Mr. Goodbody came in. The Quaker's usually ruddy face was pale. And his blue eyes reflected a level of distress Michael had never seen before.

"What is it?" Michael asked.

He offered the paper to Emily. "It's the *London Times*. I pray thee, read the editorial."

Emily turned to the editorial page and read. "'They are going. They are going with a vengeance. Soon a Celt will be as rare in Ireland as a Red Indian on the streets of Manhattan...'" Emily paled, cleared her throat, and continued to read. "'Law has ridden through. It has been taught with bayonets and interpreted with ruin. Townships leveled to the ground, straggling columns of exiles, workhouses multiplied and still crowded express the determination of the Legislature to rescue Ireland from its slovenly old barbarism and to plant there the institutions of this more civilized land...'"

Goodbody shook his head in dismay. "Does thee believe, as I do, that they are speaking of genocide?"

Tears welled up in Emily's eyes. There was a lump in her throat and she couldn't speak. All she could do was nod in agreement.

When Michael arrived at the worksite the next morning the men were abuzz with the news. The night before, Major Wicker had blown his head off with a shotgun. Earlier that day, Fergus Kincaid and his bailiff had served notice on Major

Wicker that his estates, including all chattels and goods, were now in the hands of the gombeen man.

Thirty Eight

December 1849
Ballyross, Ireland

Michael watched his father listlessly pick at his bowl of cornmeal gruel. With Mam gone, the cottage seemed oppressively quiet and sad. He knew his father had taken her death harder than the others of his family who had died. Practical, stoic men like Da knew that old grandparents would die someday, and they knew that their children would one day move out of the home to lead their own lives. But they always expected that they would live out the remainder of their lives with their wives.

Michael pushed his bowl away. He wasn't hungry either. "It's time we were on our way to the worksite, Da."

Before his father could answer, there was a thumping at the door. Michael opened it and there in the front yard stood Kincaid surrounded by a bailiff and a half-dozen constables.

"You're evicted, Ranahan," a smirking Kincaid said, making sure that the constables were between him and Michael. "You've got three minutes to clear out before I tumble the cottage."

Michael ducked through the door and stepped outside and Kincaid darted further behind the constables. "What are you babblin' about, Kincaid?"

"That's *Squire* Kincaid to you. Ask him," Kincaid jabbed a finger at Da. "He'll tell you."

Michael turned and saw his Da, leaning against the door, trembling with fear.

"What's he talkin' about?"

"Sure I didn't want to trouble you, Michael. Last week Kin—I mean, Squire Kincaid here told me we were in arrears with the rent, but I told him I didn't have money to pay and that I would—"

"And I said you would suffer the consequences, didn't I?" He waved a piece of paper in the air. It's all legal and proper. I have the decree from the courts right here in me hands." He glanced at the constables, expecting them to acknowledge how reasonable he was under the circumstances.

But the constables, fed up with being the agent of so much misery, regarded him with stony glares. If the gombeen man was looking for sympathy, he would not find it in this group. These men had become constables to uphold the law. Most of them had no liking for the peasant Irish, whom they saw as undisciplined, uneducated, and shiftless. But there was not a man in their ranks who had ever dreamed that upholding the law would include taking part in the destruction of a man's home.

Kincaid, irked that he had no support from the constabulary, turned to the bailiff. "You there, I want you to put the torch to the roof."

The bailiff, looking down his nose at Kincaid, said, "I don't burn people's homes." His response was not prompted by some heartfelt sympathy for a tenant farmer about to lose his home; it was because he was angry at Kincaid for reneging on several promised kickbacks.

Kincaid kept a wary eye on Michael, terrified that the young hothead would attack him again. Desperate to get the tumbling over with, he leaned close to the sergeant constable and whispered, "I'll give you half a crown to do it."

The constable studied the gombeen man with narrowed, cold eyes. "Are you offering a bribe to a constable in her Majesty's service?"

Kincaid jumped back as though he'd been slapped in the face. "No, no. Good God, man, no." He cursed himself. He knew the constables despised him. He'd been using them more and more to keep the peace while he tumbled cottages. And he knew they hated the duty. He'd always been careful not to give them an excuse to take action against him and here he'd just tried to bribe one of them. *You fool.*

"You misunderstood, sir," Kincaid said, scrambling to redeem himself. "I merely meant I would like to make a contribution to the widows and orphans fund."

"There is no widows and orphans fund," the constable said, grinding his truncheon in his big, beefy hands.

"Oh. Then I stand corrected."

While Kincaid had been trying to convince the constable to tumble the Ranahan cottage, the news had spread and everyone had come to see. Kincaid, desperate to get the tumbling over with, turned to the assembled farmers. "I'll offer a half a crown—no, wait..." he fumbled with his purse and held a shinny coin aloft. "A *guinea*. A guinea to any man who'll torch the cottage." *A guinea?* he said to himself. *Am I mad? A guinea will buy the services of a whole damn village of these bog trotters.*

There was no response from the sullen tenant farmers. Michael, still stunned by the realization that his cottage was about to be tumbled, was grateful that at least none of his neighbors had stepped forward to collect the blood money. If Kincaid wanted to tumble the cottage, he'd have to get a crowbar brigade from somewhere else. Then Michael's heart sank when he saw big Pat Doyle step out of the crowd.

On the verge of hyperventilating, Kincaid clapped his hands together. "Good man," he said. "Get on with it. Get on with it. The quicker you do it, the sooner you'll be a guinea richer."

Even thought Pat Doyle was as emaciated as the rest of them, he still looked formidable. He crossed his arms and faced the crowd with a scowl on his face.

"I made the mistake of tumblin' John Scanlon's cottage for a handful of coins and I've not had a minute's peace since. I'd sooner watch my children starve than put a torch to John Ranahan's home and I'll destroy any man who tries."

Kincaid groaned. *For Jasus' sake. Am I goin' to have to do it meself?*

Then, to Kincaid's astonishment—and everyone else assembled there—John Ranahan stepped in front of the gombeen man and held out his hand. "I'll do it. But I'll take the money first."

Kincaid hesitated. *What if he changes his mind? How will I get my money back?* He stole a glance at the stony-faced constables. *They'll be no help.* But what choice did he have? Reluctantly, he handed the guinea to the old man.

"Very well, but get on with it, man."

Michael stood in front of the door with outstretched arms. "No, Da…"

With a look of steely determination that Michael had never seen in his father before, Da pushed him aside. He grabbed a handful of thatch from the roof and ducked through the door.

Michael went in after him. "Da, this is your home and your Da's home before you and—"

"You were right all along, Michael." Da glanced around the room with tears in his eyes. "Sure it's not our land. It never was. It never will be." Da looked at the coin in his calloused palm. "One guinea. It's all five generations of Ranahans have to show for workin' the land all those years."

Da glanced around the little cottage that had been his home for as long as he could remember and voices from the past echoed in his mind.

"Mary, will ya be happy here?"

"Aye, John, I will…"

"It's a fine young son you have…"

"Da, can I go out into the fields with you? Can I, Da?"

"Michael, Dermot, when the time comes to get married you'll have a bit of land to build a cottage…"

"A bit of land…"

"A bit of land…"

Da thrust the straw into the smoldering turf fire and it exploded into flame. He took one last look around and, pushing Michael ahead of him, went back outside.

His neighbors stood in stunned silence. Most stared at the ground, unable to look him in the eye. The constables stood with their hands clasped behind their backs, slowly rising and falling on the toes, determined not to get caught up in the emotion of the moment.

Kincaid, scarcely breathing, watched the older Ranahan intently. *Do it, man. Do it.*

As if hearing Kincaid's silent, desperate command, Da turned to the cottage and without hesitation thrust the burning straw under an eave. The dried thatch immediately burst into flame.

Michael came up behind his father. "Da, let me do that..."

The old man, determined to do it himself, roughly pushed his son aside. Stumbling the length of the cottage, he thrust the straw under the eaves again and again, shielding his eyes as flames shot up. Soon, the entire roof was engulfed in flame.

Michael watched his Da step back from the scorching intensity of the heat and wondered what would become of him now. Michael knew he could sleep in a ditch if he had to, but his father would never survive a harsh winter outdoors in a scalp. He'd just lost his home, and he was in danger of losing his work as well. The old man, physically weakened by hunger and the backbreaking work, and emotionally drained by the death of his wife and youngest son, was incapable of doing the hard work of the road gang. Only last week, Tarpy had pulled Michael aside and warned him that if his Da didn't do his share he would be sacked.

Michael went to stand beside his father. For the first time in his life, he put his arm around him, and was stunned to feel bones through the threadbare coat.

"It'll be all right, Da," he shouted above the crackling of the fire. "We've still got the work."

December 1849
Ministry of the Treasury
London, England

Mr. Kane and Dr. Lindley made an appointment to see Trevelyan. Based on past experience, they had no expectation of changing Trevelyan's mind, but now that Playfair, the commission's spokesman had gone, it fell to them to make one last entreaty to save the destitute people of Ireland.

Trevelyan was sitting behind his desk reading a Bible when they were shown in. He closed the book and reverently put it on the desk. "Yes, gentlemen. What is it this time?"

Kane, ignoring Trevelyan's infuriating tone of condescension, got immediately to the point of his visit. "We have heard a rumor that you are going to close the public works. Is that true?"

"Yes, it is."

Addressing Trevelyan, as though he were a child stubbornly clinging to an impossible belief, a soul-weary Kane said, "Mr. Trevelyan, you cannot close the public works. This is by far the worst year of the famine. Four years of failed harvests have skinned people to the bone."

Trevelyan slammed his hands on the tabletop. "What more do you want? Dr. Kane, may I remind you that her Majesty's government has expended nearly *seven* million pounds in the last four years."

"And may I remind *you*, sir," Kane shot back, his voice quivering with emotion, "that her Majesty's government paid over *twenty* million pounds in compensation to West *Indian slave-owners* when slavery was abolished in the islands."

"And may I remind *you*, sir, that they were men of business who contributed to the economic viability of England, unlike the Irish who seem to have an insatiable appetite for the largesse of the British government." Trevelyan took a deep breath to regain control of himself. "Mr. Kane, you must understand, the only way to prevent the Irish from becoming habitually dependent on government is to bring the operations to a close once and for all."

After all these years, Kane and Lindley, bone-weary and soul-numbed, had had enough of Charles Trevelyan. Kane took an envelope out of his coat pocket and threw it on Trevelyan's desk. "Our resignations, sir. And may God have mercy on your soul."

Trevelyan glared at the envelop as though it were a dead rodent. "Accepted."

A week after the Ranahan's cottage was tumbled, a cluster of men stood in front of the Board of Works office under a gentle snow fall. Tarpy had told them to report here this morning instead of the worksite. By now, all the men knew what that meant. Reporting to the Board of Works always meant bad news.

At exactly nine o'clock, Mr. Browning opened the door and stepped out. "I have an announcement to read."

He was about to put on his glasses when he noticed the look of abject fear and resignation on the men's faces. He put his glasses away. In the four years he'd been stationed here, he'd gone from loathing these men—*shiftless bog trotters all*—to a fear of them—*they were all brutes.* But now that he'd gotten to know them, he'd learned that they weren't shiftless. In fact, he'd never seen men more willing to work at anything just to make a few coins to feed their families. And they weren't brutes. At least not all of them. Certainly there were some who were violent, but he soon realized that the violence was born of fear and helplessness. He didn't loathe them anymore or fear them. He pitied them. He decided it would be heartless to read this impersonal judgment on their lives, written by some unfeeling bureaucrat in Whitehall. He stuffed the announcement in his pocket. "Men," he said, gently. "Go to your homes. The Board of Works is closed for good. I'm so very sorry."

As he knew they would, they turned in silence and dispersed.

On hearing the announcement, Da registered no emotion. Instead, he turned away and briskly started walking up the road. Michael chased after him.

"Da, where are you goin'?"

"To the cottage. Where else?"

Michael almost had to run to keep up with him. "We don't have the cottage anymore. Remember? We've been stayin' in the church."

"Ah, what are ya talkin' about, man? Let's get out of this cold. I know your Mam will have somethin' hot for us and you know how she gets when—"

Da clutched his chest and, before Michael could reach him, the old man fell to his knees and tumbled into a ditch. Michael jumped in and pulled his Da out, wiping the freezing water off the old man's face with this sleeve. "Da, are you all right?"

Da winced in pain. "Michael, keep the family together now, you hear? Dermot's a handful, but he always listens to you. Take care of your Mam. She's a good woman." Da stopped talking as a sharp pain squeezed his heart. When the pain subsided, he continued. "Son, I didn't want to take that money you saved for America."

"I know, Da. That's all in the past."

Da dug into his pocket and pulled out the guinea. "Here, son. Take it. You go to America. For the love of God, save yerself."

Da let out a sharp cry of pain and then, slowly, his face, contorted with pain, relaxed. It had been many years since Michael had seen his Da look so peaceful.

He hugged the old man close to him and felt his life slip away.

Michael, Emily, and Mr. Goodbody stood by the open grave that Michael had dug earlier in the morning and watched as Father Rafferty struggled to conduct the service.

"Lord," Father Rafferty began in a shaky voice, "take thy servant, John Ranahan..." He stopped and his eyes welled up with tears as he looked around the cemetery, pockmarked with newly dug graves, as if seeing it for the first time. "I've buried so many people..." His voice cracked. He looked at Michael helplessly. "God help me, I don't know what to say anymore... I don't know what to believe. Just yesterday I went to the village of Killreed to consecrate a *quarry* so they could bury all their dead in holy ground... For God's sake..." Then the old priest, unable to go on, broke down, sobbing uncontrollably.

Michael stepped forward, put one arm around the broken priest and put his hand on his father's shroud-covered body. "Goodbye, Da. Maybe in Heaven, God will give you a bit of land that will be truly yours."

And together, Michael and Mr. Goodbody lowered the pathetically thin body into the open grave.

After the service, they all returned to the church to prepare the soup for the afternoon's feeding. After Emily made the tea, she sat down next to Michael.

"Michael, I'm so sorry for your loss."

"Thanks. To tell you the truth, it broke my heart to see him suffering. So, in a way I'm a bit relieved. I don't know how much more he could have taken. Is that a terrible thing to say?"

"No. It's always harder watching our loved ones suffer than ourselves."

While they were drinking their tea, Michael studied Goodbody. Michael had never met a man with a more even disposition, but now the Quaker looked uncharacteristically despondent. Michael knew he liked Da, but they weren't so close that he should react this way over the old man's death.

"Marcus, what troubles you?" Michael asked.

Goodbody looked up from his tea. "I'm afraid I have some bad news, but I did not think this the right time to tell thee."

Emily patted Goodbody's hand. "Marcus, I'm afraid we have all become inured to bad news. Please tell us."

Goodbody studied his tea cup and sighed. "The Society of Friends has exhausted its funds. It believes the problems in Ireland are far beyond the reach of private exertion. Only a sovereign government can provide the help necessary to save so many starving people." He shrugged helplessly. "I am being called home."

Father Rafferty took Goodbody's hands in his and there were tears in his eyes. "Mr. Goodbody, I for one will be sad to see you go. You, and the Society of Friends, have done much for the people of Ireland. And, I must confess, you have done much for me. I'm no longer the narrow-minded old fool I once was. God bless you."

After all this time Michael still didn't quite know what to make of this strange man with his queer clothing and queer speech. In the beginning Michael had suspected underhanded motives for his soup kitchen. It was common knowledge that some black protestants had set up soup kitchens across Ireland to lure starving and unsuspecting Catholics into renouncing their faith for a bowl of soup. "Soupers," as these traitorous Catholics were derisively called, were denounced from the pulpits of Catholic churches all across Ireland and it was understood by one and all that they would burn in Hell for all eternity for renouncing the one true faith. But Goodbody never tried to convert anyone. Indeed, even with his constant questioning, Michael had learned little about the Society of Friends. All Marcus had revealed was that the Friends were a "simple and plain people."

From the beginning, Michael also suspected that Marcus had designs on Emily. But, as carefully as Michael watched them, he never saw them do anything that would indicate that there was anything between them. Still, even now, he was convinced that *something* had to be going on.

Michael shook the Quaker's hand. "Thank you for all you've done for us, Marcus."

"I am glad that I could help thee in some small way. I see great things in thy future, Michael."

Michael saw that Emily had tears in her eyes. *Tears for the Quaker no doubt.* While she said her goodbyes, Michael went outside.

Minutes later, Emily came out and sat on a stone wall next to Michael.

"Michael, how will we feed the people without Marcus's resources?"

"I don't know," Michael snapped.

He was weary of thinking about starving people. He was weary of wondering what Emily was thinking. What *he* was thinking. What Goodbody was thinking. It was all too much. His family was gone. *Mam, Da, Dermot, Granda and Grandmam—all gone. He* didn't even have the energy to think about what he was going to do tomorrow. He just wanted to lie down and go to sleep and never wake up again.

"I guess you'll be goin' with him?" he heard himself blurt out.

"With whom?"

"Marcus Goodbody."

"And why in the world would I be going anywhere with Marcus Goodbody?"

"Because you're in love with him, aren't you? Admit it."

Emily jumped up and her green eyes flashed with anger. "Michael Ranahan, you've lost the little sense you were born with."

And on those words she marched back into the church leaving a perplexed Michael sitting on the stone wall.

The little voice in Michael's head, never failing to miss an opportunity for a dig, whispered, *"You've done it again, haven't you, you eejit?"*

Chapter Thirty Nine

The next morning Michael was at the church before dawn to help Marcus pack up his pots and pans. It would be just the two of them. Emily, who'd said her goodbyes yesterday, said she wouldn't be coming this morning because she'd be too distraught. And that suited Michael just fine. He still wasn't sure what he had said to make her so angry, but given how cold and distant she'd become after she'd stormed away from him, it was just as well she wasn't coming. After all this time, he still had no idea what went on in that head of hers. She was a great puzzle and he was well rid of her.

When they had finished packing the last cauldron onto the overflowing wagon, Michael helped Goodbody up into the driver's seat.

"Marcus, I don't know how to thank you for all you and the Society of Friends have done for us."

"Michael, I just wish it could have been more. It saddens me mightily that despite all we've done, it hasn't been enough. I must confess to thee, I am ashamed to be leaving here when there is so much yet to be done."

"You've no choice, Marcus. They've called you home and that's a fact."

The Quaker smiled down at Michael. "I have always admired the way thee deals with life. No matter the event, good or evil, thee just keeps moving forward. It is my failing that I sometimes cannot accept the way things are."

Michael didn't know what to say. In all the years he'd known Goodbody, the man had never expressed the slightest doubt about himself. It was a character trait that in the beginning Michael had found irritating. But now, hearing him confess his doubts, Michael had a new appreciation of the man. It suddenly occurred to him that they were very much alike. He, too, had his doubts, doubts that kept him awake more nights than he could remember. But the difference between them was that Michael could not, or would not, admit to them.

To break the uncomfortable tension, Michael teased, "Be careful goin' down the road, Marcus. With all these things on your wagon, you look like a gombeen man. And there's no one likes a gombeen man."

There was one more hearty handshake and Marcus Goodbody was off.

Michael stood in the road in front of the church watching the wagon, with its overburdened cargo swaying from side to side on the uneven road, until it disappeared around a bend. Then he went into the empty church to pack what little he owned. It was time for him to go as well. His family was gone. So, too, were his friends. All those men he'd stood around the fire with at Moira and Bobby's wedding so many years ago had either died or emigrated to America. He was the last young man in Ballyross.

Goodbody had been gone only minutes, but already Michael realized how much he would miss him. He truly liked and admired Marcus. He knew now that his judgment had been clouded because he'd always viewed the Quaker as a rival. But now that he was gone, Michael was astonished at the depth of sadness he felt. He realized now that Marcus was more a brother to him than Dermot ever was. He would never again stand with Marcus in front of steaming cauldrons, doling out soup. He would never again watch with amusement Goodbody reading the *London Times* and railing in his gentle way about the treachery of the British Parliament toward the Irish famine. And he would never again observe the gentle way in which Goodbody spoke to the frightened people and the tender way he administered to the sick.

Without the hectic activity surrounding the preparation and serving of the soup, the little village church seemed utterly abandoned—a place that, like its pastor, had lost all meaning and purpose. Earlier in the year, Father Rafferty, distraught that he'd had to remove the implements that signaled that this was a Catholic church, decided to put the tabernacle and the candlesticks back on the altar. The next morning to his chagrin and great anger, the brass candlesticks were gone. "Apparently," Father Rafferty bellowed from his pulpit the following Sunday, "the thieving sinners, who will surely spend all eternity burning in hell, at least had enough decency not to steal the tabernacle, God's own home on this earth."

The bare, unadorned little church reminded Michael of the mysterious, ancient beehive huts he'd explored as a child in airy mountain glens. He'd been told by Father Rafferty that medieval monks had used these huts to pray, meditate, and painstakingly copy manuscripts that would one day be the wonder of the world. But when he'd visited them, the dank, low-ceiling chambers no longer held such lofty purpose. They'd become home to the occasional fox or badger and the destination of adventurous children. Still, even as a child, he could sense that there was something hallowed about these places.

Michael stuffed his spare shirt and an extra pair of brogues into a bag and took one last look around the church that he'd attended since he'd been five. It was here that he'd made his first communion, and now he could recall with a smile the almost paralyzing fear that the host would stick to the roof of his mouth. Father Rafferty, sounding like the very voice of doom, had warned them that if that happened they were not to try and dislodge the sacred host. Better that they choke and die right there in the church, he'd told them, than to defile the sweet body of Christ with their grubby, dirty fingers.

This little church had been the center of his and everyone else's life in the village. Michael couldn't remember the number of christenings, weddings, and funerals he'd attended here. He didn't think he believed in God any more, but, still, the church did offer a modicum of solace and peace in these desperate times. And he would miss it.

As he started up the aisle, the door at the back of the church opened and suddenly, Emily was framed in the doorway. Michael's heart thumped and his poor brain was once again thrown into utter turmoil. Yesterday, he'd thought he'd seen the last of her and he'd convinced himself that it was good riddance. But now, watching her come down the aisle, he never wanted to let her out of his sight again.

She glanced at his bag. "Going I see. And where will you go?"

Michael's throat was suddenly constricted. "America," he finally managed to croak.

"Ah, your dream. So it isn't dead. Have you the fare?"

"I have a guinea." He realized that was not nearly enough to pay his passage and added, half-heartedly, "Tis a start."

"Yes, it is."

She stopped in front of him, so close that if he put his hand out, he could touch her. They stood that way, staring at each other for a long time. Finally, Michael broke the silence. "Well, I'd best be off."

"Yes, you'd best be off."

"Right. Well, then. You take care of yourself, Emily Somerville."

"And you take care of yourself, Michael Ranahan."

A smile played around her lips and he had to turn away from those beautiful, questioning green eyes. "Aye."

He started up the aisle, painfully aware that what he was doing was irrevocable. In years to come, he knew he would always regret not telling Emily that he loved her. But how could he? Da had once said that she was not for the likes of him. He'd bristled at that notion then, but now, after all that had happened, he had to admit his Da was right. She had lost her fortune, but she was still his better, a member of the aristocracy and all that that entailed—educated, cultured, worldly. Some day she would find a man of her station and marry. It was only fitting...

"*Take me with you.*"

Michael stopped, not trusting his own ears. *Did she say that or was it just that damnable voice in my head?*

He turned. "Did you say something?"

"Yes. I said, take me with you."

"Well... I don't know..." he stammered.

She started up the aisle. "I love you, Michael Ranahan."

Michael thought his heart would burst in his chest. For so long he'd dreamed of her saying those words, but he never imagined that he would actually hear her say them. "Your kind is not for the likes of me," he blurted out.

"I think I've loved you since the first time I watched you saddle Shannon in the barn."

Shafts of sunlight, shining through the stained-glass windows, highlighted her gleaming auburn hair in dazzling colors. Her face, the color and texture of those lovely, delicate porcelain figurines he'd watched her pack, seemed to glow in the light. The sight of her was almost painful. "I can't even read."

"I'll teach you."

Since that day he'd seen her riding through the village in her father's carriage, he knew he would never love anyone but her. "I'm a clod. You said so yourself." *Jasus*, the voice in him cried. *Must you always try to turn her away?*

"That can be fixed."

Suddenly she was standing in front of him and he smelled her familiar, intoxicating scent. Without thinking, he opened his arms and she moved into him. He held her tight, remembering the time he'd held her after the gombeen man told her he owned the Manor. He never wanted to let her go then. And he didn't want to let her go now. But this time it was different. Then she'd been seeking comfort. Now she was clinging to him because she loved him. She'd said so herself. And Michael knew—he'd be able to hold her for the rest of his life.

"I love you, too," he whispered into her hair.

Then the spell was broken and the reality of the world intruded. "Emily, I have no money."

"You have a guinea and I have this." She held up her mother's sapphire ring.

"But who has money to buy it?"

"The gombeen man."

"No. I'll not deal with the likes of him."

She threw her arms around his neck and kissed him and Michael wondered if it were possible to die of joy.

"You don't have to," she whispered in his ear. "I will."

Emily knew what had to be done, but still, she dreaded coming to the Manor house, fearing that seeing the house again would dredge up too many painful memories. But to her surprise it hadn't. What she'd learned gradually during the past four years, as more and more of her possessions were sold off and her station became lower and lower, was that it was people who were important, not material things. Of course, she was saddened by the loss of all those she had come to love—her father, Da, Mam, even surly, troubled Dermot. And she always would. But to her surprise, she realized that she didn't miss the tapestries, the silverware, or the Waterford goblets. They were merely trappings—*things*. And things could always be replaced.

As she and Michael sat in the great room waiting for Kincaid to appear, Emily sensed that an era was coming to a close. The famine would end eventually. It had to. But the day of the landlords and their great estates and their tenant farmers was over. She didn't know what the future would hold for Ireland, but she knew that the old ways were lost and gone forever, and she was glad of it. It had caused too much misery, heartbreak, and death. Perhaps, the famine was a necessary malevolence, sent to scour the country of an evil way of life. She prayed for a brighter future for Ireland.

As she looked around the great room, she couldn't help but be amused by what Kincaid had done with the room. The furnishing were a muddled crush of mismatched chairs, sofas, and tables, clashing in color and style. Apparently, that dreadful man labored under the misconception that more was always better than less.

The door opened and Kincaid came in wearing an orange silk dressing gown. Emily stifled a laugh. The ridiculous man reminded her of a character in a Molière satire she'd seen in London.

"I understand you have a ring for sale," he said, slipping around his desk and keeping a watchful eye on Michael.

Emily handed him the ring. Kincaid slipped a jeweler's loupe out of pocket in his dressing gown and carefully examined the ring. After a moment, he said, "It's mediocre at best. I know I shouldn't, but I'll give you fifty pounds out of respect for your late father." He slid the ring across the desk.

"It's worth four times that," Emily said, sliding the ring back to him. She had no idea what the ring was worth, but if he was offering fifty pounds, it had to be worth much more than that.

Kincaid studied the ring again. "Very well." He slid the ring back to her. "Seventy pounds is my final offer. And generous it is, I must say."

Emily put her hand over the ring and didn't slide it back. "One hundred pounds."

Kincaid saw her cup her hands over the ring and knew she was through negotiating. He licked his rubbery lips and his black eyes glistened with unbridled greed, as he pondered his next move.

Emily stood up. "Well, then."

"No—wait."

He was desperate to get the ring. He was certain it was worth at least three hundred pounds. But he couldn't bring himself to part with a hundred pounds—*a full third of its value.* He was accustomed to paying a mere fraction of a property's actual worth and he bridled at paying a farthing more, especially to this vacuous girl who obviously knew nothing about jewelry.

"You should take the seventy pounds," he said, almost pleading. "You'll not find anyone around here who'll pay more."

"I will in Cork City."

While they had been negotiating, Michael had been sitting stiffly beside her, saying nothing. She'd made him promise that he would not interfere. But it was all he could do not to reach across the desk and strangle the little weasel.

"Come on, Michael."

Michael exhaled in relief and jumped to his feet, anxious to get out of the sight of the gombeen man.

As they reached the door, Kincaid shouted, *"All right. But it's thievery, I tell you."*

"A hundred pounds?"

Kincaid nodded in defeat. "A hundred pounds it is."

As Michael and Emily made their way to the train station to catch the train to Cork, they passed through the ruined village of Ballyross. The forlorn, abandoned village looked as though it had been laid waste by some terrible plague of Biblical proportions. There was not a soul on the streets, stores were boarded up, and as far as the eye could see every cottage was without a roof—a sure sign that those who had once lived there had been evicted.

January 1850
Hampton Hall, England

Charles Trevelyan was asked to address a select group of Whig merchants about the current condition in Ireland. Speaking to a packed audience, he concluded his well-received remarks by saying, "Posterity will credit the famine for starting a revolution in the habit of a nation long singularly unfortunate. Future generations will acknowledge that supreme wisdom created permanent good out of transient evil. The Irish people have profited much by this famine. To be sure the lessons were severe, but no earthly teacher could have induced them to make the changes which this visitation of Divine Providence has brought about. The Ministry of the

Treasury has much to be proud of as well, I might add. After all, in the final analysis, the famine was stayed."

He paused to bask in the applause, and then, sticking his thumbs in his lapels, he continued in his clipped, pompous style. "Armies of antiquity have been fed before, but history cannot furnish a parallel to the fact that millions of people were fed every day by administrative arrangements emanating from and controlled by this office."

The next day the *London Times* reported that Charles Trevelyan received a standing ovation.

Chapter Forty

January 1850
Cork City

Michael and Emily took the train to Cork City. They left the train station and walked toward the quay. When they came around a corner, Michael suddenly realized where he was. It was this very same quay, five years earlier, that he'd foolishly thought they could make a stand against the British Empire.

Although the streets were now teeming with passengers heading for the quay, in his mind's eye, Michael could still see the deserted street on that rainy dawn so long ago. He heard the crunch of soldier's boots on the cobblestone and the sharp crack of rifle fire. The pungent smell of gunpowder filled his nose. He saw men falling—some dying, others wounded. He heard the echo of gunfire against the stone warehouses, the desperate screams of dying men. Painfully, he felt once again, the loss of innocence. *His* loss of innocence.

413

Emily saw that Michael had suddenly gone pale and there were beads of perspiration on his forehead. She thought it was because of the impending voyage. Earlier, he'd confessed to her that he had never been on a ship and that he did not know how to swim very well.

She wiped his brow. "Are you not well, Michael?"

He looked into her lovely eyes, now clouded with concern. He couldn't tell her about that morning. Maybe someday. But not now.

He took her arm. "It's nothing," he said, turning away from the past and leading her onto the quay.

The quay teemed with scores of dazed and cowered travelers. Most of them had never ventured farther than twenty miles from their villages, but now they were about to embark on a frightening journey across a great ocean to an uncertain future in a unknown land. The thought of the impending voyage was made all the more terrifying by the notion that they might be sailing on a "coffin ship."

Michael, too, was concerned. To satisfy his own unease, he'd gone to the front of the quay to inspect the ship. He came back to Emily smiling. "I think it will be all right," a relieved Michael said. "She appears to be a stout ship."

To pass the time while they waited to board, Michael studied his fellow passengers. Some were so destitute that they had no possessions save the ragged clothes on their backs. Others carried their belongings in old potato sacks and the occasional battered suitcase. Standing off to the side, he saw a dozen well-dressed men and women and their children surrounded by stacks of proper suitcases. A sailor had told him that these people were wealthy Protestants who would be berthed on the main deck where the cabins had windows and doors that locked.

Earlier, when they'd purchased their tickets, Michael had discovered to his dismay that they had only enough money to afford steerage. Michael, unwilling to subject Emily to the horrific conditions in steerage, suggested that they stay in Ireland until they'd earned enough to pay for main deck accommodations. But Emily would have none of it.

"You and I," she said, affectionately patting his cheek, "have survived much worse than a long ocean voyage in steerage." When he started to protest, she put her finger across his lips. "Michael, I want to go to America right now so we can begin our new lives."

Michael could only shrug helplessly and say, "All right." Over the years he would learn there was no profit in arguing with his headstrong wife.

The ticket agent handed the manifest to the captain, a grizzled man with a permanent squint from years of staring into sun-glared seas.

"Will ya look at this wretched lot?" the ticket agent said out of the side of his mouth.

The captain squinted at the crowd of his soon-to-be-his passengers and chuckled. "I almost feel sorry for the Americans. Sure they're gettin' the dregs of the country."

"Their loss, our gain," the ticket agent grinned. He looked at his pocket watch. "It's time, Captain."

The captain raised a megaphone to his lips. "Attention. When your name is called, step forward lively and have your ticket ready."

Reading from the manifest he called out the passengers' names, some of which would in the fullness of time resonate in America's history. "Crockett … Ford… Fitzgerald… Kennedy… Poe… Reagan… Foster…" And finally, "Moynihan… Barrymore… Ranahan …."

After the ship slipped her dock lines, it took almost an hour for her to tack carefully through the crowded harbor. But once freed of the constraints of the harbor's jetties, the ship, with all canvas unfurled, laid into the breeze and gently plunged through the rolling sea.

In silence and with tears streaming down their faces, almost all the passengers crowded the stern of the ship to get their last glimpse of Ireland, knowing they would never again return to their homeland.

Michael took Emily's hand and pulled her away. "Come on, Emily."

"Where are you taking me?" she said, laughing as the wind whipped through her long, auburn hair.

"To the bow. I want to see where I'm goin', not where I've been."

Standing in the bow, Michael wrapped his arms around Emily and, together, the young couple watched the brilliant sun slowly sinking toward the horizon.

"It's goin' to be a long and difficult voyage," he whispered into her ear.

She squeezed his hand. "It'll give me plenty of time to teach you how to read."

He turned her around and kissed her, still barely able to grasp that this magnificent woman was going to be his wife.

Then, arm in arm, they turned to watch the sun, now a bold red, finally sink into the rolling seas to the west.

Toward America.

Epilogue

The Great Irish Famine started in 1845 and, according to the British government, officially ended in 1850. But in truth, the impact of the famine lasted much longer than that.

Because so many dead were buried in unmarked graves and ditches, it can never be known for sure how many people died during the famine years. But, it is estimated that more than one million men, women, and children died of disease and starvation and at least another two million emigrated to America and Canada.

It is also estimated that over the course of the famine, 500,000 people were evicted and their cottages tumbled.

It was years later that scientists finally discovered the cause of the blight—a fungus called *Phytophthora Infestans*. However, it was not until 1882, almost forty years after the famine, that scientists discovered a cure for it.

For his work during the famine, Charles Trevelyan was knighted by Queen Victoria.

In October of 1852, Squire Kincaid, the gombeen man, was assassinated on the Cork road by person or persons unknown. He had no heirs, so his estates, which were considerable, reverted to the Crown.

The Great Famine sounded the death knell of the landlords. Over the next fifty years more and more landlords went bankrupt. Those who remained sold off their holdings to Irish farmers who used the land for grazing.

Michael and Emily settled in that notorious part of New York City called the "Five Points." They eventually had three sons and two daughters.

The Ranahan Construction Company, run by future generations of Ranahans, would play a part in the construction of the Brooklyn Bridge and, later, the Empire State Building, and the World Trade Center.

Descendents of other immigrants who survived the famine and the coffin ships found their own success in the New World.

One created an automobile dynasty.

May more became writers.

And several became presidents of the United States.

The End

ABOUT THE AUTHOR

Michael Grant joined the NYPD in 1962. He worked as a police officer in the Tactical Patrol Force and the Accident Investigation Squad. Upon being promoted to sergeant, he worked in the 63rd Precinct, the Inspections Division, and finally the Police Academy. As a lieutenant, he worked in the 17th Precinct and finished up his career as the Commanding Officer of the Traffic Division's Field Internal Affairs Unit. He retired in 1985 and went to work for W.R. Grace Company as a Security Coordinator.

Mr. Grant has a BS in Criminal Justice and an MA in psychology from John Jay College. He is also a graduated of the FBI National Academy.

In 1990, Mr. Grant moved to Florida where he wrote his first three novels: *Line of Duty, Officer Down,* and *Retribution*. In 2006 he returned to Long Island where he has written four more novels: *The Cove, Back To Venice, When I Come Home,* and *In The Time of Famine.*

Made in United States
North Haven, CT
28 March 2022

17626226R00233